14.

G000128375

All rights of distribution, including via film, radio, and television, photo-mechanical reproduction, audio storage media, electronic data storage media, and the reprinting of portions of text, are reserved.

The author is responsible for the content and correction.

© 2020 united p. c. publisher

Printed in the European Union on environmentally friendly, chlorine- and acid-free paper.

www.united-pc.eu

The 1st China's novel written originally in English and published in the UK
The 1st and so far only English novel from China nominated for the 2019 International Dublin Literary Award

SHENZHEN DREAM

A debut novel

Huang Guosheng

An ambitious young man's struggle to achieve his ideal life in the Chinese city of Shenzhen and too many readers
shed tears while reading it

I have a strong feeling that your novel will be well-received in the US and even worldwide. Everyone seems to know what the "American Dream" is, it's about time the world finds out what "Shenzhen Dream" is all about.

——US Xlibris House

I like the mixture of old and new in your story, *Shaking Heaven*. The folk stories at the end are wonderful.

——*Brilliant Flash Fiction*

We want you to know that we really did like your work.

——*Into the Void*

A "Shenzhen Dream" that filled with "Zhen inspiration"!

——China Writers Association & *Shenzhen Special Zone Daily*

Some chapters caused me seriously shedding tears!

——A reader

The author: Huang Guosheng (China)

About the Author

Huang Guosheng was born in Nawu Town, Maoming City, Guangdong Province, China in 1969. He once won the Liangbin Fiction Prize and took 4th place in a China National Novel Contest and was longlisted for the 9th Maodun Literary Prize (the highest literary award in China). He also won 10th place in a China National English Writing Competition, and his English poems and stories have been published and serialised in China's *Shenzhen Daily* and the American magazines *Brilliant Flash Fiction* and *Wisconsin Review*. His English novel *Shenzhen Dream* (i.e., *The Road to Shenzhen*) was nominated for the 2019 International Dublin Literary Award. He works as an international businessman and a bilingual Chinese-English writer in Shenzhen, China.

(Author's email: 1035357866@qq.com)

Synopsis

In the early 1990s Zhou Haonan, a young man from the West Canton Province of China, moves to Shenzhen to advance his career. A dutiful, kind, brotherly and painstaking man and a devoted son to his aged mother, he works as an international businessman and a Sanda boxer, and even sells his blood over the 20 years he spends working to achieve his dream. Though he has many failures and setbacks, he always finds the strength to get back onto his feet and carry on. The story examines family relationships, love and friendship as well as humanitarian and commercial matters. An inspiring and touching novel.

****

<u>A true story about this novel</u>: One reader, a Chinese middle-aged man who greatly loved this novel, unfortunately suffered liver cancer. In the end when he miserably passed away, his family found him grasping a copy of this novel to his breast. And when he was buried by his family, they burnt this novel before his tomb so that he could "take it away with him" to Heaven...

Contents

Acknowledgments

As a native Chinese who has always lived in China, I had never imagined that one day I would write an English novel and publish it in the UK and US.

First I would like to thank *Shenzhen Daily*, where many of my English works, including all the poems and some Chapters in this novel, have been published and serialized since 2015. I would also like to express my thanks to *Brilliant Flash Fiction*, an English fiction magazine in the USA, which published a short story of mine in 2016 which has become Chapter 39 of this novel.

Although I once submitted a short story (Chapter 7 of this novel) to *Shenzhen Daily* for a national English writing competition in 2000 and was awarded 10th place, I had never thought that I would engage in bilingual Chinese-English writing, let alone a work as long as this novel.

Fortunately, as an international businessman over the past 20 years, I have met countless foreign merchants in the Canton Fairs and our companies, and through them I have had many chances to develop my oral and written English. Meanwhile, as a writer for over 30 years, I had read many original English novels such as those of David Hawkes (UK translator of *The Story of the*

Stone), John Minford (UK translator of *The Story of the Stone*), Charlotte Brontë, Hemingway, Jack London, O Henry and Khaled Hosseini, from whose works I had learned much about how to write in English.

Lastly but very importantly, this is a special gift to a eight-year-old girl, Huang Shihan, my beloved foster daughter. I hope that she will read and enjoy this novel when she is older.

Huang two Sheng

黄 囝 晟

Shenzhen, China
Nov. 12, 2019

Why do my eyes often contain tears?

Because I love this land deeply…

—Ai Qing (China), *I Love This Land*

Chapter 1
A Fishing Trip

Abroad it is easy to earn a little money, but hard to earn a lot. In Shenzhen, however, it is hard to earn a little money, but easy to earn a lot.

As Zhou Haonan watched his fishing float bobbing in the ocean, he mulled over this sentence again. It was a famous wealth maxim created by Zhang Fuqiang, Haonan's childhood friend, who had been active in the city of Shenzhen for many years.

In those days, after the reclamation of Shenzhen Bay to create land, many different kinds of marine creatures colonised the water, so it was inevitable that the big fish would eat the small ones and that the small fish would eat the little shrimps.

On this afternoon near the time of the Insects Awakening division in 2008, it was still cold. Haonan, in a grey T-shirt and black trousers, had come to the seaside at Xia'sha in Futian District to fish. In the distance was the great bridge which links Shekou with Hong Kong, and overhead the planes that took off from Bao'an Airport soared and whistled past. But gradually, clouds were floating in; a thunderstorm was on its way. The people around started to leave, and Haonan was preparing to do the same.

Suddenly his mobile phone rang. It was a call from Fuqiang, from whom he had heard nothing for many months. He took the call and heard Fuqiang's laugh, as hearty as frying beans.

"I'm still alive. Haha!" said Fuqiang.

"Nobody said you'd died," said Haonan, smiling.

"I hear you've been going to Vietnam recently. Is it easy to do business there?"

"If you take 500 yuan into Vietnam, you'll be an instant millionaire," was Haonan's reply.

"Why?" asked Fuqiang eagerly.

Haonan explained, "One yuan can be exchanged for over 2,000 Vietnamese Dong. So 500 yuan is one million Vietnamese Dong." At that time one Chinese yuan was equal to about 0.15 US dollar or 0.116 pounds sterling.

"Really? Can you speak Vietnamese?" Fuqiang asked.

Haonan had studied Vietnamese intensively for three months in Dongxing, Guangxi, the Chinese frontier city close to Vietnam. When he had stayed in Vietnam, he had found that most Vietnamese spoke poor English. Haonan, who always used English as his first foreign language, had then learned Vietnamese, which made life easier for the Vietnamese as well as himself.

Fuqiang asked, "I heard that one Vietnamese man can marry several girls. And no matter what the seasons are, the Vietnamese men like to wear the green cap. Haha! As you know, we don't like wearing the green cap because it means your wife has had an illicit sexual relationship with other man or men. Haha! Anyway you're luckier than me because you can speak Vietnamese, whereas I can only use sign language. I rely on my body language if I go there and touch the Vietnamese girls. Know what I mean? Haha!"

Hearing that, Haonan said with a bitter smile, "But all I did there was manage my mahogany import business. I also travelled in Laos. That day we drove around the high mountain on the frontier between Vietnam and Laos all day long, and the car nearly crashed off a high cliff."

"Terrible! Oh yes! Are there many *Huanghua* girls being sold in Vietnam now? They're specially precious." Fuqiang was always concerned about girls.

"*Huanghua* girls? Do you mean the *Huanghua Li* wood?" Haonan corrected him. "Everyone in China knows that '*Huanghua Li*' sounds like '*Huanghua* young girl' in Chinese."

"That's right! Collect some when you go there again, please. I've heard that the Vietnamese

Huanghua Li wood is sold at one million yuan per girl. Oh sorry! It should be sold by the ton."

"Yes. But there's a strict government rule that trade in *Huanghua Li* wood is prohibited."

Fuqiang asked about other hardwoods. Haonan replied, "There're also agalwood, ebony and *Phoebe sheareri* there, but they're more difficult to deal in."

"Then let's deal in *Dalbergia cochinchinensis*. It's top-quality mahogany and very expensive. It's said that a bed made of *Dalbergia* from the Qing Dynasty is worth as much as several Mercedes Benz or Bentley cars."

"That's dark red *Dalbergia*. The wood from Laos always sells better and it's being stored all over China now."

"The Vietnamese men wear the green cap in the day and sleep on dark red *Dalbergia* beds at night. They hug girls here and there; they can drink Pu'er tea after having a good sleep. What a wonderful life! And how was your dark red *Dalbergia* deal there?"

"Oh dear! Unfortunately there are many cheats in Vietnam," sighed Haonan.

"Hum! Don't worry. When will you go there again? Let's go together."

"You're still the same. All you think about is money and girls. All right... Bye!" Haonan put down his mobile and stared at the swaying fishing rod. Then his mobile tinkled again. It was a text message from Chen Guangwei, a customer. He had not heard from Guangwei since he had come back to Shenzhen from Dongxing last year. He did not know whether Guangwei was in Dongxing or Shenzhen at present. The message said, "How are you, Zhou Haonan? The receipt you wrote me for 200,000 yuan is still in my hands."

Haonan's heart thumped wildly and he froze like a monk. Was the receipt Guangwei had made before fake? He thought hard, but he was quite certain that his signature on the receipt really was his own. He knew that no one in China could imitate his perfect handwriting, as he had always been good at calligraphy. *So, was that one I had torn only a photocopy? Did Guangwei use an exceptional photocopier to reproduce that receipt? And does Guangwei still have the original one?*

Haonan couldn't help trembling. Last year when he had been in Dongxing, because of his carelessness in writing two clauses in a contract for dark red *Dalbergia cochinchinensis*, he had put himself entirely in the control of Guangwei.

Another text from Guangwei appeared on Haonan's mobile phone. "You wait! You must double compensate me. I'll get even with you by any means. I've got the bank video of you receiving my deposit." Guangwei was like a hawk, circling high above the sky and waiting to attack a lonely crippled chick on the land.

Haonan admitted that Guangwei had the right to get evidence from the bank. He also knew that according to contract law, after the buyer hands in a deposit, if the seller cannot supply the contracted goods, the seller must return double the deposit to the buyer. Over many years Haonan had inspected countless contracts, including some English contracts which were as long as 90 pages; he always worked carefully, like a lawyer who has also trained as a judge. Unfortunately, on this one occasion, for that one page of an inland Chinese language contract, he, the middleman, had rushed it and made a mistake. As Guangwei still had the original receipt, it meant that Haonan, who had received the deposit but failed to make the delivery, would have to pay 400,000 yuan. To him this was no small sum, and enough to buy a luxury car. Last year he had gone to Dongxing, and had earned no money, in fact he had lost money. Now he needed to pay out 400,000 yuan!

Next Guangwei sent a new message with his personal photo. It showed a thin and short man, with blackened teeth caused by daily smoking. In the picture he was grinning and sticking out his middle finger. It was also last year that Guangwei had gone to Dongxing from Shenzhen and they had met up. At that time Haonan had been struggling on his own, but Guangwei, a wealthy and arrogant man, had worked with a gang. As anyone knows, "a starved camel is bigger than a fat horse."

The wind suddenly blew hard; it was getting dark now. *Will Guangwei really lodge a claim against me? Or it is just a threat?* Haonan was very agitated.

Abruptly across the sky fierce lightning flashed, as though it wanted to cut the earth in half, and at once there came a great clap of thunder which seemed to crush the sky and demolish the land. In the distance a litchi tree burst into flame and smoke. Soon raindrops as big as beans poured down. Rain like this was never seen in Shenzhen in early spring, and such shocking thunder at the beginning of the year in Shenzhen had not been heard for a hundred years. Was this an indication from the heavens that such a disaster would happen to Haonan?

Haonan looked up at the sky and an ominous premonition came to his mind. How could he escape from this terrible nightmare? He sat motionless and worried.

Suddenly a great idea seized him. He sent a message to Guangwei: "That moment when I handed the deposit cash back to you face to face and Leng Jinxiong received it, and when I tore the original receipt of mine into pieces, all of this was fully recorded on video. Didn't you notice that I wore a white steel watch at that time? Actually it has a micro infrared camera inside, which was pointing to you just then. Furthermore, there was also a video monitor at that hotel. And all the messages you have sent me just now will be used as evidence in court for your disgraceful attempt to blackmail me."

This powerful message shut Guangwei up straight away, and there was no response from him for a while.

Haonan texted again. "Meanwhile, at least four of the seven people who were there can prove the above fact. The witness testimony and other evidence of mine are in my hands. So go ahead, do what you want."

No reply from Guangwei.

"Besides, I'm also the first prize winner of the China National Hard-Pen Calligraphy Competition, and I can write diversified characters. So the characters shown on that receipt could not be proved as mine, for you have never seen my writing. And when I wrote that receipt, I used a special pen which makes the words disappear automatically. This means that in half an hour the words I'd written had fully disappeared, and changed to other new words whose handwriting did not belong to me."

The lightning continued to flash and the thunder roared forcefully. Haonan was now wet from head to toe. Guangwei did not respond.

In fact Haonan had made no audio or video recording. And as for the pen whose writing disappears, that was not true either. But Guangwei was so cunning that Haonan had to think how best to deal with him. Although Guangwei wanted to destroy Haonan and Haonan could not be sure whether Guangwei still held the receipt, how could Guangwei know if Haonan had really recorded any evidence?

The wind got more violent, with a shock of lightning that looked like a dragon coiling in the sky. Thunder rolled ceaselessly, and rain poured down. Haonan's bike had been blown over. He was like a rock standing in the sea. The thunderstorm was getting fiercer and fiercer, but he still held the fishing rod and sat motionless.

All of a sudden a cobra climbed over his right leg. He was frightened again, but he had to keep still, like a soldier pretending death among the bodies on a battlefield. He could only open his eyes and watch as the cobra crawled along, for he knew that a snake never attacks a man unless it is provoked. Sure enough, it crawled away into the underbrush.

Haonan stayed there gazing at the fishing line and the float bobbing up and down in the water. As the great waves dashed against the sky, his thoughts were tumbling.

Chapter 2
Advancing Secretly by an Unknown Path

That August when Haonan graduated and worked in the west of Canton Province for one month, he went to Shantou on business. He phoned Fuqiang before he came back. Fuqiang jumped when he received this call. He then invited Haonan to visit his Huazhou Sliced Boiled Chicken restaurant in Shenzhen. Actually the excellent calligraphy of this restaurant's name had been written by Haonan. He had never been to Shenzhen before, and he yearned for the city as much as the hot-blooded youths in the 1930s in China had longed for Yuan'an, the sacred base. So what Fuqiang proposed met his requirements well.

Haonan, however, wondered why Fuqiang had asked him to muster ten more diners, because this was neither his wedding nor a house banquet, nor the occasion of the restaurant's official opening. Haonan had no relatives or friends in Shenzhen except a cousin, Luo Zhenfeng, who worked as the lobby manager in Shanghai Restaurant in Shekou, so he phoned him, and Zhenfeng quickly made the proper arrangements.

When Haonan arrived, he saw a row of luxury restaurants lining the seafront of Sha'zui, in which he recognised at once his own calligraphy. The restaurant was full, and there were many people outside the door, each holding a small piece of paper, squatting or standing or crossing arms with each other. It was obvious that they were waiting their turn for seats. Haonan squeezed into the crowd. It reminded him of crossing a field of jute as tall as he had been in west Canton when he was a child, but he could not find Fuqiang.

Suddenly he saw somebody holding up a mobile phone as big as a brick. The man shouted "Here! Here!" It was Fuqiang. He led Haonan to a luxurious room, where Haonan met Zhenfeng and others who had obviously been drinking for a long time. In this room thirteen people had gathered. Although it was summer, because of his job, Zhenfeng, who was of middle height and had black hair, was still in suit and tie.

When Fuqiang sat down, he introduced the delicious food to the others. For the dish called "Huazhou's Sliced Boiled Chicken", he said the chickens were not fed in Sha'zui but delivered in individual cages by the long-distance bus which drove from Huazhou to Shenzhen each night, so they were native Huazhou chickens. The seasoning was fried in pure oil containing groundnut oil, soybean oil and garlic and so forth. The diners who came here were from Huazhou, Gaozhou(Gaoliang),

Maoming and Zhanjiang, and there were also Hong Kong businessmen, tourists and other visitors from mainland China.

Some claimed that the delicious taste was not only chicken. On one occasion recently a group of diners had asked the restaurant to pack the uneaten food up for them after dinner. Fuqiang thought very little could be packed because even the chickens' heads and legs had been eaten. The diners, who were still licking their lips, said they wanted to pack the oil. Fuqiang was taken aback. He would rather have presented half the chicken free of charge than give them the oil, because these diners could take it for analysis and discover his secret ingredients. But they insisted, so Fuqiang could not refuse.

Fuqiang was thin and tall with a wide, protruding mouth, and he wore a suit and a white short-sleeved shirt. He said his mouth was useful for biting watermelons and kissing girls. On the table by his hand stood his "treasure"— a mobile phone, whose top flashed enticingly. He was lucky enough to be one of the first mobile phone users in China. Once he fell and hurt himself, and had to have both elbows set in plaster. Even then, he was still grasping his mobile phone as firmly as an ant on a sweet.

Looking at this, Haonan was very envious. "You'll have one soon, *Diaotou*," Fuqiang said to Haonan, smiling. *Diaotou* was a favourite word of

Fuqiang's, a word from Huazhou in west Canton Province meaning "little creature" or "shit". It can, however, also be used in a joking way among people who are close friends. Afterwards, Fuqiang shouted, "Let's drink, *Diaotou*! Our home dialect is also a weapon of anti-corruption!"

Then Haonan related a rumour. It was said that a government official from Guangzhou, the capital of Canton Province, had once visited Huazhou. When he arrived, many of Huazhou's officials lined up to say "Welcome to *Tanguan*!" In the local dialect in Huazhou, "*Tanguan*" means "visit", but it sounds like "corrupt official" in the Guangzhou language, although this official did not know the difference. He thus suffered from insomnia that night, thinking that his guilt had been exposed by the public (actually this was not so). He rose early the next morning, and when he came back to Guangzhou, he hurried to the local Discipline Inspection Commission to turn himself in to the police. Finally he received a moderate sentence. So, such a serious case of corruption had been cracked by a simple dialect confusion. This was a popular humorous anecdote in Huazhou.

"Better speak less in the Huazhou way since we're in Shenzhen now, I suppose," a colleague of Zhenfeng's said.

Right now it was busy in these restaurants. Vessels out at sea hooted from time to time. On the sea defence embankment there was heavy traffic going to Sha'zui, so there was a constant stream of car lights flowing along the coast.

"I came here with my parents in 1979," said Fuqiang as he smoked the "Big Bamboo Pipe" which is a feature of the west of Canton. He talked about how he had made a living after he had arrived in Shenzhen and had brought a "Big Bamboo Pipe" from Maoming. Seeing this brought back childhood memories to Haonan of relaxing under the trees at the entrance to the village in hot summer. He remembered the harsh trilling of cicadas, the grandfathers who sat on their bamboo stools smoking their "big bamboo pipes", and the grandmothers waving their palm-leaf fans and showing their toothless mouths. They all gossiped and laughed about the local news.

"Huazhou congee is also a famous feature," said Fuqiang. "Not only does the congee cook well, it can be served with many side dishes: dried radish slices, sweet potato leaves, pickled Chinese cabbage, bean shoots, bean leaves, Chinese olive and starfruit, plus the fresh dried groundnut oil of Huazhou, they're all delicious!"

"Besides, there are *Jiandui, Tangnianci, Bojichui* and *Laofenpi*," someone else added. These were delicious specialities from Maoming, Canton Province. What they said made Zhenfeng want to try to these dishes very much.

"I was a little boy when I came here to deal in Huazhou congee and at that time the weeds grew everywhere," Fuqiang continued. "My parents looked after the food, and I just helped them to deliver the tea and water to the diners. I'm so weak on study that I have to do business in Shenzhen." He blew out a mouthful of smoke, and went on, "Shekou is a special zone of special zones, and the bomb between the Microwave Mountain and Tortoise Mountain was regarded as the first bomb of our national reform and opening-up. Right then I witnessed this miracle nearby, blocking my ears. There were 20 tons of explosives, which exploded simultaneously in six caves, shaking the earth."

"The day of the first bomb was July 8, 1979, and on August 26 1980, the Shenzhen special economic zone was officially founded," Haonan said.

Later he asked Fuqiang, "What did you think of Shenzhen at that time?"

"When I saw it I fell in love with it. I also love so many beautiful girls in Shenzhen, who come from every corner of China." Fuqiang blew out more smoke. "I don't have much knowledge, but I've been interested in our Chinese idiom recently. Ho ho!"

"How can you say you don't have much knowledge? Now come on, cheers!" They rose to their feet, thirteen glasses chinking together.

"You're so fickle!" Zhenfeng said to Fuqiang.

"Oh no! I'm faithful to every beautiful girl whenever I'm with her!"

"With you it's one eye on the dish and the other on the saucepan." The others burst out laughing. "One conquest breeds the appetite for another."

"All you think about is 'putting it in'!" said Haonan thoughtlessly.

"What?" they all asked eagerly.

"I can't explain it to you," said Haonan hurriedly. He dared not reveal his exact meaning.

"Oh, don't play games! Actually I want to study English as well. Now since you're all here, I wish you all car salary and a cup of water." Fuqiang smiled.

"What do you mean?"

"I mean that you may take several cups of water every day, then you'll have the money to buy a car at the end of every month."

A ripple of laughter spread through the room.

Presently Haonan said. "So many young men are rushing into Shenzhen now."

At this point a female lobby manager pushed the door and came in. When she saw Haonan, she smiled. "Why didn't you come here earlier?" she asked. "There is a saying, 'You can't get a tiger's son unless you enter the tiger's den'."

Fuqiang wailed, "Aiyo! Now this room is a tiger's den, each of us is a male tiger and if you stay here longer, you'll give birth to many tigers' sons."

She often played jokes on Fuqiang by blaming him for things. "You monkey! I'll hang you on the wall and stick you there with superglue!" She seized a stainless steel spoon to thwack his shoulder and then left. Fuqiang was still laughing. All of them were amused except Haonan, who pacified her by saying, "Don't take it to heart too much".

Zhenfeng suddenly asked, "Fuqiang, my brother, someone told me that you can drive well. When you drive the Mercedes, you can tear up an orange at the same time."

"I'm ashamed you mention that!" Fuqiang had a Mercedes Benz S180. Although it was a downmarket model, as a Mercedes it was still better than other car brands.

"Can you also cut your nails while you're driving?" someone asked.

"Even cut a toenail," someone else chimed in.

"Lads! Come on!" People in other rooms were playing a finger- guessing game. It was getting darker now, but it was still very noisy in the restaurant.

"Fuqiang! Here come your big customers!" somebody called. It was Fuqiang's parents, who showed the elegance of Shenzhen as well as the rural features of the Huazhou countryside.

Just then two men, one fat and one thin, entered from outside the door. Fuqiang said, "Excuse me," then rose to his feet and went forward to meet them. However, they had not come to dine. They sipped tea served by Fuqiang and looked around. One said to him, "Well! Business, as you said before, is not bad!"

Fuqiang replied, "Of course! What I say is always true!"

The two men then got up and walked away muttering happily to each other, accompanied by Fuqiang. After about twenty minutes of conversation, they left. In fact, unknown to Fuqiang, before they had entered they had stood outside the restaurant, observing it for half an hour. And now, although it seemed they had left, they remained hiding outside, exchanging opinions and still studying the restaurant. Fifteen minutes later, they finally drove away.

Haonan had to return the west of Canton by a long bus journey at night, and those from Zhenfeng had to go back to the Shanghai Restaurant, so Fuqiang was about to pick them up and see them off. He led them to a secluded spot and handed a red envelope containing 100 yuan to each man. They all were surprised.

"How can we deserve this favour without doing anything for it?" one of them said. They handed it back to Fuqiang. Then they all moved their hands and legs back and forth and left and right like a group of boxers practising a slow *T'ai Chi Tui Shou*. It seemed that Fuqiang used a *Yunshou*, Zhenfeng performed a *Lanquewei* and Haonan suddenly executed a *Danbian* and a Sidekick. Fuqiang couldn't deal with them by himself. He shouted, "Stop it please! Tonight I would like to express heartfelt thanks for your coming to help me. It means a great deal to me. Today most guests have been specially invited by me, and I've given all of them red envelopes."

Everyone was utterly bewildered. Fuqiang then explained, "The two men who came here want to take over this restaurant of mine. Indeed I have not received a good income from it lately, so I would like to transfer it and I'll do that soon. In order to rally plenty of people, the more the better, to demonstrate the great popularity of this restaurant to these men, I invited all my relatives and friends to come here. Now those men have decided to buy this restaurant of mine and they have given me a deposit of 130,000 yuan. They were actually among the diners who took away the used oil that time."

"Then those who sat in front of the door, waiting for their sequence numbers to be called, had they...?" Haonan asked, turning his face to Fuqiang and seeming to know something.

Fuqiang tittered. "For that troop of people? I'd already made them eat their fill. Afterwards they stayed there, so that other new diners and passers-by could see how busy we were. Haha!"

Fuqiang seemed like an anteater in the tropical rainforest, which can tell by its nose whether ants are going out to look for food or coming back to their nest to rest. When the anteater's nose touches the ants' den, it can judge which side has more ants and which less.

Haonan suddenly had the feeling of a cave being opened. "So the reason why you invited so many people for dinner here was just a trick. But aren't you worried that they will take you to court?"

"How can they? They wanted to buy this restaurant and I wanted to sell it. So it met their requirements. Additionally those two didn't know about the internal relationship among us," said Fuqiang. "I neither robbed nor stole. And even so, only the one who is caught is called a thief."

They all yelled again, like primary school children reciting – "Only the one who is caught is called a thief!"

"The environment in Shenzhen has activated your brain." One of Zhenfeng's colleagues gave Fuqiang a thumbs-up.

"I just learn from others," said Fuqiang. "Now let me tell you a story."

He told them that when he had first arrived in Shenzhen, he had once wanted to take a minibus from Gushu to Sha'zui, Futian. At that time two minibuses were available in the station. The back one was empty, and in the front only six people were sitting. Without hesitation Fuqiang got on the front one. When he sat down the steward approached to charge him for a ticket and he paid, but the minibus remained stationary. He urged the driver to start as soon as possible. Although the steward replied that it would set off soon, it still did not leave. Fuqiang could not get off because he had paid for a ticket. Only half an hour later when three new passengers got on did it begin to leave. At that very moment, however, the six people who had been sitting there all along spontaneously got off, leaving silently. They had not been required to pay the bus fare.

Fuqiang suddenly understood everything. Hearing it, everyone else understood too. Fuqiang said that from then on he knew how to do whatever the occasion demanded.

One morning when he went to Gushu from Nantou checkpoint, he did not have enough money for a bus ticket. What could he do? A trick suddenly occurred to him. He jumped onto the No. 331 bus from Shekou to Song'gang, which regularly passed Gushu. When the female steward asked him to buy a ticket and asking him where he wanted to go, he replied, "Shekou". The steward said angrily, "You are going the wrong way, please get off at the next station." Fuqiang did so, without paying. Then he jumped on the next bus from Shekou to Song'gang. Another female steward asked him the same question and he gave the same reply. After getting on and off many times, he finally reached his destination smiling, because he had completed the journey without paying anything. However, before he got off the bus he was recognised by the first female steward. She told the driver to close the door and they drove straight to the police station. He was detained by the police, and he could not be released until his parents came to pay a fine at midnight.

Haonan then said something that worried Fuqiang. "So, we must be honest and do everything properly, or we'll suffer the consequences."

"Yes. Depend on it." Fuqiang, who still had trust in luck, patted Haonan's shoulder. "Come to Shenzhen as quick as possible. Who once said that originally there were no roads on the land?"

"It was Lu Xun. At the end of his short story titled *Hometown*, he wrote: 'At first there is no road on the land, but a road will appear as more and more walkers travel across it.'"

"That's it! I'm sorry, I don't remember Lu Xun." Fuqiang punched his leg and said, "On the contrary, I think that there are originally many roads on the land, but the roads will not remain if there are more and more people walking on it."

Everyone was stunned again. Then one of them exclaimed knowingly, "You've become a philosopher!"

"I daren't claim that. As you know, Haonan is here, I daren't!" Fuqiang shrugged.

They got into the car, laughing and chatting. Fuqiang had called on another friend to drive.

They all drove to Shennan Road. Beside the road the longan and litchi trees were in darkness. Some lamps were lit in the industrial areas, and the routers and spark machines were operating noisily, as young men and women were going off duty.

When Haonan arrived at the Shennan Road, he said goodbye to Zhenfeng and his friends. They were going back to their restaurant, and Haonan was going to west Canton. They went their different ways.

"Have a good journey! I must come back to serve for those relatives and friends of mine," said Fuqiang. "Shenzhen is a magical new city, please come here to work one day soon. *Diaotou!*"

A long-distance bus to west Canton was coming. Haonan jumped on it, waving to Fuqiang.

Chapter 3
Longing for Shenzhen

The Yunkai Mountain Range lies in the crossing between the Canton Province and Guangxi, in the mountainous area of west Canton where southern fruits such as longan, litchi, mango and so on are largely planted, as well as sweet potato, mulberry, rubber tree and citrus. At the foot of lofty Liuhuang Mountain and beside the Ling River, Nawu Town is positioned in a forest of bamboo with clean hills and water, and the smoke from cooking fires curls up into the sky. The road from northern Luchuan in Guangxi to southern Huazhou County crosses Nawu Town, and along it young people travel to Beijing, Shanghai, Guangzhou, Shenzhen and abroad, to study and to work.

Haonan had lived there from birth, doing farm work for his family; he often played with his little buddies, including Fuqiang, who was three years older than him. Sometimes they fished and wandered among the streams and the forest; in the summer they went boating in the Baoshu reservoir, or climbed the Shegong mountain which stands at its centre. There was one time when they climbed

Liuhuang Mountain, the highest in Nawu, occasionally seeing the footprints of a cat; they were astonished and hurried away because they thought it was the footprint of a tiger.

Nawu Middle School was formerly called Lingxiu Middle School. In the 1970s, when Haonan studied in the junior class, a film was shown in Nawu Theatre narrating the story of Shenzhen and Hong Kong, describing Shenzhen as being almost like crossing a river to Hong Kong. Because of this, Shenzhen took advantage of the closeness of Hong Kong. Normally by then the mainland people found it hard to go to Hong Kong, but if they went to Shenzhen, they could stand on the frontier to take a look at Hong Kong.

In the 1980s when the Hong Kong TV series *Knight-errant of Huo Yuanjia* was shown on the Pearl channel of Canton TV, black and white TV was still rare, colour TV even rarer. Nawu Supply and Sales Company was one of the fortunate places which owned a colour TV set, although the screen was only 14". So in the evening Haonan, together with his classmates, often went there to watching this TV series. They admired Hong Kong, Shenzhen and their future.

At that time the people in Nawu Town often said, "Hi! How are you? I have just come back from Shenzhen!" It was usually fashionable people who said this. They wore bell-bottom trousers with styling mousse on their hair, white shirts and

Plum Blossom or "Chunlei" watches. They also rolled up their sleeves and carried the latest style of travel bag. This was how a piece of doggerel described them then:

> *Those with golden tooth fillings, whose mouths were opened often;*
> *Those who wore watches, whose sleeves were rolled up often;*
> *Those who wore white shirts inside, whose coat buttons were untied often.*

If you went to Shenzhen only once, no matter how long you stayed there, it would be something to talk about, and local people would know how splendid visiting the city was.

"Hi! How are you? I just came back from Shenzhen!" this was the glorious slogan flying invisibly above the wide, clean sky of Nawu, like a song sung by Mei Yanfang, a Hong Kong singer, several years later:

> *How I want to recognise a sincere friend of mine,*
> *To whom I talk about the dream in my side...*

But in the Nawu mountain area, which "works from sunrise and stops at dusk", the way to develop your life as a youth was to enter university after passing the college entrance examination, or join the army. If you failed in these, you would stay at home doing farm work or go to Shenzhen to do a labouring job. So when Haonan studied in high middle school, those classmates or hometown students who didn't pass the college entrance examination after graduating from high middle school had to work in different factories making electronic goods, clothing, plastic goods, hardware, handbags or mouldings in Shenzhen so as to escape the hard work of farming.

Fuqiang liked to read comic books, but was reluctant to study hard at school when he was a child. Yet he was always smart. One time when he was reaping rice with his family in the field, Yang Wu, a strong youth busy in the neighbouring field, gave him a scornful look and said, "Little creature! I want to gamble with you now."

Fuqiang asked, "What do you mean?"

Yang Wu said, "I am standing in my own field now. If you can persuade me to go to that high ridge between fields over there, I will reap one *mu* of rice for you. As you know, one *mu* is 666 square metres! Haha!"

Fuqiang asked who would be witnesses. Yang Wu said their parents would, along with the villagers who were reaping rice nearby.

Fuqiang looked around, facing many fellow villagers looking at him smilingly. He suddenly felt in trouble. He lowered his head and said nothing. Yang Wu laughed at him.

Then Fuqiang raised his head and smiled. "I would prefer to make a bigger gamble with you," he said. "I can persuade you to go from that high ridge between the fields back to your own field. If I fail, I will agree to reap three *mu* of rice for you."

"Really?"

"Why not?"

Yang Wu smiled, and immediately raced to the ridge and squatted down on it with a smile, ready for the challenge. But as soon as he squatted down, Fuqiang jumped, laughed and threw his sickle to him, telling him to start reaping. Yang Wu was puzzled. Then Fuqiang said laughingly, "Didn't you say just now that if I could coax you to that high ridge between fields several metres away, you would reap one *mu* of rice for me?"

Then Yang Wu realised that he had lost. He regretfully went back to his field, patting his head. And as soon as he stood on his own field, Fuqiang smiled again, "Look! Haven't you come back from that ridge to your own farm field now? I have won again!" Then Yang Wu had to take the sickle and reap the rice for Fuqiang.

Fuqiang continued laughing until his stomach ached. His parent was laughing too. On the contrary, the parents of Yang Wu were angry and rebuked the stupid Yang Wu.

After the autumn, Fuqiang's family moved to Sha'zui, Shenzhen, to deal with their restaurant business. Years later, a grown-up Fuqiang came back to his home town. In order to go faster and show off, he spent 1,600 yuan on hiring a taxi from Shenzhen to Nawu. What a way to spend 1,600 yuan - a special taxi from Shenzhen to Nawu! All the people in the town were dumbfounded. This red taxi with Shenzhen registration plates shuttled through the town many times. Fuqiang would have liked a sun roof so that he could have stood up and waved to his fellow villagers. Instead he stuck his head out of the side window, like a chief inspecting the troops.

After a while he got out of the taxi, took off his shirt and hung it over his shoulder, revealing his T-shirt, which simply showed the word "Shenzhen" in red. On his waist hung a pager, looking like part of his body. He grasped his mobile phone, the first that had been seen in Nawu. When he talked with fellow villagers, he held this phone and pointed in any direction, and the villagers' eyes followed it. Since the phone was always in his hand, the black antenna looked like an additional finger, the size of the claw of a black-boned chicken.

The vehicles soon formed a traffic jam, the bikes rang their bells and tractors drove slowly along making their *pangpang* sound. Those who were eating *Bojichui*, *Shuiye* and *Tuoluo* biscuit hurriedly put down their chopsticks and stood on tiptoe to watch. The hubbub was as if a puppet show was being given at the annual *Nianli* festival, a traditional annual gathering in some villages in the Maoming and Zhanjiang village areas of Canton Province.

All the people admired Fuqiang, saying, "How glorious this *Diaotou* is!"

At Haonan's home, Zhou Weiluo, his father, a thin man with withered hands and legs, frequently reminded him, "You must study hard so that you can pass the college entrance examination, then you can make a good living like Fuqiang, otherwise your only choice will be to do hard factory work or farm work for the rest of your life and going to Nawu market every day to buy agricultural chemicals and fertiliser for your little 1.3 *mu* of land pests. Do you understand?"

At that time Haonan faced the college entrance examination of the 1980s, for which more real skills were required compared with that of the 1990s. No wonder someone joked that while the recruiting rate in the 1970s and 1980s had been about 10%, later on it was up to 110%. In the past the students worried how they could pass the college entrance examination, and as time went by, it turned out that the universities, which were as numerous as the popular kindergartens, worried how they could recruit enough students.

Haonan listened and mutely agreed. He made up his mind that he must try as hard as he could to pass the college entrance examination.

At dusk one early summer evening, he strolled with several classmates along the road in front of Nawu Middle School. Since the rain had just stopped, the sky was now brilliant blue, and white mist was floating around Liuhuang Mountainside in the far distance. The silkworm leaves were green and the longan flowers, which were in bloom, spread their aroma. The air was filled with the harsh trilling of cicadas, and a herd of big buffaloes were mooing in the fields. The peasants were busy planting rice seedlings.

Suddenly a long-haul bus appeared behind Haonan, driving slowly in the direction of Huazhou County. Through the car window he saw a familiar face. It was Fuqiang. They had not seen each other for a long time, and Haonan missed him very much, but now Fuqiang was in a hurry, so Haonan just asked him, "Where are you going now?"

But he felt at once that his question had been unnecessary. The bus drove speedily on, and Fuqiang opened the car window and stretched his head out, waving. "TO... SHEN... ZHEN!" he shouted.

His voice was so loud that Haonan could hear it over the noise of the bus engine. Fuqiang was trembling with excitement and full of happiness and glory.

Seeing the bus drawing farther and farther away in the dust it was kicking up, Haonan and his classmates stood and watched for a long time.

They all wondered longingly when they would be able to get on the long-haul bus to Shenzhen like Fuqiang. Then they could take a walk and see for themselves that wealthy, highly- developed city.

After that year, when Haonan finally got a high score in the college entrance examination in Gaoliang Middle School, he went to Guangzhou to study in college. Although he was sent to west Canton to work after college graduation, whenever he heard news from Shenzhen he was inspired, like a soldier who hears the beat of the war drum. Haonan was longing to go to Shenzhen.

Chapter 4
Trial Without Pay

After Haonan returned to West Canton from Sha'zui, he went to Shenzhen on business as eagerly as a devotee of Islam rushing to Mecca. After completing the business he visited foreign companies in Shenzhen one by one, presenting dozens of his resumes and introducing himself.

Two weeks later, he went to Shenzhen again after receiving a telephone call, arriving at the offices of China Merchants (Futian) I/E Trade Co for an interview. After that, when the time approached for the festivals, he sent greetings cards to Chen Xiaomei, the manager of the human resources department of this company. Xiaomei, who had once been a journalist, was more and more impressed by him. Xiaomei was in her forties and came from Beijing with a fluent command of Mandarin. She was a fast speaker, and her actions showed that she was capable.

One greeting, one chance!

One day Xiaomei saw a beautiful greeting card pressed under the glass top on her table, bearing Haonan's perfect handwriting. At the time the company wanted to recruit a foreign trade executive, so she called him and after a few days, Haonan completed the formalities to leave his former company, rushing to Shenzhen with a red and blue bag of snake-skin strips. He was given a position in Department Seven of the company, on a three- month trial. When he worked in West Canton for one month, an apartment of 90 square metres, three rooms plus a hall, was assigned to him by the company. If he worked there continuously, this apartment would be his own. Yet he left it. Colleagues pointed out that many people never got such an apartment in their lives, but Haonan insisted that he was determined to work in Shenzhen after quitting the house.

China Merchants Company was on the second floor of Zhaozhuo Building and the office covered more than 600 square metres. Dozens of offices for the general manager, vice general manager and I/E department were divided by walls. There were also five lines of tables, used by all the foreign trade businessmen.

On a morning in late December 1991, a business mobilization meeting for 1992 was being held here. The conference room was a space of about 90 square metres, and the air conditioning was running. In the centre of the room was a rectangular mahogany table. The general manager, Hu Han'gong, sat in the president's seat. He was about fifty with a fat face, in a suit, and came from Sichuan Province. There were 82 staff working as managers, assistant managers of I/E department or as foreign trade executives attending this conference. Haonan wrote notes as he listened, sitting as upright as if he was having his hair cut.

"Now, let me introduce Zhou Haonan, the new recruit to our company," said Hu, pointing to him.

Haonan stood up and bowed to the others in turn, smiling.

"When the Shenzhen special economic zone opened up, comrade Yuan Geng sent out a call saying 'Time is money, efficiency is life', which activated people all around China. A short time ago, when Haonan was in his interview with the manager of our human resources department, he offered to work on a trial basis for one week without payment. This was a special way of promoting himself, a wonderful selling point, a new concept. I like it!"

There was applause and everyone looked at Haonan, who flushed. Hu continued, "Now Haonan has been working here for over a week. According to my observations and the response from our chief department, his performance is acceptable. We appreciated his concept of doing a working test for one week without payment, which showed his confidence and common sense. But we don't expect anyone to undergo a test without payment. Even if he had not passed the working test, we would still pay him."

Looking at Hu, Haonan nodded. Hu went on, "Our company is a comprehensive firm, and the export products are decided by the foreign trade executives themselves. The salary of the executive is 600 yuan with an additional HK$200. The task for every executive next year is to create US$3 million of foreign currency and half a million yuan of net profit. To each businessman who fulfills this task, we'll give a 20% bonus, along with a Shenzhen Permanent Residence Permit. I don't think most of you present have had such a permit, although you have always dreamed of becoming real Shenzheners. Every deal has to be charged to the businessman's account beforehand, to be repaid after the business is finished. Also, before fulfilling every deal, the executive must present a Budget Form of Cost and Profit to their department manager for signature, then to the vice general manager, Zhou Jieming, who is in charge of import and export business, and finally to me, and then you may start formally."

Jieming, a man with a full moustache who sat beside Hu, added, "The actual business charge must be almost the same as the budgeted figure. Very little difference is allowed."

The charge won't be repaid until the deal is fulfilled? Haonan mulled this over. It was totally different from the way he had worked in his former company. He had to think seriously before the business started which charges should be paid by him and which should not.

After a pause, Fu Yanjie, another executive, said, "This is the nature of DIY, do it yourself, right?"

"Yes. A work procedure needs to be done by you yourself," replied Hu.

"What's the difference between this and assigning the fields to every family in the Chinese countryside?" asked Fu Yanjie.

"Yes, it's DIY. It's like assigning farm fields to every family. The competition is fierce, we can't eat from the same big pot. Yet we don't support sole working. Instead we hope all of you will cooperate and help each other. We emphasise the nature of DIY, also we call for a spirit of cooperation. Meanwhile the logistics office, financial department, customs clearance department and bill department of the company will closely co-operate with the work of the I/E departments, and our 108 staff must be united. Certainly we only provide a business platform for you to enable you to exercise the potential business ability, this is the business policy of mine. You must hold responsibility for the company just as I do for my higher office." Hu said seriously, "This is a rule of the company, no bargaining. True gold will find its price. Regarding the business, on the whole, we only care about the result, regardless of the process."

"What an example!" one executive marvelled.

"Tax rebate of export, invoice..." somebody said.

"Cheat on tax rebates for export? You'll be caught!" someone else argued.

"Only the one who is caught is called a thief," someone said in a low voice.

Hu responded, "Hush! And be serious. Disregarding the process doesn't mean becoming a criminal. This is in the Shenzhen special economic zone, and we decided on such a rule to motivate your business drive."

All of them were silent, digesting the spirit of Hu's speech.

"With regard to export business settlement, we suggest adopting L/C terms, that is, the letter of credit. Now let's invite Haonan to introduce briefly the L/C. He is a specialist in this," said Hu.

Haonan said, "I'm much obliged. The letter of credit or L/C is one of the three main settlement terms in foreign trade, which sometimes we call international trade or international business. As to foreign trade documents, if the documents conform with each other and the L/C, the payment will be received through the bank in due course."

"So if lots of goods are shipped on board, relying on such a commercial invoice, packing list and bill of lading etc, can goods worth hundreds of thousands be received?" someone asked.

"Yes! This is bank credit," someone else replied.

"I don't believe it," said someone doubtfully.

"We must believe the bank. If the bank cannot be believed, then many will be worried," said Haonan. "Under such circumstances, we have to believe. If you worry that you can't eat fresh pork, for example, will you sleep with the pig every day?"

They all burst out laughing.

"All of you should keep control and use the L/C to make sure payment is received," said Miss Lin Min, the manager of the bill department.

"How about collection?" one executive asked.

Hu instructed Haonan to go on.

"Its safety is not as stable as letter of credit," Haonan said.

"It's best that the buyer should arrange full payment in advance, even a 30% deposit."

"But if the buyer also wants you to release the goods first, and says he'll arrange payment upon receiving the goods, would you agree?"

"Of course not!" several executives said loudly.

"So generally, considering fairness to both the buyer and the seller, the best payment terms is still the L/C," someone said.

"Regarding the L/C, it concerns so many documents that it is hard to handle. Are any payment terms more suitable than L/C?" somebody asked Haonan.

"Actually it's not complicated to handle these documents. There is a saying that 'The one who feels it's difficult can't do it and the one who can do it doesn't feel it's difficult'. The L/C isn't the best payment arrangement in the world, but with regard to fairness and reasonableness to both the exporter and importer, there is no fairer or more reasonable arrangement – not at present, not before and probably not in the future," Haonan said calmly.

Then Hu asked Haonan to talk about the "deposit", which is often used in a contract. Haonan replied, "We should manage the deposit problem properly in the contract, otherwise we'll lose much and there was once a case on this. Similarly we must pay enough attention to the deposit we'll probably receive from the buyer. It's very important that we must guarantee that we have the goods before we receive the deposit, according to contract law, otherwise we'll face double compensation for the buyer."

"This man knows more about foreign trade than Lin, the manager of the bill department," somebody said in a low voice. Lin, a thin lady, fully agreed with this and applauded Haonan.

"This has been an excellent lesson in international business," Hu said, summing up.

Chapter 5
Calligraphy and Romance

In the rest period Haonan sometimes wandered around Sea World in Shekou, then went to the Shanghai Restaurant to sit and chat. One Sunday morning, after breakfast, Haonan, who had arrived by bus, was talking with several colleagues of Zhenfeng. One said, "The pork bun in some restaurants is kneaded by the bakers with their feet. If you find a hard object when you're eating, it's probably a toenail." Then another added, "Don't think the meat you eat is delicious, you may be eating borax because it was made with bad meat."

Zhenfeng arrived. "Haonan, follow me please!" he said, before leading him to the office of Wang Zhengmao, the general manager of the restaurant. Zhengmao, who wore polished shoes and backcombed hair, was a fellow villager of Haonan in Huazhou.

He said to Haonan, "Zhenfeng once told me that you do excellent calligraphy. Last month I lent 300,000 yuan to a friend. One night I came back home too late. I forgot to take out the debt note from my trousers. Early next morning my wife didn't check the trousers and put them in the washing machine, so the debt note was destroyed."

"So what do you want me to do for you?" Haonan asked.

"It's an unusual honour of mine to have you here," Zhengmao said, showing Haonan a paper covered with writing. "This is the handwriting of that friend who borrowed money from me. Now could you do me a favour by imitating his handwriting and writing a new debt note for me? This is in case he won't acknowledge the debt, and I don't have proof."

Haonan was dumbfounded. He frowned, unwilling to do this favour.

"With your calligraphy skills, it will be so easy to imitate his handwriting," Zhenfeng said. Zhengmao looked at Haonan trustfully, smiling.

Haonan said, "You flatter me too much but, ten thousand pardons, this action is against the law, isn't it?"

Zhengmao explained hurriedly, "This is the only way, all the consequence will be borne by me."

Zhenfeng butted in. "Please set your mind at rest and write. I guarantee no harmful consequences to you."

Haonan was still hesitating. Zhenfeng and Zhengmao explained again and again. Finally Haonan agreed and wrote the text as requested.

They inspected his work. "It's absolutely one hundred per cent the same!" said Zhengmao.

"Nobody could tell it's fake. Haonan, you helped me so much! I won't forget you, ever!" He clapped in excitement.

"You must have done some good research into calligraphy, right?" smiled Zhengmao.

"Yes. The first thing with calligraphy is to imitate grounding," said Haonan. "I like regular script the best, because it's the foundation of all handwriting. The dot stroke, horizontal stroke and vertical stroke are the most basic, like the accelerator, clutch and brake when learning to drive, and the straight punch, hook swing punch and low punch in boxing, and the half-round kick, push kick and side kick in Chinese Sanda *Kungfu*. These are the most basic and also the most mysterious."

Shortly after the restaurant started to serve food, Haonan left. In the doorway, he suddenly stopped, his eyes dazzled by the brightness of a purplish-red flower-printed cheongsam. It adorned the beautiful figure of the waitress of the restaurant. He knew her name was Lin Laizhen, because he had once met her when he had been there to look for Zhenfeng.

Just then the beautiful girl turned and said, "Hello Haonan. I have heard from your cousin that your calligraphy is excellent, and your English typing is fast as well."

"Thank you! But I don't deserve it," he said. His heart was thumping wildly.

Haonan wanted to say more, but he feared he would obstruct her work, and that the others would think he was throwing himself at her. He also felt embarrassed. He would have liked to get closer to her, but was afraid of being watched by others.

Just then two diners walked into the restaurant, and Laizhen had to usher them to the appropriate table. Haonan hovered there uneasily. A cook noticed him and said, "Fuck! Looking for a girlfriend here? Who do you think you are?"

After some moments, Laizhen came back to the front desk and asked Haonan, "Will you have time free next Sunday?"

He replied without further ado, "Of course, why not?"

"I want to go to your office. Then you will teach me how to type and write calligraphy, all right?"

"All right! And I – I – I'm leaving now," he said, nodding like a little chicken pecking rice on the ground. He couldn't help feeling excited as he retreated from the scene.

During the following week at work, Haonan imagined how wonderful the appointment with Laizhen would be next Sunday. When he came back to the company dormitory he would stand by the public telephone on the second floor. Each time it rang he lost no time in answering it. He was afraid that he would miss Laizhen's call, or she would cancel the appointment, so for the next few days he became a voluntary telephone operator and messenger for all of his colleagues.

When Sunday finally arrived, it was sunny. Early in the morning he took a bath to eliminate the smell of his body, although in truth he had no body odour. As he bathed, he sang passionately a popular song originally sung by Andy Lau, a famous Hong Kong singer, *Continuous Love*:

> *Do you know that any and every glimpse of you*
> *Intoxicates me ceaselessly in all of my life?*
> *Today, could you allow me in this life of mine*
> *To still fall in love with you crazily?*

His colleagues were still asleep, including Yanjie, who used Sunday to catch up on his sleep. Yanjie got up, narrowed his sleepy eyes and asked Haonan whether he had signed a big order today. Haonan had to lower his voice to answer. After that he went out and got on the No. 204 bus to Shekou. He arrived half an hour ahead of the appointment time and waited for his sweetheart.

As he watched Laizhen slowly approach, every movement she made gave him the magical feeling of watching a lotus fairy. She was wearing a long white sleeveless skirt which impressed him as clean and pure, like a breeze blowing from the countryside. This kind of pure image, without dressing up, was just what he loved the most on a girl.

They got on the bus together and went to his offices. The building was empty and locked up, but he had borrowed a key from Xiaomei beforehand. They entered the office, sitting by the "Double Fishes" typewriter made in Shanghai, the machine he had learned to type on when he had taken college courses in Guangzhou before.

He poured her a cup of boiled water. After sitting down, he laid a copy of the English paper on the left of the typewriter. Then he fed a blank piece of paper into it. When he lightly pressed the "Enter" key, it was like a concert pianist testing the keys of a piano before playing. Then he began typing, his eyes staring sideways at the English paper instead of at the typewriter. He was typing at five to six letters per second.

"So fast!" said Laizhen.

"It's nothing," he said. "This skill is a must in our business." But he thought to himself: *fast? Let our love go faster!*

"How do you switch between capital and small letters?" she asked, pointing to the keyboard. He explained. She nodded and asked, "Are there any rules about how the fingers type?"

"Yes. It's called finger technique. Every finger has its own keys. Take the index finger of the left hand for example, it's used to type F, G, R, T, V, B and the figures 4 and 5." As he spoke, he typed.

"How about the index finger of the right hand?" She stretched out her right hand to the keyboard.

"That one is in charge of –" but as Haonan spoke, his right hand suddenly touched the tip of her index finger. Although it was the slightest of touches, he felt as though he had had an electric shock. He trembled, and saw her white and tender face colour up. The wind blew into through the half-opened window, stirring her beautiful hair, and he smelled her hair and even caught the scent of her body. He felt intoxicated.

"How about you?" she asked.

"The index finger of the right hand types J, H, U, Y, M, N and 7, 6..." he shook himself to wake himself up, as a diver tosses his head when he rises to the surface.

After that, she changed the topic, asking him how to exercise good calligraphy. Haonan became excited again as he recited:

"The right pose of writing should be one fist's distance between the chest and the desk edge and 0.33 metres between the eyes and the desktop. The body should be straight, head right and shoulders level, the legs parallel and the arms stretched out."

Hearing this, she looked at the distance between her chest and the desk edge and asked him, "Is that right?"

He rose to his feet, glancing at her, but then hurriedly looked away. She just meant that he would stretch his fist to measure for her. "Enough to me? Measure for me, please!" she added.

Haonan worriedly stretched out his right hand, but the closer it got to her chest, the harder his heart was beating. As his fist touched the edge of the desk, it was still five centimetres from his fist to her chest. He did not dare to look at her directly, so he turned his head and said, "Not yet."

Laizhen pushed her chest forward so that Haonan's fist lay in the groove between her breasts. His fist was now trapped between the desk and her chest. His fist trembled, held as it was between her breasts. He longed to unclench it into the "five claws of a golden dragon" so that he could fondle those two white and enchanting mounds, separated from him only by a layer of thin clothes. But he had to resist. Meanwhile he could feel the heat of her chest, a heat which would warm up a hibernating python. He also felt the firm elasticity of her breasts under the cloth.

Thinking he was behaving strangely, Laizhen raised her head and asked, "Enough, or not?"

Haonan, red faced, hastily withdrew his trembling fist. "En– en–enough," he stammered. She reddened as well.But he still did not dare to look at her directly. He then recited the procedure for holding the pen:

"Clenching the pen between the thumb and the index finger,

Touching the pen shaft with the middle finger.
The other two fingers bend and the palm should be empty.
Three centimetres is required from the nib to fingers."

"How do you know this rhyme?" she asked.

"This is from a book called 'The Theory of Cen's Calligraphy'," he replied. He realised that she still didn't fully understand, and wanted him to teach her hand in hand. He tried it, and when his big hand covered her small, soft one, his heart seemed to beat like a horse running free on boundless grassland. Yet he knew he had to control this feeling of his.

"Have you transferred your permanent residence permit to Shenzhen yet?" she suddenly asked.

"Oh..." he was at a loss for how to reply. "Not yet, I've only been here a short time."

"Then can you apply for it later?"

At that time when every young man wanted to go to Shenzhen, a Shenzhen Permanent Residence Permit was the first dream. Haonan was anxious to have one too, like a captain on a long journey who is always longing to arrive at the destination port. But the quota was so limited that it would be difficult for Haonan to get one.

"I'll try at the end of the year," he said.

"What credentials do you hold for Shenzhen now?"

"Only a Temporary Living Permit." Having to admit this damaged his confidence like a punctured ball.

"Do you have a house in Shenzhen?" asked Laizhen.

Haonan now felt he was getting a fiercer headache. "I'm living in the company's sleeping quarters," he said. "Do you have a Shenzhen Permanent Residence Permit?"

"No."

"Where do you live now?"

"The staff dormitory. It's called Sihai, the biggest place for immigrant workers in Shekou, eight women in a room. It's too crowded."

The day went fast, and it was dusk when they left the office. He invited her for supper in a Cantonese restaurant near Chegongmiao, then accompanied her back to Sihai.

Haonan had never imagined that he could meet such a wonderful girl. He felt she was so enthusiastic that he had a real chance of success with her. He was prepared to teach her how to learn English and type it well, and he would encourage her to take an evening university course so that she could look for a job as a secretary later on. But to get a Shenzhen Permanent Residence Permit, the supreme dream of his, he would have to become more and more accomplished in business first.

Chapter 6
Secret Ways of Getting Wealth

The continuous prosperity of Huanggang, Futian was first brought about by the expansion of export business at Huanggang checkpoint and purchasing by Hong Kong people who rushed from the other bank of the Shenzhen River.

One evening in early January, the door of the Qianlong Hotel in Shuiwei village was opened and the shining lights on the roof were spinning ceaselessly. The percussive sound of heavy metal music was deafening. The popular song *If Heaven has Love*, sung by Yuan Fengying, was played, followed by *Awakening Time* by Chen Shuhua.

In one of the rooms Fuqiang was eating bananas. "Hi! How are you?" he said as Haonan pushed the door open. Fuqiang wore a red silk tie. His real leather bag was laid nearby, and on the table stood proudly his mobile phone.

"Not bad. And you? What favourable wind blew you to my humble abode?"

"I'm still alive. Today nobody knows what may happen tomorrow, so why worry? And nobody can bring anything if he dies, so why complain? Haha!"

"Of course you don't complain, for you can always earn plenty of money," said Haonan.

"You can do what other people can't if you have enough money, that is to say, you can do anything if you have lots of money. Haha!" Fuqiang said. Haonan smiled.

Fuqiang smoothly bit off the cap from a beer bottle and said, "You hadn't got used to the beer when you were in my restaurant last time, but now there's no problem for you, right? You must make good use of it!" He poured a full glass for Haonan.

"Drinking beer? Not too bad," Haonan said, sitting down.

"Most things you do won't be too bad if you strive for them, I believe," Fuqiang said. "And no eating or drinking? That won't help you to get business."

Fuqiang, whose life was going well, had rosy cheeks and wore styling mousse on his hair. Everything he wore was a famous brand and he was wearing a large 24 carat gold ring on his middle finger, inlaid with the Chinese character for "*Fa*" (rich).

"After we sold the restaurant in Sha'zui, my parents put the money into the antiques market," he said. "Seeing that some of my friends were earning so much money in foreign trade, I engaged in it as well." This surprised Haonan. Fuqiang continued, "But I must learn it from you, for you graduated from a foreign trade college. It was said that as long as you know how the cost of foreign currency exchange is calculated, you can earn a lot of money. So, what's the cost of foreign currency exchange?"

In foreign trade activities Haonan worked in customs clearance and had been one of the first group of foreign businessmen tested and approved by the State Ministry of Economy and Trade. "The cost of foreign exchange is how many yuan you have to spend for one dollar of foreign currency," he explained briefly.

"I'd like to cooperate with you, because you can't be earning much money in the foreign trade company you work for now," Fuqiang said directly.

"We played games together when we were children, so how can I say no? And when I entered Gaoliang Middle School, you helped me so much."

"Because you're one of ours, now I'll tell you straight," Fuqiang said. He explained that he was currently dealing in the export of mechanical watch movements. As soon as Fuqiang mentioned this item, Haonan understood. It was too sensitive now because the rate of tax rebate was as high as 45%, nearly half the profit.

Fuqiang continued to explain that his method was to purchase a quantity of mechanical watch movements, then transport them to Hong Kong by container truck after customs clearance at Huanggang checkpoint. When this container arrived in Hong Kong, it would be switched to another container truck, then driven back to Shenzhen. When export customs clearance was finished, the container of goods would be exported to Hong Kong again. In this way one to five lots of goods could be handled each week. As Fuqiang needed a foreign trade businessman who was trustworthy and familiar with the process, he had immediately thought of Haonan. As to the profit, it could be shared half and half. By dint of exporting and importing the same goods, the original 45% tax rebate was almost the net profit.

Haonan was startled. Though Fuqiang was doing this deal late in life, such dishonesty in foreign trade was unexpected. It was cheating to obtain the export tax rebate.

"No need to hurry," said Fuqiang. "You think it over first. I'll wait for you." Then he said mysteriously, "In Shenzhen now, a hair salon isn't the place where you have a haircut and an envelope isn't where you put a letter. You know what I mean." Haonan listened, lost in meditation.

"Even if you refuse, it doesn't matter. We can cooperate on something else. Anyway, even if the business fails, we will still be friends," Fuqiang said. "However, if you deal with this business for a few months, will you still worry about a Shenzhen Permanent Residence Permit or a house? You can buy them. And drive a Mercedes!"

Hearing this, Haonan was excited. How tempting this was. He recalled that Laizhen had mentioned the Shenzhen Permanent Residence Permit many times. She had a modest educational background at upper middle school and worked in the Shanghai Restaurant and quota in the restaurant was rare. Even it was available, how could it be her turn? Her only hope was to have a boyfriend with a Shenzhen Permanent Residence Permit, and then she would be able to immigrate to Shenzhen after marriage. He was very keen to help her so that they could unite to form the ideal family.

Fuqiang took out a set of documents. He showed a commercial invoice and a packing list to Haonan and said, "This is a letter of credit opened to Shenzhen Fajun I/E Co from Dubai." Then he showed a copy of a bill of lading to Haonan, scrutinizing the signature of the captain. This was what Haonan understood best. This kind of deal between two banks was purely a trade in documents. The most important document was the bill of lading, the ownership certificate for the goods.

"Your calligraphy is so fine that you can successfully imitate both Chinese and English," said Fuqiang, smiling.

"Do you mean I have to imitate the signature of the captain?" Haonan said in terror, thinking that Fuqiang was intending to do "non-goods trade", that is to say, he would not ship the goods at all, just present the documents to the bank.

Haonan recalled that in normal times the executives in some shipping companies usually presented him with some blank original bill of lading, advising him that upon the goods being given customs clearance, he could type the contents of the bill of lading on by his own English typewriter, then sign the original and present it to the bank for negotiation together with the commercial invoice, packing list and certificate of origin etc. This was partly because they wanted to improve their working efficiency, and partly because they wanted to get Haonan's overseas shipping business. But this did not mean that he wanted to use the non-goods trade. Actually if he signed, even if the signature did not match that of the captain or first mate, the sum for the goods could still be received, because authenticating the signature was not the bank's responsibility. But Haonan did not dare to do it.

"We still have other ways of doing business, just depends if you dare." Fuqiang looked at the door warily, then murmured in Haonan's ear, "To be frank, we've already rented an apartment on the first floor of a village house in Shatoujiao, through which we've dug a tunnel to Hong Kong. You can go there to investigate it when you have time."

"What for?" A sudden fear seized Haonan.

"Well, sometimes when we're free we take goods from Shenzhen to Hong Kong, or from Hong

Kong to Shenzhen, including electronic products and batteries." Fuqiang patted Haonan's shoulder.

Digging a tunnel! Holy saints! This really was a new idea. Haonan remembered that one night in his childhood he had walked with Fuqiang to Nawu Theater eight kilometres away to watch the film *Tunnel Warfare*. Normally a film would be played in turn in every village of Nawu community, but the two of them just thought the sooner they saw it the better. That night when they went back home after the film was over, there was a two-kilometre stretch of dangerous road they had to pass, bordered by gloomy bamboo groves. In the dark they told each other, "Let's run as fast as we can!" They started running, holding little knives to defend themselves against the "night ghost", if there was one. The next day they stood on the grain-sunning ground of the village, describing the film to wide-eyed audiences. In *Tunnel Warfare*, a Chinese film made in 1965, the Chinese army and people successfully counterattack the Japanese invaders by using various kinds of secret tunnels in Hebei Province. But Haonan had never imagined that Fuqiang would use this approach to foreign trade. In this way goods were imported and exported without going through customs clearance or any tax being imposed. How could he think this out and make it work?

"Digging a tunnel, doesn't that mean smuggling?" Haonan said, staring at Fuqiang.

"Don't put it like that! This is goods exchange, private trade," Fuqiang said dismissively. "Anyway, I welcome you to join us. I guarantee that you will earn as much as my partner."

Haonan clenched his fist and held his chin, sucking in a mouthful of cold air.

"Abroad it is easy to earn a little money, but hard to earn a lot. In Shenzhen, however, it is hard to earn a little money, but easy to earn a lot," said Fuqiang slowly.

Haonan was astonished by this saying.

"This saying will gradually be proved true the longer you stay here. Haha!" said Fuqiang proudly. "But if you want to work a little more safely, which means you are happy to earn less, we have another operation. Your export orders, particularly stationary orders, can be brought to our company to handle, for we've already enlisted a state-owned foreign company to do stationary export business. Foreign exchange is urgently required by this company. In this way you can earn 0.3-0.5 yuan per US dollar."

Haonan said nothing.

"So please remember to bring the direct importers of stationary to trade in the name of our company if possible," Fuqiang went on. "We can work together, and we have a special advantage on stationary. There are so many projects that you'll do well even if you only choose one of them. Think it over, please!"

Haonan was still lost in thought.

"Now, let's relax a little!" Fuqiang suddenly called a chief stewardess over and asked her to bring two beautiful girls. After a little while, two girls who looked as sweet as honey sugar came smiling into the room. Fuqiang ogled them, then stood up and hugged one of them tightly, singing a karaoke song. They sang *After Losing You*, a nice song which had made Wen Zhaolun famous in Hong Kong. Fuqiang's voice was good. He was soon excitedly singing the popular song *The Love of the Boat Tracker* with modified words by Fuqiang himself:

My girl, you touched my own "thing",
We were on the bed, embracing.

The other girl sat down beside Haonan. It was the first time he had participated in such a karaoke scene and he kept her at arm's length. When the girl poured a cup of water for him, he felt embarrassed, thinking he should not trouble her for such a simple thing. Afterwards, the girl picked up a piece of an apple and put it to his mouth. He blushed as red as the apple and hastily pushed her hand away, saying, "Please don't! Let me take it by myself!"

Seeing this, Fuqiang shouted to Haonan, "Why say that? I've paid for the girl's service. You must let yourself go, then you can hug her tighter. *Diaotou!*"

Haonan's face changed instantly from light red to deep red. What Fuqiang said was like a hot potato all night long. He continued to refuse and further persuaded him to stop these activities right now. Fuqiang, however, did not agree.

Chapter 7
Turning Point

Early spring had arrived in the south of China and it was blossoming throughout Shenzhen. On the morning of January 23 1992, Haonan rose early and hastily headed for Shekou. At half past seven he arrived at the Shanghai Restaurant with an official bag and a sample.

Mohammed, a client of his from Holland, came to the dining table. Mohammed had ordered salad and coffee, Haonan a cup of Jupu tea and a big corn bread. They looked through the window at the Taizi road outside. While they dined they discussed foreign business.

Mohammed was a merchant of Middle East extraction, with blue eyes and a long nose, wearing a white headdress and gown. He had emigrated to Holland at an early age, together with his father, and set up a wholesale tools shop in Amsterdam, specialising in cheap but high-quality hand tools imported from China. This was their second meeting. Before this they had communicated several times by fax. Now Mohammed had a chance to visit Shenzhen on his way to Hong Kong.

Mohammed wanted to purchase a quantity of claw hammers from the Xinyi Kapok Tools Factory in the west of Canton via Haonan's company. This was a trial order as bulk cargo instead of as a container load. At that time very few factories had import and export rights, so their products had to be exported by the state-owned foreign trade company.

After Mohammed and Haonan had discussed the claw hammer sample, Mohammed was satisfied with the quality, and they agreed a price after concessions. Mohammed would take the sample. Now it was time to negotiating the payment terms, which was the most important of all the terms in this contract.

"I hope you can open a letter of credit to the Bank of China in favour of our company," said Haonan. His speech was as pure as aged wine. He knew the Bank of China had the advantage in international trade over the other Chinese banks.

"China Bank?" asked Mohammed. He spoke in a strong nasal tone, which sounded as if he had just recovered from a cold.

"Yes!" said Haonan. He also liked to leave out the "of" from "Bank of China", like abbreviating "Hongkong and Shanghai Banking Corporation" to "Hongkong Bank" and "Peking University" instead of "University of Peking".

He went on, "Our company has opened an account at the Futian Sub-branch of China Bank, which has many convenient branches." He pointed to a board opposite the restaurant which announced that the building was the Shekou Sub-branch of China Bank. The four characters written by Guo Moruo were still beautiful and powerful.

"Apart from a letter of credit, is there no other payment system we could use?" asked Mohammed.

"For both importer and exporter, a letter of credit is the most fair and suitable way," replied Haonan.

"I see, but the total amount is only US$3,516. I don't want the bank to earn the charge from opening a letter of credit," said Mohammed. "I hope you can accept documents against payment terms. That means I'll pay right away once the goods arrive in Holland."

"If you don't pay, nobody will pick up the goods in your port, and they will be transported back to China and double transportation expenses will be charged by our company," Haonan explained. In the meeting it wasn't appropriate for him to say directly that this condition was in case Mohammed refused to pay and disappeared after receiving the goods.

"This is only the first order, there will be a second soon," Mohammed said, hoping to persuade Haonan.

"But it must be mutually satisfied before the second order," replied Haonan.

The discussion descended into chaos. Foreign trade includes a series of points such as checking a sample, making a sample, sending a sample, design, production, packing, inspecting goods, transportation, commodity inspection, customs clearance, payment, foreign exchange settlement, foreign exchange verification, tax rebate and so on. If any of these stages goes wrong the deal fails.

Frankly what Haonan hoped most was that Mohammed would remit a 30% deposit, even 10%. Certainly it was best if 100% payment could be remitted beforehand, but he could not suggest this as he knew foreign merchants were normally reluctant. If he were an importer, would he let the exporter load the goods first? Haonan thought about this. Actually his payment terms to Xinyi Kapok Tools Factory, after persuasion, were to arrange payment within 30 days of receiving the goods. So how?

They fell silent. Mohammed lit a cigarette.

How to handle this? Haonan felt agitated. Presently he caught sight of Laizhen, who was on morning duty. She smiled to both of them. Haonan's heart was warmed. But he still could not reach a conclusion with Mohammed. It seemed that this deal would fail by one basket.

Now it was nearly 9 am, and the time for serving breakfast would be over soon.

Suddenly it was bustling with noise and excitement outside, and Haonan saw that many people had gathered by the Taizi road and some policemen were on duty. There were no vehicles on the road. Haonan had a feeling that something important was about to happen.

He was right. A few moments later, a motorcade drove up with all the cars equally spaced out. When it got to a point opposite Sea World, it suddenly stopped. It was clear that those inside the cars were pointing to and talking about Sea World, the surrounding industrial area and Shekou.

"Deng Xiaoping! He is visiting Shekou!" someone exclaimed.

The restaurant staff put down their bowls and dishes and watched through the windows. Some of them even stepped outside and wandered along the busy roadside, but none of them crossed the road. Some people's view was blocked by those in front, and they would tap the shoulder of the person in front, who took no notice, so the person behind had to stand on tiptoe to see, stretching like a duck being carried by its neck. Others jumped into the air so as to not miss such a historic scene.

Afterwards the motorcade set off again, moving slowly in the direction of Shekou port.

History had been made in an instant. The opportunity had appeared in a flash of lightning. Haonan's heart beat wildly all of a sudden. He knew from the TV that Deng Xiaoping had already arrived in Shenzhen by special train on January 19 and investigated the International Trade Centre Building, Splendid China and Fairy Lake Botanical Garden. The previous day, January 22, he had personally planted a Ficus altissima in Fairy Lake Botanical Garden, to bring to Shenzhen his hope of reform and opening-up. Now he was going to Zhuhai City via Shekou. Haonan was now so excited that he said tremblingly to Mohammed, "Do you know who Deng Xiaoping is?"

"Of course!" said Mohammed respectfully, "All the people in Holland know this wise and great Chinese leader."

"Take a look, please!" Haonan lost no time in pointing outside. "This year is the 12th anniversary of setting up Shenzhen special economic zone, and this is the second time Deng Xiaoping has visited Shenzhen and Shekou. Our nation is so stable, the whole of Shenzhen is thriving. So what are you worried about?"

Mohammed was also touched by this historical point. He rose to his feet, pressing on the window glass with his tall body facing Taizi road. The motorcade had gone now, but swarms of people remained, reluctant to leave, their faces shining with excitement and happiness. Some people suddenly jumped up again, hoping to see farther, but they were too late, and there were pitiful expressions on their faces. Then someone ran off, trying to catch up with the motorcade.

"I believe your nation, your company and you," said Mohammed excitedly. "But I have decided not to open a letter of credit."

"Still not? The price and quality of this business are better than you expected, but you still won't agree to open a letter of credit?" Haonan's mood sank abruptly from excitement to despair. He was so angry that he turned and walked to a toilet several metres away. But Mohammed followed him into the toilet, dragged him back to the table and said, "No no, I don't mean that! I won't open a letter of credit because I will arrange to pay 100% of the goods' value to you, then you can start to produce the goods."

Haonan was astonished again. He said, smiling, "I still want to go to the toilet, but I will sign the contract with you at leisure when I come back."

"Alright."

Afterwards Haonan sat again in his seat and unfolded the draft of the English contract. For many years he had been able to write with perfect control, like a brave general commanding all the soldiers in a military camp. At this moment, however, he could not control his hand, and his signature had become a wild cursive script. When it was Mohammed's turn, his finger was also trembling, although his English signature was as elegant as always.

Mohammed said, "Please let me know your personal bank account details. I'll pay you as soon as I'm back in Holland."

Haonan said no, the amount should be remitted to the company's bank account. As a businessman, he could not receive money for goods from any of his company's customers. Mohammed nodded and smiled appreciatively.

Haonan unfolded the company's bank account information, which he had prepared well beforehand, advising Mohammed that before remittance the contents must be checked carefully: the beneficiary's full name, the account number and the receiving bank's full name, otherwise the amount would be returned and the banking charge would be wasted. Then he felt assured.

Finally they both rose to their feet. The blood rushed around Haonan's body as he seized hold of Mohammed's big hand.

"I'm going on ahead," Mohammed said, and went outside. Facing the direction in which the motorcade had gone, he crossed his palms and prayed for a good while.

Chapter 8
The Beloved Mother and Her Dutiful Son

It was dusk one Sunday in winter in the early 1980s in West Canton, and a low sun was shining on the Chengbian village of Changling. In a yard with a tile-roofed house made of mud brick, which faced south, three rooms were horizontally aligned. Water could be drawn from a well inside the enclosure. In the kitchen, a woman was cooking. She boiled water in a pot using firewood, then put in some green water spinach which she had got from her own vegetable patch. When the leaves were boiled through after some minutes, she picked them up with chopsticks and laid them down in a big basin, spreading them out. After that she grasped them and squeezed the water off by hand, as if wringing wet clothes. Then she laid them down in a big white bowl, scattering the leaves with chopsticks. Finally she soaked them with fried relishes that included salt, garlic, ginger, soy sauce and peanut oil. Then the delicious aroma could be smelled.

This woman was Haonan's mother. She shouted outside, "Haonan, it's time for supper now!" She had never studied at school, so she could only speak her native language.

"All right, A'shen," replied young Haonan. This was the traditional term used when addressing your mother here. He put down his big holdall, which was packed full with rice, clothes and textbooks and walked into the kitchen.

Haonan's father, a country doctor, was out seeing patients in the mountain area. His elder brother and sister were still planting sweet potatoes in the field. A'shen looked at Haonan and gasped in fear. She asked him, "Why are there blood streaks in your eyes?"

"Really?" Haonan said. He walked over to the stove, bent down and raised the wooden lid of a big iron pot of congee. At that time, owing to a serious grain shortage, congee was all that was usually available to his family. And because of the shortage of rice, the congee was mostly water, so the cover of the mixture was as clear as a mirror. His family was reluctant to buy more daily items such as a mirror, so Haonan used the water surface instead.

He pushed his eyelids wide open and looked into the pot. He clearly saw that there were indeed some blood streaks in his eyes, caused by a recent beating. He said, "It doesn't matter. I'll go to bed earlier tonight to make it up."

"Good!" said A'shen, pushing him. "Hurry and have your supper please! You need to walk to school."

Haonan had been studying at Nawu Middle School since graduating from Changling Primary School. Every Saturday afternoon he came back home on foot, returning on Sunday evening. In those days all the students dreamed of owning a bike with the Phoenix, Forever or Kapok brand. Those who possessed such bikes would ring their bells noisily on the way to school, to make sure everyone knew they had bikes. Haonan envied them, as to him a bike was just a dream.

After supper, he put a glass bottle full of dried radish slices into his luggage bag. The bottle had originally been used by his father to hold sodium bicarbonate. Although he had washed it many times and filled it with boiling water, there was still a smell of medicine inside. In the coming week this bottle of dried radish slices would be his main daily dish. There were other options for him such as salty pickled cabbage, dried cucumber, beans or taro stem, together with several pieces of egg. He ate mainly the dried radish slices, and once these had gone, he could only eat rice with soy sauce or salty congee.

In school only a big bowl of congee was available as breakfast. In the early morning when the students came back from running exercise, they used their meal tickets to buy big bowls of congee in the school dining hall. Then they came back to the dormitories, taking out the dried radish slices to eat. For lunch and supper, most of them used a rectangular food container made of aluminium to hold the rice, and after washing them and adding water they put them into the steamer of the school dining hall, class by class. When lessons were over later, the rice was well cooked. Then the students carried their boxes back to their dormitories and ate the rice with the dried radish slices. Haonan had lived like that day after day and year after year.

That evening when he stepped out the house bearing the heavy holdall, his father, elder brother and sister had not yet come back home. The sun had gone down and it was cold. As usual, A'shen insisted on seeing him off. They both wore thick winter clothes, with green cloth shoes.

"You still see Haonan off to school despite the cold," a neighbour said.

"Yes," smiled A'shen.

Ding—ling—ling! One of Haonan's classmates rode up on his bike, given to him by his parents. As he shot past, he said to Haonan, "See you in school tonight!" Those who had bikes were reluctant to pick anyone up. Sometimes Haonan was lucky, he could get on a bus as it passed by. But now, when they looked behind, all they could see were several pedestrians walking in the dust. He would have to walk again today.

After a while Haonan and his mother reached a big lemon- scented gum tree. He said to A'shen, "You go back home, please! I can go on alone." A'shen said she would go back, but she still kept walking. It was a little darker now, and they continued for a few dozen metres.

"You go back, please! It's very cold now," he said.

"All right," replied A'shen, but still she marched forward. She said seriously, "Let me take the bag for you for a while."

"Oh no, it's light."

"How can you say it's light? It's packed with so many textbooks and so much rice," A'shen muttered. "Sometimes you might go to the Nawu foodstuffs station and buy a bowl of pork soup. You won't study well unless you have good health. Do you have enough money with you now?"

"I'll go, and the money is enough, father gave me some already," he said. Actually he did not have much money in his pocket, nor did he ever buy pork soup. At Nawu Middle School those students who had better economic backgrounds could eat eggs from time to time. The eggs were normally laid down to be steamed in the aluminium meal box together with the rice, or broken into a cup to be steamed with water or beans. For those from the best families, once the class was over at noon, they rode on their bikes with one hand on the handlebars and held their boxes of steamed rice above their heads with the other hand, ringing their bells. They rushed to the Nawu foodstuffs station to buy bowls of pork soup for 0.50 yuan. Haonan and most of the other students would drool as they bit their dried radish slices in the campus.

"And bread, you might buy some," said A'shen.

Hearing the mention of bread, Haonan drooled again.

Every morning when the second class was over, the school broadcast a sad and melodious song by Deng Lijun, *How much sorrow?*

When would the spring flowers and autumn moon be gone?
How much of past events had you known?

At that moment in front of the campus door there arrived, as usual, some vendors who sold bread, made of quality flour, with shredded coconut, groundnut, sesame and sugar inside. As it had just been baked, steam was rising from it. It would be delicious. Most of the students swarmed around to buy some, but Haonan stood in front of the door of classroom hesitating. Though the bread only cost 0.10 yuan per portion, how could he get even this extra money every day? So generally, he could only retreat and watch as other students ate the bread. Now, however, in order to avoid worrying A'shen any further, he simply replied, "Yes, I will. Father has already given me food money."

"That's good, that's good," muttered A'shen.

They walked on again. He tried to persuade her one more time to go back home, but she refused, and they continued shoulder to shoulder.

"Is there hot water available in school?" A'shen asked eagerly.

"Yes," he said, but he felt ashamed, for he was lying again so as not to let A'shen worry about him any more. Hot water was available in school, but there was not enough to go round, and the female students had priority. So after the self-study course was over on a winter's evening, Haonan went to the well, together with a few classmates. By then the bitter north wind was blowing, yet they only wore shorts and T-shirts. Soon they stood in a horse- riding pose to fetch water with a galvanised buckets from a deep well. They washed their heads and faces, and after rubbing themselves dry they dipped towels into the water and rubbed their chests until they were red and scalding. Finally they poured buckets of cold water onto their chests. In the cold wind, steam rose from their tender bodies. If it was extremely cold, they would run wildly along before taking a bath, or exercise by doing one hundred push-ups. Someone might shout at the top of his voice, singing hysterically *The Spring of the Northern Nation* or *The Song of the Peony* for encouragement. Haonan took a bath every day from his childhood on, a habit which built a good foundation for his future health.

Now it was growing late, and the north wind threatened to pierce their marrow. A'shen and Haonan had reached the path a kilometre or two from the village, and Haonan was now worried about A'shen going back home alone. He said, "I'll see you off home."

"No, don't say that," A'shen said. "I hear you were bullied recently?"

Hearing that, Haonan was astonished. "No," he said.

Compared with other students of his age, Haonan was small and thin. He had a classmate named Chen Lingfang, which sounded like a girl's name but was not – on the contrary, he was the tallest and strongest male student in the class, with a good family background, and he was very rude, often getting Haonan into trouble for no reason. At the beginning of the term, Haonan, who had been working on farms in the summer holidays, had had a deep tan. As he was chatting to classmates in the dormitory, Lingfang jokingly said, "Welcome to this student from South Africa!"

Hearing this, Haonan dared not react. Then Lingfang yelled loudly, "Beat down the child born after the death of his father!"

Haonan's parents were alive and well, but a few classmates continued to call him that, which

93

hurt him terribly. However, the more they called, the more Haonan ignored them. This made Lingfang more arrogant, so he went up behind Haonan and pinched the back of his head, then turned away and sat down on the edge of a bed, pretending that nothing had happened.

Haonan ached so much that he had to squat down. Many students laughed. Haonan knew it was Lingfang who had done it, but he was afraid to challenge him. However, the pain and the insult fired him up, so he went up to Lingfang and asked, "Was that you who bit me?"

Lingfang tilted his head to one side and said, "So many of our classmates are here, how could you prove that it's me? *Diaotou*!" Haonan said nothing, just looked around the dormitory. Lingfang then just stood smiling. He was a head taller than Haonan. Lingfang stretched out his index finger and poked Haonan's forehead. "Yes! It's me! So what? You fatherless *Diaotou*!"

"I have never bothered you, so why did you want to beat me?" Haonan was angry.

"I look down upon you. This is the reason why I bit you and I'd like to throw you into the pond to feed the fish. OK?" Lingfang was fearless.

Anger seized Haonan's heart, and he was finally beyond endurance. He seized Lingfang's right hand so as to pull him to the class director's house to be judged. Lingfang naturally twisted Haonan's right wrist behind him. Haonan's tears ran down his cheeks. Someone even applauded and shouted, "Fight! Fight!" Lingfang became more aggressive, and fiercely pushed Haonan forward, making him fall with a thump on the ground.

Blood oozed from Haonan's forehead. He rubbed away his tears. Finally an urge to resist rushed through his body. He picked a brick up from the ground, rose to his feet and pounced on Lingfang. As Haonan's arm holding the brisk rose, Lingfang seized it in a flash, and the brick fell to the ground. Lingfang lifted Haonan's right arm upwards until Haonan's legs left the ground and he was hanging in the air like rabbit being carried. Lingfang yelled, "How dare you take a brick to beat me!"

When Lingfang got tired of carrying Haonan, he threw him out and he fell badly once again. Then Lingfang went over to the window, held up Haonan's rice bucket and threw it down. The bucket broke with a loud crash on the ground, the white rice sprayed everywhere and the agate-coloured glass bottle smashed into pieces. The dried radish slices were thrown out too, and a strong odour spread around the dormitory. Seeing all this, Haonan, with no way of fighting back, lay on the ground crying. Finally he staggered to his feet. Lingfang still held his arms akimbo and his head up. Haonan walked out the dormitory and headed outside the campus. A low red sun was shining on the campus wall, and the buds of the kapok tree were fluttering gently down. On the mountain a short distance away, a crow was calling sadly. Haonan walked to a pine tree a few hundred metres away, twitching with emotion.

After this incident, Lingfang was severely punished by the school, but Haonan kept it secret from his parents in order not to make them worry any more.

The shadow of evening had now almost covered the land, and all the people had returned to their homes, lighting their kerosene lamps and having supper. Haonan was still walking along the mountain road with A'shen.

She knew this road very well. Unless there was a storm, she went every day to the mountain a kilometre away to cut firewood, which she sold in Nawu Market eight kilometres away. On the road she would walk for a while and then stop, then walk again. Sometimes she would stand under the shadow of a big tree, cooling herself by waving her straw hat. Her clothes got wet, then dried again, then got wet again. Salty drops of water would roll down her back and drip onto the road, so she would place a towel under her clothes, with one end across her right shoulder, so that when she sweated heavily on the road, she could easily rub herself with the towel. It took her two hours to reach the market, yet all she got for her load of firewood was two yuan or a few taels of rice (a tael is about 50 grams).

When A'shen had been pregnant with Haonan, she would still go out on the mountain, cutting the firewood and carrying it to Nawu to sell. After he was born she would carry him on her back. A'shen cut firewood stems as tall as an adult, up and down, wielding the knife continuously. Meanwhile Haonan played nearby, plucking the wild, blood-red Gu'nian'zi, a mountain fruit, and mulberries to eat, or pulling the white and tender root and sucking their sweet juice. Occasionally he would see a snake dashing away. The first time this happened he cried in terror, but he gradually got used to it as he learned that the snakes would not attack him without provocation.

After finishing her work, A'shen left the hillside, carrying the firewood on her shoulder and Haonan on her back, and headed for Nawu Market. Haonan either slept in the straps that held him, jolting up and down, or narrowed his eyes, his little hands and head pressed firmly against A'shen's spine. He lay quietly without crying or sulking. When A'shen grew tired, she laid down the firewood and put Haonan down, feeding him and playing with him for a while, their laughter mixed with sweat. Then she started walking again. Sometimes there were bikes and tractors passing by, but she always had to walk.

Now they came to a long and steep uphill stretch where the road turned left. Again Haonan urged A'shen to go back. Finally she slowed her step. He said loudly to her, "I'm almost dead with cold, you must go home right away!" A'shen stopped and stood, as motionless as a statue, transfixed by her son as she watched him go farther and farther away. The road was getting steeper, and with his heavy holdall it was hard going. Yet he still turned frequently, waving to A'shen.

Shortly after that he stopped to reposition the strap of the holdall. He massaged his right shoulder, which was aching because of the strap, and moved the holdall to the left shoulder. Then he straightened up again and went forward. He had made up his mind not to look back again, but when he made a sharp turn to the left along the hillside, just as the hill was about to hide him, he couldn't help turning again. He could still see A'shen standing watching him in the dark.

Several years later, Haonan left Nawu Middle School to study in the Remedial Class at Gaoliang Middle School, the most important middle school in West Canton. As it was 130 kilometres from Gaoliang to Nawu, he always stayed on the campus. That June he felt God was teasing him, because he failed by a single mark in the pre-examination for the college entrance examination to qualify to take the main examination.

One morning in October 1986, it was sunny in the campus. On the third floor of the teaching building, branches of trees waved their green leaves across the windows of the classroom where the English class, the fourth session of classes of the liberal arts remedial class in the morning, was being held. Haonan, sitting next to last beside the corridor, stood and recited a passage in English from *A Million Pound Note*, by Mark Twain. He pronounced the words correctly, his voice rising, falling and pausing. His classmates listened carefully, following the text.

Suddenly a woman carrying a bulging woven bag appeared outside, looking into the classroom. Seeing this, the teacher stepped out and asked, "Aunt, who are you looking for?"

The woman put the bag down, panting for breath, and replied, "I'm looking for Zhou Haonan."

"Zhou Haonan!" all the classmates shouted together.

But Haonan had already walked out to the corridor. As soon as he had looked outside, he had recognised his mother.

The teacher went back into the classroom, leaving Haonan and his mother standing face to face outside. Though the hot summer had passed, sweat still broke out over her body like rain. She had carried a big bag of rice from the first floor to the third, and she was out of breath. She wore blue clothes with a plaid pattern, and a big yellow and white towel was stuck under the back of her dress, half of it laid from her right shoulder to her chest. Now she withdrew the towel, rubbed the sweat on her face and smiled at him.

"How did you travel such a long way?" said Haonan. "I can buy rice here."

"The rice here is expensive, and ours is better, you like it. But I came here mainly to see you," said A'shen.

Haonan untied the bag. He could see this was the latest rice harvest, which he loved to eat best; it included the rice bran which had not been removed by the blowing cabinet. Additionally there was a bottle packed with golden dried radish slices. To bring him this bag of rice, A'shen had travelled over one hundred kilometres by bus and on foot.

How painful his heart was now. If he had not failed to get that one mark in the pre-exam, he could have gone to the college, and then his mother would not have had to come to this school. The more he thought about this, the more ashamed he felt.

"You really shouldn't have come here," he said. "But at least you should have let me know in advance so that I could go to the bus station to pick you up, for you don't know the road. If you had got lost, how would I find you?"

A'shen grinned at him. "Before daybreak today I got on the tractor of a fellow villager to Nawu. Then I got on the bus from Nawu to Gaoliang."

"But you can't read, how could you find me? This school is so big."

"I asked the doorkeeper, and he told me at once where you were. He also wanted to carry the rice for me, but I said no need."

Haonan knew that though A'shen didn't know any words in another language when she went away from home, she was good at asking people. Furthermore she didn't suffer from car sickness. Sometimes when she went to a new place she did not leave the bus station, but just stayed inside and waited. She would telephone or convey her words through other people so that she would be picked up soon.

Haonan put the rice on his shoulder and accompanied A'shen to his dormitory.

At noon he took a box of rice as lunch for A'shen from the school dining hall. A'shen said, "It'll be enough if you have tried your best in your studies. Of course it'll be best if you can go into the university next year. Your failure this year is in the past now, so don't think about it any more and don't give yourself more pressure."

He nodded thoughtfully.

At 2:00 pm, he showed A'shen the way to Gaoliang bus station, where he insisted on guiding her to Nawu. Hearing this she said it would affect his studies, adding that since she had come to Gaoliang alone, it would be easier for her to go back alone. He had to agree then, and he bought the bus ticket for her.

Before driving he guided A'shen into a restaurant, where he bought a cup of native soup, a local food speciality, for her. A'shen declined, but finally they shared it. After this Haonan went to the toilet, and when he came back, he saw that A'shen was carrying the used bowl and chopsticks back to the kitchen and had rolled up her sleeves, preparing to wash them. The waitress, surprised, hastily said there was no need. Then when A'shen came back to the table, from habit she picked up a piece of rag and wiped the dining table. Haonan said this would be done by the waitress. A'shen smiled and said, "I've got used to doing it after every meal." Seeing this countrywoman in town for the first time, the other diners were very amused.

Afterwards, when they sat down on chairs in the bus station waiting room, A'shen fished out a little red cloth bag, opening it layer by layer, and took out three notes totalling 30 yuan. As soon as Haonan saw them he knew that what she was about to do. He refused to accept it.

A'shen was angry. "Take it, please! I only came here to bring you the rice and the money."

Realising that she would be sad if he did not take it, he finally agreed. He clutched the notes, which still retained her body heat. He knew that it was the money she'd earned by her own sweat and toil, carrying firewood for 15 days and walking 240 kilometers. He lowered his head, saying nothing for a long time.

At length she got on the bus, which drove slowly out of the bus station. She put her head out of the window, waving to him. "Study hard, just try your best, it'll be enough. Everything depends on it!" she said.

He watched the outline of the bus going farther and farther away until it disappeared. In public view he stood by the roadside with tears in his eyes.

Chapter 9
Hard Work

After starting work in Futian, Haonan arrived early every morning and was the last one to leave at night. It was he who turned on the light on arrival and he who turned it off on departure. Thus he became the ideal person to clock in and out on behalf of his colleagues, but he refused all requests. It was said that clocking in and out using fingerprints would be adopted soon, and his colleague Fu Yanjie said amusingly that he would rather cut off half his finger and hand it to Haonan so that Haonan could clock in and out for him – a large commission would be paid. Haonan replied, "If they introduce clocking in and out by facial recognition, perhaps you will cut off a layer of your face and give that to me?" They both laughed.

Li Feng, the secretary of the office, was in charge of receiving and sending faxes for the whole company, so only she kept the key of the fax room. She came from Zhejiang province and was just over 20 years old. She normally spoke in a low voice, never wishing to argue with anyone. Every day when she went to work, she carried a small bag on her shoulder, and she lowered her head while walking, with her high-heeled shoes strutting in little steps. If Haonan arrived before her, he anxiously watched through the window of the fax room as the faxes spat out of the machine. Sometimes he jumped up to watch, his hands pressing on the glass and his face sticking to it like a gecko. He watched with his sharp eyes to see if his name was on any of the faxes or to identify from the fax number who had sent it. If the number was 0082 or it showed the name "Winners Trading Co", then he thanked God it was for him, from a Korean customer who had been discussing an order for ramie fabric, made from the ramie plant, an ancient plant also known as China grass and used for open-weave garments. One or two faxes were exchanged between them most days, and if there was no fax from this man, Haonan was very disappointed.

After Haonan had been with the company three months, he had successfully handled a profitable export deal with Mohammed on the claw hammers, and he received the full goods amount before shipment, which made Hu very satisfied. However, although Mohammed had said that the quality and business relationship were good, he did not place the promised second order, so Haonan had to look for more customers.

Through an introduction by a classmate who worked in Guangzhou, he made acquaintance with

Mr Kim, a new customer, who acted as the president of Winners Trading Co in Korea and was interested in importing ramie fabric from China. They mainly originated in Jiangxi, Hunan, Hubei and Sichuan provinces, and some was made by machine, some by hand. In summer in those provinces that planted the ramie, hand-made looms for making the fabric stood in front of the doors of most homes. The Koreans were fond of wearing summer clothes made of ramie, so the fabric was in strong demand there. Haonan got in touch with Liu Xianwu, a supplier from Hunan Province.

"Haonan, you're wanted on the international phone, I've put it through to your extension number. It's the one who speaks English," said Huang Lijuan, the tall, thin receptionist of the company. She was also the switchboard operator. If she received an important telephone call, she would go inside the offices and call for the person who was wanted.

As soon as he heard this, Haonan knew the call was from Korea. Sure enough, Kim was on the phone. He told Haonan in English that he had received the letter Haonan had airmailed ten days before, and asked, "Can you really supply the ramie fabric?"

Haonan advised Kim to send a detailed enquiry by fax, and it arrived half an hour later.

"Haonan, what's the country code for France?" Li Feng asked Haonan in an affectedly sweet voice. She was sending a fax to a businessman as Haonan was entering the fax room. Everyone lifted their heads, looking at him.

Since Haonan had worked for the company, he'd become a living directory. If an executive could not remember the long- distance telephone code of the mainland factory, or wondered what the country code of an importer was and was too lazy to find out, he would ask Haonan. When some executives received a foreign merchant's enquiry mentioning world-famous ports such as Odessa, San Jose, Gdynia and Constanza, they didn't know which countries these ports belonged to, so they all asked Haonan. He also knew the foreign exchange rates between Chinese RMB, US dollars and pound sterling, and he responded to their questions at any time. This greatly improved the company's efficiency.

"0033," Haonan told Li Feng immediately.

"Thanks a lot! I'll let that Korean customer of yours send you more faxes." Li Feng smiled.

"My pleasure. If you can."

But Li Feng was still having problems. "I got the telephone code for France, but why couldn't I still send the fax out?" she said. Haonan went closer, scenting her aromatic perfume. He picked up the fax paper and glanced: 0033 023. "Have you also dialled 023?" he asked.

"Of course. Doesn't it say 023?" she said, staring sideways at him.

"It's wrong. This is the code of another city. You probably don't know that if there's a 0 in front of the city code, you needn't dial it. Similarly, if you call or send a fax to Shenzhen when you're abroad, you needn't dial the 0 of 0755, the city code of Shenzhen, either."

"Oh, fantastic!" Li Feng opened her eyes wide, biting the shaft of the pen.

"Fly abroad right now, and call back Shenzhen as test," Yanjie said to Li Feng. Yanjie was a young man with serious acne, and his black cheeks were as high and steep as the western Gobi, the place where he was born, but he was cheerful all day long. He worked in I/E department 7 and sat near Haonan.

"I'll kick you!" said Li Feng. Yanjie fled rapidly.

Then the vice general manager, Wen, appeared by the fax room. "He knows all the staff extension numbers and the foreign countries' telephone codes," she said, praising Haonan. "Many foreigners probably don't know their own country codes."

It was Xiaomei who had recommended Haonan to Hu, and before Hu had made up his mind, it was Wen who had persuaded Hu to accept him after viewing his resume, together with confirmation by Xu Yanwei, the manager of I/E dept 7, of Haonan's business ability.

Vice general manager Wen, who was in her forties, came from Dalian City. She had short hair and wore long skirts, making her look professional and capable. She had graduated from Dalian Foreign Language College, and had always worked in the watch business. Almost every other day a foreign merchant came to sign an order with her.

Every day after finishing work, some lads gathered in the company conference room to play cards. They enjoyed themselves with games such as "Striving for First Place", "Fighting the Landlord", "Playing Upgrade", and others.

"Haonan, you must improve your consciousness and join our holy team," said Li Rentai, a colleague of Haonan's, who was dissatisfied with Haonan sometimes.

"Your business is so smooth that I don't think I will have your luck," replied Haonan, smiling.

Rentai had worked originally in the Lanzhou Chemical I/E Co, engaged in the business of exporting phthalocyanine blue, a dye. Before Haonan had joined the company, Rentai had seamlessly transferred all his business from his former company to this China Merchants Company. Then his phthalocyanine blue products were transported from Lanzhou to Shenzhen Goods Station by train, and to Shekou port by truck to be loaded into containers. Finally the goods were moved on board and foreign exchange was received without effort. Rentai felt so free after getting off work that he had time to play cards. However, Haonan had only recently joined, so he had to develop customers all the time, and although he went to work as early as he could and stayed as late as possible, he still felt there wasn't enough time.

"Haonan, we'll wait for you to play *Mah-jong* in our dormitory this weekend," said Kuang Ming, who came from Hunan Province. In any case they always warmly invited Haonan to take part in various kinds of spare-time activities, but Haonan was too busy to join all the time. They were staggered to find that Haonan didn't even know how to play *Mah-jong*. Oh my God!

Fu Yanjie, who didn't play cards, went up to Haonan, patted his shoulder and said cheerfully, "Well! Some of our colleagues were dissatisfied with you a while ago because you get to work earlier than others and leave later."

Haonan smiled, ignoring him and concentrating on drawing up a fax.

"That day I saw you wandering around the company dormitory with a most beautiful girl. Who was she? Were you two looking for a place to have illicit sex? Tell us, please! If you confess you will be treated leniently; but if you deny it, you will not!" Rentai yelled to Haonan. They couldn't help laughing loudly.

"Just an ordinary friend," said Haonan.

"Ordinary friend?" Kuang Ming recited cheerfully:

"The first time you two were new to each other,
The second time you two became more familiar,
And the third time under the quilt you two
finally slept together."

They all laughed crazily again.

"Rentai, you're wanted on the factory telephone!" called Lijuan, who was about to leave the office. She was going to transfer a call to him, but Rentai had just drawn a good hand of cards. He replied sharply, "Tell him I don't have time, I never receive business calls after work, and tell him to leave a message on my pager if it's urgent." Hearing that, Lijuan did so and hung up the phone.

"There is a Niu (girl) following me..." Yanjie sang loudly. He went closer to Haonan and nudged him. "Don't get curvature of the spine!" he said. "You should stand up to rest a while if you get tired of sitting." He was afraid that Haonan didn't get it, so in an official tone he said loudly to him, "Do you understand what I mean?"

"Yes, I understand," Haonan looked up and laughed at him.

"Haonan, it's nearly nine o'clock at night. Go back home, please!" said Wen, coming into the office with a foreign merchant. Haonan was still calculating the CIF Busan price of the ramie fabric.

"All right, thank you very much!" replied Haonan, lifting his head.

The voice in the conference room suddenly dropped. Soon they had all left. Wen chatted jokingly with the foreigner in her office.

In the end Haonan finished the price calculation and made it clear for a quantity of ramie fabric loaded into one 20-foot container. He then pulled out his drawer. The faxes exchanged between him and Kim over the past three months had made a pile 10 centimetres thick.

Chapter 10
Two Hours of Love Without Refuelling

Like Haonan, Laizhen, who was born into a railway family in Shaoguan City, Canton, had always longed to go to Shenzhen. She had often played beside the railway line from Beijing to Guangzhou. She would ask, "How far is it from here to Shenzhen? Is it strange in Shenzhen?"

After failing to enter college after graduating from high middle school, she had come to Shekou. Because of her beauty, she was given the job of waitress.

When you climb to the top of Bijia Mountain on a sunny day, all the views of Futian can be seen. One Sunday that summer Haonan went there with her; it was their second date. The further they climbed, the fresher they felt. The hillside, however, was so steep that Laizhen grew tired. She wore a short-sleeved shirt and a long skirt, and her face was pink and sweating. Seeing this, Haonan seized hold of her soft hand. She was surprised and instinctively drew it back. But seeing his firm gaze, she then stretched out her hand obediently and soon felt his strength transferred to her. Haonan, grasping her hand tightly, wanted to guide her to the top of the mountain, which seemed the pinnacle of their life.

When they reached the top, they slowed down, and breathed more easily. There were tourists packed in groups. The sky was high and there were enough clouds to dilute the strong ultraviolet rays. It was much windier here than at the foot of the mountain. Haonan walked shoulder to shoulder with Laizhen, sometimes deliberately walking backwards, so that he could take in her figure and appreciate her slim waist and rounded buttocks. Then he would walk beside her again. At first she thought this was a little strange, but then she understood what he was doing, so when she saw him admiring her behind she would carry on walking forward with a smile, letting him see what he wanted.

"Let's take a rest," he said at last. They came to a pavilion and found a stone bench to sit on, where they began to chat.

"Let me tell you a story," said Haonan. "Is it very interesting?"

"Why not? Here it is. In the west there was a young, passionate but unfaithful woman, who secretly met a young man in her family while her husband was away. But suddenly another lover of hers came to see her, so she had to hide the first one in a cupboard. However, her husband suddenly came home as well. Thinking quickly, she said to the second lover, 'You take this sword and rush to the door, saying "Let me see where you can run!" then you'll be able to escape easily.' The second lover did so. When her husband saw her, he asked in surprise, 'Who is that man? What did he come to our home for?' This woman then released the first lover from the cupboard and said, 'That man is hunting him and wants to kill him, and by chance he ran into our home, so I had to shelter him in the cupboard.' So both lovers fled safely.

"This story was published in The Decameron, by Pocarque, an Italian writer," Haonan explained.

Laizhen laughed. Looking at her, Haonan felt love rise in his heart. Staring at her white hands and well-rounded chest, and smelling the fragrance of her hair brought to him by the wind, he was so intoxicated that he stretched out his hand to clasp her to his breast. She did nothing to stop him.

In this carefree mood he recalled a wonderful love story in which a beautiful girl and her boyfriend lost their way while travelling. They had soon pledged to each other that they would stay together for their whole lives. That night they slept in a house with a tiled roof. The man let the girl go inside the house, while he remained outside. The girl was not sure if she should close the door before going to sleep. After thinking about it, she drew out the door bolt and replaced it with a fragile straw, then fell drowsily asleep. When she woke up

115

early the next morning, she saw that the straw had not been broken, and the man was still sleeping outside the door. He was waiting for her, as well as protecting her.

Now Haonan was thinking that if they travelled like this couple, losing their way at night, Laizhen would do as the girl had done and he would do as the man had done. He too would not try to open the door but would stay outside, as if protecting a holy candle.

"What are you thinking?" she asked.

"Nothing."

He also recalled that at their first meeting she had mentioned the matter of a Shenzhen Permanent Residence Permit. He had now been working for the company for more than six months and had had some success in business, but he had little to show for it. So he had to ask himself, how could he get such a permit? And a house?

It was now nearly twilight, and the rest of the people were going back down the mountain. So did Haonan and Laizhen. While they walked they talked, until they reached a remote and quiet place where only the birds sang in the woods. They spontaneously hugged each other. Irresistible impulses now seized them and their lips slightly touched in their first kiss. Her delicate cherry of a mouth was created by nature, not by lipstick. He liked this natural feeling. His hand started to stroke her waist. There was a little sweat on her body, mixing with her faint fragrance. She pulled her hairclip off, shaking her head and letting her long hair drop slowly onto her shoulders. He hugged her so hard that she was almost unable to breathe. "Be gentle," she said, raising her eyebrows, her mouth trembling. Happiness was written on her face and her hands pressed lightly on his shoulders.

Finally he felt an unbearable impulse, and began to fondle her chest. It was like touching two ripe apples. "This is not the place," she said, pushing his hand away. He drew his hand back. His face was as red as the setting sun.

They turned and began to walk back, heading for Haonan's little room in Futian.

On that Sunday evening his colleagues had not yet returned home. He shut the door and the window, and they hugged each other eagerly. Her burning eyes told him silently that she needed love. Their desire was now beyond control, and she took off her clothes to reveal that her body was as smooth and flawless as a peeled onion. Trembling, he clung to her like a leech, holding her on the bed, but it was a crude iron bed which squeaked terribly. What was more, he feared it might collapse at any time. He also feared that when his colleagues came back they would hear them. So he lifted her to on the clean ceramic floor, letting her sit, and put a thick towel under her as padding. She lay silently, like a dry seedling waiting for rain.

He was sweating heavily, so he hastily turned on the electric fan at the highest speed. She blushed, not fearing to open her eyes, and experiencing an excitement she had never known before. She was opening her arms, like falling down into a valley from the top of a cliff, or looking down at the world from the clouds, she was like Chang'e, a young and beautiful woman of Chinese ancient legends who lived on the moon, strolled in the moon palace and danced in white gauze. The feeling was wonderful.

Soon, feeling intoxicated, Laizhen fell dreamily into sleep.

After a long while she awoke. It was now dark outside, but the street lights revealed that Haonan was still riding her body, his eyes excited with love.

She lay appreciating Haonan in the dark. Thanks to a great deal of physical exercise, he had strong biceps, back, chest and stomach muscles, and very strong arms. His stout legs were working like a well-oiled engine. She was deeply attracted to all of this. The feeling of his skin excited her, and she began to pant and her body started to writhe. His passion was lit again, and he kissed her and hugged her. Now she felt she was floating in the sea. Her fingers seized hold of his arms digging her fingernails into his muscles, drawing blood. But he did not feel it.

At last she relaxed and took her hands away. "How can you go on for two hours?" she asked him.

"What do you mean, 'go on'?" he said.

"Like just now."

But he was still teasing her. "What's 'just now'?" he said.

She picked up the pillow and hit him with it. He put up a hand to block it, explaining, "It was like continuing on a journey without refuelling."

"But I don't understand how you can go on for two hours without refuelling. I'm just asking you how you could keep going for so long," she was angry now.

"Well, I found this skill by chance, I didn't try to develop it. Perhaps it was because I encountered many setbacks when I was a boy. And perhaps the stronger the dedication to one's work, the more intensive this ability is. Anyway, I can control the time and tempo."

"Have you secretly taken medicine to intensify your sexual ability?"

"Quite the contrary, I daren't. I'm a vegetarian. Normally even eating an egg can make me stronger. So if I eat more meat to strengthen myself, my hormone secretions would be more excessive."

"Are there many men like you who can continue for so long?" she opened her eyes wide with interest.

"As far as I know, it's only me. I've a friend named Zhang Fuqiang who told me that the whole process for him was over in two minutes. So I'm the one no one can beat," he said smugly.

"Two minutes for him, but for you, two hours?"

"You didn't lose out though. How many times did you come just now?"

She hurled the pillow at him. He protected himself with a hand, giggling. In the end she admitted that she had come nine times. She said, "It was said that there was a painter who was also too vigorous."

"That's true. He was named Qi Baishi and he became a father again when he was 83 years old."

"Oh, my God! But I bet you could do that at 93."

"It depends on how well you cooperate with me."

"Well, I would rather leave this position to other better women if I live to that age. At any rate you can go to Japan to make a video, and battle with those Japanese girls for 360 rounds day and night."

"I don't deserve that!" He smiled. Then he helped her up gently, taking a long towel to clean her snow-white body. What's done cannot be undone. "We're enjoying our ride and have got on the 'loving car', so let's buy another 'ticket', all right?" he said.

She said nothing, lost in thought. She was admiring his heroic features, his strong body and his extensive knowledge. She was satisfied with him. However, she was thinking that she would not let him "buy another ticket" until he had a

Shenzhen Permanent Residence Permit and a house.

Looking at her expression, he understood. He was soon lost in meditation.

Chapter 11
A Desperate Queue

In the summer of 1992, the buzzword around Shenzhen was "stock". Everywhere people were talking about stock names such as Bao'an of Shenzhen, Yuanye and Jintian, and magazines and newspapers were selling out. It was said that 500 million yuan of new stocks would be published by the method of selling sheets of drawing lots, which would be carried out in 302 places including every bank, insurance company and stock exchange organization around Shenzhen at the price of one hundred yuan each, to be purchased by individual Residence Identity Card.

As an immigration city, there were originally many tycoons who came from all over the country to gather in Shenzhen. Once the news spread that lots would be drawn for the stock, nearly a million people, including people from Chaozhou and Shantou cities, Sichuan Province, the north-east and the north-west, suddenly rushed to Shenzhen. Although they knew that purchasing the lots did not mean they would really earn much money, they still turned up, bringing their dreams. They stayed in hotels or inns large or small, patiently waiting. Those who worked and lived locally started to borrow Residence Identity Cards from those further away. From the end of July to the beginning of August, the main items among the registered letters in the post offices of Shenzhen were Residence Identity Cards sent from every corner of the country, with the warnings "Be careful!" or "Don't fold!" clearly written on the envelopes, some with big exclamation marks. The staff in the post offices worked night and day and got sore arms from sorting them.

"Haonan, can you lend your Residence Identity Card to me?" said Fuqiang. At that time Fuqiang had already collected eighty cards from people in the country. He seemed like a woodpecker which always knows where the insects are hidden.

Then Fuqiang changed his mind. "No, you don't need to lend it to me. Let's queue up to buy one," he said. "Just go to the first floor of China Merchants Bank and queue up. *Diaotou!*"

There were people lined up in front of some spots who had been waiting three days. They sat on a small bench in the day and slept there at night. Provisions were brought for them by their relatives and friends.

That August 9 was a Sunday. Haonan remembered that when he had written the essay before, he had written, "I got up from bed as smoothly as a jumping carp". How could a weak human jump as strongly as a carp? Yet he did so early this Sunday morning and prepared to set off. He had made an appointment with Zhenfeng and Laizhen to line up to buy the sheets of drawing lots.

The nine-storey China Merchants building, shaped like a boat, was the landmark feature in Shekou, and on the first floor was the headquarters of China Merchant Bank. Haonan couldn't help laughing when he thought of the sayings "Don't say you are early" and "There is always someone who is earlier than you". Fuqiang and his father, together with other people from the country whose names were unknown to Haonan, had been queueing since early morning. In front of the building a long line had formed of people of all heights and ages and both sexes. Haonan let Laizhen step in in front of him. In the clamour Haonan faintly heard someone calling him. He turned and saw that Fu Yanjie, Li Rentai and Kuang Ming, his colleagues, were gathered, and surprisingly, their leader was Hu.

Haonan nodded to him and smiled. "So you're here too?"

"Yes." Hu shrugged, reddening with embarrassment. Haonan had never imagined that Hu, the eminent general manager of the company, would have to stand in line with ordinary people.

The sun was rising slowly, and the people were beginning to feel hot. People were joining the queue one after another, bringing bags in which there was cash, food and drink. Those who came from the south or north of the Yangtze River and inside or outside the Great Wall normally did not have the chance to meet each other in daily life, but now, in order to realise their common desire, they felt close and could say anything they wanted.

"How much are the sheets?" asked one.

"One hundred yuan each," one answered.

"How many sheets you can buy will depend on how many Residence Identity Cards you have, but no one can buy more than ten sheets. Yet certainly you can buy them by getting someone else to queue for you."

The long queue was creeping forward, and everyone wanted to get to the selling area. There were several red cloths covering the working desks, in front of which there was a high step. As soon as you got onto the step you could buy a sheet. In the bank the clerks, all in the same uniform, were busy counting the money. The cash was thrown sack by sack onto the counter. Though the air conditioning had been turned to the lowest temperature, they still felt hot. The currency counting machine had been running so long that it was too hot to operate, so it was replaced by hand counting. As a result most of the cash was stained with the sweat of the person who had bought the sheet, and it carried their body odour, mixed with the fish smell of local fishermen in Shekou. The clerks had to put the notes on the desk one by one, drying them with tissues and towels and blowing them dry with electric fans, as if caring for a baby.

At that moment those dealers with sheets of drawing lots in their hands began shouting, "Three hundred yuan each!" "Five hundred yuan each!" or "One thousand!"

No sooner was each voice heard than the sheets were sold out. There was a growing pile of rubbish in front of the bank, including torn plastic bags, a plastic bench which had been stamped into pieces, a sweaty abandoned T-shirt, even a damaged Residence Identity Card.

The long line moved slowly towards the bank door, like a bicycle chain with all its parts interlocking. Haonan hugged Laizhen in front of him, and Laizhen was pressing against a woman in front of her who was about 40 years old. Behind Haonan was a girl who was as young and beautiful as Laizhen. Haonan spoke to her and found her name was A'chuan. She could not help pressing against Haonan with her white and tender hands, and after turning back and seeing this, Laizhen complained a little. With A'chun was her boyfriend, A'bing, and he held A'chun from behind. He was afraid his sweetheart would be squeezed out of the line, so he would rather have her in front of him than standing behind him being hugged by another man.

"Jumping the line isn't allowed!" shouted one of the officials who were keeping the line in order.

"Mineral water! Who wants it?" the vendors who wandered beside the queue were shouting constantly.

"How much is it?" one asked.

"Thirty yuan."

"So expensive! It's two yuan normally," another said.

"I'm not forcing you," said the vendor.

"OK, we're so thirsty. Give us five bottles."

In the late afternoon, the sun passed behind the clouds and it started to rain, but all the people were still queueing. Someone held up a sunshade as an umbrella. Haonan took off his shirt to shelter Laizhen, so the upper part of his body was naked. Fortunately the rain soon stopped.

Presently Fuqiang and his father, Hu, Yanjie and Kuan Ming had all managed to buy sheets of drawing lots and had left. After their long wait it was finally the turn of Laizhen, in front of Haonan. But then a rumour suddenly spread along the queue, which caused a commotion among the crowds. As Laizhen stretched out her small hand to take the sheet of drawing lots from the clerk, a flood of people surged upon her from behind. She stumbled and fell. Haonan was busy fishing his money out, and when he realised what had happened he was too late to help her. Laizhen rolled heavily on the ground, pressing her belly with her hand. Haonan was horrified to see blood dripping down her trouser leg. He shouted in horror and helped her up to the roadside, where he rapidly hired a taxi to take them to the Union Hospital nearby. Other people pitifully watched them leaving.

The sheet of drawing lots which had originally belonged to Laizhen and Haonan was finally purchased by Achun. It turned out that the reason for the commotion just now was that the sheets had been sold out.

Laizhen was soon out of danger after emergency treatment, but it was too late to save her baby. That night Haonan stayed beside her sick bed, watching her on a drip. She lay quietly, and he constantly consulted and comforted her but she was expressionless.

That evening, the authorities in Shenzhen declared that five million drawing lot sheets for the new stock had already sold out. There were, however, many people who had not bought any yet. Through the hospital windows Haonan could see the crowds of people on the streets who still wanted to buy. They didn't disperse but kept wandering in front of the selling spots, demanding more sheets.

Nobody slept in Shenzhen that night, because of the noise of the wild celebrations of those who had bought sheets and the disappointment and anger of those who had failed. The same sadness was written on the faces of Haonan and Laizhen.

The next day the assistant of the Shenzhen Mayor appeared in public to try to pacify the crowds, announcing five clauses of notices of Shenzhen municipal government and guaranteeing that an additional 500,000 sheets would be distributed around the city so that the purchasing pressure could be relieved. On the night of August 11 Shenzhen officials announced on television that all the necessary arrangements had been made.

Chapter 12
A Battle in the Canton Fair

The hot summer gradually went by, and the days were growing shorter. At night the wind was cooler, blowing gently into millions of families' houses through their windows. Under the sparkling neon lights along the streets the leaves fell off one after another, their faint rustle seemingly announcing that autumn was stepping into the world. Everywhere in Guangzhou swarmed with people,and it was apparent that foreigners of many different colours had come from around the world. It was a sign that the 72nd annual Autumn Fair was approaching.

When there were only five days left to October 15, the day the fair was opening, Haonan found that most of the contents of his department's catalogue would have to be amended. But how was he going to do this in such a short time?

Wen snapped, "Just do it now, even if it means overtime!" The printing workshop would be decided in Guangzhou, and the new catalogue must be fulfilled before October 15.

Haonan and Xu Yanwei at once drove to the Guangzhou office of the company, which was in Tongxin Road. Xu Yanwei was scholarly and elegant, 1.75 metres tall with gold-framed glasses, a big nose and a wide forehead, showing the full face of good fortune. This department consisted of five persons including Haonan. Everyone in the company was in charge of his own work. Xu Yanwei, who acted as the department manager, had his own business and managed the whole department, so this work of reprinting the catalogue was mainly the responsibility of Haonan.

So from October 11 on, Haonan entered an intensive state of almost military readiness, editing the pictures and revising the Chinese-English language. An older woman in Guangzhou office took charge of cooking so that he could focus on his work. When his neck was sore, he tossed his head; if his eyes grew tired, he exercised them. Sometimes he rose to his feet and walked over in front of the window, looking down at the bustling streets of Guangzhou and recalling the scene when he had first arrived in Guangzhou after passing the college entrance examination years ago —

Early that morning, with the admission notice of the college entrance examination packed in his luggage, his parents, elder brother and sister had seen him off to the big bus from Nawu to Huazhou. He wanted to report for study at the Guangzhou Foreign Trade College. However, when he asked for a ticket, he was told that they had been sold out. How was he going to reach Guangzhou the next day? Suddenly he saw that a coach showing the route from Huazhou to Guangzhou was driving slowly of the bus station, but when he went to inquire, the answer was still the same - no seat was available.

The driver told him that this was the last bus to Guangzhou, so he had to get on in a hurry. When he looked inside, however, it was bulging with passengers standing on the corridor. This "Yellow River" coach was supposed to hold 45 people maximum, but it held more than 90, so he had to stand. He knew he would have to remain on his feet for a night or longer before he arrived in Guangzhou.

The coach went to Xinyi County in the north, then, turned east to Luoding County, swinging from left to right on the winding road up the mountain. Along the road there were a few cars which had fallen down the cliffs. Soon Haonan saw that the two drivers were swapping over. They did not even stop the coach. While one driver rose to his feet, still grasping the steering wheel with one hand, the other sat down to take the wheel. All the passengers gasped with horror.

As the coach moved on, the passengers heard the inspiring song *Every Section of Road* played, sung by Lv Fang from Hong Kong. At 11 pm when the coach reached the border of Heshan County,

Haonan began to doze. But as soon as he fell asleep he woke again. He had bumped his head on the upright column and his knees couldn't bend. How could he sleep like this? In fact there was not enough space for him to fall, let alone lie down. And there was no fresh air either!

Presently the coach slowed down and joined a queue waiting to get onto a ship. Lights flashed in the dim night. Haonan heard the voices of people selling things - "Sugar cane juice, chrysanthemum tea, cream bread!" Some of the vendors tapped the coach windows, or lifted their baskets high to display their wares. From this Haonan knew they had arrived at the legendary Jiujiang ferry crossing, which usually involved a long wait.

After thinking hard for a while, he fished out one yuan from his pocket, tied tightly by the leather belt given him by his parents. Then he bought a box of chrysanthemum tea.

Because there were so many vehicles and people, normally there was a two-hour wait here. The coach crept as slowly as an ant and the wait extended from 11 o'clock at night until dawn. "Sugar cane juice, chrysanthemum tea, cream bread..." many years later this long-drawn-out voice still lingered in Haonan's brain.

At noon the next day, he arrived for the first time in Guangzhou, the capital of Canton Province. When the coach entered the Zhongshan Road 8th bus station of Guangzhou from Baihedong and

Fangcun, he got out to see many high buildings towering over him. He stared and wondered. As a lad who had grown up in a rural village, he suddenly felt like a submariner rising to the surface after a long time down on the sea bed; everything was up above him. Red-eyed and dragging his tired feet, he got out his map to find the way to the college...

In order to get ready for the Autumn Fair, he rushed around day and night. However, it was easier now because he had a seat. He began to edit and revise the documents more seriously.

He now recalled what his father had said, that before the Chinese liberation his unmarried father, together with Zhou Weiding, his uncle, had fled to the South Pacific to avoid the military riots. In the confusion his uncle had got on board and escaped. His thin, weak father, however, was pushed over the ship's rail and never seen again, so from then on the two brothers were separated by heaven. "You engage in foreign trade and you have many chances to go abroad," his father said several times. "If you go to the South Pacific, you might try to find out your uncle's whereabouts."

Haonan had now endured three days and nights without sleep or rest. When finally he had finished revising the last pictures and words early in the morning, he was as excited as the two men who finished weaving The Emperor's New Clothes after spending the whole night at their task, as in

The Emperor's New Clothes by Hans Christian Andersen from Denmark, although the two jobs were entirely different. After Haonan had presented the catalogue film to the man at the printing factory who had been waiting for it, he had a meal, took a bath and fell asleep until early the next morning, sleeping for 24 hours.

On the morning of October 14, he plunged into the busy work of exhibition preparation. But then he overslept and got up too late, so when he showed two workers bringing five cartons of samples to the door of the fair, it was 12 noon, which was past the specified time allowed to enter the exhibition halls. Two security guards unceremoniously stopped them outside. If the samples could not be put on the company's stand it would be empty when the Autumn Fair would open tomorrow, and all their efforts would be useless. What was he going to do?

The two workers told him that as they were not permitted to enter, they would have to leave, but Haonan told them to wait. He showed his exhibition preparation certificate to the two security men and asked again for permission to come in, but he was still refused. He then went to the kiosk to phone the company, but still could not arrange entry. He was getting more anxious.

Just then a number of exhibitors who had finished the samples exhibition inside the halls came out one after another. Haonan suddenly glimpsed a notice on the wall describing the rules to be followed during the fair. In the bottom right corner was the signature of Li Zefu, the chief of the security section of the Canton Fair; the security office lay on the south-west side of a hall.

A sudden whim seized Haonan. He surreptitiously took the notice, folded it carefully and put it into his chest pocket. Then he told his two workers, "You two stay here and guard the samples for me. I'll be back in 20 minutes. Don't go away, otherwise I won't pay you the carrying freight." The men agreed, and urged Haonan to hurry.

Haonan could enter the hall with his certificate as long as he was not carrying samples, so he hurried to the security office. The two security men watched him doubtfully. After about 15 minutes he came back, handing them a paper which read:

This is to give approval for comrade Zhou Haonan from China Merchants (Futian) I/E Trade Co to enter the hall to place samples. He must finish before 2 pm today and leave the hall, otherwise the samples will be confiscated and all responsibility will be borne by him.

Li Zefu, Chief of the Security Section of China Import and Export Commodity Fair
Oct. 14, 1992

Having read it, one of the security men said, "OK, since it has been approved by the chief, come in, but to be quick!"

Haonan nodded, sweating. He then led the two workers, pulling the cart of samples into the halls. He swiftly found his company's stand, cleaned the display window and put the samples and catalogue in order. They left by another exit. He looked at his watch; it was 1:45 pm. He smiled secretly at having unexpectedly finished the work ahead of time. He then reported to the leaders of his company, without mentioning how he had got into the halls. He knew the company only cared about the result, not how it had been achieved. They praised his success.

Before he and the two workers went their separate ways, one of them said, "It's lucky that you could get approval from that chief. If you know him, why didn't you mention it before?"

Haonan said mysteriously, "I might say I know that chief, I might also say I don't."

"What?" the men looked puzzled.

"I only know his writing," Haonan said, smiling.

"How would that help?" they were even more confused,

"You must keep this secret for me," said Haonan. "The Approval Notice was written by myself, imitating his signature."

They both grinned and stuck their thumbs up.

Now Haonan, feeling entirely relaxed, went back alone to the Guangzhou office. Amid the flow of traffic and people he hummed a song by Andy Lau, *Thanks for Your Love*. In his heart he did want to express thanks to the chief of the Autumn Fair. And he suddenly felt fonder of Guangzhou.

On the morning of October 15, the 72nd session of the China Import and Export Commodity Fair (Autumn Fair) was opened in the China Foreign Trade Centre in Liuhua Road, Guangzhou. There were red slogans hanging above the roofs and balloons were floating in the sky. In front of the doors of the Autumn Fair, after addresses by the leaders of the Ministries of Economics and Trade of China and Canton, ribbon-cutting began. There was much applause, with loud music from drums and gongs, and the lion dance was performed. Foreign merchants from all over the world gathered together.

China Merchants had three stands, one of which was in the hardware hall on the 4th floor of Hall No. 9. Haonan, wearing "Exhibitor" on his chest, was sitting with Wen, Xu Yanwei and others. As the location was off the beaten track, not many visitors were coming and few orders could be signed.

"We can't wait like this, it's like sitting under a tree waiting for a hare to crash into it," Wen said.

"We must go out to invite foreigners to come and talk to us." She asked Haonan to do this.

Haonan took a look at the catalogues on the table, the fruit of three days and nights of painstaking work. He rose to his feet, carrying a bag of catalogues on his shoulder and holding handfuls of them. He stuck his name card on the catalogue's cover, showing the booth number and the location of his company, and set out to deliver them on the bustling corridors. But the security guards walked beside him, carrying black truncheons and warning him that he could not deliver catalogues like that. Haonan reluctantly had to pull back. He clutched his catalogues, walking on the red carpet which covered the corridors. He stared at the many foreign merchants who were arriving or leaving, wishing he could find out if they were potential buyers.

Passing by some famous national import and export companies, he saw that their stands were located beside the corridor of the first floor, along which all foreign merchants had to pass. Many of them were inspecting the samples of light industrial and mechanical parts displayed on the stands. However, the mainland foreign trade businessmen were just joking with each other and paying no attention to deals. How could these businessmen act like that? When one merchant asked, "How much is this one?" and pointed to a sample in a cupboard, nobody bothered to answer, so the merchant shrugged and left.

"Are you interested in hardware?" Haonan said, swiftly catching up with the man and presenting him with a catalogue.

The merchant took a look at the catalogue and accepted it. "Yes, I'll contact you later," he said. Haonan smiled in his heart, feeling that he had reaped a small harvest. He knew that everything would begin from the catalogue, and everything would depend upon it.

He came to the second floor of Hall F, where he saw a foreign man kneeling on the carpet, praying. This was a Turkish merchant. Haonan stood nearby, listening to his prayer, and when the man finished and rose to his feet, Haonan walked towards him and presented the catalogue.

"No, I don't deal in these goods," the Turkish merchant said and was about to throw the catalogue away. Haonan hurriedly took it back.

The corridor was crowded with people. Standing in front of booth No. D4326, which belonged to Canton Province Machinery I/E Corp, Haonan was certain that an Arab woman inside this booth, whose head was wrapped in a white towel, was an importer of hardware. He approached slowly and waited. The woman was negotiating in detail with the Chinese businessman, holding a calculator. Forty minutes later she was still there. It was obvious that they were still bargaining. Haonan got so tired that he would have liked to give up. But he did not want to do that, so he stayed, pacing back and forth.

"*There were seven steps from the entrance to the window, and there were also seven steps from the window to the entrance.*" Haonan suddenly recalled this text from *The Report Under the Gallows*, written by Julius Fucik from Czechoslovakia, in which the prisoner had no choice but to pace back and forth across the floor of Punk Latz prison. So Haonan did now. He turned from time to time, paying attention to the Arab woman.

Close by there was a stationary booth in an excellent position. In it a middle-aged man with a round face, big ears and a thick neck with a black mole on his chin was talking to a foreign merchant who had a full beard. It seemed that the middle-aged man did not speak English, so he just worked on a calculator, showing the price displaying on the calculator to the foreign merchant. But the foreign merchant clearly thought the price was too high, for he said "No no!", snatched the calculator, tapped in some new figures and showed them to the middle-aged man. The middle-aged man laughed, snatched back the calculator and tapped it again before showing the new figures to the foreign merchant. The actions reminded Haonan of slow *T'ai Chi* boxing like that performed by *Shan*

Tong Bi, Shuang Feng Guan Er and *Ye Ma Fen Zong.*

After several rounds of this, the middle-aged man was clearly tired. He sat down, unfolded the contract and wrote down the simple terms and conditions concerned for both signatures. It was clear that the joyful foreign merchant had got a good price. He fished out an armful of US dollars to hand in as a deposit. The middle-aged man wiped his sweating brow and put the cash in his pocket. Haonan was surprised to see that the foreign merchant was able to pay in cash.

After that both of them wanted to talk about something else, but they were finding it too difficult to find anything in common, like a chicken talking to a duck. The middle-aged man caught sight of Haonan watching and signalled by his expression that he was looking for help. Understanding this, Haonan went over to offer to interpret. The foreign merchant was asking his customer to guide him to see the sights of Shenzhen after the Fair, in particular to see the legendary and beautiful Splendid China, the Fold Culture Village and the Window of the World. Hearing this, the middle- aged man, who had gained a great deal of profit from the order, just kept saying "OK".

Haonan was still keeping an eye on the woman on stand D4326. At last he saw her stand up. This was his chance. He hastily went over and followed her, and as soon as they were out of sight of stand D4326 he bravely went up to her and said, "Excuse me! Do you engage in hardware?"

"Yes," she said, stopping.

Haonan showed her his catalogue. "Please contact me if you have an enquiry," he asked.

"Sure, thanks." She took the catalogue and walked away. Haonan thought he had made a further good harvest.

Just then, another foreigner, a man with a white beard, passed by, dragging a wheeled case. Seeing a hardware catalogue among the luggage, Haonan concluded that he must also be a potential buyer. He went decisively over and offered the man his catalogue, but the man paid no attention. Haonan wished this foreigner would take the catalogue in case the products in it might meet his requirements in the future. It didn't matter if there was no order right now, the key time would be in the coming days. But perhaps this man had kept too many catalogues, because for whatever reason, he waved it away and kept on walking. Haonan could only keep talking to him by walking backwards in front of him. Taking a catalogue in his right arm, Haonan opened it to show to the foreigner. But this man walked faster, still firmly shaking his head.

Haonan suddenly stumbled on a bulge in the carpet and fell. His catalogues were scattered on the ground. The white-bearded man took the chance to escape, and disappeared. Haonan was disheartened, and heaved a deep sigh. The businessmen who were sitting inside the nearby booths all laughed with amusement. Haonan lowered his head. An image now appeared in his brain. In a booth situated in a busy place, like the Malacca Strait through which all the ships must pass to get from the South Sea to the Indian Ocean, various kinds of hardware samples were displayed in the shop windows, catalogues were laid on the tables and foreign merchants of various colours were in queueing in front of him, waiting to sign contracts...

"Beep beep!" Haonan's pager brought him back to reality. It was Wen telling him to go back to the company's booth – there was an order available now! He jumped up like someone on a trampoline and pushed through the crowds in the congested hall. When he got to the booth, it turned out that a foreign merchant had come to the stand holding one of Haonan's catalogues. The price and sample terms had been discussed and the contract was to be signed soon. However, when it came to signing, the merchant did not pay attention to Wen, instead insisting that the contract must be signed by Haonan, otherwise he would worry about the quality and delivery time. Haonan's spirits soared. After quickly looking at the contract, he wrote his signature — "Bruce Zhou", like a dragon flying and a phoenix dancing.

Chapter 13
Double Happiness

One early morning two days after the Autumn Fair, a minibus driving from Shekou port to Luohu railway station made a 90-degree turn onto the Shennan Boulevard. Haonan got onto it at Zhuzilin station. He was going to meet a foreign merchant in Luohu District.

After getting off at the International Trade Centre Building station, guided by the usherette, he took the sightseeing lift to the top floor of this fifty-three-storey building, the highest in Shenzhen right then, a revolving restaurant, where he chose a suitable seat. While he waited for the merchant, he looked down at the landscape. The rising sun burst glowing rays in all directions. There were bustling pedestrians on Shennan Road Central and Renmin Road South, and cars big and small shuttled ceaselessly past. The Luohu checkpoint had been opened, and people travelling between Shenzhen and Hong Kong were walking like shoals of swimming fish. There were wispy white clouds of smoke floating above the mountain on the crossing between Shenzhen and HongKong. The high buildings that emerged like bamboo shoots after spring rain represented the prosperity here.

At the Autumn Fair Haonan made acquaintance with Pario, a merchant from Portugal. Pario did not deal in hardware; he purchased only Chinese oil paintings to sell in Portugal. Before returning to Portugal, he travelled to Hong Kong via Shenzhen, where he had arranged to meet Haonan at the International Trade Centre Building.

Pario attended the Canton Fair twice a year. He was of medium height with dark skin, and had a black growth as big as a mushroom on the back of his neck. Pario at first wondered if it was a malignant tumour, but was reassured that it was benign. However he had been told by the doctor that it could become malignant at any time. He refused to have the operation to remove it because it was near the large artery of his neck.

Soon Pario came at the table. While he was drinking his coffee, he ate an oatcake. Haonan had a steamed bun with black rice and a cup of orange.

When Haonan quoted CIF Lisbon terms, he was surprised that Pario just said "Really?" before happily agreeing. It seemed that his style was generosity instead of bargaining. The contract, amounting to just over 3,015 US dollars, was only a small trial order for transporting bulk cargo by air. Haonan checked the contract draft in the business bag he had with him.

Presently Pario signed. He was left-handed and Haonan saw that he wrote the "r" of his name beautifully and finished it at once. It looked like a small snake which had raised its head and put out its tongue.

After this Pario pulled 3,015 US dollars from his pocket. This surprised Haonan. "He has not investigated my company, so why does he trust me so easily? Doesn't he worry that the company may not deliver the goods after receiving payment, or fear that I would go off for a holiday after taking it?" Haonan thought to himself.

Pario saw Haonan's doubt and smiled. "After seeing your honest face and your business spirit, I trust you," he said.

Haonan expressed his thanks.

"I saw how painstakingly you delivered the catalogue in the Autumn Fair," continued Pario. "I went to your booth and met your vice general manager, Miss Wen, who spoke fluent English. I trust your company and you. Daren't you accept my money?"

"Of course I dare, even if you add a few zeros to the amount," Haonan joked.

"The delivery must be on time, as per the quality and quantity we agreed. And I won't inspect the goods at that time. I believe that you will satisfy me."

After taking the payment, Haonan wrote a receipt for Pario. Later, Haonan saw him off at the

Luohu checkpoint. Then he got on a minibus to take the payment to his accounts department. When he arrived, everyone was busy. Seeing him, Fu Yanjie burst out shouting, "Haonan! Good news for you!"

Fu Yanjie had a fax for him. It was from Kim, the Korean merchant, saying that he had received the ramie fabric sample sent by Haonan, was satisfied with the quality and was placing an order. Haonan looked down the list. The total for one year amounted to 10,150,000 US dollars. With a profit of 2.2 yuan per dollar, he would realise a profit of 22,330,000 yuan for the year. The annual target for the whole company was 20,000,000 US dollars, and this one customer would fulfil half of it. Not only would Haonan far exceed his own yearly target, he would get a bonus of 4,460,000 yuan, according to the 20% to 80% profit sharing proportion between him and the company. It meant that he would earn more than a daily average of 10,000 yuan. This was a huge event for the company, as great as when Pangu, the magical figure in ancient China's folk myths, separated the sky from the earth in ancient China.

Kim advised Haonan to prepare the contract carefully, sign it and fax it out, in the meantime claiming the banking information from Haonan's company for receiving the letter of credit. Haonan decided to use the Hong Kong & Shanghai Banking Corporation as the advising bank for the letter of credit, the negotiating bank which would bear the responsibility of presenting the documents and receiving and transferring the foreign exchange. Kim would open the letter of credit at sight from Hanil Bank of Korea. Haonan knew that now this order had reached the last stage before the deal was concluded.

"Who said that no double fortunes would come? They have come to me now," Haonan said to himself quietly. How happy his heart was!

In accordance with what Kim planned, provided the first order went well, future orders would come rolling in. Certainly everything must be done right from the beginning. Since the first order was a trial, Kim would fly from Seoul to Shenzhen to inspect the goods. From the second order on, formal inspection would be handled by a trusted agent proficient in the Korean language, or probably be exempted.

After acknowledging this good news, Wen came up to Haonan and warmly patted his shoulder, saying, "Well done!" Meanwhile Hu smiled warmly through the window of his room.

Seeing the order plan and putting the fax down on Fu Yanjie's table, Xu Yanwei sighed and slapped the table. Unfortunately his hand struck a drawing pin. He shrieked and hurriedly drew the pin out, leaving a spot of blood in his palm.

Haonan was shocked. "You have paid for this order in blood," he said. Fu Yanjie helped Xu Yanwei to remove the blood with a pad of cotton.

Haonan put the fax in his drawer, locked it, then calmly walked out of the office. He went over to the grass area to the east of the company's building and strolled across the lawn, smiling happily. Now it was past 11 am, the air was clean and the sun was warm. The trees cast shadows on the grass. The zigzag paths led to secluded places. In the north there had been snow, but here in the south it was still autumn, with green views everywhere. On this verdant lawn where Haonan often strolled, larks sang in the trees and butterflies gently danced over the grass. A light wind blew through the tops of the king coconut trees. On the flagged pavement, lovers walked hand in hand towards an arched door. Haonan breathed deeply and raised his head to the sky. Up in the deep blue sky, white clouds floated slowly, and a big aeroplane drifted past.

He said to himself, "A Shenzhen Permanent Residence Permit and a house. It seems they will soon be within my reach. Laizhen, just wait for the happy life I'll create for you!"

Chapter 14
From Triumph to Despair

On Haonan's table was a ramie fabric letter of credit opened by Kim to Haonan's company, amounting to 60,000 US dollars for the trial order. The happiness he felt at receiving it was as great as when he had received his notice of admission to college. He also felt like an official in ancient China, holding a heavy and holy imperial edict which he had to obey.

The document was an A4 sheet of golden copper-print paper engraved with a dragon pattern, on which English was printed in detail, stating the rights and obligations of both importer and exporter. The documents which had to be presented under the letter of credit included a commercial invoice, packing list, certificate of origin, bill of lading, beneficiary's statement and an approval inspection certification signed by Kim. These six documents had to be presented to the Hong Kong bank, Shenzhen Branch, and if there was no discrepancy between them and the letter of credit after they were dispatched to the Hannil Bank of Korea by Hong Kong Bank, Shenzhen

Branch, the amount deposited in the Hannil Bank of Korea by Kim would be remitted to the account of Haonan's company.

After this Haonan became a superstar in the company, the great foreign trade businessman in Futian and even in Shenzhen. Every day when he arrived, all his colleagues greeted him in a friendly manner, some fearing that Haonan would overtake them.

Soon, many beautiful young women from the big banks, usually dressed in clothes as thin as a cicada's wing, were coming to see Haonan to urge him to let their banks handle his letter of credit business. Meanwhile beautiful women from the shipping companies, dressed in colourful suits, came to look for him, hoping for his sea shipment business and saying the freight charges would be discounted by 80% or more. They laid down many original bills of lading to Haonan, telling him smilingly that he could sign them on behalf of the captain after making shipment, then present them to the bank for negotiation.

Following them came yet more girls from the insurance companies, hoping to win business from Haonan at a favourable insurance rate, which would be subject to satisfaction by Haonan. They also offered many original insurance policies for his signature if required.

One evening several days later, Haonan went to the Xindu Hotel in Luohu District. As soon as he stepped into the lobby, he found that there were many pretty girls standing there. He mused to himself that it was past ten o'clock at night, so what were they waiting for? They did not look like hotel staff. Afterwards, a girl who was as beautiful as a flower came over to him, asking, "Would you like to do business here, sir?" It surprised him that she knew his intentions. He replied, "Yes, I am going upstairs to do business."

No sooner had he said this than the girl rushed into the elevator with him. He was bewildered. Why was she so enthusiastic? He stared at her open-mouthed. But the girl sighed and said, "Don't look at me like that! Haven't you seen a beautiful girl like me before? I'll let you see how I look naked very soon."

"See you naked? But..."

"Don't say any more! When we are in the room, you can show me with actions, not words. Everyone knows the price here. My skin is white and delicate. I'll provide good service, and I will play your flute."

"Everyone knows the price here? How did you know my price? Play my flute?" He was even more confused. She smiled. She had not expected him to be a virgin.

The elevator reached the ninth floor, and he said politely to her, "I must go into the room to meet my customers now. They have been waiting for me. You go back, please!"

"Stupid man, stinking man! You have wasted my time!" She was suddenly angry. She went back into the elevator.

Many years later when Haonan recalled this scene, he was still amazed by it. It was so strange to him that he still did not understand what business this girl had been doing. Later on when he talked about it with friends, Fuqiang explained her occupation. Fuqiang also criticized him sharply for not taking the chance he had been offered.

Now Haonan lightly knocked on the door of room 906, saying, "Nice to meet you, Mr Kim!"

Kim was about 1.7 metres tall. His wire-rimmed spectacles were so expensive that he had them on a cord around his neck. He wore a black suit and kept spraying himself with perfume, like that wafting from the various foreign merchants in the Canton Fair. After shaking hands, he gave Haonan a miniature microscope he had brought especially from Korea, as this would be used as an inspection tool in the coming business activities. Haonan expressed his thanks.

"My pleasure!" Kim replied.

Behind Kim was a thin, older Korean named Hu Wanzhong. He neither knew Chinese nor English, but he was a big buyer of ramie fabric from Kim in Korea.

That night Haonan invited the two men for a Chinese meal at the Xindu Hotel at his own expense. When he left the hotel, he saw the girl he had encountered earlier still standing in the lobby. She angrily clenched her fist as if she wanted to beat him. He gave her a warm smile.

It was midnight when he arrived at his dormitory, and the Big Dipper was hanging in the dark sky. Early the next morning he rose while Venus was still shining, completed his toilet, then rushed hurriedly to the Xindu Hotel. After inviting his Korean customers for morning tea, he hired a taxi, driving them to the Meiyuan warehouse in Shenzhen.

He sat in the passenger seat and warmly introduced Shenzhen to the Korean merchants as they drove. They were very interested in this magical city. Then Haonan's pager rang. It was news from Xu Yanwei that Hu would prepare a banquet for these Korean customers tonight, and would be waiting for the good news that the business was successfully finished. Haonan's spirits were buoyed up at once.

For many years ramie fabrics had been stored in Meiyuan warehouse and could be freely selected by buyers. Payment might be effected after the goods were delivered, and even 30 days' credit allowed to reputable companies such as Haonan's company.

They three arrived on the third floor, where the cargos of Liu Xianwu from Liuyang Supply & Sales Station of Hunan Province, the supplier of Haonan, were situated. Kim jumped on them, randomly choosing a bolt of ramie fabric. Then he jumped down, fished out a mini microscope to check the count quantity, which was the total quantity of warp thread and weft thread. It should be same as the sample. Now Kim and Hu Wanzhong were talking about it in Korean, and Haonan could not understand. Gradually Kim's face darkened. "Are these the goods you took a sample from to send me?" he asked.

"Of course," was Haonan's reply.

"The sample you sent me had a 1,200 count, but this is only 1,000," Kim said.

"Impossible," said Haonan. He clearly remembered some days before drawing out a sample at random from these goods. He had checked with the warehouse keeper that these goods, which belonged to Liu Xianwu, were always piled up here, and were never changed. So how could they be different from that sample?

He asked Kim, "Can you show me the sample I sent you before?"

"I didn't bring it with me from Korea." Kim shrugged, unfolding his arms.

At that moment Liu Xianwu arrived. He was a quiet and gentle man, originally a businessman at the Liuyang Supply & Sales Station. Since there was hot demand for ramie fabric, he had set up a business office in Shenzhen to deal with it. Haonan now rushed over to ask, "Have you ever changed these goods?"

"No," Liu Xianwu confirmed.

"No change, same size, quantity and quality," said the warehouse keeper nearby.

"But the quality does not meet my requirements," said Kim.

Haonan was staggered. He gazed dumbstruck at the big pile of cargo. He blamed himself most. He should have asked Kim to sign, stamp and return the sample, or to bring it with him from Korea. Now whether the goods qualified or not depended entirely on Kim's subjective judgment.

Later it was time for Haonan to invite them for lunch. He reflected that there were similar ramie fabrics in the nearby Sungang warehouse and Sichuan building warehouse, and decided to show them later.

In the afternoon, however, after they had checked several further lots of goods, the conclusion from Kim and Hu Wanzhong was still the same: the goods could not be approved. Haonan was confident that more goods would be available the next day, but Kim said this was impossible because his visa had only one day to run. They had to leave today for Hong Kong and fly back to Korea tomorrow, and their air tickets could not be changed.

Standing on Bao'an Road North in front of the warehouse, Haonan wondered how he could do this. It was busy with cars and people, but none of them could give him an answer.

"So what shall we do now?" Liu Xianwu asked Haonan.

"Today there is nothing we can do. Let's see them off to the Luohu checkpoint," Haonan said.

Before they set off, Haonan received a further pager message from Xu Yanwei: "Hu has booked the banquet tonight for celebrating. Is the inspection done?" Haonan then went to the public telephone kiosk and called to tell him what had happened. Xu Yanwei sighed, and Hu cancelled the booking.

On the square of Luohu railway station in front of the Luohu checkpoint, there was a big turning area where many *Bougainvillea glabra*, the city flower of Shenzhen, were planted, blooming all year round. At nine that evening, Haonan and the two Korean merchants stood on the square. Because of the hurry, they had cancelled the supper. It was approaching the end of the year and winter was coming. It was hot in the day but cold at night. Haonan was wearing only summer clothes and he suddenly shivered. He was still trying to think of a way to solve the problem before his customers left.

He insisted again that the goods he had shown them were indeed those from which he had taken the sample, but he had no evidence. Kim would not change his mind. He declared that he had made the journey only for the inspection, because this was the first order he had placed with Haonan. It had cost him about five thousand US dollars. He had also spent a thousand US dollars on opening the letter of credit, regardless of whether it would be negotiated.

Haonan was silent.

Liu Xianwu had already circled the turning area many times. The flow of traffic was busiest on the square so parking was strictly prohibited there, but he was reluctant to abandon Haonan.

The evening wind blew cold inside Haonan's short sleeves and trousers. He had to hug himself tightly to keep warm. Perhaps Koreans, who lived in a colder climate, were more used to winter.

Haonan did not usually mind a cold bath in any season, but tonight he was feeling a chill he had never suffered before. They heard the shouts of those wanting them to stay at a hotel, buy various household supplies or ride the long-distance bus, but the vendors all left in disappointment after seeing the three of them standing there as still as statues. However, they managed to stick in their bags and pockets many flyers advertising "House Renting", "Foreskin Incisions", "Eradication of Prostate Inflammation" and so forth. Kim and Hu Wanzhong found on their luggage boxes advertisements for breast

159

enlargement, plastic surgery and transgender operations. When Kim's wife saw these colourful name cards and telephone numbers later, she would wonder if her husband had seen a prostitute during his visit to China.

Those who had come to the square to see somebody off had left, and those who had come to pick somebody up had also gone. Finally Liu Xianwu in his circling van stopped asking if Haonan was getting in but just looked at him in pity. Haonan kept signalling Liu Xianwu to leave, saying he would take a bus later. But Liu Xianwu was still reluctant to do so. He also kept hoping Haonan would find a solution to his problem.

"Maybe I could print the Inspection Certificate and sign it myself?" Haonan mused, thinking this would be a lifeline. Kim saw his smile. "Is there a solution?" he asked, peering at Haonan. But such behaviour was definitely cheating. Haonan thought a moment and shook his head. "No, not yet," he said. Both Koreans sighed pitifully.

On the square people were hurrying to and fro, the colourful lights blinking, but Haonan's face was dim. He was wishing that the two Koreans would stay in Shenzhen tonight, then everything would be possible tomorrow, as he knew that there would be more fabrics to inspect.

There were faint sounds from Haonan's pager, but he ignored them. He knew that at 11:00 at night, the Luohu checkpoint would be barred. When he looked at his watch, it was 10:55.

"We have to leave now," said Kim. He shook hands with Haonan and walked slowly away. Everything was over, despite all Haonan's hard work.

Haonan stared at Kim and Hu Wanzhong as they walked away, his heart was heavy and full of disappointment. After a long sigh, he looked up at the night sky and roared, "What have I done wrong?" The heavens gave him no answer.

The van finally stopped near Haonan. He had been standing there for two hours. After looking again in sadness at the people hurrying in the direction of the checkpoint, he dragged himself over to the van and sat absentmindedly down on the passenger seat. His enormous order had vanished into the void, for no reason.

Inside a building at Sihai, Shekou, in a room on the fourth floor, there was a dormitory for the staff of the Shanghai Restaurant, in which four sets of two decks of iron beds were placed by the wall. Eight female workers had gathered together around a three-pound of taro root birthday cake laid on the table. Today was Laizhen's 20th birthday. However, there was sadness on her pretty face. Haonan had promised her that he would come here to celebrate her birthday with her, bringing the news of his business success. But she had not heard from him. She only knew that he had gone to meet two Korean customers. She had called his pager several times, leaving telephone numbers and messages.

"Did he forget your beauty after meeting a foreigner?" said one colleague. "That's the influence of the US dollar."

"He speaks English so well that he can meet foreign girls. I've heard he can make love for two hours, which is unthinkable in China," another butted in.

"You...!" Laizhen rebuked her in embarrassment. They burst out laughing, then looked at the clock on the wall. It was nearly midnight, and her birthday would soon be over.

"Don't wait any longer. Let's blow the candle out now," someone suggested. Soon the light was turned off. They lit nine candles for Laizhen and sang the Birthday Song. Afterwards Laizhen blew the candle out. She was worried that the loving fire between her and Haonan was dying away.

In a room in the Hunan restaurant beside the Shennan Road, Haonan had not swallowed one piece of rice or one mouthful of water since the afternoon. He was clinking wine glasses with Liu Xianwu, trying to get rid of their sorrow. He was wondering why he had been so unlucky as to encounter this disaster, and why there were no clues.

Chapter 15
Humiliation at the Year-End Conference

Some days later, on a day in January 1993, all the staff of China Merchants gathered together in the company's official hall for a conference to summarize the past year and encourage work in the coming year.

On the rostrum, Hu, Wen, Zhou, Liu and Li sat down in sequence. The conference was recorded by Chen Xiaomei. Hu rose to his feet and said, "Business was thriving in the foreign trade field around China in 1992, in which, however, some were still alive but some died. All of us were united while performing individual responsibilities. In 1992 we had fulfilled the task by earning foreign exchange of 20.12 million US dollars for our country. Meanwhile a large number of senior managers were successful, such as Miss Cao Chunhua, who exported linen; the shoe business of Liu Xiaoquan; the marble business in Fujian Province dealt by Zheng Weiping; the rabbit fur in Anhui of Xu Yanwei; the dried ginger and white fruit in Guizhou of Ma Zhimin; the bamboo and willow woven arts & crafts products in Guangxi, handled by Yu Minru; the seat cushions made of wood pearl in Zhejiang Province and the soft-toy shoes from Anhui Province; the chemical phthalocyanine blue in Gansu Province of Li Rentai, and the bicycle chains of Fu Yanjie. We consistently obey our rule 'Only the result matters, regardless of the process'."

Hearing Fu Yanjie's name, some female staff laughed secretly because it sounded like a woman's cleaning tool.

Haonan dispiritedly wrote the conference record, sitting in his own post.

Liu Xiaoquan was the manager of I/E dept 4, whose shoe business was easily done. He understood neither English nor letter of credit. He had graduated as an accountant and always worked as one. God knows how he made acquaintance with an Argentine buyer who purchased shoes from him, from sports shoes to slippers and from flat shoes to high heels, with continuous big orders. It seemed that it wasn't required for him to work hard; after signing the contract, the goods were transported to Shekou and customs clearance was handled by Li Huo, Huang Zhuo and Li Jianqiang, who worked in the customs clearance department of the company. Later on Liu Xiaoquan enrolled Li Bin as business manager in the department, implementing computerised system management for the company for the first time. By these methods his business was flourishing. In this department there was an additional executive named Huang Changshui and a professional Japanese translator, Miss Hong Fang.

Miss Cao Chunhua's father was managing director of a linen factory in Mohe city, Heilongjiang Province. This introverted north-eastern woman, who was not skilled at business or socialising, had once supplied linen to Haonan. Although the deal between her and Haonan failed, she flew from the remote north of China to Shenzhen, joining Haonan's company, where she did very well at business.

Fu Yanjie, who sat beside Haonan, always did poorly at business. Nobody took any interest in the cycle chain samples he displayed in the Canton Fair. Several times after the fair had closed, he had angrily heaved his samples into the dustbin. By chance, a chain sample he left on a friend's stand caught the attention of a merchant from the Middle East. Fu Yanjie's business card was on the sample, so the merchant contacted Fu Yanjie by fax, firstly ordering a small quantity and then placing a larger order. Gradually Fu Yanjie became successful.

Zhang Yanyi, who dealt in canned foods, once attended the fair with Haonan. On one occasion a Malaysian merchant walked into the booth and pointed to a can of luncheon meat, asking Haonan and Zhang Yanyi about it. Haonan went to the toilet, and when he came back, Zhang Yanyi had already won an order. The Malaysian merchant had originally thought that it would be the same no matter which businessman he signed with. But to Haonan's surprise, the god of fortune smiled on Zhang Yanyi. What was more, thanks to this unexpected order, Zhang Yanyi's business grew bigger and bigger. Now Haonan was heartbroken. He blamed himself for not holding onto his bladder for a little longer at that time.

Li Sufen dealt in sesame oil produced in Hubei Province. At first when Haonan worked for the company, he had been trusted by Wen to assist her with customs clearance. One day Haonan and Li Sufen got on a No. 204 bus to the Wenjingdu customs clearance building. He helped the customs clearance operator to fill in the clearance sheet, commercial invoice, packing list and cargo receipt and the driver's notebook, and was waiting for the result after eating rice. The work didn't finish until nightfall. Then he called Li Sufen's pager, hoping to go back with her. However she had already got back home and was lazily relaxing on a swing on her balcony after supper.

Although Sun'ang had married and fathered a son, he was still a casual lad who did things in a hurry, so he did not notice if he lost a shoelace while walking. Xianju County in Zhejiang Province was famous for seat cushions made of wooden pearls in China, and these were transported to

Shekou by truck one by one. Tapping his calculator to work out the charges, he told the customs clearance department of the company to arrange shipment. But he was so careless that whenever he copied his Shenzhen Residence Identity Card, he lost it, for he would take the copy but forget to take the original from the copying machine. Owing to his carelessness, Haonan was on one occasion entrusted by the company to temporarily assist him, flying directly from Shenzhen to Shanghai. That was the first time he flew. Afterwards he escorted three trucks of imported expandable polyethylene, driving them to Mingguang Arts & Crafts Factory in Jiashan County, Anhui Province. This would be used as padding when making animal- shaped shoes for export.

Wanwei had majored in Chinese at Henan Normal University, and although he was not good at commerce he worked on import business for the company. At that time there was a hot market for Panasonic fax machines from Japan. As soon as Wanwei joined the company he seized this opportunity to import fax machines in containers from Hong Kong, then sell them to mainland China. He later recruited total five people as his import department, and even set up a branch office in Luohu district which did excellent business.

Yu Minru, an innocent young lad, had been idle since graduating in Spanish at Guangzhou Foreign Language College a year before. Yet how would he get a chance to meet a foreign merchant who spoke Spanish? Knowing that other foreign businessmen usually chatted in English, he regretted his choice of language and wanted to resume learning English. As he had received no orders for his bamboo and willow woven products for a long time, he was sometimes teased by Fu Yanjie. With this company's "do-it-yourself" approach, if you hadn't won an order for three months, you would be too ashamed to stay. Yu Minru decided to leave after the Autumn Fair of 1992.

The Canton Fair is always a grand ceremony, which various elite people rush to attend; it's also a fierce furnace, in which people can perish or be reborn. On the morning of October 30 when the fair was about to be closed, Yu Minru sat in the company's booth, his face as dark as black clouds, because his products had attracted no attention from any foreign merchants after fifteen days. On the negotiating table were three more exquisite samples which would soon be packed away.

Wen said, "Let's get ready to leave". No sooner had she spoken than two foreign merchants, one fat and the other thin, both heavily perfumed, came in.

"What can I do for you?" said Wen.

But they did not answer. It seemed that they were only brokers wanting to purchase cheap samples during the confusion of the closing minutes of the fair. Afterwards Wen communicated with them by sign-language. She had met many foreigners, and she had no difficulty in speaking with them. However, there was a barrier between her and these two brokers now.

The thin, depressed-looking one held up a bamboo basket sample from the table, but Yu Minru snatched it back immediately, saying in Spanish, "Don't take it!" This was the first time he had had the chance to use his Spanish.

"What are you talking about?" the thin one replied, also in Spanish, signalling to Yu Minru to say it again.

"Don't take it!" Yu Minru said again, angrily and loudly. But the thin man told the fat one behind him, "Give it to him! Give it to him!" The fat one fished out a thousand dollars from his pocket and stuffed it into Yu Minru's chest pocket.

Was it so easy to get money just by glowering at foreign merchants and speaking in Spanish? Yu Minru, Wen, and Haonan, who had come up to assist, were all open-mouthed. It turned out that the two merchants belonged to a large import and export company in Brazil and they had come to buy woven bamboo and willow products. During the seven days they had been at the fair, although they had seen many of the products they required, they knew only Spanish, so they could not communicate with the Chinese businessmen, who only spoke English. On this last day the fat one had persuaded the thin one to give up and go back to Brazil. The thin one was reluctant, so the fat one told him he would pay him a thousand dollars if he succeeded. The thin one accepted, but the money was paid to the man who could speak Spanish. So it was Yu Minru who got this money.

But this was only a tiny thing. The most important point was that by this chance, the two foreign merchants would place a big order with the one who could speak Spanish. One sentence can be worth thousands of dollars. At that time English translators were warmly welcome, for by guiding foreigners they earned the price difference between that of the foreigners and the factory, and sometimes there was commission from the factory to pay as well.

By now Yu Minru felt he had just awoken from a dream. He did not care about the thousand dollars. He hastily unpacked the cartons in which the samples had already been sealed and poured them out again so that the two merchants could take a look.

This was the first time Wen had seen her businessman talking to foreigners in Spanish. Haonan, who was also watching, even felt an impulse to learn Spanish himself.

After forty minutes, Yu Minru signed a huge order with the two men. Relying upon his Spanish, after coming back to the company he carried out the order he had signed at the fair and from then on he received new orders constantly. So good fortune followed his calamity. Later he established a new import-export department with foreign exchange earning up to five million dollars a year, and this became a company legend.

When the conference was about to end, Hu announced the task for every businessman in the new year. Later on, he awarded, on behalf of the company, a VW Jetta car to Cao Chunhua, along with a ceremony to hand over the keys. Chen Xiaomei took a photo.

At the conference Hu reported that the company had a quota for six Shenzhen Permanent Residence Permits. Liu Xiaoquan, Sun'ang and Yu Minru already had permits, so the first went to Cao Chunhua, which enabled her to move from Mohe in the northernmost part of China, where the northern lights of Russia could be seen just by opening her window, to Shenzhen special economic zone. The second was for Li Rentai, to enable him to move from the remote mountain area of Gansu Province to Shenzhen; the third was gained by Zhang Yanyi, who focused on the exportation of canned foodstuffs. The other three were allocated to logistical staff.

Hu added, "Haonan originally had a big export order for ramie fabric, but the trial order failed. The reason was his lack of experience. It was regretted by all of us. However, our rule is, only the result matters, not the process. So we can only hope that he will take the lesson on board and recover from his setback."

All the staff gazed at Haonan sympathetically. He listened carefully throughout, lowering his head. Actually his heart was bleeding and he wanted to cry. He was silently recalling what had happened in the last year. Apart from the dreadful failure of the ramie fabric deal, the business between him and Pario had also vanished. Pario had arranged full advance payment for the first two orders, to win the trust of Haonan's company. But when it came to a third order, Pario said that because of temporary cash flow difficulties, he wanted shipment first. Haonan asked Hu and got his agreement, for all the leaders of the company thought it was unnecessary to worry about such an excellent buyer. However, when Haonan tried to fax the export documents, the number supplied did not exist. It turned out that Pario had disappeared after picking up the third lot of goods. He had built up trust with the previous two orders in order to avoid payment for the third.

The company decided to penalize Haonan by stopping his wages for six months, although they still allowed him to live there. Later he borrowed money from Fuqiang and Zhenfeng to pay the supplier for the goods. So now he had no chance of getting a Shenzhen Permanent Residence Permit, let alone a house. And all his hopes would have to depend on his struggle in the coming year.

Chapter 16
Shocking Encounter in a Restaurant

It was a night in early summer, and beautiful lights twinkled in Shekou. At a "Good Dream" coffee shop, Haonan and Laizhen sat next to the window sipping tea.

"Somebody told me they are carefully checking personal credentials at the checkpoints of Nantou and Buji now," she said, worried.

Haonan indeed had much experience of this. Many times when entering the city downtown through Nantou checkpoint, he had taken a small Frontier Pass, which was like a special entrance ticket enabling him to go into Shenzhen. Later on he had successfully applied for a Temporary Living Permit in Shenzhen, which was better, but only someone who held a Shenzhen Permanent Residence Permit was a real Shenzhener. "What credentials do you hold now?" he asked.

"The same. But our restaurant is applying for Temporarily Living Permits for the workers now," she said sadly.

"Those who don't have Temporary Living Permits in Shenzhen will be detained at the police office and then repatriated to Shaoguan prison," said he anxiously.

"I really don't want to pay to be sent back to my hometown," she said. "How about you? You can't get a Shenzhen Permanent Residence Permit in your company? Obviously not, because your big order from Korea failed."

"Yes." He had to turn his face away. After Kim had gone back to Korea, Haonan had tried to make him come back to Shenzhen to inspect the goods, and even said he would pay half his travelling expenses. However, to his dismay, Kim had suggested that Haonan should first send a shipment to Korea, and if the goods qualified he would sign the Inspection Certificate and send it to China by courier. This enormous risk was unacceptable to Haonan.

"Oh, the Shenzhen Permanent Residence Permit!" she lowered her head, muttering to herself. "Now we can't get Shenzhen Permanent Residence Permits, so there'll be no welfare house offered to us."

"Yes, we have to do it step by step. Permanent Residence Permit first, then the house."

"So you won't get a new quota until the end of the year, or next year?"

"Yes, but I'm not certain if it'll be allocated six months later."

"If it's not available for six months, I'm afraid I'd be in the menopause by then!" she joked.

The environment in Shekou was peaceful, but their hearts were troubled. After a while she said, "I'm going to make an investment, but I don't have the money. Can you lend me ten thousand yuan?"

"Ten thousand?" he blurted out.

"Yes."

He fell silent, and they gazed at each other.

She had made this request partly because she wanted to test his finances and partly to see if he would lend her such a sum. But Haonan was still struggling financially, as his business costs had to be borne by himself; he would be repaid by the company after the business was profitably completed, together with getting a bonus. So he always had to be frugal. Just then he had more than a thousand dollars with him, worth more than ten thousand yuan, which was a deposit a foreigner had handed in today. It could be presented to the company a long time later, so he could lend it to her. Ever since he had met his beloved, he had been ready to save her from any difficulty. However, it occurred to him that she might want to invest the money. If he said he was so poor that he could not lend her the money, would she leave him? He decided to test her then said wistfully to her, "I'm sorry, at present I can't lend you such a large sum."

"Oh dear!" Her disappointment clearly showed. Then she murmured, "It's late at night now. I must get back."

During the rest period a few days later, before getting off work, he phoned her. "How about we both go to the temple of Guan at Chiwan in Shekou tomorrow? The sea view of Mawan nearby is nice too, and we have never been there before." But there was no enthusiasm from her, as there had been before. She said in a low voice, "I need to work all day tomorrow," then put down the phone.

He knew he would have to spend a lonely weekend.

Haonan did not wake up until noon next day. After lunch he felt lonely, so he went to the Shanghai Restaurant again, not only so that he could see Laizhen but to chat with Zhenfeng. When he arrived, however, he saw that the waitress on duty was not Laizhen.

Doubtfully, he entered the restaurant. It was three o'clock, lunch was over and only a few diners were there, sipping tea leisurely. When he saw Zhenfeng, he asked, "Didn't Laizhen come to work today?"

"Come to work? Isn't that her sitting sipping tea?" Zhenfeng pointed. Haonan was shocked. At a table near the window, the one where Haonan had sat talking to Mohammed, Laizhen was sitting. She wore black sunglasses and a short white skirt, and her snow- white skin could be seen from far off. She was looking at the view outside the window.

176

Opposite her was a young man of about 20, a little shorter than her, with hair dyed yellow. He was wearing jeans and a short-sleeved shirt in a flower pattern bearing the word "Japan" and had a heavy gold ring on his finger.

"You must prepare for this news," Zhenfeng said to Haonan. "He is her new boyfriend. She met him only three days ago. His name is Chen Guangwei, and he is a native of Shekou. He is rich and has property in Futian too."

Although Zhenfeng spoke in a gentle voice, Haonan felt as if he had been struck by lightning. All the workers here recognised Haonan and knew he was Laizhen's boyfriend. Yet no sooner had she finished with Haonan than she had met a new man. It seemed she had regarded Haonan as of no importance.

Haonan was very confused. He rushed into another room and collapsed onto the sofa, staring open-mouthed like a dead fish. His brain was filled with bleakness.

A colleague of Zhenfeng's pushed the door open and came in. "Control your grief and accept what has happened," he said bluntly.

Haonan suddenly felt he had lost everything. A Shenzhen Permanent Residence Permit and a house were given to people like Guangwei by nature, along with the big share dividends allocated by the village committee every year end. These natives would lazily drive in their Mercedes

S Class or BMW 7 Series cars to expensive restaurants to sip fine tea. The only culture they needed was the ability to distinguish real money from fake. How could Haonan compete with Guangwei?

Haonan could see through the crack between the double doors how happy Laizhen was in conversation with Yellow Hair. She was giggling melodiously. Yellow Hair inclined his head, admiring her. After a while, he stretched out and kissed her forehead as delicately as if he was sucking the sweet tortoise herb jelly of Guangxi. Horrors! Under the watchful eyes of Laizhen's colleagues, they were so harmonious and gentle together that Haonan could not bear the pain.

"It's hard to accept such a change," said a man coming in. It was the cook who had been watching when Haonan had first plucked up the courage to strike up a conversation with Laizhen. He went on, "How could you fall for a waitress standing in front of a restaurant and studying countless people? Laizhen understood how to judge a man's wealth by his clothes. The longer she stayed here, the better she could tell by the food the diners ordered how much money they had."

Haonan was so astonished that he couldn't say a word. Over the year they had been together he had failed to see through her. He sat there lost in the realisation that he had indeed been wrong in the beginning to choose a waitress like this as his girlfriend.

"Have a cup of water, please." Zhenfeng handed a cup to him. Haonan took it, as expressionless as a cow eating hay.

Zhenfeng added, "Laizhen has gradually undergone a complete transformation. As her desire for money increased, she colluded with the two cashiers of the restaurant in a plan whereby Laizhen was in charge of looking for ideal diners. If she made a triangular mark on the top right corner of the order slip, this was a secret signal to the cashier that this diner would be suitable for overcharging. This was mainly aimed at diners who had drunk too much alcohol. Laizhen was as skilful at judging these diners as a butcher with his knife. The diners normally paid no attention to the amount they were drinking, so extra charges of dozens, even hundreds, of yuan would be shared by Laizhen and the cashier who was on duty. If the diners found out the error, Laizhen and the cashier would pretend to be surprised and say 'Sorry for the mistake, we were in a hurry counting'. They would repay the extra money, and Laizhen, as beautiful as a flower, would sweetly smile and brush the male diners' shoulders with her plump chest. The male diners' anger would disappear, and they would happily pay the bill and leave."

In this way Laizhen had made a lot of money. Zhenfeng explained that when Laizhen had met

Haonan, she had seen how fluently he spoke English and thought a businessman like him must have millions of US dollars or pounds sterling in the bank. She did not know that in fact he was so poor that to rely on him getting a Shenzhen Permanent Residence Permit would be like expecting a dead horse to climb a mountain. So, in this money- driven society, how could she love him?

Haonan nodded, painfully closing his eyes.

Black clouds were now building up in the sky outside, and it was hot.

As 4pm approached, Haonan and Zhenfeng walked out of the restaurant. By chance, in the parking area in front of the restaurant, they met Laizhen and her new boyfriend standing by a Crown car. Laizhen now saw Haonan at last. She was a little nervous, but quickly recovered. Scrutinizing her, Haonan felt that the beautiful girl in front of him now suddenly become alien to him. The memory of the electricity he had felt in front of the typewriter, the advice "It should be one fist's distance between the chest and the desk edge" when teaching her calligraphy, the warmth of the hug and kiss at Bijia Mountain, the two hours of making love on the floor of his single room – all of these were gone with the wind.

"You recognise these men?" asked the yellow-haired man.

"One of them is my colleague. As for the other, I – I don't recognise him," she said dismissively.

Haonan looked at Zhenfeng in shock, his heart beating fiercely.

"*Zhen*, let's go!" said the Yellow Hair. He started the engine of the Crown, and Laizhen sat in the passenger seat as meekly as a little bird. She glanced quickly at Haonan, then turned away. There was nothing to explain. Her eyes were calm and cold, as if nothing had happened. The Crown moved off and roared away in the direction of Shekou port.

Inside the restaurant, all the workers had been watching the scene.

"'*Zhen*'? Why could he call her '*Zhen*'? But her given name is '*Laizhen*'!" Haonan angrily muttered. He suddenly felt dizzy and began to fall. Zhenfeng hurriedly helped him back to his feet.

Haonan wanted to feel again the happiness he had shared with Laizhen, but he could not. Nothing was the same. She had changed so quickly.

After saying goodbye to Zhenfeng, Haonan went over to a stone chair next to a shrubbery beside the bathing beach, where tourists were coming and going. He stayed there the whole afternoon, crossing his hands on his chest, saying nothing, not moving.

This was a summer of cloudy weather. As dusk approached, a gentle sea breeze blew. It stirred Haonan's clothes, but it could not drive away his melancholy mood. From a nearby video shop he heard a song, *I'd Still Rather Wait after Loving and Aching*, sung by Pang Ling from Hong Kong. Her desolate soprano wafted through the air over the beach. In the music Haonan's melancholy seemed freeze-framed in front of him, like the nearby sculpture of *Nv-Wa-Bu-Tian*, the female god mending the sky in ancient China legend. (*Nv-Wa* means a person, *Bu-Tian* means mending the sky). Its lyrics sounded like:

> *Once smilingly said and playfully said but reluctant to separate,*
> *Once loved and ached but still wished to wait,*
> *In this life of mine I'd rather die for you without any hate...*

Yes, he had once loved and ached and he still wished to wait, but for whom? And who would want Haonan to wait for her? The beautiful girl he had wanted to wait for had just thrown herself onto another man's bosom. Haonan buried his face in his hands. Tears fell ceaselessly between his fingers and dropped down into the grass beneath.

Soon it was dark, and Haonan rose slowly to his feet and walked across the lawn in front of the Naihai Hotel. In the woods a pied hornbill was sadly chirping, like a child who has lost its mother, and it seemed to be crying for Haonan. Little bird, he thought,   how he wanted to be like Gong Ye Chang,   the   ancient man who was supposed to

182

talk to the birds, so that he could talk to it through his heart to get rid of his sorrow.

He remembered the many weekends when he had strolled here with Laizhen. They had paddled in the shallow water and explored the gaps between the stones, watching the skipping crabs and shrimps and looking at the colourful conches, mussels and pearl shells. They had picked them up and exchanged them, hugging each other. He was grateful for having had the chance to get to know such a wonderful girl. And how he longed to grow old with her, together for life. Now this love, like a delicate flower, had vanished as soon as it had appeared. It had not been able to survive the harshness of life's reality, and like a wall collapsing for lack of a firm foundation.

It was now late at night. Haonan had no interest in supper. On the lawn, infatuated lovers walked past hand in hand. Motor boats roared past towards Shekou port. Haonan wondered why he had not agreed to handle the watch movement export business with Fuqiang. And many other friends in Shenzhen foreign trade had invited him to join their export tax rebate businesses, dealing with importing cars and car parts. Why had he been so silly as to turn them down? Otherwise by now he might have had that Shenzhen Permanent Residence Permit and a house. And Laizhen.

It was soon midnight. He could see the faint lights of boats on the sea between Naihai Hotel and Hong Kong. Someone was playing a song called *You Were My Everything* sung by Wang Jingwen, another Hong Kong singer, his favourite. Yes, he thought, Laizhen had been his everything, but now? The words cut his heart:

Probably when I lost you,
I felt the past days were the most beautiful,
You were my everything;
Probably when I lost you,
I found that your love had died.
You were my everything...

He staggered on, shaking his arms, like paper blown by the wind. Presently his shoulder bumped into the rough bark of a palm tree. He stood there still for some while. His face was streaked with the marks of tears. He looked bewildered up at the unfathomable night sky. There was no moon tonight, and the bright stars were reflected in his tears.

He dropped to his knees on the sand, holding his face in his hands, and roared in a heartrending voice, "Lin—Lai—Zhen!"

Chapter 17
Praying for Help from God

The next morning when Haonan went to work, he was late for the first time. He seemed a different man. Eyes red with tiredness, he lowered his head and said nothing all morning. His colleagues' inquiries soon revealed what had happened between him and Laizhen the previous day.

"Congratulations! You're free to select other nice girls now," said Li Yijun, the thin deputy office director.

"Congratulations?" Haonan was shocked. It seemed to him that Li Yijun was rubbing salt into his wounds. He did not know that Haonan had not slept the previous night, or how painful his heart was.

Fu Yanjie could only comfort Haonan by saying, "There are so many nice girls in the world now. If you were with one who doesn't suit you, better split up sooner than later." Haonan understood the idea, but it was hard for him to feel like this.

Wang Li, who sat behind Haonan, was engaged in the export of T-shirts. She had noticed his haggard appearance, and as a sincere Christian, she thought she would take on the responsibility of helping him to overcome his sorrow. She was approaching 30 and recently divorced. At the beginning her husband had had an extramarital affair and she had lodged a lawsuit against him. They had fought over custody of their daughter, and the evidence indicated that she would lose. Fortunately she was guided by a kind man who prayed for her. When she won custody of her daughter, she said Jesus had arranged it, and the courage to recover from her painful and defeated marriage had come from the power of Jesus. From then on, therefore, she was committed to a Christian life. She always remembered to pray when she was not working, and before picking up her chopsticks at each meal.

Now she asked Haonan, "Do you have time tonight? I'll show you a place where you can set yourself free of mental burdens." Haonan knew how kind-hearted Wang Li was. He felt so depressed that he agreed to go with her.

That evening Wang Li led Haonan from Zhuzilin to a residential area named Leigongling in Shekou and showed him into a flat on the third floor. It was an apartment of about 40 square metres, and outside the balcony was a large area of litchi trees. Inside it was bulging with people. There was a blackboard on the wall on which hung a picture of Jesus suffering on the cross. Wang Li guided Haonan to a platform at the front and introduced him to Mr Li Qinjian, a priest.

"I'm glad to meet you." Li Qinjian's voice was gentle. He stretched out his hand, "God will be grateful for your coming here tonight."

"God knows I've come here?" Haonan said doubtfully.

"Yes, God knows everywhere you've gone or will go."

"Can God know if I go to the toilet?" Haonan asked.

"Don't talk about that."

"If God closes a window, he will open another for you," Wang Li butted in.

Glancing inside the room, Haonan saw that the people were mostly women between 30 and 40. They sat on stools, smiling and chatting. Each was holding a small book in her hands, a Christian holy Bible.

"This is for you," Wang Li said, giving one to Haonan. "Now that we're all here, we are brothers and sisters already. Relying on Jesus, we come here together."

Haonan found a seat and sat down. He flipped the *Bible* open. It was the Chinese-English version, and he saw Chapters of the *Exodus from Egypt*, along with text about Jerusalem, Jehovah, the Gospel according to Matthew and Noah's Ark.

"Sit down, please! Let's begin our meeting!" said Li Qinjian from the platform. "Jesus created the human being, and all things in the world originate from Jesus. So we must be thankful to Jesus. We must treasure all we possess today. Now let's pray!"

Haonan saw that all of them had closed their eyes, lowered their heads, crossed their hands and put them in front of their chests, murmuring. He lowered his head too, but it was difficult to close his eyes. He opened his eyes narrowly from time to time, casting sidelong glances around. After about three minutes, all of them said loudly "Amen!" to signal the end of the prayer.

"You must be calm and know how to forgive, then you might get out of your sea of bitterness," said Wang Li beside him.

Haonan did not fully understand, but he nodded politely.

"Now, let me help you to pray." Wang Li put the hollow of her left palm on the back of Haonan's right hand and slightly closed her eyes, uttering, "God! The great Jehovah! Please forgive Haonan's offence!"

Offence? I have never stolen or robbed, he thought to himself. Then he heard Wang Li say, "O God! Today I brought Haonan to you. We would like to kneel down before you, listen to your guiding words. We hope that you can feed us, lead us! We'd like to follow you. O holy God! Please accept him to your broad chest. Lead Haonan, take care of him so that he will follow your call. Amen!"

Although he did not know what offence he had committed, Haonan mechanically repeated, "Amen!"

"Are you feeling better now?" Wang Li asked.

"It seems almost the same," he replied.

"Don't hurry, you'll calm down and feel no desire soon."

"No desire? And what offence am I guilty of?" he traced to ask.

"Once a man has desire, he commits an offence. Before great Jesus, all of us are criminals."

"Criminals? How could we be without desire? I still hope for a Shenzhen Permanent Residence Permit and a house, and I still hope that the relationship between me and Laizhen can be resumed." he said.

But no sooner she replied, "Take it easy! Everything will be all right!"

Presently Li Qinjian started to speak about the story of how Jesus rescued him. Then it was time for a hymn, a praying song, and then they all lowered their heads and sang together:

God of mine, how treasured you are,
God of mine, you're the sunlight on the land.
God! Almighty God!
Please lead us to go to the far...

This song, not loud but sung in harmony, drifted through the window, passed the litchi trees, and floated into the colourful night sky above Shekou. Haonan was not used to this kind of worship, but seeing how involved they all were, he decided to follow and take it seriously.

"You can devoutly pray, and before Jesus you can say whatever you want," said Li Qinjian. "Jesus can hear what you say because he is always with us, any time and anywhere."

Haonan rose to his feet, seizing Li Qinjian's hand tightly. Suddenly he saw that he had a clear knife scar on his left wrist. Seeing Haonan's puzzled expression, Li explained that when he had come alone to Shekou from the north-east seven years before, he had deeply loved a girl here. However, just before the wedding banquet, this girl fell in love with a foreigner, so the despairing Li Qinjian tried to kill himself by cutting a vein. Fortunately he was found and rescued in time. After that, once his broken heart had recovered, he had devoted himself to Jesus and become a priest saving people in Shekou. Then Haonan understood.

After this they prayed again. In a faint voice Haonan suddenly blurted out, "God! Please kill Chen Guangwei right now!" Everyone at once stopped praying in alarm, and turned doubtful eyes to Haonan, who wondered what to do.

"Who is Chen Guangwei?" they asked one after another.

"He is my rival in love who stole my girlfriend, I hate him so much!" Haonan replied angrily.

Wang Li hurriedly said to Haonan, "God is benevolent. He doesn't advocate grudge or murder. God helps us to love everyone." She lowered her head and murmured, "God! Please offer happiness to Chen Guangwei! Please accept him, hug him with your limitless love!"

Haonan was surprised. But no sooner had he spoken than Wang Li stopped him, grasping his hand and saying, "God! Please forgive Haonan's ignorance and his offence, because he only came here today."

"Is this also an offence of mine?" Haonan questioned.

"More serious," someone butted in.

"If somebody strikes your left cheek, you then turn your right cheek to be struck?" Haonan remembered this sentence. He really didn't understand why she prayed to Jesus to forgive the one who had harmed him so much. He thought to himself: *Doesn't forgiving my enemy mean hurting myself? Take the Japanese invading China, for instance, would I pray to Jesus to forgive the Japanese invaders? Fuck no! Why do I need to pray for Chen Guangwei, who has stolen my happiness? He's lucky to have Laizhen, isn't that enough?*

He remained perplexed about this for the rest of the evening. However, he then went back to his company's dormitory in Xia'sha village, reflecting on what had happened that evening, and gradually felt calmer.

Most of his colleagues were already asleep. Before going to bed, he suddenly wanted to pray by himself. As the Christians tonight had done, he put his palms together and lightly touched his forehead, and facing the faint light from the window, he spoke heartfelt words. At that moment he felt he did not need to worry about anything. He felt that under the broad sky God was looking down at his people and knowing all their thoughts.

His heart was a little quieter, but he could not yet close his eyes. He felt there was a big gulf separating him and Laizhen, for he had neither a Shenzhen Permanent Residence Permit nor a house.

"Since I'm unable to bring her happiness, I don't have the qualifications to give my love to her," he said to himself. "So I pray that God will grant happiness to Laizhen. Oh God! Punish me please! Beat me dead please! The harder you do it, the more chance I have of being reborn and gaining everlasting life." After he had spoken, although he still felt heartache for Laizhen, he could calm his feelings.

"Forget her, please!" he finally blurted out to himself. He thought that only in this way could he end his sour and bitter feelings, and only in this way could he throw himself back into his life and work. He stood up, turned on the light and picked up the address book on the table. He found the name, address and telephone number of Laizhen, written in his own elegant handwriting, took a bottle of correction fluid and painted the words out one by one. Then he stared foolishly at the area of white which had appeared among all the contact information for relatives, classmates and friends. Now all his history with Laizhen was buried under the strong-smelling correction fluid.

"Laizhen, I'll forget you forever!" he said to himself as he closed the address book.

That night he didn't think any more. He only noted that overhead there were two lines of wild geese flying freely in the sky.

In the end he fell sweetly asleep.

Chapter 18
Trapped by Loving Feelings

Time and time again, I ask myself,
I ask myself: where in nature is your good?
Where is your good?

Not long ago a popular TV series, *The Beijingers in New York*, was played on screens around China. Its theme song lingered in the air long after the performance, and the story of these characters in New York moved all the people of China deeply. It chanced that one day when Haonan rode his bicycle past the Honey Lake, he saw a big Lincoln car parked there. It carried the number plate LA 1937. Haonan knew LA was the abbreviation for Los Angeles, so it was apparent that this sedan was from Los Angeles. Had it been transported by ship? How could such a sedan appear in Futian District? Gazing at it, he naturally thought of *The Beijingers in New York*.

One day a thin man walked into the offices of Haonan's company. He took off his shirt and hung it over his shoulder, leaving only a white vest on the upper part of his body. He was twisting a Mercedes key fob in his finger. He said to Huang Lijuan, who sat at the front desk, "I'm looking for Zhou Haonan."

"What's your surname, please?" Huang Lijuan asked politely, holding a pen to write it down.

"Zhang," he said.

"And your given name?"

"Fuqiang."

"Fu — what?"

"Fuqiang!"

"Fu — what?"

"Sounds like 'rape'!"

Huang Lijuan blushed. She hastily showed Fuqiang to the reception room, then told Haonan, who came out to see his surprise visitor.

"I was passing here to make a shipment, so I came to visit you," Fuqiang said to Haonan. "But you look as if you have aged, what's wrong with you?"

This greeting made Haonan's heart sink like the collapsing bank of a river. He tried hard to keep calm, but his eyes betrayed him. He rose to his feet and turned his chair so that his back was to the door and window, so that colleagues could not see his face.

"Alas! Fuqiang, Fuqiang," Haonan said in a low voice, "you're the childhood friend I hunted frogs with. You're my relative in this strange land of Shenzhen. A friend in need is a friend indeed. But Fuqiang, why did you only appear just now? In those lonely days I was so without hope that I almost jumped from a building to my death. If you had been with me then I would have cried and hugged you." From the failure of the ramie fabric deal to splitting up with Laizhen, Haonan told Fuqiang all of what had happened.

Fuqiang sighed sympathetically, for although he always liked to have fun he was now sad as well. After a pause he patted Haonan's strong shoulder and said, "Forget it. Let it be. A new girl won't come until the old one goes."

"It's easy to say that," Haonan said, sighing dejectedly.

"But I can do it, and in fact I did it. You also know that I don't lack a girlfriend." Fearing that Haonan didn't believe him, Fuqiang added, 'Don't give up a forest because of a tree. And as long as you own a forest, you'll have plenty of trees."

Haonan smiled bitterly. Gradually he began to relax. Their conversation turned to ramie fabric. Haonan said, "I'm at a loss to know what to do now. You always have many tricks, so what do you think about it?"

Fuqiang said, "Show me the signed contract between you and the Korean customer." Haonan went back to fetch it. After scrutinizing Kim's signature on the bottom right, Fuqiang said, "You're very good at imitation. There is a solution here. The Inspection Certification could be signed and issued by you as per Kim's handwriting. You can present the documents to the bank after you have delivered the goods to Kim, then get the letter of credit amount. In the meantime, you can apply for an inspection at Shenzhen Import and Export Commodity Inspection and Quarantine Bureau, who can confirm that these goods are qualified at a 1,200 count instead of 1,000. This will confirm that the goods conform with the requirements of the contract. Then you have no fear of having to pay compensation."

Haonan said, "I can apply for the Inspection Certification in Shenzhen Import and Export Commodity Inspection and Quarantine Bureau. But I cannot imitate the signature of the customer. It would be illegal, that's why I didn't do it at the time."

"If I were you, I would sign it. I'd first get the payment, never mind what happens later," Fuqiang said.

"But this conflicts with the rules and principles of contract law."

"If he was talking about it, why didn't he come back to inspect the goods? According to the contract between you and him, since he didn't come here to inspect the goods, he breached contract law. The goods have been stored in the warehouse waiting for his inspection, but he never came to see them again." Fuqiang knew what he was talking about.

"Yes, I can ask him to come here again, but imitate his handwriting? I can't do that."

"You're still so inflexible. Can you still remember what I said in front of you and Zhenfeng beside my restaurant when you first came to Futian?" Fuqiang tapped the table. "Only the one who is caught is called a thief. *Diaotou!*"

But Haonan still shook his head.

"OK, forget it! Don't mention it again. Don't be so sad, please! I'm now going to tell you an interesting story about me." Fuqiang began to relate how he had almost been detained by the police. The night before last he had earned much money after a customs clearance at Huanggang checkpoint, so with his partner, he had gone to celebrate in the nearby Huanggang village. How should they celebrate? They decided to look for girls for sex. He had gone into a single room on the fifth floor of a building. No sooner had he unbuttoned his clothes than suddenly the alarm bell rang everywhere, and the building was surrounded by the police. As there were more than 20 rooms in this building, there were more than 20 pairs of prostitutes.

Instantly the doors were closed and locked. The policemen rushed in, checking the rooms one by one. If anyone was reluctant to open the door, they ordered the accompanied locksmith to force it open. As soon as the door was opened, the suspect and the evidence were grasped and put into a police car without explanation.

"You were detained and released again so soon?" Haonan asked.

"Let me tell you the rest of the story," Fuqiang said. He explained that his partner had been one of those detained. Suddenly Fuqiang hit upon an idea. He told his girl not to be nervous, and promised she would be OK. They put their clothes in order, opened the door wide, switched on all the lights, and switched the TV on with the volume up. Then they sat on the sofa in the living room, crossing their legs and picking their teeth with toothpicks, watching the TV series *The Blue Sky of Bao*. When the policemen passed, they saw the door wide open and two people inside watching TV. They did not even go into the room.

"I did want to invite them to watch the wonderful *The Blue Sky of Bao* together," Fuqiang said, smiling, and then, imitating Bao's voice in the TV, he shouted, overjoyed, "Well! Come on! Wang Chao, Ma Han, open the fodder chopper!"

Haonan was not interested in this. He said, "Just now you talked about customs clearance. Does that mean the mechanical watch movement business?"

"Yes, you can join us if you still want to. You could still earn a great deal of money. We lack your professional talent. My partner would welcome you too. He will be detained by the police for 15 days and the three of us can resume cooperation after he is released. Join us as soon as you can. Once you get a lot of money and you can buy a Shenzhen Permanent Residence Permit and a house, will you still worry that Laizhen won't come back to you? Hurry, my brother! Time waits for no man! It won't only be Lin Laizhen but Chen Laizhen, Wu Laizhen and Deng Laizhen queuing up to marry you!"

It seemed that a light suddenly flashed in front of Haonan. Facing such strong temptation, his heart beat wildly. After a moment, he said calmly, "But I still hope that you can stop at once for those businesses, let alone the deal under the tunnel in Shatoujiao."

"This..." Fuqiang was in difficulty.

After seeing Fuqiang off, Haonan buried himself in the work of preparing a set of export documents on activated carbon, applying for customs clearance documents from the company. After the failure of ramie fabric, Kim placed an order for activated carbon with Haonan. The letter of credit had been received, and because Kim did not request the inspection certificate, he did not have to fly to Shenzhen to inspect the goods, for activated carbon was produced by machine rather than being hand-made. The goods were made by the Yushan Activated Carbon Factory of Jiangxi Province and would be exported as soon as Haonan got the goods ready.

The previous August when Haonan had gone to Jiashan County, Anhui Province on business, he had made acquaintance with Zhu Xianmin, the managing director of Mingguang Arts & Crafts Factory, and found they had much in common. Zhu was middle-aged, with rich experience and strong passions. The factory he had been operating for more than 20 years did not have import and export rights, so various kinds of arts and crafts toys, shoes and soft toys were indirectly exported by the agent of the import and export companies inside or outside the province. Several days before, Zhu had phoned Haonan to say that the factory had established a joint venture company with Zhu Tianrui, a merchant from Los Angeles in the USA. In this way the factory would trade directly. According to the constitution, the factory would entrust a foreign trade businessman who would stay in Los Angeles a long time. Zhu hoped to find one who was sincere and creditworthy with excellent English, and familiar with international trade. He thought of Haonan. However, he said that before flying to LA, this man must stay in Jiashan County for three months to get used to the production processes of the factory and most importantly, he must check material costs and the finished soft toy products, to help the business in the US. Zhu appreciated not only Haonan's fine character but his professional skills. He called him many times, pushing him to make a decision as fast as possible.

"Can I make a living there?" Haonan said doubtfully.

"A dog can't die of hunger as long as it runs," said Zhu, quoting a proverb from Bohemia.

"Let me think it over," Haonan said.

Haonan continued to work hard all day, and in the evening he often followed Wang Li to Shekou, attending the gathering, praying devoutly and singing Christian songs.

One month passed, and he still felt the same. He had to think to himself: *When would Jesus arrive? When would Jehovah save me from my sea of bitterness? Would Jesus grant me a Shenzhen Residence Identity Card and a house? Great God, can you let Laizhen draw back her heart and come back to me?* Although he had sworn that he would forget Laizhen, he began to miss her again, uncontrollably. The sun rises and falls, the tide flows and ebbs, but there was an unspeakable bitterness in his heart. *Laizhen*, he thought it again, *I neither see you nor hear you, so any news about you will produce great comfort for me.* He finally realised that missing her was like the pendulum of a clock on the wall which never stops, and how silly it had been to paint out her details with correction fluid.

At this thought he fished out some solvent and painted it carefully on the blanked-out words. Pungent as the solvent was, he imagined it was the aromatic smell of her body. Presently her name, address and telephone number appeared again before him. He stared at the words and read them silently. It brought him a little comfort and satisfaction.

However, it wasn't quite enough. Upon the cup he used every day, his desk lamp, wardrobe, pillowcase, the door and the window, he either wrote or stuck the name "Lin Laizhen" in his elegant handwriting. As a result, one day when Fu Yanjie walked into this room, he misunderstood and thought he had entered the room of a new female colleague. When Haonan came home from work or in the stillness of every night, when the moon and stars shone, he would look at her name and recall his lover. When he stroked her name, he felt he was once again massaging her snowy-white skin. But then he would realise that it was only a hallucination. Afterwards, he would lie heavily on the iron bed where she had once slept, moaning, "Lin Laizhen, Oh Lin Laizhen!"

Chapter 19
Let Me See You One More While

Haonan never imagined that Futian, the place he had rushed to like a stream trickling into the sea two years before, would unexpectedly become just a way station in his life.

That morning Hu saw laughingly several guests off at the doorway of the company, then came back to his office and ordered Huang Lijuan to summon Haonan to his office. Haonan, sitting at his desk, heard the laughter, but when he entered Hu's office he saw that his boss's face was as cold and hard as ice. Facing Haonan, Hu rebuked him thoroughly for the business that had gone wrong. At first Haonan didn't know why, but he later found that Hu had at first demanded his resignation. This would mean the company would not need to pay him three months' salary.

It turned out that Hu had received a phone call from Chen Guangwei that morning. Guangwei had demanded that Hu should fire Haonan, declaring that otherwise he would stop leasing his building to the company or raise the rent by 30%. Hu had asked why, but Guangwei had given no reply. Hu originally thought that Haonan must have offended someone in the society. Transferring nearly one hundred staff to another place would be a lot of trouble, so Hu was willing to sacrifice Haonan, and he agreed to Guangwei's demand.

After all his defeats Haonan was so disheartened that he agreed to leave the company the next day. The whole conversation lasted less than two minutes, making it the fastest resignation in Shenzhen. It shocked Hu, too.

As a native of Shekou, apart from owning ancestral property there, Guangwei also owned a building in Xia'sha village, Futian District. He was a playboy who enjoyed a rich and comfortable lifestyle, going hunting, racing and so on though he was only 20 years old. He had learned about Haonan's relationship with Laizhen and hated him for it, which was why he had forced Hu to fire him.

Haonan's employment papers had not been transferred to Hu's company and were still kept by his previous company in West Canton, so it was as simple to handle his departure as checking out a hotel guest who had not checked in. He went back to the dormitory to collect his belongings. That night, Haonan packed his bags and sat silently on the edge of his bed. He stared at the ceiling, then the narrow grey walls, asking himself again and again, "Shall I leave here soon?" This six square metre house, the little home where he had so often dragged his tired body back after work, had become dearer to him.

For supper, his usual habit was to wash some rice and put it into the rice cooker. Meanwhile he prepared a cleaned crucian carp on a stainless steel plate, together with ginger, onion, soybean sauce and groundnut oil, and put it on top of the rice when the rice was almost cooked. Then he covered the lid of the rice cooker again for a while. In this way the crucian carp and the rice would simultaneously be well cooked. When he took off the lid, the steam with the delicious smell of fish would fill his nose. This was the simplest and the most useful cooking method, taught to him by Zhenfeng.

However he had been so busy today that he had not had time to buy a crucian carp in the market. So that evening, he cooked eight taels of rice and he put it in a bowl with three slices of dried radish. The radish was extremely crisp and tender, and each time he bit into it, it made a tweeting sound like a small bird.

He sat on a tiny stool next to the small table biting into the dried radish slices and listening to the tweeting sound of the bites floating out through the window. It was so crisp, tender and rhythmic that he thought that outside it must sound like the song of a turtledove.

Suddenly he saw the barrel of an air rifle at the window. Someone must have thought there really was a bird in the room. Haonan heard a laugh, and the barrel was withdrawn. Clearly the hunter had realised it was a person making the tweeting noise and not a bird. The owner of the rifle gave a snort of contempt. He was a young man with yellow hair. It was Haonan's enemy, Chen Guangwei, who sometimes came to inspect his own building. And now when Guangwei saw Haonan eating his radishes, he said scornfully, "Shit! It's you! Why are you still here? Get out of my building before I beat you."

Haonan rose to his feet, closed the window tightly, then sat miserably back to resume eating. Tears began to trickle down into the bowl, and the rice that was left slowly formed a congee, as wet and salty as his tears.

After supper, at the entrance to the village, he met Xiong Libo, a clerk in a forwarding company, to make a monthly settlement for sample freight. He handed over 800 yuan in cash packed in an envelope to this young man, who had only recently started this work. The previous week Haonan had sent out a bag sample of mixed cotton and yarn to a new customer of Pakistan via Xiong Libo.

"The settlement time between us has not expired, so why do you pay so early?" Xiong Libo said. He was riding a motor tricycle laden with many packages.

"I have resigned," said Haonan.

"Really? Why would such a capable lad as you resign?" Xiong Libo was shocked.

"Yes, it's true."

"Well I wish you good luck," Xiong Libo said, sighing. He felt a deep respect for Haonan, as he knew that Haonan could easily have escaped without paying him.

Next Haonan met Huang Yong, an executive with the Shenzhen Wantong Shipping Company, to return to him five sets of original blank bills of lading. If he had presented them after typing and signing by himself, together with other documents, to the bank, payment for the full amount for the ramie fabric would in due course have been received by his company, but he did not want to play this trick.

Once everything had been settled he went back to Shekou, hiding in an area of mangrove trees which faced the Shanghai Restaurant across the Taizi Road. The summer air carried the smell of the seaside and the wind blew through the trees and into his clothes. There were few people and cars about. Although it was nearly closing time for the restaurant, he saw from the trees that a new waitress was on duty, and she and her colleagues were still busy. Once the diners were leaving, the waitress bowed to them and smilingly saw them off. He wondered where Laizhen was and what she was doing. He looked for the Crown in the parking area, but could not see it. Perhaps they were having fun in a night club. Hiding among the trees and staring longingly at all this, he felt his heart surge with pain as if cut by a knife. Finally he murmured, "Good-bye, Shanghai Restaurant. Good-bye, Lin Laizhen."

He returned to the dormitory and said goodbye to some colleagues of his. Fu Yanjie, who had always teased him, compressed his lips in sorrow, and gave him a long handshake. Haonan went to his room, packed his bags and took out a paper and pen. He tried to write something, but in the end he tore the paper into little pieces.

Early the next morning when Haonan woke up, he used the rice cooker to heat three red sweet potatoes he had cooked the previous night. After having these as his breakfast, he carried his snakeskin bag out into the morning fog and headed for Futian bus station. The luggage was heavy, but his heart was heavier. He did not want to leave, but he had no choice. Here he could not get a Shenzhen Permanent Residence Permit or a house, let alone the love of his life.

As he walked to the station on foot, he looked back sadly at the buildings behind him, hoping to keep these familiar views in his memory. He did not know when, or if, he would return, so this was a precious moment.

At Futian bus station he got into a bus full of passengers. When it started off the driver put on a

CD, and he heard the sad voice of Liu Meijun, a female singer from Hong Kong:

Again — let me see you one more while,
Smiling in tears...

He suddenly thought of something, and putting his hand in his pocket. He fished out a piece of paper. On it was a poem he had written the previous night:

Presentation to L Before Leaving

Before leaving, I told you
I'd rush to the faraway north, good-bye!
When it would be autumn and the chill would hit you,
The missing from me to you
Would become that line of wild geese above the blue sky.

Before leaving, I also told you
I'd fly to the far side of the Pacific Ocean, good-bye!
When you would stroll again
the seashore that we once walked hand in hand many times,
The blessing from me to you,
Would blend with the waves that beat the beach, heavy and high.

Before leaving, I even told you
My soul would rise to the heaven after many years, good-bye!
When the stars would sparkle in the silent night,
And humankind would lift their heads and look up,
Seeing all the stars shining in the sky.
There would be me among them.
I wouldn't close my eyes even if I died,
And I'd be reluctant to leave you alone.
That's when I'd turn my head to look at you again,
My eyes, my pupils and my soul would all be flashing thereby.

Miserably he tore it into pieces, then stood up and cast them through the window. He wanted to leave these heartfelt words here. The fragments were blown here and there, flying into the treetops and up into the sky.

Then he suddenly recalled that he still had something important to do. Before the bus left Zhuzilin, he asked the driver to stop, and got off along the Shennan Road. Carrying his luggage, he walked into an area of litchi trees. It was still early in the morning, and few cars were on the road. A flock of birds flew overhead. "The early bird catches the worm," he thought. But he recalled

that this saying had been modified by Fuqiang –
"Only the early worm gets eaten by the bird".
Haonan smiled sadly and looked around.

Presently he raised his head, staring at the
remote Bijia Mountain. Then he looked in the
direction of Shenzhen Bay, and then towards the
heights of Nan Mountain. He imagined he could
see the slim form of his beloved in the dense and
towering conifers.

Abruptly, in front of a big area of
Bougainvillea glabra, the city flower of Shenzhen,
he knelt down. His eyes half-closed and his palms
crossed. He began to murmur with the devotion of
Mohammed at prayer and the attitude he had
taken when he had been a Christian. He was
praying now, hoping that this land could witness
his sincerity. He was trying his best in the hope of
somehow staying here a little longer.

Some time later he dug his fingers into the
turf and scooped up a handful of soil. After sealing
it inside a plastic bag, he put it carefully into his
luggage. Then he rose to his feet and muttered
fondly. "Goodbye Futian! Goodbye Shekou! And
goodbye Shenzhen!"

Then he got onto another bus for Guangzhou,
passing through Overseas Chinese Town, Dachong,
Nantou, Xi'xiang, Fuyong and Song'gang. He felt
his heart was broken.

That night an express train from Guangzhou
to the west of Nanjing City in Jiangsu Province

drove out of Guangzhou at full speed. In a seat next to the window in the middle of the train, Haonan sat, sadly staring out into the darkness. On the small table before him was the small bag of soil he had dug from Shenzhen.

Chapter 20
Freezing Cold in a Luxury Bedroom

Though the midsummer noon was as hot as fire, in the presidential suite at the Nanhai Hotel in Shekou it was comfortably cool. The air conditioning had been set on 16 degrees all night, and the guests had to pull their cotton quilts over their heads. Unless the telephone rang, they did not wake up, nor did they realise that the sun was high in the sky.

One guest stood in front of the window of his room in his Japanese kimono-style nightgown, his sleepy eyes blinking at the glaring sun outside. The window faced the mighty Shenzhen Bay, and he could see the mountains, rivers and tall buildings of Hong Kong. On the sea many buoys were floating, and several light pleasure boats were sailing towards the eastern side of Shenzhen Bay. The guest suddenly realised that his brown hair had become tousled during his sleep, and he could also see that it needed to be dyed yellow again, so he walked over to the mirror and used an exquisite horn comb to put it in order. Then he shaved his beard and rotated the big and heavy golden ring on the left middle finger of his, then fiddled with the golden necklace around his neck, as big as a rosary. On the bedside cupboard stood a huge and heavy cellular phone, specially made to order in 24K gold. There was a large mirror in the bathroom, and in it he could see in the background that from beneath the snowy-white quilt there peeped a curl of long hair. The hair was Lin Laizhen's. Her white floral skirt lay on the floor.

The man looking in the mirror was Chen Guangwei.

Three days after Laizhen had met Guangwei, she had moved into his private western-style building in Shuiwantou, Shekou from her dormitory at Sihai. Another week later she had resigned from the Shanghai Restaurant. From then on she had spent all her time either travelling around in the Crown with Guangwei or sleeping with him, as though she wanted to make up for the sleeping time she had lost while working in the restaurant.

She had suffered badly from her miserable abortion, but after that Guangwei had led her to enjoy an entirely new life. Just now, the air conditioning was so cold that she had goose pimples and she was trembling.

Guangwei, barefoot, walked aimlessly across the red wooden floor. As the temperature was so low and he was reluctant to turn off the air conditioning, he wore an additional set of silk nightwear. He began to look for the Rolex watch he had lost somewhere in the suite last night, which had cost him 300,000 Hong Kong dollars. It was half past twelve when he found it, and by then he felt hungry. He was not prepared to dine outside the room, so he pushed a button by the bed and demanded, "Bring me some breakfast!"

After Guangwei's parents had escaped to Hong Kong many years before, they had lived in Hong Kong. Guangwei was their only son, and he had left the campus for good after almost graduating from primary school. Every day after that he drove his car wherever he pleased, treating all the grand restaurants as his dining rooms.

Now the doorbell rang and at his summons, a female servant brought a plate of snacks into the room. Guangwei fished out a red one hundred Hong Kong dollar note to give her as a tip. The woman took it, thanked him and left.

It was the summer harvest season in rural Canton. The previous night, because the roof insulation in Guangwei's home was relatively slow in dissipating heat, he had got into the car and brought Laizhen to stay here, in the Nanhai Hotel.

Slowly drinking his Coca Cola, he started to worry that he had nothing to do. He slid back under the quilt and began to make love to Laizhen again as she slept.

Later on, he wearily got up and fished out a box of cigarettes. He put a cigarette between his lips, and reluctant to light it in the usual way, he took a roll of paper money amounting to a hundred yuan and lit it with a match, then used it to light the cigarette. Then he threw what was left of the note into the toilet, urinated on them, and pressed the button to flush them away.

After a while, still not feeling happy, Guangwei walked into the living room and sat on a rattan chair. He took out a piece of tinfoil, on which he put some white powder. He used his lighter to light the powder, half-closed his eyes and sniffed at the fumes from the burning powder.

At 2 pm the golden phone rang. It was Hao Zhiyue, the cashier from the financial department of China Merchants. "Mr Chen, are you up?" he asked.

"Yes."

"I happen to be in Shekou. Where shall I hand the money to you?"

"Bring it to the Nanhai Hotel."

About twenty minutes later Hao Zhiyue, short and smartly dressed, arrived with a black plastic bag containing 20,000 yuan in cash. He sat down on the living room to let Guangwei count the money. The bundles of one hundred yuan were fresh and there were paper slips tied around them by the bank teller and stamped with a red rectangular seal. Guangwei picked up the notes one by one and tossed them into the air. The money fluttered down into his palms. "It's enough, no need to count," he said. He threw the money onto the bed. The notes slid along the smooth fabric and came to rest against the pillows, like tiles skimmed across a pond.

"We always hand over the rent on time, right?" Hao Zhiyue said, smiling.

"Yes, not bad. Your company has been renting my building for three years now," Guangwei replied.

"Yes, as an old customer of yours, I hope the rent will be kept the same," Hao Zhiyue said. When he turned he noticed Lin Laizhen's head peeping from the bedding. Wasn't that Haonan's girlfriend? What was she doing here? But soon he realised what had happened.

"All right, I'll keep it unchanged for the present," Guangwei said. Then he asked loftily, "Is Zhou Haonan still in your company?"

"You recognised him?"

"Shekou is a very small place," Guangwei said, laughing. "He once imagined he could love my girlfriend, but he did not realise that he is not qualified. Haha!"

"Really?"

"How could he compete with me? Haha!"

"He has left our company, and he has also left Shenzhen."

"That's good, that's good." Guangwei was slightly surprised. He slowly paced back and forth. "It's better like this. Otherwise he'd be sad when he saw me. As you know I'm not someone who cares about psychological counselling. Haha!"

"All right, enjoy yourself. I must leave now. Monday is the busiest day of every week for us." Hao Zhiyue walked out the room, looking at the receipt Guangwei had written for him. The handwriting was crooked, like the marks of a chicken's claws.

On the way back Hao Zhiyue stopped at the Futian Sub-branch of the Bank of China, where he collected a letter of credit from an importer in Pakistan. On arrival at the company, he handed it to Hu.

"Who's in charge of this letter of credit?" asked Hu. "With such a big order we'll make a partial shipment. It's a long-term order with a high profit." He began to phone the departmental managers.

Xu Yanwei came in the office. "The mixed cotton and yarn, this is the letter of credit Haonan did," he said.

Yes, this was a new order handled by Haonan. The Sheraz Company, an importer from Pakistan, received the sample he sent. After confirming the quality, they silently opened a huge order of a letter of credit. If such a large letter of credit had arrived before Haonan had left, it could have saved him. It would even have brought him a Shenzhen Permanent Residence Permit and a house.

At that moment in the presidential suite in the Nanhai Hotel, Guangwei cleared his throat and turned on the Karaoke machine, playing a popular song by Chee Pai Hui, *Reading You*. He sang:

> *Never tired after reading you a thousand times,*
> *The feeling of reading you is like in March...*

He couldn't get used to this Mandarin song, so he chose a song called *The Story of Modern Love*, sung by Julian Cheung and Maple Hui:

> *No right or wrong when separating,*
> *No more explanation is required if I want to leave,*
> *Now it's very silly to talk about "forever love".*
> *As that night passed by,*
> *The spark of my love was already gone,*
> *It's impossible to pay out a long time as all life of mine...*

He made such a racket with his singing that Laizhen slowly turned her snowy-white body and awoke. "I'm cold!" she shouted. She hurriedly wrapped herself in the thick cotton quilt and asked Guangwei to give her a silk quilt as well.

Before leaving, he rubbed his leather shoes with a white hotel towel. This polished the shoe like new, but it blackened the towel. Then he spat into a glass and urinated into a tea cup.

Every day they seemed to be competing in a marathon sleep competition, as if to see who could sleep longer. For her, this was a protest at the hard life she had been living before she had met him. Now she could enjoy a life of luxury and dissipation. Her morning started from the afternoon, and her afternoon ended in the early morning.

Chapter 21
A New Start

At ten o'clock in the evening the minibus from Nanjing City to Jiashan, Anhui Province, was jolting along a bumpy mountain road, throwing the passengers alternately up into the air and back down into their seats. Suddenly there was terrible screaming from the passengers, and Haonan realised that the bus had left the road. He passed out and remembered nothing more.

When he woke up, he found himself lying in a hospital bed, with a nurse standing over him. She told him he was in Chuzhou People's Hospital in Anhui Province, and he was lucky to be alive. It turned out that he had been unconscious for three days. The driver had been tired and on this terrible road he had lost control of the bus, which had left the road and plunged more than 20 metres down a cliff. All but six of the thirty passengers had been killed.

Haonan could remember being thrown through a window of the bus. Fortunately he had held tightly onto his luggage, and like an air bag it had saved him from worse injury. He had been knocked unconscious and rolled into a cave. When he came round, he was in darkness, and hungry and thirsty. He also found it difficult to move. He had taken out a bottle of mineral water from his luggage and drunk it, but it soon ran out, and he had nothing to eat. Finally, desperate with thirst, he had begun to drink his own urine.

He lay there, afraid that poisonous snakes would bite him, until at last, when he was near the point of death, he was found by rescue workers lying in a pool of blood.

That night, after a good sleep and a meal, he felt that he had almost recovered. He massaged the wound on his body and climbed to his feet. There were no nurses around, and the other patients were asleep, so he pulled out the syringe needle which had been inserted into his vein, put his clothes on and walked out of the hospital with his luggage. He walked to the bus station and got on an old bus from Chuzhou to Jiashan. After a long drive, however, when the bus arrived at a station named Zhangbaling, the driver declared that the bus had broken down and everyone would have to go their separate ways. There were no further buses which would take passengers, so Haonan set out on foot into the darkness. The only light he could see was from glow-worms.

"Do you want somewhere to stay?" a man asked him after a short distance. He was bareback, tattooed and was sitting on a stool in front of a three-storey building.

"Yes," Haonan replied. Looking at his watch, it was already three o'clock in the morning.

"Single rooms are available for ten yuan or less," said the man coldly. Behind him Haonan could see several girls cooking a meal.

Haonan's motto when he went out on business was to save money whenever possible, and it would be daybreak soon, so he chose the cheapest room, five yuan.

"Take this candle and go down to the one with the open door," the man said, handing a candle to Haonan. "Use the cooks' fire to light it."

The room was down in the basement. The further Haonan descended, the darker it became. The candlelight showed him two small rooms, separated by Polyboard, and there was no ventilation, so they gave off a mouldy, rotten smell. There was no sound; either no one lived here or the occupants were asleep. He walked into the room with the open door, which had room only for a single bed. When he closed the door, he found there was no bolt. He could secure it only by putting his luggage and a broken chair against it. At least if someone tried to push the door open, the sound of the chair moving would wake him.

No sooner had he sat down than a mouse suddenly squeaked and jumped over his shoulder, then fled. There was no electric fan, mosquito net or mosquito trap. But now he couldn't think any more, he had to get to sleep as soon as possible.

When he had blown out the candle, he suddenly felt as if he was in the bowels of hell, although nobody could describe what that was like. He had never experienced such a terrifying blackness.

He tried to sleep, but kept waking up in terror. However he was relieved at the thought that nothing terrible would happen, because at that time he was worth nothing to a thief.

Mingguang Arts & Crafts Factory occupied more than ten *mu* in the west of Jiashan County. Most of the 300-plus workers were female. At the doorway of the factory that morning, a middle-aged man paced back and forth. His hair was wiry and curly and he wore a white undershirt, blue trousers and leather sandals. It was Zhu Xianmin. When he caught sight of the tricycle approaching, he hurried to meet it and said loudly, "Haonan, you have finally come here. You have taken a lot of trouble."

"Managing Director Zhu, long time no see, one year. How are you?" Haonan wiped the sweat from his forehead. Zhu led him into a three-storey building, where he would occupy a room on the top floor. This was always a vacant building. Then Zhu showed him the workshops.

In the sewing workshop, Haonan saw many piles of clothing fabric and piles of soft toys such as chickens, ducks and bears. On the ground, dozens of young female workers were sleeping. Some of them were using sheets of expandable polyethylene as pillows, and some were not properly covered. The wind from the old ceiling fans blew their upper clothes and skirts about and revealed the white skin of their legs and stomachs.

Haonan was surprised and asked, "What's happened to them?"

Like a hen sheltering chicks with her wing, Zhu said painfully, "In order to finish a batch of goods, they had to work all night. They have only just finished."

Just then a big container truck rolled up to collect a load of goods.

After coming back from the workshops, Zhu introduced Haonan to the deputy managing director, Shuo, and showed him the departments for supply and sales, technology and materials. Some of the staff already knew Haonan.

That day flashed by, and at the end of it Haonan was at last able to have good night's sleep. From the next day on he worked in the workshops, getting familiar with the different kinds of production technology. In the early evening he came back to the spacious building where he was to sleep, which was 40 square metres in extent.

In Anhui Province in summer, the daily temperature difference was great; in the daytime the sun was burning hot, but it was cool at night. That night Haonan slept for some while before being suddenly woken by a cracking sound. He opened his eyes, got up and went over to the window. It was still and silent inside the factory, and the shadows of trees were dim. Under the faint electric light the doorkeeper was dozing. Seeing that there was nothing to worry about, Haonan went back to bed. But no sooner had he fallen asleep than there came again the cracking sound. He listened carefully, feeling that it came from the ceiling. *Are there mice here?* He thought, tossed and turned, then fell quietly asleep.

The third night he was awoken again by the sound. But this time the location was different, sometimes in the east of the ceiling, sometimes west. He still had no idea of the cause and went back to sleep.

The next morning he walked out to the roof to check. It was paved with flat cement, with no thermal shroud, and nothing else could be seen. "How can there be anything wrong?" he asked himself, laughing.

Yet the same sound continued the following week. He could not endure it. That night he went downstairs to talk to the doorkeeper, describing what he had heard. The doorkeeper, who wore an old army suit and had once been a soldier, said, "I daren't turn on the electric light there in the evening. Last summer a businessman from a company in Nanjing was staying in the same room. At midnight he heard the same sound and came rushing down wearing only briefs and sandals, leaving his luggage behind. He moved to the hotel outside. Not such a brave man! It was not until the next day that he came back to collect his luggage. The noise is terrifying, but no one can work out the reason."

Hearing this, Haonan felt his scalp was tingling. That night he could not sleep, and just hugged his pillow. He faintly heard a girl singing a sad song at the top of the building. He clearly remembered that he had shut the door before sleeping, but the next morning he found it was wide open. When he looked in the mirror, his face was green.

Haonan always took an interest in science, but he could not work out what could be causing the noise. He did not mention it again until one day Zhu came back the factory after a business trip. Zhu saw the dark rings round Haonan's eyes and asked him why. Haonan explained. Zhu laughed so loudly that the workers in the workshops all peered round to look. Zhu didn't know the reason for the sound either. He thought for a moment and then said, "This building is low down. In 1992, when the East China floods took place, the water reached the third floor. After the floods receded, the corpses of two young women were found in the room where you live now."

Although it was daytime, Zhu's words made Haonan's legs weak.

"Move out now and I'll arrange a new place for you," said Zhu. "If you suffer this distress every night, how can you work?"

Haonan relaxed.

One morning the following year, under a blue sky, it was busy at Hongqiao Airport, Shanghai. Boeing, Airbus, McDonnell-Douglas and Concorde aircraft were taxiing, taking off or landing as ordered by air traffic control.

In the international departure lobby, the America-Chinese Zhu Tianrui wore a black suit with whole body of perfume, and gold and silver tying on his fingers. Zhu Xianmin had already taken off his leather sandals; his appearance was similar to that of Zhu Tianrui because he was going abroad. After they had checked in their luggage, they chatted as they waited to go through security. Zhu Tianrui was about to go back to the USA, but Zhu Xianmin was only visiting to investigate the toy market there.

Zhu Xianmin was beginning to worry. He had Haonan's passport and air ticket in his hand, but Haonan had gone off to look around the airport half an hour earlier and he had not yet come back, and the time to board was approaching. Zhu Xianmin hurried to the airport communications room.

A few moments later a voice announced, "Attention please! Flight number S3527 from

229

Shanghai to Los Angeles will close for boarding soon. Could Mr Zhou Haonan please check in without delay?"

Haonan was about to fly to Los Angeles to set up a branch of the toy company in the USA. This would begin a new era in his life. Along the road from Auhui to Shanghai his heart had been shouting "New York, Los Angeles, Las Vegas, the White House, Capitol Hill, Statue of Liberty, I'm coming to see you". And during the journey a song was being played constantly:

Time and time again, I ask myself,
I ask myself: where in nature is your good?
Where is your good?

He was also thinking that he was going further away from Shenzhen. So he remembered a poem of his:

Seeing you off

Standing on the railway platform,
I was seeing you off,
Shaking hands with you.
My eyesight then
followed the figure as you stepped on the train,
Then traced the train, which roared off faraway.

From now on, I knew,
We would live in different faraway places.
You would have your own work,
And I would continue my own life.

Well! Seeing you off,
Is like a spring made of love,
You're at one end,
I'm at the other end.
The further it pulls,
The tighter it shrinks.

At the moment when he was about to leave he suddenly felt a surge of sorrow and love for Shenzhen. He recalled that his uncle and father had separated for so many years that his father hadn't known where his younger brother was. He also thought about his mother, who was older than ever. Why would I travel further away from my mother? He thought to himself.

At that moment a picture flashed into his brain. Under the burning sun, on the zigzag mountain path from Changling to Nawu Town, a woman was carrying a heavy bundle of firewood. As she walked, she wiped away her sweat with a towel over her shoulder. She walked and rested, then walked again, fanning herself with her straw cap from time to time. Sometimes a tractor or a bicycle passed, but she didn't have the chance of a ride.

Haonan's heart suddenly felt more painful. How was that purple-red floral flag? Where was it fluttering now?

"No! I can't leave China!" he said to himself in a low, decisive tone.

The message to travellers to board urgently was repeated.Haonan knew Zhu Xianmin must be looking anxiously for him.

"What's wrong with him?" said Zhu Xianmin, inside the plane. He was sweating after hurrying.

Zhu Tianrui said, "We've wasted an air ticket."

"I can't imagine that," Zhu Xianmin muttered.

"Zhu Xianmin, my boss, I'm extremely sorry! But I'll compensate you," Haonan said, sitting on a remote seat of airport, bowing his head. "I can't go to Los Angeles with you, for Shenzhen is waiting for me, and I can't go any further from my mother."

That night a special fast train from Shanghai to Guangzhou carried Haonan back south. He sat on a down bed next to the window, with no intention of sleeping. As he saw the scenery they were passing, his heart followed the roaring train, flying with it to the south.

Chapter 22
Love Without Touching

After coming back to Shenzhen, Haonan first lodged at an inn in Futian for ten yuan a day. He did not want to be upset by seeing the familiar places he had left behind, so he decided not to go to Shekou yet. Time is an effective medicine for a bitter heart. For more than a year he drifted around the north, his pain gradually easing.

Soon he was recruited as a foreign trade businessman with the Shenzhen Zhongcheng Electric I/E Company located at Huaqiangbei, on a basic salary of 800 yuan per month, excluding food and accommodation. So he had to rent an apartment nearby. That day he saw a "To Let" notice on an electricity pole along the street. It also said "Boys only". Was it a notice to recruit students for a kindergarten, so the gender was restricted? He dialled the number and was answered by a girl. She confirmed that she had a room to let, but was reluctant to tell him the price, saying that there were too many people asking, but she invited him to check the apartment and gave him directions.

He tried to find the place by following up the information she had given, and finally arrived in front of an old building in an industrial area behind the Hualianfa building in Huaqiangbei. He could see that there were electronics shops on the first floor, offices on the second and third floors and dormitories on the fourth floor, where different kinds of underwear and men's and women's jeans were hanging. The fifth floor, an extra floor which had been added later, was walled with red brick and painted with white powder; the roof had coloured galvanized sheets that warmed the building in winter and cooled it in summer. He went a long corridor and knocked at the door of room 519. The door did not open. He had a feeling that he was being inspected through a peephole on the door by someone inside.

Finally the door was opened by a slender, attractive girl in a white flower-pattern skirt. She showed him to the room, describing it as two bedrooms and a living room. He could see a medium "Good Dream" mattress, a simple cabinet and a white dressing table made of basic materials. She said, "You look a bit familiar. I think I once saw you in Huaqiangbei."

"Really?" He grinned. After chatting, he found that she knew the company he had worked for. He felt closer to her. "Where is the room you want to rent?" he asked.

"It's this one, and it's 800 yuan per month," she replied.

"Could you give me a concessionary price? As a businessman I often go out on business, so I seldom use water and electricity. And when are you moving out?" he asked.

"No, the price cannot be reduced. I'm not going to move out, I'm going to let half the room," she said.

Haonan was mystified. "How can you let half of it? Will you divide it with a board into two rooms?"

"No, you and I will live here together," she said calmly.

"What? Live with you?" He opened his eyes wide in shock.

"Do you think I'm going to eat you?" she smiled. "It just means we will both sleep in this bed. You can afford 400 yuan, and so can I. I just want someone to share the rent." She spoke quietly, looking at the mattress.

"Only boys allowed? Cohabit in one room? Sleep on the same bed?" Haonan was even more mystified.

"As the saying goes, the well water can't poison the river water."

"You're the well water and I'm the river water?"

"You might say so."

"The well water cannot poison the river water, I agree; but the river water can flow into the well," he said mischievously.

"How dare you!" she said, raising her head in anger.

This rent-sharing idea had provoked his curiosity. This girl didn't look like a devil, so maybe he should see what would happen. However, he decided to pretend not to accept the idea, and made as if to leave, like a customer pretending to refuse to buy from a merchant in order to reduce the price.

"Are you afraid to live here?" she asked.

"That's funny! Afraid of whom?" he responded, laughing.

She replied, "Five or six other men have been here to check the room, but none of them looked good enough to me, so I refused to open the door. I'm not a casual girl. To be frank, you're the first one who has entered my room."

"Thank you very much!"

"I'm sure I haven't misjudged a boy like you," she said directly.

Boy? He thought to himself. That seemed funny, as he was 24 years old. "Boy?" he said.

"You want to share with me because I'm only a boy?"

"What are you worried about? Do you think I'll steal your wealth? And rape you?" she said defiantly.

"It depends on you. Anyway, don't call me a boy."

"All right, I'll call you a man." She giggled. "Anyway, the more you respect me, the more I will respect you."

They finally reached an agreement. She told him her name was Li Shuwen and she came from Chengdu, the capital city of Sichuan Province. She was 1.60 metres tall with white, clean skin, and under her long hair her face was as perfectly shaped as a goose egg. It was said that girls from Sichuan Province were naturally beautiful, and Haonan thought that must be true - seeing is believing. She had just graduated from a university in Chengdu and was a clerk in an electronics company in Huaqiangbei, which didn't offer accommodation. So she rented this house nearby, and although the rent was on the high side, she could walk to work, and she enjoyed avoiding traffic jams.

Haonan began to feel that once again he had been struck by Cupid's arrow. In order to avoid suffering another painful defeat, he decided to control himself and not to plunge too deeply in.

After getting off work the next day he took his belongings packed in the red and green snakeskin bag and moved in with Li Shuwen. Once everything was in order, she began to cook. They had agreed to share the costs of meals. The Sichuan dish she cooked was so hot and spicy that it made Haonan sneeze. He told her he would soon get used to it. She told him she would get to like his Cantonese food because the dishes he cooked smelled as soft as the southern wind in a summer night, particularly his crucian carp steamed in the rice cooker. She hoped he would often be busy in the kitchen.

Shortly after that the two women who lived in the next room came home. Shuwen told him in a low voice that they were sisters who came from Chaozhou and Shantou in Canton Province, and they worked in drain clearance. They spoke in the accent of the area, in which "*fapiao*" (invoice) is pronounced in Mandarin as "*huapiao*".

After Haonan had finished cooking, it was the two sisters' turn to use the stove and dining table. They peered curiously at Haonan, who smiled faintly. Owing to the occupation of the two sisters, the stove and dining table smelled slightly, but the odour was soon driven off by Shuwen's sweet smell.

When Haonan went to bed that night he felt a strange excitement. Never in his life had he shared a property like this. Sitting on the edge of the bed, he smiled to himself.

"In accordance with the gentlemen's agreement between us, you should now turn your back to me and close your eyes," she said.

He did so. She turned off the light, took off her clothes and changed into a thin nightgown, then turned on the light again. Under the thin nightgown he could see the curves of her body, and this made his heart thump like a deer.

He asked Shuwen to close her eyes while he changed into briefs and a vest, although in fact he would have been happy for to keep her eyes open. He wasn't used to dressing like this for bed unless it was cold, so he asked if she would mind his upper body being bare. She agreed and he took his vest off, revealing his strong muscles. She looked at him appreciatively. Later Shuwen told him that she had chosen him to share with her because she hoped to have a man who could protect her.

They got into bed, but they kept a line between them which could not be crossed, nor could they touch any part of the other's body.

This night was the watershed of another loving life of his, in which the half of the mattress was fire, and the other was sea water. When he faced her back, he felt as if he was on the edge of a crater of temptation. At midnight, in order to keep his promise, he had to get up and take a cold bath to cool himself down. After this he went to the balcony and looked at the night view of Huaqiangbei. Posts were being rammed in to form the foundations of the Diwang Building. Time passed and when it was nearly daybreak, he dragged himself back, getting quietly into bed again to sleep on his side. Shuwen was still curled up asleep, as if trying to make up for many nights of lost sleep.

When they awoke the next morning, they looked at each other and smiled. Then they left to go their separate ways for work.

The next night, rain had cleared the sky above Huaqiangbei. The electric fan by the bed blew out gusts of cool air, which woke Haonan, dressed only in his underpants. Beside him Shuwen was lying on her back in a deep sleep, hands down by her sides. Her young girl's soft perfume was wafting from the nightgown, which was as thin as a cicada wing. By the light from the street lights he could see her attractive figure, especially the curves of her breasts. When the wind lifted the edge of her nightgown, he glimpsed her long white legs.

Suddenly her soft hand reached out and alighted on his stomach. A lonely man and a lonely girl living in the same room and sleeping in the same bed – how could he bear such temptation? He moved closer to her, but then he remembered their arrangement and the unwritten rule between them. He gently lifted her hand and put it back by her waist. Then he turned and fell asleep with his back to her.

He did not see Shuwen gently open her eyes and smile in sympathy.

They each had keys for the outer door and bedroom. Usually when she was not in the apartment, he wore only briefs. If he heard her coming back, he would hurriedly put on a pair of shorts. If it rained and she had left any clothes on the balcony he would hurriedly bring them inside, otherwise he never touched any of her belongings, even when he was there alone.

They both went to work every day. Sometimes he was late home. Her company was nearer, so usually she would go shopping in the Vanjia department store and cook before he got home, waiting to dine with him. Afterwards they would work out the costs of the food and share them. He gradually got used to her Sichuan dishes and she got used to his Cantonese food.

At the end of the month, they each contributed the agreed 400 yuan for the rent. The relationship between them had by then become so close that the sisters in the next room thought Shuwen had found a boyfriend. Yet neither Haonan nor Shuwen crossed the line between them. She often saw him tightly holding the pillow he had brought from Anhui Province. She asked him why he did this, but he just smiled, keeping it secret. Sometimes when she woke up at midnight, she found he was sleeping with his back to her, and the bed was moving, because his body and hands were moving. She did not raise her head to see what he was doing, but she guessed that he was masturbating... She sighed from deep in her heart and began to fondle her breasts with her fingers...

One night when he came back to the room, he found a note on the table saying: "I'll be away for a few days, I'm missing you!" For the next few days, he did not see her. While she was away he woke up many times and tossed and turned until daybreak.

One Wednesday Haonan served a Brazilian customer who wanted to purchase a PCI card, an electronic product, from China, helping him to inspect and select the goods and accompanying him to buy digital equipment in Aihua, Huaqiang and Seg Electronic Markets, which kept him busy until 11 o'clock at night. When he came back to the apartment, he saw that the door was open and the light was on. Shuwen was back!

But Haonan was shocked to see that with her in the inside room were two tall, strong men with crewcuts, dressed in black. When they saw Haonan, he felt their eyes stabbing him like knives. Shuwen hurriedly stood up and came to the door of the room, asking Haonan, "Hasn't your cousin come back yet?"

"What cousin?" Haonan was puzzled.

"Isn't the person who lives in the next room your cousin?" As she spoke she had her back to the two men. She put her finger to her lips and flashed her eyes at him. "Wait for your cousin in the living room, please!" she said. "You can't come into my room whenever you like. It's late and I have guests."

Haonan was about to question her, but he saw her fearful expression and realised that something dangerous had happened, so he returned to the

242

living room. She closed the door with the three of them inside.

Haonan was curious and worried. He pricked his ears, trying to hear what they were talking about. Sometimes voices were raised as if they were quarrelling, but he couldn't hear clearly.

About forty minutes later the crew-cut men marched angrily out and left.

"What's the matter?" he asked Shuwen.

She replied in a low voice, "I'm in great danger."

He was thunderstruck.

She explained, "I've been stupid. These men were originally Snakeheads who illegally organized prostitute traffic to Hong Kong. They told me that I could have work in Hong Kong at a salary of more than ten thousand Hong Kong dollars per month. I flew back to Chengdu to apply for a certificate to travel to Hong Kong. Only when I arrived in Hong Kong did I find out that I was required for prostitution. They said the men in Hong Kong were particularly fond of girls from Sichuan. Anyway, I refused. I lied that I was having my period. Fortunately I had a chance to escape back to Shenzhen. But before I could go through my door they appeared with sharp knives, demanding 30,000 yuan as double compensation, otherwise they will kill me. What can I do?"

Haonan was astonished. He was trying to think.

"I said it was too late tonight to get the money, as the banks had closed," Shuwen continued. "So they are coming back before daylight tomorrow, expecting me to go with them to the bank to withdraw the money. I don't have that much money, and even if I had I would not give it to them. But if I cannot give them this money, they'll kill me. They can do anything they like."

Haonan paced to and fro. It was now one o'clock in the morning.

The light shone on Shuwen, standing motionless in fear.

He went over to the window. On the Huaqiangbei road the lights were blinking. There were only a few people and passing cars. Most of the restaurants had closed.

He suggested reporting it to the police, but she thought she didn't have sufficient evidence. And if these two men were detained, they would have accomplices who would come after her instead.

They stayed silent, but their hearts were beating fast. He was thinking furiously. Her face was bloodless and white as snow.

All of a sudden a great idea seized him. "Didn't you once say you had a cousin living in Shangbayue village, outside the Buji checkpoint in Shenzhen?"

"Yes, I did."

"Let me accompany you there. You go now. Get your luggage packed immediately!" he said.

244

She jumped up as if she had been given an electric shock, clapped her hands and said excitedly, "OK!"

They acted without further ado. She got all her clothes in order, simplifying everything. He even moved some heavy belongings of hers to the living room so that the room gave the impression that there was no female living there.

It was two o'clock when they left. First he turned off the lights and went downstairs to check. He circled the building twice and looked around. After confirming that there was no danger, he went upstairs and helped her to carry her luggage down, holding her hand as they went. She was still in a state of shock, although she felt a little safer after Haonan's strong hand took hers. This was the first time their skin had touched.

Along the road it was still. Most people were indoors asleep, and only those who were preparing breakfast in the shops were busy. They met several cleaners with big reed brooms over their shoulders. After a few minutes they reached Huaqiangbei road. There were a few taxis left, and the driver of a Jetta car approached them and offered to put their luggage in the boot.

They started to drive along the Huaqiangbei road, but after two seconds Haonan realised that there was a Nissan in front of him. When the Jetta turned left, it turned left; when the Jetta turned right, it turned right. Haonan's heart suddenly sank again. Had the crew-cut men noticed them running away? Haonan asked the driver to pull up along the roadside. The Nissan did the same, which made Haonan even more worried. To take the initiative, he told the driver he wanted to drive himself. The driver was tired after a long day, and he sleepily took the passenger seat.

When Haonan set off, so did the Nissan. After a while they stopped at traffic lights, and when they started again there was only two metres between them. Haonan put on his left indicators and accelerated past the Nissan on the left. The Nissan accelerated too. When Haonan slowed down, so did the Nissan. Finally Haonan stamped on the accelerator, overtook the Nissan on the right and hit the brakes, and the Nissan was forced to stop suddenly behind him to avoid a crash.

Haonan opened the door, got out and walked back to the Nissan. He was going to ask the men what they wanted. But then the Nissan went into reverse and shot suddenly backwards, then turned to the left and roared past Haonan, fleeing off into the night.

Haonan got back into the car. "They were bumper men," Haonan said. "It's a dodge to get money from people. The bumper men crash deliberately into your car and then demand money. Very few drivers can get away from them."

"Really? But we got away just now. Well done! I just started this taxi business a short time ago and I've never experienced such a case before. It was terrifying."

"I think your heart was beating at 140," Haonan said. Then he drove off.

It was nearly four o'clock when they arrived at Shangbayue village. Haonan left the Jetta with the driver, asking him to wait while he accompanied Shuwen upstairs. When she saw her cousin, she gave a smile which told Haonan she was feeling safe again. He said goodbye to her and turned to go downstairs, then got into the Jetta to return to Huaqiangbei.

Once in bed, he soon fell asleep. Early the next morning, he got up to go to the office.

He didn't see the two men again. He heard from the two sisters that they had returned the next morning, but they told the men that Shuwen had moved out. They did not believe this and insisted on coming inside to check, seeing that the room was empty except for some rubbish left on the floor. They saw Haonan, but they did not know who he was, let alone that it was he who had helped Shuwen to escape. They were angry and kicked the wall fiercely, shouting obscenities, but in the end they had to leave.

It would have been hard for other people to believe that Haonan and Shuwen had shared a bed for more than a month without sexual intercourse.

Neither of them had ever imagined that one day she would conceive his child.

Chapter 23
The Bumper Men

Fatty Liu, a long-distance driver in a Dongfeng truck with an Anhui Province registration plate, had arrived at the Chang'an, Dongguan section of national route 107. He was delivering a load of soft toys, the goods ordered from Haonan by Zhu Xianmin for export to Belgium, to Meiyuan warehouse in Shenzhen. Haonan was now trading in soft toys as well as electronic items. In order to make up for the previous loss of the air ticket, he had given Zhu Xianmin a good purchase price.

When Fatty Liu changed lanes at a roundabout, he did not switch on his indicator, and a traffic policeman approached. He pointed through the window at Fatty Liu and said, "*Diaotou!*" Liu went round the roundabout, but when he got back to the traffic policeman, the officer said again, "*Diaotou!*" Liu went round yet again, and the officer again angrily said, "*Diaotou!* What in hell are you doing?"

Fatty Liu stretched his neck out of the cab and said apologetically, "Weren't you telling me to turn the car around?"

The traffic policeman was originally from Huazhou, the West Canton province, and what he said was often mixed with the dialect. He thought only those who came from Huazhou could understand his dialect. When he said "*Diaotou*", a joking term among Huazhou people, it sounded like the Mandarin for "turn", so no wonder Fatty Liu kept turning. Finally the officer understood. "Sorry, go ahead," he said. Watching Fatty Liu drive into the distance, he said to himself one more time, laughing, "*Diaotou!*"

When Fatty Liu arrived at the Huangtian section of Bao'an District, Shenzhen, on national route 107 he switched on his right indicator to enter the right-hand lane for the fuel station. While he had been driving in the right-hand lane he had come up behind a black Mercedes with the number Canton B 66666, driving very slowly. Fatty Liu sounded the horn, but the Mercedes ignored it. Fatty Liu sounded his horn again, but it made no difference. Seeing that there was no car in the middle lane, Liu angrily switched on his left indicator and turned into the middle lane. He stepped on the accelerator and his giant truck roared up to overtake the Mercedes.

Normally the big trucks were the bullies on the roads. Fatty Liu in his truck always looked down upon smaller vehicles. Yet now the Mercedes was in his way again. Liu returned to the right lane, but as his right front wheel crossed the white line, he was staggered to see that the Mercedes had stepped on the accelerator. The rear left of the car scraped the truck's right bumper, and a white scratch formed on the Mercedes.

The two cars pulled up simultaneously.

Now Fatty Liu was sweating, for he had damaged an expensive car. He hurriedly got out to check. As the left-rear door of the Mercedes had been struck, only the other three doors could be opened. Five men got out of the car, looking relaxed. The driver, wearing sunglasses, was tall and thin, but the other four all looked very tough and powerful. To Liu's astonishment, the driver did not even look at the damage. It seemed they all knew what had happened. Instead the driver walked to the roadside and made a call on his cellphone, while the other four walked over to the roadside with their backs to the Mercedes, standing or squatting down smoking.

If they had been angry and started arguing with him, Fatty Liu would have found that normal. But they did nothing of the kind, which made Liu more worried and made him wonder who they were, for their Mercedes was an S320 costing more than one million yuan. Looking again at the spot, Liu knew that it was he who had crossed the white line, violating a traffic rule, while the Mercedes had correctly stopped in the middle of its lane.

One of the men approached him. "How come you hit my car?" he said gently. His kind voice

251

made Fatty Liu feel worse. He could say nothing. If he called the traffic police, they would say that it was he who had broken the traffic code.

"You decide what to do," another man said.

"We have something urgent to do," said the driver. He did not take off his black sunglasses. The calmer they were, the dizzier Fatty Liu felt.

"Give us 20,000 yuan, *Diaotou*!" said the driver. He spoke Mandarin with the accent of Huazhou.

This *"Diaotou!"* was not the command for Fatty Liu to turn the truck round. Facing this huge demand for compensation, he felt as if he had driven his truck over a cliff. He did not have that kind of money.

A few of the passing drivers decelerated and wound down their windows to see what was happening before shaking their heads and driving away. Fatty Liu would have liked to call the traffic police, but he feared his driving licence would be confiscated, which would be a disaster. Although it was a cold spring day, he was sweating. By contrast the five men were still so calm as they stood on the roadside dialling, strolling about or smoking. They were behaving as if nothing had happened. The more in control they seemed, the more puzzled and afraid Fatty Liu felt.

Under all this pressure, after bargaining, Fatty Liu finally paid them 10,000 yuan. As soon as he drove off, the five men burst out laughing. In fact the Mercedes had been bought second-hand for

200,000 yuan. After polishing, waxing and glazing, it looked as fresh as a new one. The driver and owner was Zhang Fuqiang, Haonan's friend. The other men were his employees.

After getting Fatty Liu's money, Fuqiang drove at a leisurely speed down the Bao'an section of national route 107. He was in no hurry to get the car repaired because he knew that it would be fresh as before once the scratch had been painted, which would only cost only 200 yuan. His driving technique had been perfect, and he had made sure that the damage was confined to a scratch and there was no dent.

"Fuqiang, you did well there!" said one of the men with him.

"Constant effort brings success. But first of all you need to understand psychology. Anyway, we must remember that we prefer to choose cars that are not from Shenzhen," Fuqiang explained.

"How did you find out this way to earn money?" another asked.

Fuqiang smiled. "In the 1980s there was a Japanese TV series called *Suspected Blood*, with Yamaguchi Momoe, a Japanese actress, in the lead role. She played Sachiko, the daughter of Oshima Shige, who suffered from leukaemia but could not afford medical treatment. Oshima thought of a solution. He pretended to bumper some cars, then demanded compensation from the drivers. That was my inspiration."

Fuqiang had been one of the first people in China to have a cellphone, and now he was the first Chinese man to practise the "Crash for Cash" trick.

"Aren't you afraid of being caught if you keep on doing this?" said one of the men.

"We'll stop before that happens. After lunch I'll show you another good trick, as long as you co-operate with me like just now."

After a good meal at a nearby restaurant, Fuqiang phoned his friend A'min and asked him to come. Driving a BMW 730, which had also been renovated and had the registration plate Canton B 33333, A'min also belonged to the younger generation. Seeing the gaiety and splendour of Shenzhen, he dreamed of earning a lot of money. They worked together in the section from Dongguan to outside the Shenzhen checkpoint, sometimes separately and sometimes together. When A'min arrived, Fuqiang said, "Let's change cars."

They drove along the three-lane section from Fuyong to Song'gang. The Mercedes, now driven by A'min, and Fuqiang in the BMW ran along the middle lane. As Fuqiang drove he was scanning the other vehicles with eagle eyes. He noticed a car with the number Hunan C 31981 driving in the right-hand lane. It was a Toyota hatchback driven by a woman on her own.

Fuqiang called A'min, who moved into the right-hand lane in front of the Toyota and slowed down. The woman in the Toyota indicated left to pull out, but found the BMW blocking her way. Then the BMW slowed down. The woman again tried to overtake, but the BMW dashed forward as quick as lightning. She tried to turn back, but it was too late; the BMW struck the Toyota.

She put her hands over her face and shrieked. As Fatty Liu had done, she got out to see that the car that had struck her was in the correct lane. Fuqiang got out of the BMW holding a red warning triangle and put it on the ground 100 metres back. The other four men just stared at the Toyota, saying nothing. Then Fuqiang took out his cellphone and started dialling. According to the evidence, it was the Toyota which had violated the traffic rules no matter which policeman came to deal with.

Fuqiang told the woman that she could not leave until she had paid 12,000 yuan. With no other choice, she finally had to pay up.

Then Fuqiang separated from A'min and drove the Mercedes. Presently he found another solo female in a Mercedes S Class with a number which wasn't from Shenzhen. They stopped her with the same method and got out of their car as usual. But to their surprise, the woman just locked her door and sat inside the Mercedes, dialling her cellphone.

Seeing this, the men felt that they had hit trouble and wanted to leave. But Fuqiang remained calm. He smiled at his accomplices. "Don't worry, we'll just wait," he said. The four men waited, still nervous.

About twenty minutes later a Volvo drove up. The four men rushed to their car for their knives and sticks, but Fuqiang was still calm and smiled at them. "Relax," he said. When the Volvo stopped, the driver, a middle-aged man, wound down the car window and held out 20,000 yuan in notes. "Is this enough?" he asked.

Fuqiang smiled coldly. "Of course not, but I'll accept it. And please tell her to drive more carefully from now on."

"Yes, yes!" The middle-aged man nodded furiously, like a chicken pecking rice. Then he drove off, with the woman following.

The four men relaxed and laughed again. "You get it right every time, Fuqiang," said one of them.

"Not every time. The other day I lost to a man driving a Jetta. He stopped the car and got out before I could hit his car."

That evening the men went to a karaoke room in Ban'an and splashed out some of the money they had made out of the innocent drivers on a big meal. Fuqiang suddenly decided to contact Haonan, so he called his pager, but he received a message saying Haonan was away on a business trip.

That night Fuqiang and A'min left together, having picked up a girl to keep them company, and Fuqiang asked A'min to go for a drive. Fuqiang put the rear seats flat, and lay down on them with the girl. Their heads were towards the front of the car, their feet stretched out in the boot. Every time A'min braked, Fuqiang thrust deeper into the girl, every time A'min pressed the accelerator, Fuqiang withdrew a little from hugging the girl, and every time A'min swerved to one side, they turned over so that the girl was on top, and when A'min swerved back, Fuqiang was on the top again.

After Fuqiang had had enough, they swapped places, and Fuqiang drove while A'min took his pleasure with the girl in the same way.

Chapter 24
The Five-Star Bank

In the early days of Chinese reform and the opening up of export businesses, companies could earn much foreign currency; all they needed was a calculator to negotiate with foreign buyers. But if they did not own factories or property, they gradually disappeared. This was how the company Haonan worked for, Shenzhen Zhongcheng Electronic I/E Company, had gone bankrupt, and why Haonan had to look for a new job.

In Shenzhen there is a place from which, along Shennan Road Central to the east up to Xiaomeisha, or along Shennan Boulevard to the west up to Nantou, the distances are almost the same. This is Gang'xia in the Futian District, where the tall buildings and affordable houses are served by convenient traffic facilities. Separated by Caitian Road South, Gang'xia is divided into two areas, Louyuan in the east and Heyuan in the west. Whenever you walk into this "village in the city", you can see advertisements for everything from restaurants needing management to cures for syphilis.

So Haonan moved from the thriving Huaqiangbei area to Gang'xia. After settling in he went to Shangbayue village to see Shuwen, but her cousin told him that the two crew-cut heavies had appeared at Shangbayue and for her personal safety, Shuwen had returned temporarily to Chengdu, her home town. Haonan had to forget about her. It was fortunate that he had not become too involved with her.

Then Haonan had an unexpected opportunity to work in a foreign bank. In a suit and tie, he went in on his first day full of enthusiasm. The bank had taken over the third floor of the Xindu Hotel, and when he arrived there he was amazed to see that when he put out a hand to push open the glass door, it opened automatically for him. The lights were as brilliant as those in an operating theatre. On a board, the words "Singapore Union Bank, Shenzhen Branch" were inlaid in gold. Under the board was green Brazilian ironwood and fine carpet covered the floor, so new and clean that he was afraid his shoes, carefully cleaned that morning, would dirty it. He entered to see many dark red rosewood office desks, arranged neatly with computers, office files and stationery. On the doors of the rooms facing the windows were gold signs stating "President's Room", "Vice-President's Room", "Secretary's Room" and "Conference Room" and so on. This was much the most impressive business environment Haonan had ever worked in.

Because of the slump in foreign trade across China, it was difficult to get a job in import and export businesses. Recalling his damaging experience with the ramie fabric deal, Haonan decided to leave foreign trade. Once he had presented his resumé, he was recruited as letter of credit collector and inspector for this bank.

Haonan, who had now been working in foreign trade for several years, knew many of the companies involved, and the bank's president, Wu Menghua, appreciated this experience, which could help to expand the bank's letter of credit business and the bank's deposit and loan business.

Another reason why Wu Menghua employed Haonan was that he had seen his excellent calligraphy, the Liu Gongquan style, on his resumé and envelope. He was very fond of Chinese culture and in his home and office there were many calligraphy works by Qi Gong and paintings by Zhang Daqian. This president, who had been sent to work in China by the headquarters in Singapore, was a member of the board of directors and the bank's second biggest shareholder. Haonan's luck in being selected from the countless applicants by the president was as fortunate as an appointment by an emperor of ancient China.

When Haonan had the opportunity to join this bank, he felt he had been awarded a mountain of gold. He had always felt that banks, particularly foreign banks, were the epitome of importance, wealth and leisure. The working day passed in a leisurely manner and every day there was a buffet with fruit and beer.

That morning there were nine staff members sitting in the conference room, waiting for a meeting with the president and the vice president. Liu Xinyu, Zhou Lei and two staff from the international department were talking. Wu Menghua was thin and in his fifties. Probably because he spent much of his time buried in his work, he looked slightly unhealthy. Now he came over, taking small steps, and suddenly saw a piece of scrap paper. As he was in too much of a hurry to look for a garbage can, he put it in his pocket first; he would rather soil his clothes than the office.

After he sat down he was followed by the vice president, who was as tall and thin as a bamboo. His surname was Luo, and he also came from Singapore. Wu said, "Please welcome Zhou Haonan, our new recruit. We hope he will bring new business for our bank." They all clapped, which gave Haonan a warm feeling. Wu went on, "Regarding the financial department, Miss Deng Xiaoyan will be responsible for handling loans and trying to avoid bad debts. Miss Wang Jun is to be in charge of human resources, hunting for more talent for the bank. Liu Xinyu and Zhou Lei are to continuously inspect letter of credit. The international business of ours will have a better future, I believe, because of the powerful new energy being invested in it from today."

At the end of the meeting, Wu addressed the women and said, "In order to maintain the good image of the bank and impress our customers, from tomorrow when you come to work, you must not wear your trousers."

They all looked at each other in astonishment. Among the eleven employees present, apart from Wu, Luo, driver Lai and Haonan, all the others were females. Looking at their expressions, Wu fiercely repeated, "You must not wear trousers! Do you hear me?"

The women all blushed. Luo then murmured to Wu in Malay. Wu blushed at this and hurriedly corrected himself. "I mean you must wear skirts instead of trousers, not wear nothing!" he said. "But long skirts, not mini-skirts."

They all burst out laughing, even Wu. After that they returned to their workplaces.

Haonan found the office extremely quiet. Unless there was a telephone ringing, he could hear his colleagues breathing and the sounds of files being opened and moved around. Sometimes he could hear typing as the latest bank report was being produced.

At lunchtime delicious meals were brought by a woman who was responsible for daily cooking for the bank's staff. After that there was time for a nap or a chat.

"In this wonderful environment your work will be stable," Zhou Lei, who sat behind Haonan, told him. "You'll have a steady income and your salary will be increased yearly. Unlike the foreign company in which you had such difficulties before, this is foreign enterprise, where you work from 9 am to 5 pm. It's steady work which most people don't have the luck to get. You'll appreciate it very much."

Haonan was given a monthly salary of 8,000 yuan, which after a trial period would rise to 10,000 yuan. After two or three years he would receive a yearly wage of 500,000 yuan, which was more than most young men dreamed of. However, he was still wondering about one important thing. He asked Zhou Lei, who was making up her eyes in the mirror, "Can the bank allocate a quota of Shenzhen Permanent Residence Permits?"

"No, but a house allowance is available," she said. "After you become a qualified clerk, the bank will provide you with a loan to buy a house." She put down her eyebrow pen.

"So I can solve my housing problem. I won't need to rent any longer," Haonan gratefully sighed.

"Yes, you have been selected by Wu from more than 300 candidates. Everyone here has bought a house with a bank loan. If they can't do that, how could this be called a bank?"

"Whose name will be registered on the Property Ownership Certificate?"

"Yours, of course."

"Great!" Haonan's heart was bursting. He bowed his head and joyfully thought to himself: *if Laizhen knows I am likely to have a house soon, she might come back to me!*

"Please teach me how to do calligraphy," said the clerk next to him, Tian Mingjuan, stretching out her neck and holding a pen and paper in her hand. She had just graduated from financial college, so everything was fresh to her.

"You are flattering me, but let me try," said Haonan. "First, you are holding the pen wrongly."

"How?"

"All you young women press the end of the pen with the bottom of your thumb, as though you fear it will slide to the ground. You're hugging the pen instead of holding it, which is tiring. The correct way is like this." He showed her. "The tips of the thumb and index finger and the top of the first knuckle of the middle finger must press together on the same spot on the shaft, about 3 cm away from the nib. This may vary a little with different people. The fingertips must not leave the shaft. Meanwhile, you must not press the shaft with the knuckle of your thumb. Generally speak, the pen might lean on the part between your thumb and index finger, or the third knuckle of your index finger, or anywhere between the two. It's slightly different with different people."

"How complicated calligraphy is! It's more tiring than driving," said Lai, the driver, butting in. All he had to do each day was pick up the two presidents.

"This is the basic requirement for handwriting, just as wearing slippers isn't allowed when you're driving, right?" Haonan said. "And there are similarities between them. The legs should be extended to the width of the shoulders, the knees must be at a 90- degree angle, head straight, chest out..."

He wrote down the two mnemonic rhymes he had taught Laizhen, letting Tian Mingjuan recite them. But of course, in public Tian Mingjuan didn't want Haonan to measure the distance between her chest and the desk edge.

When they heard that Haonan was working for a foreign bank, Fuqiang and Zhenfeng came to see him. Zhenfeng wore a suit, but Fuqiang was dressed casually in a shirt and soft shoes. They whispered to each other, heaving deep sighs from time to time. When they had gone, Wu rebuked Haonan for Fuqiang's appearance, as it was not appropriate to the bank's image. Wu kept muttering, "stupid!" Haonan had to apologise.

Chapter 25
A Vital Decision

At the end of 1995, Sanda boxing was introduced for the first time to the night club scene in Shenzhen, at the Happy Park Disco Night Club in Zhongxing Road, Luohu District. One night when Haonan was there it was very crowded, and the song *Man Must Be Self-Strong*, sung by Lin Zixiang from Hong Kong, was played repeatedly. Hearing this and seeing the fierce fighting on the platform, Haonan recalled watching the TV series *Knight-errant of Huo Yuanjia* with his classmates. Everyone used to come off the streets to watch it.

The miserable experience of being bullied at school by Chen Lingfang now flashed back into his mind. After years with no outlet for his anger, it had built up like the pressure of lava under a volcano. He clenched his fist, muttering grimly to himself, "I want to fight!"

In the beginning when Haonan had worked in Futian, he had known of a famous Chinese martial artist named Shi Qingliang who lived in Shekou and specialised in Nan-Quan, T'ai-Chi-Quan and Xing-Yi-Quan, three kinds of Chinese traditional martial arts. He had begged Shi Qingliang to train him in his spare time, and for a charge of 100 yuan per month he had taken lessons one night per week. At that time Shi Qinliang taught ten students only. Haonan had learnt some established skills and tricks from this. He had shown talent and gained Shi Qiangliang's affection. What he had learnt, however, was only how to train without fighting with his friends; he had not learned real fighting.

One lunchtime a year later as he walked to the dormitory, he heard the sound of a quarrel at the entrance to the village. Following it, he found three young men had surrounded a middle- aged man and were about to attack him. One of them picked up a club and struck the man in the waist.

"No!" shouted Haonan. But when he rushed in to prevent the attack he suddenly felt his legs go weak with fright. The skills he had learned did not help. From then on he understood that martial art training could be useful for the body's health, but it was no good when encountering real fighting, so he made up his mind to learn the useful fighting technique of Sanda boxing.

Later, when working in the Mingguang factory in Anhui Province, with Zhu's permission, he went alone to the Tiechanmen Sanda & Fighting Club in Jiangsu Province, several hundred kilometres away. That winter he experienced snow and freezing temperatures for the first time. He underwent intensive, systematic professional training for three months. During this time he exercised harder than his friends under the same coach. Whenever he smashed his fist into the punchbag, his heart shouted for Lin Laizhen. His feet shed blood, but his heart was bloodier. His anger was an inexhaustible engine, especially the anger from being bullied when he was young, and it encouraged him to punch with the force of a thunderbolt. Finally the rope that held the punchbag broke under the force of his attack. Haonan lost his balance and fell to the ground alongside it, howling, "Lin Laizhen!"

He fought with his friends every day. When he was wearing boxing gloves they were enemies, but when he took them off they were his brothers again. They learned from fighting and fought from learning. The coach and the other pupils did not understand why Haonan was so aggressive. Even those who were taller and heavier than Haonan dared not fight with him, so he often won despite his light weight.

Now that he worked in a bank, he had plenty of spare time to fight.

One evening in January 1996 as Haonan was changing into his Sanda shorts and putting on his boxing gloves, the song *Man Must Be Self-Strong* began as usual in the Happy Park Disco. As soon as he heard this song, he felt the blood rushing through his body. He was wearing nothing but the shorts and gloves. The assistant helped him put on the red cloak. He waited for the instruction to walk out, skipping to relax his muscles.

Soon the song stopped, and the master of ceremonies on the platform picked up a microphone and announced: "China is great and she has lasted for five thousand years, with many upheavals. The ancient Great Wall never falls and the water in the Yellow River, one thousand miles long, never stops flowing. Tonight, our first match is in the 65kg class. The fighter in red is Zhou Haonan. He comes from Canton and has the nickname of 'the mastermind on the platform'. The man in black is Lei Dong, from Hunan Province, and we call him 'the angry tiger rushing down a mountain'. Now let's welcome the two of them!"

After thunderous applause, *Man Must Be Self-Strong* broke out again. Haonan stepped out of the changing room and walked steadily to the ring. At this moment of excitement, a brilliant image of the "Old One-Armed Man", Chen Zhen, who he had watched on TV in his childhood, came back to his mind. Suddenly a flurry of searchlights shone on Haonan and his strong muscles were revealed to the audience. A bodybuilder's muscle represents only dead physical strength; for a Sanda athlete, however, each muscle is charged with dynamic power.

The crowds applauded again. Haonan waved his hands in thanks. Using a small wooden ladder linking to the platform he walked into the ring, and the workers raised a second rope so that he rolled into the ring. He stood up and waved again to the crowds, side-stepped around the ring and stood in his corner with his arms hanging over the rope.

But when Lei Dong in his black cloak entered the ring, Haonan began to tremble. Lei Dong was a huge man with a crew-cut whose height and weight seemed a third more than that of Haonan. Surely he must be well into the 85kg class, even if he had lost a little weight. The night club was in uproar. But the fight could not be cancelled and Haonan had been thinking of nothing except plunging into the fighting.

Then two beautiful girls in bikinis appeared, holding up boards and circling the ring. The host said, "That's enough of these girls, now it's time for a fierce struggle between two strong and well-matched opponents!" Haonan and his opponent took off the cloaks.

"Start!" shouted the referee.

The one in black was expressionless. He seemed as deadly if he was looking for the man who had killed his father. Without hesitation, he ferociously sprang upon Haonan, punching with both fists at Haonan's left and right temples. They were not orthodox punches, more those of a streetfighter. Lei Dong's strength originated from his waist. When Haonan had practised Sanda in the north he had won more than a hundred fights, but never in his life had he experienced such heavy blows. Lei Dong had not only strength but fighting technique.

Then a punch from Lei Dong hit the corner of Haonan's left eye. Haonan was so dizzy that he felt the night club was spinning and he could see stars overhead. He fell to the floor.

The referee immediately shouted "Stop!" to prevent any further attack from Lei Dong. But Haonan stood up and continued to fight.

"Come on! Come on!" shouted the crowds to Haonan ceaselessly. But Haonan had been dazed by the punch. He circled the referee, wondering what to do. This soon brought a warning from the referee.

Lei Dong attacked again with fierce punch on the corner of Haonan's right eye, and Haonan was knocked down again. Again the referee shouted "Stop!" and signalled that Lei Dong had won. So one round was enough. The crowds hissed at Haonan, and someone even threw an empty bottle at him.

When Haonan took off his boxing gloves in the changing room, the staff hurriedly apologised to him for the mistake. Haonan's opponent should have been a 65kg fighter, but when Lei Dong had appeared they found he was in the 85kg class. But it was too late to find a substitute, so they had to let the fight go ahead so that they would not have to give the audience their money back. It was therefore inevitable that Haonan would be knocked out.

He impressed this Lei Dong from the beginning of the fight. Finally he realised that Lei Dong was just one of the crewcut men he had met that night who had tried to force Li Shuwen to pay compensation. Haonan couldn't help feeling afraid.

When Haonan arrived at the bank the next day, smelling strongly of medication, his female colleagues spontaneously cried, "You have two black eyes!"

Haonan bowed his head, forcing himself to smile and saying that he had sleepwalked the previous night and had bumped into a table. He did not dare to tell the truth. They all laughed.

He bought a big bottle of *Tianqi* liquid medicine to treat his wounds. He also had to stew herbs and apply them to the wound, and every day he wrapped a hot boiled egg in a dry towel to massage his black eyes. Afterwards he stood on the balcony, looking at the streets. He kept recalling the fight and being knocked down, and like a wounded soldier he kept thinking about the battle in which he had been injured. Did he still want to fight or not?

In fact he was back in the ring only two weeks later, his injuries barely healed. His opponent this time was from the Southern Shaolin Martial Arts Gymnasium, a man who had once been champion of the 65kg class in the Fujian Provincial Sanda Competition. He was taller than Haonan but not as strong as Lei Dong. Seeing the reputation and achievements of this opponent, Haonan was very wary. From the beginning of the first round, he kept watching his opponent rather than fighting, so he was reprimanded by the referee and two points were deducted.

When the second round began, Haonan found that his opponent often punched straight left and right to keep his feet too steady, and he seldom kicked. So Haonan kept blocking him with a middle sidekick. He remembered that his coach had taught him that in resisting someone who was tall with long arms, it was best to keep your distance so he could not attack directly. Then, not only could he kick his opponent's waist and abdomen, since the opponent couldn't punch straight at Haonan, he could not score many points.

In the third round when his opponent was working out how to defend against middle sidekick, Haonan twisted his body at 180 degrees all of a sudden and with a right back half-round kick he struck the big artery on the opponent's leg. In the blink of eye his opponent went into spasm and got down on his left knee as if he was saluting a returning king. The gong was sounded and the referee held Haonan's right hand up. He had won!

Applause broke out at once. Haonan had tasted a great victory.

But when he signed to receive the winner's bonus of 500 yuan, his hands trembled as if he had Parkinson's disease and his muscles went into spasm. This was because he relaxed suddenly after a long period of tension. His own handwriting seemed wild and strange to him.

When he put the money he had won into his pocket, a sudden spasm of pain swept through his chest. In a flash he remembered his mother far away in west Canton. If she knew he was fighting like this in a Sanda boxing ring, would she feel terrible sadness? They say all sons and daughters are the heart muscles of their mothers. It was as though Haonan's own mother had been injured by the punches and kicks. Would his mother sense his pain? Now Haonan did not feel pain for himself, but only for his mother.

One morning a few days later, Haonan sat in the conference room opposite Wu and Wang Jun. Wu's Mandarin was not very fluent, so sometimes Wang Jun had to explain his meaning. Wang Jun had graduated from a financial university in Wuhan City, Hubei Province, and during the three years she had worked in this bank, Wu had greatly appreciated her excellent abilities in finance and human resources. So she was soon able to get a bank loan to buy a big apartment, and now she was about to get married.

Wu said to Haonan, "Recently your letter of credit business has been increasing, and your ability to inspect letter of credit has improved greatly. You have successfully passed through the trial period. Congratulations! You will have a good future."

Wang Jun applauded. Haonan expressed his thanks, smiling.

Wu went on, "But on the other hand, the night before last, I saw you fight in the night club."

Haonan's heart sank.

Wu went on, "I like boxing, especially Thai boxing, but I don't want you to take part. It can kill an adversary with one punch. Thai boxers often die in their fifties because of their extreme training and the cruel fights. In the Philippines and Mexico, it was often said that the boxers who were knocked out in the ring died soon afterwards. Chinese Sanda isn't as cruel as Thai boxing and occupational boxing, but Sanda boxers are cruel too. Generally what you do in your spare time is not the concern of the bank, but fighting is so risky that you might beat an opponent to death or be killed yourself. You have purchased no life insurance, and this bank will not provide it."

Wu had seen Haonan's black eyes and he had sometimes seen him limping. He also knew that the fight had been held in Shenzhen, and he had heard that Haonan had practised Sanda. So he guessed that Haonan must have been engaging in fighting in his spare time.

Haonan thought that what Wu said was right. His fighting had worried the bank.

"Now I realise that I can't approve a house loan for you," Wu said. "If there is a death when you fight, your loan will be the bank's bad debt. Prevention is better than cure. I must be responsible for the bank. Do you understand?"

Haonan nodded.

"So now you have two options. The first is to write a letter of commitment, in which you guarantee that you will attend no more boxing matches in any night club in Shenzhen. The second option is to leave our bank. Think it over before making your decision. You can reply to me in three days. I sincerely hope you choose the first option."

Haonan did not want to give up such a highly-paid job, for once the house loan was approved, he would own a satisfactory apartment. For so many years he had dreamed of this. If he left the bank, he would probably have no chance of owning a home. He would have to return to foreign trade. But with the long hours working in foreign trade, how could he find the time and energy to fight in the evenings?

Yet fighting was one of his greatest desires. His youth would soon be gone in a blink of eye, for he was almost 30, and in two years' time it would be too late to enter the ring again. The quiet and civilised banking environment was an excellent stable for a horse, but he was a powerful horse who wanted to run wild and free and was reluctant to lie down in the stable for too long.

Three days later, in the same conference room, the same three people met again. Haonan said seriously, "I've decided to choose the second option." Wu shook his head repeatedly, strongly expressing his disappointment. He angrily threw his oil-painting pen on the carpet, heedless of the black ink which leaked out and began to stain the carpet.

Wang Jun said sympathetically, "Actually a house loan for you amounting to 1.5 million yuan has already been approved by Wu. But if you still want to fight, there will be no house. I feel sorry for you, too."

"Thank you," Haonan said.

Wang Jun went on, "As the official clerk here, you earn ten thousand yuan monthly. Apart from the house, you can enjoy yearly travel to the Chinese mainland and abroad, visiting Guilin, Singapore, Malaysia, Thailand, the Maldives, the USA, the UK and so on. Why did you make the choice to fight? It could kill you at any time."

"Did you hear that? Wang Jun has just broken the rules of our bank by telling you in advance,"

Wu said with ashen face. "You can think about it for a little longer. I'll wait."

Haonan lowered his head and said, "I have chosen the second option. I am very sorry."

Wu rose to his feet, agitated. As he left, he snapped, "Stupid! Stupid!"

Haonan left the bank with great regret. He felt he had abandoned a most important thing in his life, and all his colleagues were sorry as well. As a matter of fact Wu had been mulling over another plan, to appoint Haonan to train in financial organisations in UK and after that, to cultivate him as his successor at this bank. In contrast, Haonan had made another surprising decision that he would temporarily give up work and engage only in fighting and make a living from boxing.

After that, from the next day on, he usually stayed at the Dajiale Sanda and Fighting Gymnasium to the north-east of Litchi Park, the special training gymnasium of the Shenzhen Sanda and Boxing Association. Every day he ran, skipped and punched fixed and mobile punchbags. He also had real fight practice with his friends from time to time. After four hours of daily training, he was often so tired that he had a sore waist and an aching back, and even fell to the ground. But in the evening he was frequently active at many night clubs in Shenzhen, such as the Happy Park Disco. Fortunately he won more often than he lost.

Chapter 26
Love Strikes Like Lightning

Since Haonan was away from home, if nothing special was happening he would call his mother at 10 o'clock every morning. So when it was approaching 10 o'clock, no matter how busy his mother was, she would temporarily stop work and wait for the call. She always asked if he had made any plans for marriage, and it always disappointed her that he had not. At holiday times she would be waiting for his return, hoping he would bring a girl with him. He never did.

At that time at the entrance to Gang'xia village there were two phone booths facing each other. From each you could hear clearly what the person in the other was saying. After Haonan had finished talking with his mother one morning, he heard a voice say from the other booth, "Why can't I get through?"

He turned and saw that the speaker was a beautiful young woman. She turned to him and their eyes met. Haonan felt as if he had been struck by lightning. She asked him, "Can you help to dial for me? I've just come to Shenzhen and I don't know how to use this phone card."

Haonan went over to dial for her. The line was busy, and several minutes passed before the call was finally put through. She started talking happily on the phone in a dialect he did not recognise.

He decided to call his mother again. Finally they both hung up at the same time and turned to face each other. Once again he felt a flash of lightning. They both started to talk at the same time.

It turned out that her name was Fu Xiaohong and she was from Chongqing City in Sichuan Province. She had no work at present and was staying with her cousin in Badeng Street, Futian. They walked as they talked, and when they separated, they gave each other their pager numbers. Haonan's heart was beating furiously.

That night Haonan was busy washing clothes and doing odd jobs until midnight. Early the next morning he was awoken by the pager, which was dancing on the pillow and bumping against his forehead. He answered the phone, and heard a sweet voice say, "Hi, handsome! Where will you go to play today?" It was Fu Xiaohong.

"Today I am just planning to catch up on my sleep," he replied.

"How about we go to the Fairy Lake Botanical Garden?"

Since his setback with Lin Laizhen and his encounter with Li Shuwen, Haonan had not had a girlfriend for a long time – and of course Li Shuwen had not been a girlfriend, although they had slept in the same bed. Now another charming girl was interested in him, how could he say no? And his mother was still worrying about his marriage prospects. Perhaps she had arranged for someone to introduce this Chongqing girl to him. He accepted Xiaohong's invitation.

It seemed that Haonan had not dug a well, although he had felt thirsty. But the well had now been dug for him; it seemed as well that now that he had been standing by a pond hoping for a fish, the fish had now jumped into his pot.

Legend says that Chongqing was a cradle in which beautiful girls were born. If in Shenzhen beautiful girls were as common as clouds, this girl was a new kind of cloud. Xiaohong, who came from Jinyun Mountain in the Beibei District of Chongqing, had grown up bright with beauty and at 20 her body was perfectly shaped. Some years before Haonan had been to Chongqing on business, but he had been in too much of a hurry to appreciate the beauty of Chongqing girls. Now life had put in front of him a Chongqing girl who was as beautiful as a flower.

They sat side by side in the minibus on the way to Fair Lake Botanical Garden. Enjoying the envy of people watching, he breathed in her delicate aroma.

At the Botanical Garden, the sun shone warmly on the greenery. They strolled along the hillside, stood on the pavilion, climbed into the temple and looked up to the far distance. Afterwards in the Daxiong Palace they devoutly burnt incense and knelt down to pray for health, safety and wealth. Haonan prayed especially for a Shenzhen Permanent Residence Permit and a house. Tired, they sat down on a stone stool under a banyan tree halfway up the hill, drinking orange juice and chatting.

"What's your job?" she asked.

"Fighting."

She was surprised by this, but looking at his strong arms, she believed him. Then she asked, "Now that you are a fighter, will you treat your wife like a punchbag?"

He grinned. He was often asked this question. Now he replied, "Would a policeman treat his wife and children as targets for firearm training? Actually the most important thing is the mind, which controls the actions."

She nodded and said, "How many people can you fight on your own?"

"You can't judge fighting ability like that. Take a 60kg Sanda fighter for instance. He can beat a man of 85kg who doesn't practise Kungfu, but he cannot compete with an 85kg man who is a

Sanda champion. Lightweight and middleweight fighters can't generally beat heavyweights. So how many people you can beat should be judged within the same weight class."

"I see. The one who practises martial arts can fly up into the sky and leave the earth, like those *Kungfu* stars."

"You've read too many martial arts stories! Actually Sanda is different from the actions shown on TV and films. Sanda concentrates on efficient fighting, with the aim of beating the opponent at the fastest speed and the lowest price. The fights shown on TV and in films are carefully arranged beforehand, so they never really fight in the ring. In our Canton province there were many outstanding Sanda fighters such as Li Zhimin, the 75kg of national Sanda champion and Liu De, the 60kg champion."

"I didn't know that."

"The action, take Bruce Lee for example, is real *Kungfu*. It's a pity he died so young. It was said that Bruce Lee and his son, Li Guohao, were both killed by small Japanese men. How can we explain how his son could be shot dead by a bullet when he was acting in a film?"

"It was said that Huo Yuanjia was murdered by the Japanese too," said Xiaohong. She bent the upper part of her body, showing her cleavage, the skin as white as a jade. Haonan felt his blood pumping as vigorously as the oil in a twelve-cylinder Mercedes.

It was twilight when they arrived at Badeng Street and went into a Chongqing restaurant for a meal. As soon as they sat down, she phoned two other girls and invited them to join them, saying they were friends from the same town. When they arrived, the three girls chatted like sparrows in the Chongqing dialect and paid no attention to Haonan, who could not follow what they said. The girls then decided to order many different seafood dishes, all with chilli. Fortunately Haonan, who had travelled all over China, enjoyed all kinds of Chinese food.

Xiaohong took a photo from her bag and showed it to her friends. He could see that it was a family group, in which the husband was lovingly hugging his wife and a cute daughter. Haonan thought the woman in the photo was very like Xiaohong.

Xiaohong, who appeared slightly flustered, gave the two girls a special look, as if signalling something. Then she pointed to the woman in the photo, saying to Haonan, "This is my elder sister, taken when she was young. I have a good relationship with her."

"You look very much like her," he said. The other two said nothing, but an odd, secretive smile was on their lips. Haonan felt uncomfortable.

When he asked for the bill, it came to 936 yuan, which made his heart sink. He had never paid so much for dinner for his own friends, and he had never met these girls before. The girls went on talking happily as if the bill was none of their business. Still, he reflected that without investment, there is no harvest, and perhaps this expensive meal was worth the money.

The next day when he phoned to his mother, he happily told her about his new girlfriend. At the other end of phone his mother, thinking that her efforts to get him married had met with success at last, gave a big smile. After putting down the phone, she went to the mini-store and told her neighbours about Haonan's new girlfriend as if she was holding a news conference.

After training in the Dajiale, Haonan went to the club to watch fights. Sometimes he took Xiaohong. Inside the club they sat on high stools, holding hands on a little round table and eating almonds, cashew nuts and odd-tasting beans and drinking beer. The spotlights were colourful and the waitresses bustled through the crowds. In the ring a fighter in red and one in black were vigorously fighting, and the spectators were shouting. Haonan jerked and moved his body along with the fighters. His arms and legs never stopped, as if he was in the ring himself.

Watching the matches began to excite Xiaohong. At first, when she saw the blood and sweat, she hurriedly covered her eyes with her hands, but soon she got used to it and began to clap her little hands and yell. Her gentle white face was full of happiness. But then she quietly drank a bottle of Coca Cola, lost in thought.

"What's wrong?" Haonan turned to ask her.

"Nothing special. It's only that no one can help me now," she sighed.

As soon as he heard that, tender feelings for her replaced his excitement. He stopped watching the fight and asked her why. Finally she told him the truth. Her beloved niece, the little girl in the photo, had been diagnosed with leukaemia. This news had come like a thunderbolt on a sunny day, as huge medical fees would be required for her treatment. Haonan felt distressed at this news.

"Could you lend me any money?" she said, looking up at him pitifully.

Haonan could not possibly find so much money. He said nothing.

"I'll marry the man who can help me," she said.

He whispered in his heart, *selling yourself to save a relative?* But her eyes pleaded with him. "Try as hard as you can, please!" she said. "I'm raising money everywhere now. The day after tomorrow I must go back to Chongqing."

He calculated that he could afford 43,000 yuan, which was his total boxing income so far. However, he had only known her for ten days and knew very little about her. But how could he not extend a hand to rescue her?

At last he said, "What if I lend you 43,000 yuan?"

"Really?" Her mood immediately changed from sorrow to happiness.

The next morning they went to the China Merchants Bank on the first floor of the News Building on Shennan Road Central. In 1995 when the bank had first promoted its one-card pass Haonan had applied for it, so he was one of the first holders, though he had only a small balance. Haonan stood in a queue holding his pass while Xiaohong sat on a sofa nearby.

When he handed over the 43,000 yuan, he was seized by serious anxiety. They had met such a short time ago. What would he do if she never returned to Shenzhen? How would he find her? But her niece's leukaemia came again to his mind. He had to help her.

Xiaohong happily took the money. They walked out of the bank and saw a mobile blood donation car parked nearby, with a slogan in red saying, "Donating a bag of blood can save a life!" and "O type blood is urgently required!"

Haonan felt he had plenty of blood to spare and it would be better to donate it here than waste it in the boxing ring, so he stepped into the car with Xiaohong. There were only a few people in the car. Xiaohong sat silently while he filled in the form, then the doctor jabbed his finger to take a blood sample. The nurse gave him a carton of milk.

"It's O-type blood, the transaminase enzymes are normal, liver function is normal... all is normal," said the nurse a few minutes later after the health check report was done.

When the big needle was inserted into his vein, it felt less painful than the jab in his finger. He always hated his finger being pricked. In fact he would rather be punched.

"Please come back and give blood again in three months," said the nurse as she saw Haonan off. Another nurse said, "Once you have donated, if you or your relatives need blood in the future it will be free all your life."

"Really?" Haonan was pleasantly surprised.

"How much blood did you draw just now?" Xiaohong asked. "400ml, same as everyone."

"I cannot give blood. I go dizzy if someone sticks a needle in me."

Soon they arrived at the air ticket office near the Hualian Building. He fished 810 yuan from his pocket to buy a ticket to Chongqing. Then they wandered into the rainbow department store, where Xiaohong took a liking to a real leather Italian bag costing 520 yuan and a pair of children's shoes costing 300 yuan for her niece. She also wanted to buy a real leather jacket as gift to her elder sister. She tried it on, saying they were the same size, so it would fit her sister. This cost him another 4,000 yuan.

He asked to see her that evening, but she said she wanted to get together with her cousin before she left. Suddenly Haonan felt as if someone had poured a basin of cold water over him. He stood still, dumbfounded for a while. He had given up training and competition to spend time with her that evening, but she didn't want to see him.

Early the next morning, it was overcast and raining slightly. The No. 330 airport bus drove them to Huangtian airport in Bao'an and again he could detect her faint aroma. His sadness grew as they drove. He had no idea when she would be coming back, and he wondered what he would get in return for his love and his money. Meanwhile Xiaohong was happily looking at the views outside as though her niece's life had already been saved. He wondered why she did not appear to feel any sadness over leaving him, or for her niece, who was still waiting to be cured. But then she would arrive home soon and perhaps be able to save her niece, so there was no need to cry all the way to Chongqing.

In the airport lobby he joined a long queue to pay the 50 yuan airport fee for her, applied for the boarding pass, weighed her luggage and loaded it. She sat behind waiting. He was sweating outside when all this was done, despite the cold wind. He stopped at the gate and watched her moving forward in the queue. He still had so much to say to her, but it seemed she had no feelings for him. She did not look back at him even once.

Finally she coldly called goodbye and disappeared into the tunnel to board the plane. He still stood there, watching her receding figure until she disappeared. Then he wandered back into the lobby. He had never paid out that kind of money before even for his beloved mother. He had not even touched this girl's hand.

He stood in front of the airport window watching her plane soar into the sky and listening to the fading thunder of the engines. His money had vanished, and now so had she.

Chapter 27
The Sanda Fighter

One night when Haonan passed the Fierce Dragon Night Club in Futian, he saw a board in front of it advertising "The 1st Session of China, Korea and Japan Fighting Platform Competition", along with pictures of five classes of fighters from Korea and Japan. This was called a "communication match", but since they were coming a long way to set up a boxing ring here, it was actually a challenge match designed to attack the reputation of the Chinese Sanda. This worried Haonan, who had now been fighting for a year, but it also gave him an incentive, so he quickly applied to fight.

This tournament between three countries was the highest level of competition since Sanda and boxing matches had been introduced to night clubs in Shenzhen. A demonstration by the away team was arranged for the first night, and Haonan watched it carefully. These fighters from Korea and Japan were highly aggressive and could break bricks with their heels and penetrate wooden boards with their bare fingertips, which terrified many spectators.

It was arranged for Haonan to fight in the first match the next night, against Changtaek Park, a Korean black belt seven in Taekwondo, who liked to use the famous down split kick and reverse kick. Nearly one thousand spectators gathered beside a ring which was one metre high and sixty-four square metres in area, and there was a referee on each side of the platform.

The heavy bass of *Man Must Be Self-Strong* broke out again, sounding as if it was coming from the earth's core. Haonan, who had been waiting in the changing room, now slowly walked out. In his red cloak he walked steadily along the gangway to the ring. Colourful spotlights shone on him, the music mixing with the cheers. Inspired by the song, his heart surged wildly, but his face was calm.

Soon both fighters stood on the platform. The host first introduced Changtaek Park, who responded to his name with a down split kick. His left leg described a perfect arc in the air, which made the spectators cheer again. But when it was Haonan's turn to be introduced, he stayed calm. He just raised his hands, smiled and waved to the audiences, making himself look slow-witted. They faced each other and mutually saluted by putting their right fists in their left palms, then stood face to face.

The first round was usually when the two fighters checked out each other's condition and decided how much energy to expend in each of the five two-minute rounds. None the less, within two seconds of the referee shouting "Start!", Haonan put his right heel behind his left heel while raising his left knee and stretched straight out his left leg. This action was called "padding step for sidekick". In the blink of eye, his left foot landed a kick on Changtaek Park's chest. The Taekwondo fighter was not familiar with the Chinese sidekick, one of the three main kinds of kick in Chinese Sanda, so when he realised that he should raise his hands to resist, it was too late. The move was so fast and the kick was so accurate that nobody could have stood against it. Changtaek Park soared over the 1.5 metre-high rope and flew like paper blown by a whirlwind, to fall heavily on the carpet in front of the spectators. All the people shouted, and the staff who stood by the ring to guard the fighters were too slow to react and just looked helplessly at Changtaek Park down on the ground. The referee hurriedly rushed down and began counting, "One, two, three..."

Terror and regret were written on Changtaek Park's face. When the referee had counted to 10, he was still lying on the ground, shaking his head. The referee rose to his feet and waved in the air: the winner and loser had been decided.

This national Taekwondo champion had won many fights over several years. It was hard to believe that he had lost so quickly. Never in his life had he experienced such a fighting technique. The spectators broke out in wild cheering for the Chinese team. Some people were still returning from the toilet and wiping their glasses, and when they found that no sooner had they sat down than the match was over, they protested strongly to the organization committee, demanding either a refund or for the match to be fought again.

The next morning the headline on newspaper front pages around China reported, "Chinese Sanda Fighter Zhou Haonan Knocks Out Korean Taekwondo Champion in Two Seconds". Many people wanted to know where the Fierce Dragon Night Club was, for they were keen to see this kind of fighting.

The rules of the tournament provided for the winner of each fight to go through to the next round. After five days of competition the Chinese team and the joint Korea-Japan team had equal scores. On the sixth night Haonan faced a tough match against Suganao Hitoshi, the 65kg Japanese national Karate champion.

Outside the night club on the night of the fight the ticket- dealers kept shouting Haonan's name to attract customers, like the children who waved copies of the Gazette on the streets of Chongqing before China's liberation, shouting ceaselessly, "Extra! Extra!"

Haonan arrived early at the match organization committee offices, where he discussed key fighting points with Yang Xiaolong, his coach, and four friends. Yang Xiaolong was of middle height, strong and dark with heavy upside-down eyebrows. In the Sanda world he was known as the Tyson of Shenzhen. He was the leader of the five members of the Chinese Sanda team.

Suddenly a man wearing black clothes and carrying a black bag appeared. He ushered Haonan out of the offices and took him to a quiet corner.

"What do you want?" asked Haonan, puzzled.

"Someone here is offering you 200,000 yuan to lose the match tonight," replied the man in a low voice. He held up the bag. "Here is 20,000 as a deposit. You can keep it."

Fake fighting? Haonan thought to himself. He understood that some people had gambled secretly. It seemed that most people had backed Haonan as winner, so if he lost anyone who had backed his opponent could earn a great deal of money. "You fight for money, don't you?" the man in black said. "Losing this match will make you more money than winning for six months." Seeing no reaction from Haonan, the man went on, "You think it over. 200,000 yuan!"

At midnight that night, the grand final was about to start. The spotlights all shone on the ring, and after the host had introduced Haonan and his opponent, Suganao Hitoshi, the song Man Must Be

Self-Strong broke out again. On hearing it, Haonan felt his blood pumping.

The gong sounded, and another bloody fight began. The fighters kept their left fists and left legs in front, opposing each other. Suganao Hitoshi had long hair and a full beard and was taller than Haonan, but not as muscular. Haonan lightly slide-stepped in the Sanda style, looking for a chance to attack. It was obvious that Hitoshi was worried that Changtaek Park had been knocked out by Haonan within two seconds and this would happen to him too, so when the match began, he went into a serious defensive position. The first round was just a test between them, and there was little action.

Sitting down on his stool in the corner of the ring, Haonan laid his hands over the ropes while the assistants massaged his hands and legs to relax them. He turned his head to glance at the crowds. He saw that in the nearest seat to the west of the ring a woman was sitting, wearing a long purplish-red dress with a floral pattern. She was staring back at him. Their eyes locked like two lasers in the night. He knew that beautiful face and that long hair. It was Lin Laizhen!

He thought wildly to himself that she probably knew that the reason he had entered the ring was just to send a meeting signal to her. And one year later she had finally received this signal and come! *Oh! My sweetheart! I love you so much!* He thought.

Beside her, however, a man was sitting, a man with yellow hair, one arm draped over her shoulder. It could only be Chen Guangwei. He was smoking in a leisurely way, making smoke rings one by one. Haonan's happiness at seeing Laizhen immediately turned to anger. When the gong for the second round was struck, he stood up with a flourish, his eyes fiercely concentrated on his opponent.

In the second round when Hitoshi raised his leg to kick, Haonan obstructed it with a low sidekick. Hitoshi then ceaselessly looked for angles for kicking. He would make a feint to one side, then attack from the other. After 37 seconds, Haonan suddenly made a reverse rear swing punch, his body turned at 180 degrees, and the back of his right fist fiercely struck Hitoshi's face. No sooner had he defended than blood streamed from his nose, which brought a cheer from the crowd. The referee hurriedly signalled a temporary stop, letting the medical assistants stop the bleeding. Afterwards when Hitoshi returned to the platform, he had to concentrate all his attention on defending his head with his hands. In next to no time Haonan lay on the floor and his right leg swept from back to front, hitting Hitoshi's heel so that he fell on his back. Kicking like this from a lying position was seldom used in fighting, if it was used well, the result could be wonderful. As

Hitoshi rose up to fight again, the second round was over.

In the next round, the fight became one-sided. Haonan was so dominant that it was as if he was getting help from God. However, although the scores were very different and Haonan was confident of victory, Hitoshi was still fighting; perhaps he would make a comeback. Sure enough, when the match entered Round 4, Haonan realised that since he had not knocked his opponent out, he would need to save his energy for the fifth round, so in this round he mainly focused on defending, which was also the instruction from his coach, Yang Xiaolong.

At the break Yang Xiaolong gave Haonan no more instructions. Instead he went over to the referee. At that moment, the man in black clothes appeared again. He walked over to Haonan and pointed out a man a short distance away. "Your performance dissatisfied my friend," he said. "Now he wants to add an additional 100,000 yuan, totaling 300,000. What do you think of that?"

Haonan's handsome face was expressionless. Guangwei wanted Haonan to lose, and badly. When he had read about his brilliant victory in the newspaper, he had been unhappy. Guangwei did not care what it took to make Haonan fall, especially in front of Laizhen.

The gong for the last round was sounded and somebody in the crowd waved a red five-star flag.

When Haonan saw it he was inspired, remembering how great his responsibility was. Yet now at last Hitoshi came out fighting. In the 12th second he seized a chance to make a rapid and fierce push-kick which struck Haonan's left ribs. Haonan wanted to grab the leg and throw him down, but he was too late. What was worse, it was the same rib that had been heavily kicked by his coach in training and the wound had not yet healed. He gave a grunt and fell to the floor.

"One, two..." The referee began the countdown. As Haonan lay on his side, he saw Guangwei and the man in black jump out of their seats and cheering. But Laizhen was covering her face with her hands, and her eyes were open wide. At that moment Yang Xiaolong rushed to the edge of ring and banged the floor to rouse Haonan. At the same time, as if the mountains and the sea were whistling, all the spectators shouted together, "Hold on, China!" It was apparent that this fight was now an honour match between China and Japan.

The referee continued counting. Haonan bit his teeth and breathed deeply. On the count of nine he rose to his feet and stood steadily on the platform. He looked at Laizhen. And Laizhen smiled at him!

The referee signalled for the match to continue, and the crowd reacted with thunderous applause. Haonan had learned his lesson. When Hitoshi advanced, Haonan slide-stepped back. Hitoshi thought this meant he was abandoning the attack because of his injury, and fearlessly punched forward. But Haonan suddenly brought his left leg up and made a straight sidekick at his opponent's head - this is a classic backslide-step sidekick in Sanda. No sooner had Hitoshi recovered than Haonan twisted his waist and turned his hip, and his Gai-quan struck Hitoshi's left temple. The kick and the punch one after the other confused Hitoshi. Then Haonan delivered another Gai-quan to the left side of Hitoshi's head. Hitoshi's hands fell down; his eyes were dull and he was swaying. Haonan took this opportunity to slide forward, muttering to himself, "I'll punch your 300,000 yuan!" He gave Hitoshi another Gai-quan. Finally his opponent fell. The referee began to count down, "One, two, three..."

The spectators held their breath. When the count was complete, Hitoshi was still lying motionless. The referee raised Haonan's right hand in victory. The Chinese team had beaten Korea and Japan by one point. With one voice, all the spectators began to sing *The March of the Volunteers*. Haonan looked out of the ring to see that Guangwei had turned to leave, but Laizhen was still there, smiling and applauding for Haonan.

Haonan put his right fist inside his left palm, greeting the audiences on all four sides. Then he ran two steps and suddenly leapt into the air, his left leg straight out and his right leg folded under, looking straight ahead, his right fist touching his left palm.

Gradually the spectators began to leave. It turned out Suganao Hitoshi had to be sent, on a stretcher then in an ambulance, to the nearby people's hospital with severe concussion.

Haonan could now hold the gold cup for the 65kg class in the 1st China, Korea and Japan Fighting Platform Competition. Though the cash prize was only 3,000 yuan, it was worth far more to him than Guangwei's dirty 300,000 yuan bribe.

When Haonan walked down from the platform, a tall foreign- looking man with blue eyes and a big nose followed him. When Haonan went into the dressing room to change, the foreigner stood at the doorway, as if he was preventing girls from breaking in. The man asked his translator to invite Haonan to sit in a room. The translator asked, "Do you have an English name?"

"Bruce Zhou," was Haonan's reply.

"You must have been inspired by Bruce Lee," the foreigner said in English.

"Of course. That's why I call myself Bruce."

The foreigner gave Haonan a card with the name "William Jackson" printed on it. Haonan had collected more than a hundred American business cards, and on none of them was a US country name or phone code printed. It seemed that the Americans believed that everyone in the world knew the names of their fifty states and their country phone code, 001.

William asked in surprise, "How come you speak such fluent and smooth English?"

"I was a translator in my previous work," Haonan replied in English. As the two continued to talk, the translator was left on the sidelines.

William said he had read that in Shenzhen, for the first time in China, Sanda boxing matches were being staged in a night club, so he had flown specially from the USA to watch. He had seen all Haonan's splendid matches and found that his technique was not only practical but stylish. So he had decided to invite him to fight in Las Vegas, the great US gambling city.

"Las Vegas?" Haonan said in excitement.

William explained that he was a boxing promoter like Tang King, who had handled Mike Tyson. If Haonan signed with him to fight in Las Vegas, he would be the first Chinese fighter in the USA. He was sure he knew how to develop Haonan into a worldwide lightweight superstar boxer. In Las Vegas the prize money from one match was more than any in night clubs in Shenzhen. He said the boxers who had signed with him all owned Ferraris and seaside villas. US dollars and beautiful American girls would all be waiting for Haonan. After finishing his speech, William tapped his chair and waited for Haonan's happy agreement.

Haonan had made up his mind to fight in Shenzhen. He had not expected this new opportunity to get rich quickly. MGM Hotel? Muhammad Ali? Evander Holyfield? Mike Tyson? Printing money by boxing? Was this way to enjoy a life of luxury, like the kings of boxing? This had been his daydream, but now it seemed within his reach. His heart thumped with excitement, thinking of the reputation and money he could gain. When he came back to Shenzhen in the future and saw Laizhen again, would Yellow Hair still be so arrogant? A smile floated on his lips.

But if he moved to the city of gambling, he did not know when he would come back to Shenzhen again; maybe one year, maybe two, or even longer. Now that he had this chance to go abroad, he suddenly felt a boundless love for his native Shenzhen and his mother, still in West Canton.

And then that picture of the old peasant woman carrying heavy firewood along the long mountain road to Nawu came back to his mind. He remembered how she had carried a boy on her back as she laboured and sweated... He had already left his mother far away, and now he was thinking of going even further from...

At last he made his decision. He would stay in Shenzhen. When he explained, William gave a deep sigh. But before leaving, he said, "I've come a long way. I watched several days of matches and among all the boxers in China, Korea and Japan, I chose you because you are second to none. You are giving up a golden chance. Such a pity! But I respect your decision."

After that Haonan said goodbye and walked out of that room. Wherever he went he was respected as a hero, and people were all in a hurry to shake hands with him. The girl fans showed their white backs so that Haonan could sign their bodies in ink.

It was about two o'clock in the morning, and Yang Xiaolong and the four friends had left. As usual Haonan left alone. The breeze blew. Colourful lights shone on the streets and there were a few taxis but no pedestrians.

Suddenly four men got out of a saloon car and blocked his way. Their leader was Guangwei. Beside him was the man in black who had tried to bribe him. The other two were Lei Dong, the man who had once knocked him out, and the boxer from southern Shaolin whom he had defeated.

"Little fool! You refused us!" the man in black said.

"You could have made 300,000 yuan, but you turned me down," Guangwei said angrily.

"Why should I accept?" replied Haonan.

"No one turns me down and gets away with it," Guangwei sneered. After the match he had called Lei Dong and the man from Shaolin. Lei Dong could easily knock Haonan down, and the Shaolin

304

man just wanted revenge. The two fighters advanced on Haonan, the Shaolin man holding a stick.

Haonan recoiled a little and flicked his hand to his back, drawing out a hidden weapon – a pair of stainless steel Nunchakus, 76 cm long, its A and B clubs linked by a chain. He had been carrying it in case he needed to defend himself against a Japanese attacker. He now held the deadly Nunchakus in his right hand, and took up the right stand-by posture of Sanda fighting, his right side forward. *You won't defeat me unless you have a gun*! Haonan thought to himself.

The two men stepped closer and Haonan raised his right hand, holding the B club and striking out with the A club in the action known as "the green snake emerging from its cave". The A club struck the wrist of the Shaolin man, who howled in pain. As soon as the A club swung back he struck it out downward to strike Lei Dong. Lei Dong was hit on the right elbow, which disabled his right hand. Two blows in two seconds had put them both out of action. Haonan rushed upon Guangwei, filled with anger, Haonan swiftly kicked him down to the ground.

The man in black, like a dog that always follows its master, hurriedly got into the car with the other three. Guangwei sat in the car, hardly believing what had happened but knowing it was time to get away. The contemptuous look on his face seemed to say, "Haonan, let's wait and see what I'm going to do!"

The car roared off and vanished like a puff of smoke. From the open rear window Laizhen watched Haonan worriedly in the wing mirror.

That night when Haonan returned home, he took a bath, then rubbed his body with the bone-setting liquid. Then he slept through until the next afternoon. His waist was sore and his leg ached. Knocking out a Japanese national Karate champion and then dealing with his later attackers had exhausted him. After getting up he cooked Tianqi steaming chicken, to soothe the sinews and quicken the blood.

As he was drinking the soup, the landlord brought him a letter. This was a surprise. He seldom received letters because most things were communicated by phone. When he opened the letter, it was from Xiaohong, who was still in Chongqing. He had thought she would be coming back to Shenzhen soon. He unfolded it and read it.

Dear Haonan,

It's only a short time that we were together, so we did not know much about each other. At that time I didn't tell you the truth about myself. Actually I got married at the age of 19. I gave birth to a daughter and she is four years old now. Because of gambling, my husband had a lot of debts. That money you gave me has been used to repay his gambling debts, otherwise he would beat our daughter.

The letter went on to explain that on the photo Haonan had seen, the lady who looked like Xiaohong actually was Xiaohong. She did not have an elder sister. The so-called niece was her own daughter. The leukaemia was also fiction.

Haonan had never imagined that with that slim and graceful body, Xiaohong was married with a child. He realised now that when she had pretended she didn't know how to use the phone, she was just trying to trap Haonan.

The letter had hurt him more than being punched in the ring. He threw it on the table and lay almost paralysed on the bed. He pressed his chest and muttered bitterly, "Who would think this powerful body would suffer like this unbearable blow? First Lin Laizhen and now Xiaohong, why do I always sacrifice myself?" He also thought he would have to explain this to his mother, as all the country people knew he had fallen in love with a beautiful girl from Chongqing. But how could he explain it now? Would they think he had lied?

He rose slowly to his feet, walked over to the balcony and looked dizzily down. Gang'xia, this "village in the city", was very like a downtown area of Shenzhen, where shoulders rubbed shoulders and heels touched heels, particularly in the afternoons. He could hear an assortment of music from the stores. One song was very loud:

> *How can the lovely flowers long stay intact,*
> *Or, once loosed, from their drifting fate draw back?*

This was *Sobbing for Fallen Blossoms* from *The Story of the Stone,* a TV series. It was sad and lingering and accurately reflected Haonan's desolation.

Chapter 28
Almost a Man of Property

Haonan had now been fighting for over a year, and he was planning to go back to working in foreign trade. One day he received a message from a man called Li Guoxiong from the Shenzhen Medicine and Health Products I/E Company, inviting him to talk about something. He took a bus to Shangmeilin.

Guoxiong had met Haonan in the Canton Fair. He was the middle-aged man who didn't know English but just pressed his calculator to discuss prices with foreigners. He was a stationery exporter and was doing good business. He rented room 616 in the Aiguo Building on the Meihua road and was in charge of his company's stationery department, bearing the responsibility for profit and loss. There was a screen separating room 616, where Guoxiong sat inside next to the window, and Mrs Li sat near the door.

When Guoxiong had seen Haonan's painstaking approach in the Canton Fair, he had thought Haonan would make a good assistant, if he would work with him. After the fair closed,

Guoxiong and Haonan happened to walk out of the fair together. As they passed Liuhua Park, in the stream of people and vehicles Guoxiong suddenly ran like the wind after a passing taxi, but it was reluctant to stop. Guoxiong kept running until he caught up with the taxi, then tapped the window until the impatient driver pulled up and opened it. "What's the matter with you? Are you sick?" he shouted. "Can't you see my car is full of passengers? If you want a taxi, why don't you queue?"

"No! I don't want a ride. It's just that a bolt has fallen off your right front wheel."

Guoxiong ran back and picked the bolt up, then went back to the driver with it. The driver thanked him and apologised. Seeing all this, Haonan naturally thought what a kind heart Guoxiong had.

When Guoxiong knew Haonan was giving up fighting, he made an appointment to meet him. Guoxiong, a fat man with big nose and long ears, was talkative and knew about astronomy, geography and current affairs. From Saddam's tyranny in Iraq to the 8·10 stock case in Shenzhen, he had his own unique insights. The tall, thin, pale and gentle Mrs Li told Haonan that her husband's knowledge was acquired from reading the newspaper every day. He always spent one to two hours on this, and read it from cover to cover.

As a matter of fact, Guoxiong had been reading and researching *The Romance of the Three*

Kingdoms for many years, and he knew he needed a capable foreign trade businessman, but he also worried that after person he hired had become familiar with the stationary business he would set up his own company to take his business for himself. There is a saying that "A man being used can't be suspected, while a suspected man can't be used", but he could not do both. Haonan seemed an ideal man for the job. Not only was he good at foreign trade, he would not steal the boss's business. There was no doubt that Haonan was the right candidate and had a loyal heart.

They chatted freely for a long while, and then Guoxiong asked about Haonan's requirements. Haonan replied, "Nowadays what I want most is a small house, one room with reception hall is enough. I also want a Shenzhen Permanent Residence Permit."

Guoxiong said, "That's easy. If you join us, I'll buy a house for you. And since our department has been creating so much foreign exchange currency, I can also get a Shenzhen Permanent Residence Permit for you."

Haonan listened happily, feeling as if a spring breeze was caressing him.

"The salary I'll offer you will be 2,500 yuan monthly. At the end of the year there will be an additional bonus of 20,000 yuan, whether we make a profit or a loss." In fact in many years of foreign trading, he had never made a loss.

Haonan nodded.

Guoxiong went on, "At the end of this corridor there is a small attic, used as an annexe to room 616. Although only one bed can be put inside, you can stay there. But you'll have to use the public toilet. Anyway, as soon as you buy a new house, you can move. So start looking into getting a new house, and decide on the location. I'll pay the full price of the house, and it will be deducted from your salary in installments."

"I have a deposit of 46,000 yuan which can be used as the first payment," said Haonan. This was his boxing winnings.

"That will be better," said Guoxiong. "The name on the Property Ownership Certificate will be yours and we'll work together, so what should I worry about?" Optimistic and extrovert, he laughed so loudly that Mrs Li on the other side of the screen laughed too. Haonan thought happily that his distant dream would be realised soon and he would bring his mother to live with him in Shenzhen. *But Laizhen, where are you now? Will you still reject me because I don't have a house?*

"What are you smiling for?" asked Mrs Li.

Haonan got a grip of himself and hurriedly expressed thanks to Guoxiong. "Sure! You have a kind heart," he said.

"The banks in Shenzhen will soon be providing mortgages, a new way of buying a house," said Guoxiong.

"You are my bank, and you're even more reliable than the real bank," said Haonan, smiling. When he had worked in the bank, the remuneration had been so magical that he had felt as if he had won the first prize in a lottery. But in this company he could feel his remuneration was what he created for himself.

"Don't mention it. We'll work side by side. The money can't be earned by one man alone," said Guoxiong, laughing again.

Haonan would get a house in his own name, along with a Shenzhen Permanent Residence Permit by the year end. And as for Guoxiong, he would have an excellent professional assistant who would create more business for him.

Guoxiong rose to his feet and opened his window, and fresh air blew in. Outside construction was under way. A long crane jib was lifting a big bundle of shaped steel bars and the scaffolding was going up layer by layer. In this rising city Haonan would possess his own space. He was grinning from ear to ear.

One week later, carrying his belongings, including a pillow brought back from Anhui Province, Haonan moved from Gang'xia to Meihua road. He was to live in the attic Guoxiong had mentioned. It was less than five square metres, but at least it was rent free.

In the dim light of early morning, there were few pedestrians on the street. Haonan rode his bicycle down the Meihua road on this cold winter morning. Without gloves, his hands were frozen stiff on the handlebars. He had to risk taking his hands off sometimes to knead them enough to bring back a little warmth.

He had got up very early, and he would have liked to sleep a little longer under the quilt. But finally, after giving himself "just one more minute" several times, he had to force himself to get up without further delay, for he had to race against time. This morning he was required to be the first one to arrive at the customs clearance office in Huanggang, and his documents of customs clearance had to be the first ones to be handed over at the window for inspection, because one container load of pencils had to pass the customs checkpoint, then be loaded in Hong Kong and shipped to the port of Felixstowe, UK, where an importer needed them urgently.

After getting off work he rode to his future home, taking a tape measure with him, because he was trying to work out how he could create a separate space for his mother to stay in. To do this he had to walk in and out of the construction site, and in his safety helmet he looked like a new worker there, which made the construction manager frown, thinking he had employed a strange worker. At last he chose room 739 Feixu

Garden on Bagua 2nd Road, Futian District, an apartment with one room and one reception hall totalling 50 square metre. As a new building, its unit price was 5,000 yuan higher, amounting to a total of more than 200,000 yuan.

One warm April day under a deep blue sky, Haonan sat in Guoxiong's van. They were going to arrange full payment for the property. Inside the Industrial and Commercial Bank on Meihua road, Guoxiong, smiling, stuffed many bundles of green bank notes into a black bag. Then they rushed to the sales office, following a bus. Suddenly the bus braked hard. Guoxiong stamped on the brakes too, but he could not stop the van in time and it hit the back of the bus. The two vehicles stopped. It turned out that a tricycle had run a red light, and the bus driver had had to do an emergency stop. The tricycle rider had run off.

Guoxiong frowned. Although there was little damage to the van, he was a great believer in fate, and he felt the accident was a sign of bad luck. Normally when he sneezed, he would immediately say loudly in Cantonese, "*Da-Ji-Li-Shi*" (good luck).

There was no need for this to be dealt with by the traffic police, as Guoxiong was fully responsible. He phoned his insurance company about the claim.

Guoxiong was still depressed when he arrived at the sales office, where he received a phone call. Then, sitting down on the sofa with a gloomy face, he said to Haonan, "My wife suggested that although the house has been bought, your name can't be put down as owner, instead it should be mine. However, you can keep the Certificate of Property Ownership."

Hearing that, it was as if thunder had suddenly echoed across the sunny sky. Haonan said nothing for some time.

"I don't have a choice," said Guoxiong. "I must obey my wife because she finances the business. I hope you understand. When you have fully paid for the house, I'll transfer the Certificate of Property Ownership to you, and I will pay the charge."

Haonan was wondering how he could sort this out. He and Guoxiong had agreed that Haonan's name would be on the certificate of property ownership, even though most of the money for the house was being paid by Guoxiong. He still believed that Guoxiong had a kind heart. Meanwhile Guoxiong stressed that he had purchased the house purely to help Haonan. Finally Haonan nodded silently. After the house had been paid for, they went back to the office.

In order to prepare goods for inspection, they often went to Zhejiang Province, where they took the national *Yun* Seven aircraft and visited many stationery factories. In summer it was hot in the plane, so Guoxiong would fan himself with a cattail leaf fan.

They held receptions in grand hotels for foreign businessmen they had met in the Canton

Fair, and Haonan made good use of his English. Afterwards he looked after the buyers step by step, including handling the faxes, quoting and sending samples, signing the contracts, drawing up the export documents, arranging customs clearance, checking the foreign exchange currency, arranging payment to the factories and applying for export tax rebates. During this process the business information were all recorded on CD. As time went by, profit and foreign exchange currency creation was snowballing.

Several months later in their offices, Guoxiong said to Haonan, "The Certificate of Property Ownership is available now". He took out a red notebook and presented it to Haonan, who took it and examined it. How attractive it was, and it still gave off aromas of plastic and ink.

"But I still have to keep it for now," Guoxiong went on. "However, as soon as you make the last payment, I'll transfer it to you and pay the charge."

It seemed to Haonan that after a clap of thunder, hailstones were suddenly falling from the heavens like rocks. *Why can Guoxiong not let me keep it? Does he think that I will try to sell it by myself?* Haonan thought, staring at it longingly, like a baby who had been abandoned by the roadside hungrily crying for milk.

After that happened, Haonan felt the relationship between him and Guoxiong had ended.

He painfully made up his mind that he would have to leave.

He had three disks of data ready to hand to Guoxiong, but now he hesitated. The disks contained full sets of all the standard foreign trade forms used in China, along with all the information relating to their business, including commercial invoices, packing lists and so forth. He suddenly remembered that Fuqiang had once told him that if he had direct stationery importers, he could transfer the business to Fuqiang's import and export company. After the business was smoothly transferred, huge profits would follow. He also knew that if this information was transferred, Guoxiong's business would soon be destroyed. However such behaviour would breach his principles of honesty and trust. So he handed over the disks to Guoxiong and assured him that he had not copied them.

The reason why Guoxiong had changed his mind about the Certificate of Property Ownership was that his wife had pointed out that Haonan's calligraphy was so excellent that he could imitate Guoxiong's handwriting perfectly. If he wanted to he could forge Guoxiong's signature to sell the house, without them knowing. When Haonan learned of this later, he said to himself that he would rather cut off his finger than be accused of this fraud.

But one more thing Guoxiong's wife worried about was that she couldn't be sure when this aggressive young man would go back into the ring to fight at weekends. It would be wonderful if he could always be victorious, but even the boxing kings such as Muhammad Ali and Mike Tyson lost their crowns eventually. Haonan had no medical insurance, so if he was badly hurt in a fight, his employer would have to pay the bill for treatment.

So after getting back the payments he had made on the house, amounting to 46,000 yuan, Haonan left Guoxiong's company.

At that time a girl named Xiao Fang had recently been introduced to Haonan, and they had begun a relationship. She worked as an accountant in a trading company and had a Shenzhen Permanent Residence Permit. At first she was not happy that Haonan did not have one, but she thought this would be granted if they married. The most important thing was that he had a new house, though it wasn't big enough.

Soon everything was ready for the wedding. They had booked the wedding dress and car and had prepared the wedding invitations, which would be sent to their relatives and friends once the day was confirmed. She had heard that a great deal of money could be gained by holding a wedding banquet, so she was busy arranging one.

The evening after Haonan left Guoxiong's company, he invited Xiao Fang to dinner in a restaurant, where he was going to talk about his feelings, hoping to be comforted a little by her. Soon after he had arrived at the restaurant he smelled her jasmine perfume, and in came Xiao Fang. She was gorgeously dressed, with earrings, rings and painted fingernails, and carried a leather handbag. After ordering their meal, he told her, "I have lost my house."

"Pardon?" she asked. He explained, and Xiao Fang was shocked. They did not speak for a time.

Not long after, the food arrived and Xiao Fang ate without speaking. After finishing, she said she was going to the toilet. But time passed and she did not return. Finally Haonan paid the bill and went to the doors of the women's toilets, calling her name. There was no reply. He then went over to the service desk and dialled her cellphone.

"Where have you got to?" he asked.

Xiao Fang replied, "I've come back home, don't call this number again."

"But I have things to talk to you about."

"I don't care what you want to talk about, don't call this number again."

"Then what number shall I use?"

"No number!"

"You're regretting marrying me?"

"Marrying you? You even never fondled my breasts!" was Xiao Fang's firm reply.

"What's happened to you?"

"Nothing. I just think we are incompatible, so let's separate. Don't bother me again!" She hung up. Hearing the beep from the handset, Haonan stared dumbfounded at the handset. What on earth had happened? It was as if the handset itself was questioning him: *why are you still holding me? Put me down!*

Next day he moved back to Gang'xia, and made up his mind that he would never leave there unless he could settle somewhere else for good.

Haonan's elder brother had heart disease, and he was going to use the 46,000 yuan he had saved to pay for treatment in Zhanjiang, but the surgery had been put off to allow Haonan to buy a house. Shortly after Haonan had settled in Gang'xia, his elder brother had a heart attack, and he was told by the hospital that surgery must be carried out at once. Haonan hurriedly rushed to Zhanjiang at midnight bringing the money, plus other money his family had borrowed, making a total of 80,000 yuan, to save his elder brother's life.

At that point mortgages had not been introduced by the bank, so Haonan missed another chance to become a property owner in Shenzhen. He never imagined that in the coming years house prices in Shenzhen would rocket skywards, which would have probably given him the chance to make as much as one million yuan just by selling this apartment at the right time. So missing this opportunity would make him feel great heartache.

Chapter 29
Vanished from the Earth

One day in June 2001, Haonan arrived on the 21st floor of international trade & residence building, bringing his CV to apply for the job of foreign trade businessman with the Shenzhen Dongqi Industrial & Trade Company.

It seemed to him that he had once known this company, which had the same name as the agent through which he previously "exported" the ramie fabric, but the address was different. The general manager was Wang Gexin, who had a big "wealth mole" on his chin and smiled whenever he spoke. This private enterprise sold import and export licences, and made a great deal of profit. Its current main business was importing emulsified refinery oil from Korea, with the customs clearance right of import and export around China.

Wang Gexin began, "Our oil resources are in the Middle East or Singapore, and the import port is Qingdao, which is the largest collecting and distributing oil base in China. It'll be enough if you can be in charge of following this business. In a few days we'll fly to Qingdao together."

Haonan's colleague was called Kuang Dawei and he wore a pair of thick glasses for short sight. He had come from Hubei Province and graduated in English, and he sat beside Haonan. They got on well as soon as they met. Wang's secretary, Wei Jianpin, and Miss Deng, the accountant, were all from Sichuan Province, and were both relatives of Wang. Only five people used the whole floor, so there was too much space.

"Our business volume is so large that we will have to recruit more staff soon, so this office space still isn't enough," Wang said. "The tables and chairs here are rented and they will be changed soon. Our only computer is for Wei Jianpin's sole use."

"That's good," was Haonan's reply.

"I've never seen a man who dealt with oil who was poor," said Wang. He was brimming with energy and vitality. "We have abundant capital, so there are many more businesses for us to deal with such as D2 from Russia, a cathode electrolytic copper from Zambia, urea from Ukraine, charcoal from Indonesia and iron ore from Brazil. What we're dealing in now is real international trade. With reference to the hardware tool you once exported, honestly I don't have any interest in it."

Strictly speaking, Haonan and Kuang Dawei were foreign trade documentary handlers, with salaries of RMB2,000 but meal and accommodation excluded. The two of them often communicated in

English, with the result that their two female colleagues often smiled at these two "fake foreigners". If no customers arrived at the office, Wang would seldom appear. So basically there were two men and two women sitting in the office, and because business had not started, they were able to relax.

The day after Kuang Dawei returned to his home town, Wang handed over a pile of contract drafts to Haonan, requesting him to check them. There were nearly 60 pages. Under the captioned contract was 10,000 metric tonnes of emulsified refinery oil, which meant chartering a ship of 10,000 metric tonnes for transport. The total amount for this contract was US$5 million. According to Wang, after deducting the import duty and value added taxes, the net profit per metric tonne would be more than RMB300, so the profit for the whole contract would be up to RMB3 million. Since 10,000 metric tonnes would be imported monthly and six vessels would be chartered within six months, a profit as high as RMB18 million would be realised.

Haonan spent half a day translating the contract correctly, then put it on Wang's table. When he returned to his desk, his heart was still thumping wildly. Just then Wang returned. He walked over to Haonan and patted his shoulder, smiling encouragingly. "Follow me, there'll be a bright future for you soon!" he said. Haonan was touched.

The next day in the conference room, Haonan attended the business negotiations between Wang and the sellers. Wei Jianping made notes, while the Korean sellers sat on the south side of the long table and the Chinese buyers on the north. When Haonan stepped into the room he was astonished. It was Mr Kim, and Hu Wanzhong! These were the Korean customers he had sold the ramie fabric to.

Haonan was dizzy. He had never imagined that he would see these men again. His heart roared like a tsunami. The previous setback with the ramie fabric export business still hurt. When he shook hands with them, his hand was trembling. Nine years on, the two men looked older, and the lines of ageing were clear on their faces.

They looked at Haonan in surprise. After the ramie fabric, they had begun to handle emulsified refinery oil. They were now operating as a joint venture.

The past, let it be. I must look forward to the future, Haonan thought to himself.

"Do you know each other?" said Wang, seeing Haonan's expression.

"More than that, we have even signed a contract before," Haonan said sadly.

"How come?"

"We'll talk about it later."

Kim said, "Regarding this oil, the specifications, such as ash, flash point, gravity and sulphur content, all meet your requirements, and we can provide the SGS Inspection Certificate. We can even arrange for the China I/E Commodity Inspection Bureau to check them abroad, it will be no problem."

"That's good," said Wang.

"Regarding the L/C (Letter of Credit) at sight under this contract, we hope you can open a transferable L/C to us," Kim said.

"No problem," Wang replied.

"No, we cannot," Haonan contradicted him. "if your bank transfers this L/C to the next supplier and no goods are available, our opening charge, which is 0.15% of the L/C amount, totalling US$7,500.00, will be wasted. We need you to have the goods but not transfer our L/C to the next supplier. Of course if you don't have the goods but have capital, you may use our L/C as mortgage in your bank by which to open the new L/C to your next supplier. This is called back to back L/C in the banking business. So the L/C we open must be non-transferable."

"Yes, we'll open a non-transferable L/C," agreed Wang.

The Korean customers had to accept. "Before you open the L/C, we require that you issue a bank credit letter to certify that you have capital and the ability to open the L/C," Kim said.

"All right," said Wang.

"No, we can't do that," replied Haonan. "We must first receive the 2% PB of yours issued by your bank. You worry that we don't have capital, but likewise, we fear that you don't have the goods to be supplied. How can you prove that you really have the goods? Have you sold this kind of goods before? For this you can let us have a copy of your previous B/L (Bill of Lading), because the B/L is the certificate of goods ownership."

"Yes, we must check a B/L copy," Wang declared.

Kim took out a document from his office bag, "This is the B/L copy for your reference. These goods were exported by us last year."

Haonan took it and scrutinized it for a while. Then he shook his head, "This is a fake. Actually you have never sold this kind of goods."

Wang opened his eyes wide.

Kim said angrily, "You must give us respect! How can you say that our B/L copy is fake?"

Wang threw Haonan an angry glance as well.

Haonan lifted up the B/L copy so that Wang and Wei Jianping could take a look. He pointed out a sentence, saying to Kim, "Take 'Clean on Board' for example. It means that the goods are clean and have been loaded on board. Only by reading it can I judge that this B/L copy is fake."

Kim looked flustered but asked angrily, "How did you judge?"

Haonan explained loudly, "If the goods had been shipped on board in order, there's no need to type 'Clean' on the B/L. But you had typed it already. That means you don't understand the L/C requirements and indeed, you never shipped any goods on board at all."

Haonan spoke so reasonably that Wang and Wei Jianping were amazed. The two customers didn't know what to do for a moment. Finally Kim had to confess. "It's actually not a real B/L, it's only for your reference," he said.

"It can't be regarded as a reference either," Haonan replied promptly. "However, if you do have goods, we still want to conclude this deal with you."

"After signing the contract, we require you first to open the L/C, then we'll issue our 2% PB," said Kim. "After all, you also know that if we don't have the goods to be supplied, a fine of 2% of the contract amount will be paid to you. This is bank credit."

"Certainly," Wang said without hesitation.

"We can't do that either," said Haonan. "Once the contract is signed, you must first open a 2% PB. If you first open a 2% PB but we don't open L/C, you'll lose the bank handling charge of 2% PB, and that will be only US$150. But if we first open L/C but you don't provide us the 2% PB, we'll lose US$7,500..."

Facing such an expert on foreign trade, the Korean customers could find no grounds to refuse.

That evening Wang invited their guests for dinner. After that, Wang left and Haonan saw them off by taxi. Before they went into the hotel, Kim said, "We'd like to give you a book as gift, which was written by Mr Lee Kuan Yew from Singapore." Haonan received it thankfully. When he got back to his lodging, he opened it to find a bundle of cash in the back – 10,000 yuan!

His heart suddenly felt glad. He was so poor just then that he did need the money. After all, it was just these old Korean customers who had hurt him, and 10,000 yuan could scarcely make up for his loss... Nevertheless, it was a commercial bribe. It was apparent that their customers wanted to give him the money to persuade Haonan to relax the rules for future business with them. But that meant he would have to sacrifice the interests of the company.

When Haonan went to the office the next morning, he explained what had happened to Wang and handed him the 10,000 yuan. Wang would never have imagined that Haonan would give him this money. Staring at it, he said happily, "Well done! Please rest assured that I'll hand back this money to our Korean customers."

In the blink of an eye a month had passed, and it was payday for Haonan. But Wang said, "Please wait a little longer. I'm preparing the capital for 10,000 metric tons of oil, and I'll pay your salary a little later." In order to support the business, Haonan and Kuang Dawei accepted this.

Haonan went downstairs. Apart from a bank in the first floor of international trade & residence building, there were also three small offices used by a real estate agent, an air ticket company and a name card printing business. Every day when Haonan passed, the girl who sold the air tickets smiled brightly. Sometimes she asked him, "When will you book a ticket to Qingdao?"

"Soon," he answered.

One day on the way to work he bought the *Southern Metropolis Daily*, which carried a horrible picture of a plane crashing into a high building. This was the terrorist attack on the World Trade Centre in New York. In the days that followed, Haonan and Kuang Dawei talked mostly about the "9/11 disaster".

The draft contract on Wang's desk had not been signed yet. Wang said that the capital for opening the import L/C would be got ready soon, but the emulsified refinery oil was transit-trade, which was mostly purchased by Korean customers from the Middle East, then transshipped to China. Now access had been blocked by the US, so they had to wait.

Two months passed, and still the salaries had not been paid. Wang still told Haonan and Kuang Dawei to wait a little longer. They were unhappy, but they had no alternatives.

Time passed. Soon it was approaching the end of the year, and almost six months had gone by. Since he had not been paid, Haonan had to find the money for all his meals, lodgings and traffic charges. His original limited deposit was running out, and he had to borrow money from friends. Wang told him to wait a little longer, for the effects of the 9/11 disaster would soon pass. He patted Haonan's shoulder, saying, "What are you worrying about? I'll pay you for six months all together. Then you'll get a big red envelope, which will be so heavy you will hardly be able to lift it." Haonan could only lower his head and smile bitterly.

After one sleepless night, Haonan did not finally wake up until nine o'clock. On the road to the office sitting in the minibus, he felt a little chilly. Though the sun shone brightly, the pedestrians all wore winter clothes. Glancing anxiously at the buildings as he passed, Haonan dialled Wang's mobile phone, wanting to explain why he would be late. But the phone was switched off. Haonan thought that perhaps Wang had not yet got up.

Haonan normally bought two steamed buns and a cup of soybean milk for breakfast, but that morning, he decided to go straight to the office in case Wang or a customer was looking for him. When he passed by the breakfast store, the owner stared at him, as though wondering why he was not buying his usual breakfast. On a space nearby, a security chief was shouting to a group of security officers. "Stand upright!" he shouted. "Take a rest!" Then, "Look forward smartly!"

But Haonan didn't hear these words. What he heard was, "Take the interest!" and "Look forward to the salary!"

When he ran into the first-floor lobby, there was a long queue in front of the yellow line, where people were carrying bags of cash ready for depositing; the beautiful girl from the real estate company said to him, "The new apartments are available now, when will you arrange your first payment?"

"Soon," he smiled.

"Why did you run so fast? When will you buy a ticket to Qingdao? Remember to support my ticket business." She patted the table, murmuring to him in her sweet voice.

"Soon," he hurriedly replied again, edging himself into the elevator, which was full to the limit. Inside the elevator, the electric fan above was running slowly. Haonan smelled the taste of perfume and men's body odour. A girl behind him was probably a newcomer, as he had never seen her before. Her high breasts touched his back, so that each time the elevator started up he could feel a pleasant vibration against his spine which reminded him of Lin Laizhen.

When the elevator reached the 21st floor and Haonan walked forward, he somewhat regretted that he had hurried. It was past 10 o'clock, but the glass door was still locked. *Is Wei Jianping, who is in charge of the keys, late as well today?* He couldn't see Miss Deng or Kuang Dawei either. *Are they all later than me today?*

But when he looked inside he saw that all the office equipment had gone. The chair he normally sat on was lying on the floor, abandoned. Waste paper littered the floor. An old and torn file bag lay against the glass door.

A sense of foreboding shrouded his heart. "The company has moved, just like that?" he murmured disbelievingly. He hurriedly pulled out his mobile phone to call Wang, but the response was a recorded message: "The number you dialled does not exist".

Haonan was trembling now. No wonder Wang had kept putting off payday. He had vanished from the earth, and the salary of 10,000 yuan that Haonan was due for half a year had disappeared like a puff of ash.

He called Kuang Dawei, who was on leave to handle the formalities of divorce. Dawei was shocked. "What about the emulsified refinery oil?

Earning three million for every deal? Fuck! Wang is a con man!"

Haonan imagined that the 10,000 yuan he had presented to Wang had not been handed back to the Korean customers, but kept by Wang himself.

After some while, Haonan picked up the torn file bag, went downstairs and left the building, lowering his head so that the girls in the real estate and air ticket offices didn't recognise him, which saved him another round of gentle calls to buy from them. He walked towards the railway station at Dongmen Road South. The winter sun shone on this prosperous city, and the International Trade Centre Building and Sunshine Hotel stood out majestically. People hurried to and fro.

He sat down on a bench and opened the file bag. It was a pile of I/E contracts and customs clearance documents from long ago, dated 1993. He saw the words "ramie fabric". Did Dongqi Industrial & Trade Company also export it? At that time he had purchased the export licence for ramie fabric from this company, but the goods had never been exported. Of course they themselves owned the licence, so they could export ramie fabric directly. He searched through the papers. The importer: Winners Trading Co. Then he saw the names: Kim. The joint signatures of Hu Hangong and Wang Gexin. Three years of contracts...

Haonan shook, and the files fell to the ground. He bent down to piece together the evidence.

That night years ago on the square of Luohu railway station, after Kim and He Manzhong had left for Hong Kong, had they returned to Korea next day? No! Hu Hangong had already arranged for them to come back to Shenzhen the next day. Later Hu Hangong had done the deal in the name of Dongqi Industrial & Trade Company, gaining huge profits.

Haonan walked into an IC kiosk to pretend to dial someone, but really he was crying secretly. Unfortunately he was soon impatiently ejected by a little girl behind who really wanted to phone. He had to leave, and cried tearfully to the sky, "Oh! In Shenzhen I even can't find a place to have a loud cry..."

Chapter 30
The Golden Bed

When Haonan walked to Dongmen, hanging his head in sadness, he saw a small poster sticking on a wall announcing: "MALE SERVANTS WANTED IN THE HOTEL, MONTHLY INCOME RMB20,000". He had seen it hundreds of times before, but never paid it any attention. But now, a sudden thought seized him. He stopped and pulled out his mobile phone to call the number on it. He was answered by a man with a deep voice who asked him, "Can you last for up to two to three hours every time?"

"Yes, I can control the time and tempo," was Haonan's reply.

"I've never heard of such a superman! Please go to the lawn in front of the Hubin Hotel on Hubei Road and wait for me!"

Ten minutes later, Haonan arrived at the appointed place and stood on the lawn. His phone rang, and the same voice asked, "Is that you on the side of lawn, middle height, strongly built?"

"Yes."

About five minutes later, a man with a tattoo on his wrist walked up to Haonan and said, "Follow me, the customer is waiting for you." He led Haonan to a coffee shop two hundred metres away, where there were only a few clients. The man then made a call on his phone, in a tongue that Haonan didn't understand.

Shortly after that, a black woman of middle height came in and sat at their table. She was fat, with legs as big as buckets, but she pushed her black glasses to the top of her head like a movie star. She wore a gold necklace and huge gold earrings which looked as if they belonged in a circus. Her lips were painted with thick lipstick. As he looked at her, Haonan felt dizzy.

After a while, the woman nodded to the man and opened her big red mouth. Then she went to the toilet. The man said to Haonan, "Congratulations! She has chosen you. You can go to work immediately. And if you can do three hours as you said, you will earn three thousand yuan."

"Three thousand yuan?" Haonan was dumbfounded, wondering how he could get such good business.

"The customer will go to check-in in the hotel. Remember, she may make a special request, or use the leather crop and handcuffs. If you can satisfy her, you will earn an additional two thousand yuan."

"Special requirement?" Haonan didn't understand at first, but gradually he got it. He bowed his head and sighed. Now he had nothing of value except his prick.

"Please feel free to do it! We still have more customers, it just depends on your ability," the man said, laughing. "Take a cup of water first!" Haonan drank from the cup...

A few moments later, Haonan found himself opening the door of a hotel. The glitter of gold was so dazzling that he hastily had to cover his eyes with his hand. This was the first time he had entered such a big, luxurious room. The tables, chairs and crockery were all in gold. A bed beside the wall was covered with a golden Raschel quilt, the soft carpet was golden and even the washing basin and toilet bowl appeared to be in pure gold. The woman he had met appeared and asked him to close the door. The golden quilt was slowly uncovered, and the woman sat there in nothing but a gold-rimmed bra.

"Come here, baby," she said.

Haonan walked shakily towards the golden bed. She said, "Don't be afraid. I'm still a virgin today."

Normally if Haonan had heard this, he would have laughed, but not today. He obeyed her impatient summons and mounted her body. It was like piercing a tortoise's shell.

"How elastic your strong muscle is!" gasped the woman. "And how smooth! What an attractive six-pack you have! Your chest muscles are even bigger than my breasts!" The woman talked without ceasing, seeming as intoxicated as if she was tasting a bottle of excellent red wine.

Haonan closed his eyes and pumped like a piston. "You can't stop!" demanded the woman. "Oh my god!"

And so it continued. A little later she murmured, "That was my sixth orgasm in an hour. It's the first special experience I've had in more than forty years. All my husbands together could not compete with one round of yours today."

Haonan pretended not to hear. Sometimes when he felt he would have to "shoot", he slowed the tempo a bit, but the woman protested, "Don't slow down!" and he then had to accelerate again hastily. His treasured weapon was like a diamond drill used in porcelain works, hard and hot. As he had been preventing ejaculation for so long, his penis was becoming seriously congested.

At last the three hours had passed, and the woman under him shook his shoulders and burst out howling like a volcano exploding. "No need for the leather crop and handcuffs, that's nine times! Fantastic!" And then, like two marathon runners finishing shoulder by shoulder, they collapsed on the golden bed. Yet while she was happy, Haonan was sad. He had exhausted himself, yet he had not eaten even a grain of rice that day.

After a moment, the woman stood up and fished out a bundle of cash from her handbag. It was 10,000 yuan. She drew out half of the notes and threw them down on the bed, then patted his shoulders, opened the door and left.

Haonan impatiently picked the money up, counting it faster than a bank counting machine: it was exactly 5,000 yuan...

Haonan woke up suddenly. Someone was shaking his shoulder. He looked around the dim coffee shop. "Wake up, please sir!" said the waitress. "We're closing now."

It turned out that before the man had left, he had put a sedative into Haonan's glass of water and he had slept all afternoon. What he had experienced just now had all been a dream. Alarmed, he touched his pocket. "Oh my god!" he murmured. His mobile phone, along with several hundred yuan, were all gone.

He went hurriedly to the counter and dialled the number he had used before. But all he got was a recorded message saying the phone was switched off. He put down the phone and walked shakily to the door, but the waitress stopped him. "Sir, you have not paid the bill. Coffee, water and dessert for three people, total 240 yuan."

Haonan stopped, turned his head, forced a smile and searched his pockets. There was still 250 yuan left at the bottom of a secret pocket. It was enough to pay the bill, but it left him with only 10 yuan. He walked out onto the street, and the sorrow rushed back. Full of remorse and self-reproach, he walked to the bus station, paying two yuan for his bus back to his flat. Without taking off the clothes, he threw himself onto the bed, burying his head in the pillow. Now he had a better place to cry, but he had no tears left. Gradually he fell into a miserable sleep.

When he finally awoke and heaved himself sleepily up, it was eight o'clock in the evening, and he was extremely hungry. His head seemed heavier than ever and all he had was eight yuan. What was he going to do? He stood at the window and stared down at the scene below.

In a "village in the city" like Gang'xia, eight o'clock in the evening was the busiest time for everyone. A loudspeaker in front of a Chaozhou hardware shop was playing 24 hours a day in the typical Chaozhou mandarin style, saying, "This is the last day of our clearance, don't miss your chance!" A board in the nearby shoe store announced, "The price of jumping off a building for the last day!" The characters of that one had been written by Haonan at the owner's request, in return for a pair of "Old Man" shoes costing 200 yuan. After he had been wearing them for two weeks, water got into them when it rained.

Opposite the shoe shop was a Meizhou restaurant. Since its menu was also written by Haonan, he sometimes went there for fast food, for which he got a ninety percent discount.

Haonan's gaze moved on, to a clinic, which he always passed on his way home. Seeing this gave him an idea, and he headed downstairs. First he went to the restaurant for a meal of Fungus Fried Meat for seven yuan. Normally he ate four or five bowls here - the rice was always free - but today he ate eight bowls, like a hungry wolf. This was his breakfast, lunch and supper all together.

While he ate he was still thinking what had happened that day. Finally he walked to the wash basin to wash his face. He raised his head, sadly looking at himself in the mirror. A serving girl who was passing stopped to ask, "Why are you crying?"

He hurriedly lowered his head and poured a handful of water to his face. "Who said I was crying?" he said. "It's water!"

Haonan finished his food and left quickly. He now had only a single yuan. He walked into the clinic next door and stood by the birth control counter.

"Hey, young man! Do you want Durex or Natural Latex?" a middle-aged woman wearing a white gown asked him. "One yuan each, you can buy in bulk. You don't need to be shy. Durex is really good, it's thin and durable," the woman continued, as if she had much experience of it.

"No, no." He walked away and went inside, saying to a female doctor, "Are you still in charge of blood?"

The doctor smiled understandingly. She guided him into a quiet room, where the light was dim and various medicines and items of medical equipment were on the table. She told him to take a seat, then disinfected his left middle finger with alcohol. Then she used a sharp piece of glass to cut his fingertip. Immediately his blood sprayed into her face, like a water pistol.

"Shit! Why did you spray so much blood?" she said. She took some tissues to wipe her face. Then she took the blood to inspect it. After some time, she came back. "It's O type. The transaminase enzymes are on a little high side but still in the normal range. You didn't have much sleep last night, did you?"

He nodded.

In Europe there is a sort of horse with protruding veins which is highly regarded. Now Haonan had just such prominent veins. When the needle was inserted into the big vein at the corner of his left elbow, he didn't feel much. His blood flew slowly into a bag, which was constantly shaken by the doctor without ceasing. When the volume was up to 800 ml, she withdrew the needle and let him use a piece of absorbent cotton to press the wound for fifteen minutes.

He stood up, and the doctor gave him 600 yuan. She told him, "As long as you feel well, you may come here. For most people, at least three months are required between donations, but for you, a month or two is enough."

He nodded. This was the last day for him to pay the rent. From what he had earned by selling the blood, he used 500 yuan for rent. That evening the landlord appeared in his Mercedes S320 to collect the rent, and wrote a receipt for him. The money from his blood wasn't even enough to fill a tank of gasoline. Suddenly Haonan felt that his landlord's car was filled was his blood instead of oil.

In the days that followed, he survived by eating dried radish or soy sauce rice. He tightened his belt day by day.

It was more than twenty days before the lunar New Year arrived, the first time Haonan had returned home for it so early. For every Spring Festival before, he had always regretted not being able to stay at home longer. This year, he did not have to worry about returning to Shenzhen immediately for work afterwards. He stayed at home, and each night he took a long sleep, saying he was catching up on his rest. When his relatives asked him what had happened, he said little. He was like a Buddhist monk lost in meditation. If he had to go out, he always looked outside carefully before stepping outside, like a rat looking around before crawling out of a cave. When he appeared in the village, he scurried around like a spy because he was afraid of meeting people who would ask him how he was able to take so much holiday. He liked it when it rained, because he could hide under an umbrella.

On New Year's Eve there was happiness in the villages, but in Haonan's family kitchen, it was very different. He sat on a short stool facing the burning firewood with his mother. The branches and bamboo twigs were crackling, and the blazing fire shone red on their faces. His mother clipped several burning lumps of charcoal into a "warm basket" held under her knees, then her hands covered the charcoal for warmth; this had been the traditional way of getting warm in West Canton for thousands of years.

She asked again what progress he had made towards getting married, and when he told her there was none, she gave a deep sigh.

"How's your work?" his mother asked.

Haonan could not hide the truth any longer. He had to describe how Wang had vanished without paying him. However, he did not tell her he had sold his blood. He had planned to do that one more time so that he could earn the money for New Year shopping for the family, but he had not completed the recovery period.

Facing his mother, who was getting older and weaker day by day, he muttered, "A'shen, I didn't bring anything to you this time." Then he buried his head in his hands. Formerly he had always brought a bird's nest, ginseng or deer's antlers for his parents.

Mother was dumbfounded. "Haonan, you're silly!" she said warmly. "I don't know how you have spent your time. Anyway, coming back here healthy and safe before the lunar New Year so that I can meet you is the best gift you can give me."

Soon his father and elder brother came and sat with them. Haonan described his experience again. His father, who always took hardships and insults lying down, said nothing and his elder brother ground his teeth. Haonan recalled his father's bitter experience many years before, and how his mother had supported the family alone. Now Haonan could not stop the tears any longer. They dropped like pearls on the burning firewood, making it crackle and give off wisps of black smoke.

Not long after this, on top of a building in the distance, some children lit a huge rocket gun, and it whistled into the sky, exploding into colourful flowers. Then a firecracker went off with a loud bang. The new spring had arrived.

Chapter 31
Conscience

One March afternoon, Haonan appeared in the Shenzhen talent market. He needed a job. It was afternoon, and most people had already left.

He came to a booth where two women were working. One of them asked him, "Are you interested in a job as a foreign trade executive?" He presented his resumé.

"How long have you worked in the foreign trade?" she asked.

"About ten years."

"Then you must know what FOB stands for?"

"Yes, Free on Board."

"OK, you can report to work tomorrow."

At nine o'clock the next morning, Haonan arrived at the new company, which was the American NDN International Holding Group, Shenzhen Branch. He arrived at the 22nd floor to find that the whole floor, as well as the one above, belonged to the NDN Group. The offices and corridors were full of people. The staff all wore suits and ties and all were hurrying, carrying A4 sized cases. The floors were divided into areas of fifteen square metres by screen, and each had eight office tables joined back to back, two employees sharing each one. Fortunately the air conditioning was running and the air pump was busy circulating air, otherwise it would have been stifling. Only in the Canton Fair had Haonan seen such a busy scene before.

One of the women he had seen in the talent market appeared and introduced herself as Shen Wenying. "The executives here don't have salaries, and the company don't pay for food and lodging," she explained. "But the business profits are shared half and half. The work is challenging. The NDN Group is in charge of helping Chinese factories to expand their export business. We sign export agreements with them, and for this we charge a fee of 40,000 yuan. Afterwards we'll promote their products in the US, even sell to the government purchase group from the White House. You're very professional and you have a lot of experience, so you'll be able to do this well."

Haonan had never done this kind of work without a salary before, but a profit based on half-sharing was attractive to him. NDN's location in the International Trade Centre Building, the golden area of the Luohu district, told him it must be a powerful company.

Old Li, who sat nearby, said, "Provided you get the sample from the factory and they sign the agreement with us, after they pay, we are certain to export their products to the US". He was over sixty with white hair, and very experienced.

"But before the price is agreed, and before the American importer confirms the sample and the payment terms, does the factory expect us to pay us the 40,000 yuan as an export working fee?" said Haonan doubtfully.

"These are only small problems," said the vice general manager, David Wu, who was next to Lao Li. His thick hair was neatly combed backwards. Later Haonan learned that Wu and old Li always appeared together in every discussion of the company, and they were known in NDN as "Two King Kong". Whenever the two of them attended negotiations, they won the trust of the factory.

"You can do some good business here," Wu and old Li jointly encouraged Haonan.

Shen Wenying said, "You invite the factories to come here one by one. I, Wu and old Li will work with you together. We're a team."

Haonan finally made up his mind to try the job. He could always leave if conditions were not favourable. After all, this was work, not being kidnapped. He thought to himself: *I'm not worth enough to be kidnapped.*

No sooner had Haonan and Shen Wenying come back to their small office than Xiao Chen, one of the foreign trade executives, jumped on his office table and waved his arms, exclaiming, "I did it! I did it! I got paid already!" Several colleagues applauded him. Several executives who were waiting to send faxes, stopped to join in the celebration.

It turned out that Xiao Chen had signed an export cooperative agreement with a textile factory in Jiangxi province yesterday, and he had just been told by the accounting department of NDN Group that the RMB40,000 had been received from the factory. Xiao Chen would immediately get a bonus of RMB20,000 from the accounting department – even the 20% personal income tax would be exempted.

Then a cheerful voice was heard from the next room. Another executive had also received payment from the factory.

Haonan was impressed. The bonus from just one order was equal to his salary for a whole year.

Every day after that, Haonan worked with a group of ten colleagues, all relying on a single phone. He contacted factories they recognised or knew from the Yellow Pages directory. Always you heard the same thing: "How do you do? This is American NDN International Holding Group, Shenzhen Branch, we're in charge of promoting your products in the USA market..."

Haonan soon realised that although they were hungry for money, they knew nothing about foreign trade and spoke no foreign languages.

Haonan wondered how they could engage in foreign trade, and he reported his concerns to Wu.

The result of this was that the next day all the executives gathered in the conference hall and sat at small tables, arranged by Wu so that Haonan could give them a lesson in foreign trade. This was the first time he had taught like this, but since he was so familiar with foreign trade he could face such a crowd with confidence, knowing he could be questioned by anyone about anything.

"In foreign trade activity, what price terms are generally used?" someone asked.

"We use mainly FOB, CFR and CIF," Haonan said briefly.

"What does an export quotation consist of?"

"It has four parts: price terms, currency symbol, price figure and counting unit. For example, US$5.00/Pc FOB Tianjin." He wrote this on the white wall board with a black oil pen.

"Teacher Zhou, how can you write Chinese and English so well?" someone asked.

"Thanks for your praise. The most important thing is interest, then practice," Haonan went on. "One thing to be noticed is there are six points for the ellipsis in Chinese, but only three for English. This is one of the differences between Chinese and English. In a foreign trade letter, 'look forward to' can't be followed by the original form of the verb, instead it should be the gerund or noun. 'Deposit' and 'Down Payment' are similar but different…"

Then Wu stood up. "You don't have to speak so professionally and profoundly," he said.

Haonan replied, "Fair enough. These points can't be grasped within a short time. For an international trade major at college, four years are required. At work, let's learn on the job."

But after finishing the two-hour lesson, Haonan felt sad. Many years later when he recalled the above scene he couldn't help laughing secretly: he had never imagined in such a so-called international trade holding group that apart from him, nobody had graduated as foreign trade major. How could such a company engage in foreign trade?

One day a couple of weeks later, Haonan received a phone call from Zhu, the managing director of Mingguang Arts & Crafts Factory in Anhui Province. He said he had just arrived in Shenzhen. He was bringing a big bag of soft toy samples, and he would reach Haonan's company soon.

"Hi! Long time no see." Haonan shook hands with Zhu in the conference room of NDN. "I'm so sorry I didn't go to Los Angeles with you that year. How is your business now?"

"Growing little by little, but it could be better. Without your help, how can we do better? However, now that you can help us to exploit the export market, it's more than I had expected."

Wu and old Li came into the room, and Haonan introduced them to Zhu. When they discussed the export agreement with NDN, Zhu asked, "Shall we hand in the export work fee before we export our goods?"

"Yes," old Li said hurriedly.

"Why can't you deduct it from the amount received after concluding the deal? We may pay NDN commission after that," Zhu said.

"But who will do the initial work? We must send your samples to the US to conclude the deal with the importers," Wu said.

"In the event of the deal failing, we'll double compensate you, that is RMB240,000. But don't we have here the most trustworthy man to supervise the deal for you?" He indicated Haonan.

Zhu was still doubtful, but he felt that what old Li said was reasonable. The most important thing was that Haonan was present. So finally he signed the agreement.

"We'll certainly give you the ideal payback. Please get ready for customs clearance soon!" said old Li excitedly, holding Zhu's hand tightly.

After Zhu left, Wu, old Li and Shen Wenying congratulated Haonan. "You've made a good start," said Wu.

So Haonan had finally signed an order. According to the rule in NDN, there was an export work fee of as much as 120,000 yuan, and when Zhu's payment was received, Haonan would get half this as bonus – 60,000 yuan. It was like rain finally falling after a long drought. This bonus would be vital to him. After the bitter shock of Wang's disappearance, Haonan had entirely lost his drive, so he now had a profitable deal to bring back his confidence.

That night Haonan invited Zhu for dinner, and they happily drank much wine. "Can you still remember the crackling noise on the top of building when I lived in your factory that summer?" said Haonan. "I talked about it with others after that. We concluded that it must be expansion and contraction with heat and cold."

Zhu laughed. "I thought at first that there were two lonely young girl ghosts who were stealing your virginity!"

Early the next day Zhu returned to his factory. According to the agreement, he would arrange payment by the third working day. So that day Haonan waited for the money to come through. However, he felt anxious, for he had seen that after his colleagues received the working fees from the factories, they transferred all their energies to new factories and entirely forgot all the factories they had signed agreements with before. Similarly, NDN paid no heed to this matter. How could they be promoting sales for the factories who had signed? The more Haonan thought about this, the worse he felt.

On the way back from the rest rooms, he passed Wu's office and saw through the window that there was a collection of Zhu's animal toys, the little bear, the mouse, the cat and so on. Haonan was surprised. These were the samples Zhu had brought two days before. Why hadn't they been despatched by courier to the US?

Haonan recalled that when he had given his lesson, none of the employees, including Wu and old Li, knew anything about foreign trade. He also recalled how when he was in the Zhu's factory all the female workers had lain on the ground exhausted after a night of working overtime. Furthermore, he thought about why the foreign workers were mostly from Nigeria and Bangladesh and lived in little rented houses nearby...

Suddenly Haonan understood that none of these people were real foreign merchants. They were just here to enable NDN to operate its deception.

He hurried downstairs and walked into an IC kiosk, where he dialled Zhu's mobile phone.

"Have you arrived at the factory?" he asked.

"Yes, but no need to push me. I've arranged for the accountant to go to the bank to make the payment."

"So have you paid yet?"

"Don't be so nervous! Don't you believe me? The payment is being made now. So please get your accountant to check in your bank. It'll be OK."

"You really are paying 120,000 yuan?"

"My god! Isn't that what we both signed for? Do you think it's not enough? If so, I could consider arranging an additional ten thousand or two for you," said Zhu.

Haonan took a deep breath and suddenly howled, "Zhu – don't make the payment!"

"What's happened? You're not keeping your word? But we have both signed the agreement."

"No, I don't mean that. Don't arrange payment!"

"You want to breach the agreement between us again?"

"No, I don't mean that." Haonan did not know why it was so difficult for him to find the correct words. He was also afraid that he might be overheard by someone from NDN nearby. He hastily looked around.

"So what the hell has happened?"

Finally, Haonan bellowed into the phone, "NDN is a dishonest company!"

Zhu was as shocked as if he had been struck by lightning. He immediately ended the call and phoned his accountant, who was arranging the payment in the bank. "The payment must be stopped right now!" he ordered.

"Why? I have nearly completed it," replied the puzzled accountant.

"Stop right now! Tear the draft up!" Zhu cried hysterically.

"All right, no problem!"

When Haonan dialled Zhu's phone again, he was told that the transfer had been stopped. Now he could breathe a sigh of relief. When he left the kiosk, he was as relaxed as a prisoner who has just got out of jail.

He looked up at the sky, feeling that his heart was as high as the heavens. Yet he was trembling again. He hastily went to the Luohu police station opposite, saying to the officer on duty, "I'd like to report that on the 22nd and 23rd floors of the International Trade Centre Building, the NDN company is involved in a huge foreign trade swindle."

After giving his statement, he walked out in confidence. For his personal safety, the police told him not to return to the NDN office. He did not.

Once they had assessed the case, the police promptly took action to seal off the NDN Group. David Wu, an oversea Chinese man, was detained as a criminal. There would be a public prosecution for commercial embezzlement.

It was said later that according to Wu's verbal confession, the real boss, who never appeared at NDN, was Chen Guangwei. It was he who had made the investment to set up this dishonest company. Since so many debts around China had to be compensated, he was almost bankrupted and was sentenced to six months in prison.

Chapter 32
The Struggle in Dongxing

The autumn sun shone from a blue sky on to the Beilun River, which is spanned by Dongxing City, Guangxi and Mangjie City, Vietnam. The friendship bridge between China and Vietnam is the only road between these two cities. The Dongxing side was full of black Vietnamese women who wrapped their faces in towels. Speaking in poor Chinese, they ceaselessly promoted various Vietnamese native products, or offered to exchange Vietnamese dollars for RMB. With the trading agreement signing between China and ASEAN, foreign trade activity between China and Vietnam was increasing.

In August 2007, Haonan went to Dongxing again; he had once spent three months there learning the Vietnamese language for daily and business use. He went with his business partner, Leng Jinxiong, who was in his fifties and from Hunan Province. Jinxiong was a big man with an explosive temper and he dealt solely with business in Shenzhen.

The first time they met, they sat in a noodle restaurant in Futian and ordered noodles and drinks. After negotiating for an hour they signed an agreement, in which there were clauses that charges would be borne individually, customers mutually sharing and profits being split equally. When it was time to pay the bill, which was only 30 yuan, Jinxiong started picking his teeth with a toothpick and pretended not to notice, so Haonan paid it without more ado. Then they went out to the bus station.

"I have two coins in change for you," Haonan said to Jinxiong, to express his enthusiasm. Jinxiong had thousands of yuan in his pocket, as well as loose change, but he replied happily, "How thoughtful of you," and stretched out his hand to take the coins. Unfortunately they fell to the ground and rolled several metres away. He hurriedly bent down and hunted for them, and finally picked them up and clutched them tightly. Seeing this gave Haonan an uncomfortable feeling.

The following month they went to Xinning on business, and all their business expenses were borne by Haonan, with money he had borrowed. Jinxiong visited Haonan's home several times, using it to receive airmail and packages. Haonan wondered why he did not use his own address. Would he also use Haonan's home to receive marijuana and heroin? Several times Haonan passed by where Jinxiong lived, saying he would like to visit, but Jinxiong always said, "I'm leaving now," so Haonan never saw his home.

Haonan had never imagined that in Dongxing he would meet Chen Guangwei again. Jinxiong had mentioned that there was profitable business to be done there in mahogany, as it was popular for furniture. But when they reached Dongxing, Jinxiong told him the buyer was Guangwei.

On hearing this, Haonan wanted to leave immediately and return to Shenzhen. But Jinxiong said, "Are you wealthy now? Why do you regard money as an enemy? What's wrong with earning money from Guangwei? I'm not asking you to sleep with him." Then Haonan had to accept.

One day in November Haonan signed a contract to supply Guangwei with a large quantity of dark red Dalbergia cochinchinensis, obtained from a man called Yefeng. It filled three forty-foot containers. Haonan was only a middle-man. Haonan purchased a total of 1.4 million yuan, then sold it to Guangwei for two million, making a profit of 600,000. This was a joint business venture for Haonan and Jinxiong. Jinxiong had gone to Indonesia for another deal, so Haonan was responsible for their business in Dongxing.

That afternoon at the ABC Bank's Dongxing sub-branch near the Dongxing checkpoint, three parties met to conclude the transaction. Haonan had not seen Guangwei for many years. He was grasping an old-style mobile phone as big as a brick, and wore a heavy chain round his neck. Haonan disliked him intensely when he saw him, but thinking that as Jinxiong said, he should not regard money as an enemy, he controlled his feelings. At least Lin Laizhen was not with him.

Haonan suggested that Guangwei should sit in the east of the bank lobby, and Yefeng in the west. Yefeng was a young man with a clean face who came from Guangxi. He had purchased this lot of *Dalbergia* from a Vietnamese merchant.

As Guangwei waited to draw the cash while holding the bank's sequence number in his hand, his slanted eyes ceaselessly scanned Yefeng. He wanted to get closer to him, but owing to the presence of Haonan, he couldn't; likewise, Yefeng well understood what Guangwei meant. Before keeping the deposit from Guangwei, Haonan knew that if Guangwei had a chance to get closer to Yefeng, even if only for a minute, and the price was revealed, the deal would immediately fail.

Finally, half an hour later, Guangwei's number was called by the bank loudspeaker. He picked up 200,000 yuan from the bank teller. Then he pulled out a deposit receipt printed well beforehand and asked Haonan to sign it.

Having looked at it, Haonan pointed out that "Deposit" had wrongly been printed as "Deposition". Guangwei insisted that it was correct and no problem, but Haonan stood firm. He wrote down a new receipt describing it as a

"Deposit" and signed it. After that they exchanged the receipt and deposit cash.

Presently Guangwei left. Haonan drew 150,000 yuan to hand to Yefeng. The balance of 50,000 was kept by Haonan as his profit. Yefeng wrote down another deposit receipt to Haonan. The deal was looking successful.

The next morning, Jinxiong, Haonan and Guangwei all met at a delivery place which belonged to the Luofu goods yard. It was managed by Dongxing Customs, and many cargos such as timbers, rubbers and dried fruits imported from Vietnam were stored there. In the north-east corner stood a huge pile of dark red *Dalbergia cochinchinensis*, which had been lying there in the open for nearly six months. Dozens of buyers had been to inspect this timber. As a matter of fact Guangwei was also a middleman, as he was planning to sell the wood to a buyer from whom he had already received 200,000 yuan as deposit. So the deposit he had given Haonan was not his own money.

When Haonan approached the stack of timber, he saw a group of people beside it. One man grasped a big knife and split one of the timbers. The cross-section was red, like blood. Then an old man in glasses put his nose close and smelled. After a while he walked over to Guangwei and disappointedly shook his head.

"It isn't dark red *Dalbergia cochinchinensis*, just looks like it," he said. "And it isn't from Laos, it's Swartizia from Africa. For the real thing the price would be 30,000 yuan, but for Swartizia, it's only 3,000."

"What?" gasped Haonan, feeling a chill in his heart. Jinxiong was expressionless, and Guangwei smiled faintly.

"We can't buy it," the old man said. He was the man who had been going to buy it from Guangwei.

Haonan's heart sank. The men discussed the problem, but there was nothing to be done.

The next morning no news came from Guangwei that he would pay the balance and deliver the goods. Haonan and Jinxiong had to wait.

The autumn sun was shining on the wall of the Donghai Hotel as vehicles drove slowly to the Dongxing checkpoint. In room 602, Haonan and Jinxiong were talking after lunch. Jinxiong sat beside the window picking his teeth, while Haonan half lay on the bed.

At the age of twenty, Haonan had once laughingly talked about insomnia with others. He had wondered how there could be such a thing. If a person was tired enough, how could he not sleep? Yet he had suffered insomnia in recent years. In Dongxing, although he was tired day and night, it did not drive him to fall asleep. The previous night he had not been able to sleep until he had swallowed a sleeping pill. However, the side-effects had made him feel weak in his hands and feet and his brain was still dopey.

"That 50,000 yuan deposit, you must hand it to me now," Jinxiong said to Haonan murkily.

Haonan turned. "Pardon?"

"I said you must hand in the deposit to me now."

"Don't you trust me? The deposit was in my hand."

"I told you to give me the money. You must do it!"

"Aren't we going to share the profit when the business is completed?"

"No! You must go to the bank now and withdraw the cash for me!"

Haonan still lay on the bed. "If that is so, let us be clear that this August in Haiphong, Vietnam, the *Dalbergia* was our first business. I wasn't in Vietnam then, I was in Shenzhen handling the anthracite business. It was a pity that the anthracite deal had failed, but the *Dalbergia* deal made 300,000 yuan of profit. According to the agreement between us, I should get 150,000 yuan. Why haven't you given it to me yet?"

Jinxiong was so sly that when the *Dalbergia* was almost finished, he used the pretext of importing the anthracite to get Haonan to go back to Shenzhen to charter the vessel. That prevented Haonan from attending when the deal for the *Dalbergia* was concluded in Vietnam. Jinxiong invited a Vietnamese translator instead of letting Haonan do this free. It was like killing a donkey after it had finished pulling a millstone, and it allowed him to keep the whole profit.

Jinxiong was flustered at Haonan's challenge. "So what?" he said, jumping up suddenly. Then he dashed across to Haonan and punched him on the head.

Haonan was staggered! Jinxiong did not know that the man he was attacking had been a powerful Sanda killer, but the previous night he had seen him swallow a sleeping pill. Haonan instinctively jumped up, but he was still sleepy as a result of the pill, so he could not fight properly.

They stood there at a stalemate for a moment. Suddenly the door was pushed open, and a man they knew called Chen Xinsui came in. He rushed between them. Jinxiong went back to his seat and Haonan sat on his bed, confused.

"I'll beat you to death!" said Jinxiong. "I know everyone around here. If I just make a call, your bones will be sawn into powder and you won't have a place to bury yourself."

"Keep calm! Keep calm!" Chen Xinsui urged Jinxiong, still standing between them.

"Hand in the deposit right now, otherwise I won't set you free!" Jinxiong howled. Haonan slowly but firmly shook his head.

"Ok, you wait!" Jinxiong put his luggage in order and headed for the door, followed by Chen Xinsui. He turned and shouted to Haonan again, "If you don't hand it in today, tomorrow I'll refuse to receive a penny of it. And you wait! You know what'll happen!"

Haonan did not understand why Jinxiong had attached him. But he knew it was time to leave. He checked out and moved to the Shanghai Beach Hotel, near the Dongxing bus station.

That evening, Yefeng called Haonan. "When will you make delivery?"

"Something unexpected happened, my buyer didn't confirm the goods," Haonan replied.

"That's not my problem. After all, you confirmed it."

"Can we put it off a little longer?"

"The latest day is at the end of this month, so you have sixteen days left. If you don't deliver the goods, I'll sell to other buyers and your deposit won't be returned."

Haonan had no choice.

No sooner had he put down the phone than Guangwei called in. He ignored the delivery issue but just asked, "Why did you fight?"

"When will you pick up the goods?" Haonan hurriedly wanted to know.

"Pick up the goods?" Guangwei said. "It's Swartizia instead of dark red *Dalbergia*. My buyer has pulled out."

"But you had inspected the goods and signed a contract with me."

"So what? Isn't the description 'dark red *Dalbergia cochinchinensis*' written on our contract?"

"But you handed me the deposit, so you had confirmed the name and quality of the goods."

"Don't you understand? There is no time limit on the contract between us, it's effective forever." Guangwei smiled.

Haonan hurriedly took out the contract and studied it. Although before signing he'd confirmed it contained the clause "Valid until the end of this month" with Guangwei, together with "The goods will be delivered within seven days". But now it was unimaginable that these two clauses had not been written in the contract. So this contract would be effective forever. Not only did Guangwei not need to deliver the goods but once the end of the month went by, Yefeng's goods would be sold to other buyers, so Haonan would have no goods to supply. According to Chinese contract law, the seller who receives the buyer's deposit but is unable to supply the goods described must pay double compensation to the buyer. That meant Haonan would owe Guangwei 400,000 yuan.

"Could you make an exception in this case?" Haonan asked.

"But who will give me an exception? You're smart!"

Haonan felt as if he had lost his balance and was falling over a high cliff.

Chapter 33
In the Timber Yard

Only in Dongxing are there so many hotels, big and small, at favourable prices in China. In a single room at the Shanghai Beach Hotel at eight o'clock that evening, Haonan sat on the edge of his bed reflecting what had happened. He kept motionless, but his mind was in a whirl.

"The validity expires at the end of this month," he murmured. But why didn't it say so in the contract with Guangwei? How could he have signed it? What could he do?

Midnight passed, the time when he had usually brushed his teeth, taken a bath and fallen asleep. Tonight, however, he had no intention of taking a bath, despite his sweaty smell. He was still sitting on the edge of bed, tightly holding the pillow he had brought from Shenzhen. At three o'clock that night he was still sitting there. In the next room there was a fat man whose wheezes shook the hotel like a mountain moving. On the other side someone was talking in his sleep. It was not cold tonight, but Haonan was trembling. In this strange land, he felt more and more isolated and helpless. *Contract law, validity time at the end of this month, seven days delivery...* he was still murmuring randomly.

At last the night passed, and Haonan heard the noise of the bus station. The sound of motor-bicycles spread over the streets, mixing with a babble of Vietnamese chatter. Never in his life had Haonan experienced such a night; he had sat unmoving the whole night long. His brain had been labouring endlessly, and he felt a horror he had never faced before. Finally he told himself: *I can't sit like this waiting to die. I must contact a lawyer!*

Along the Beilun Boulevard and opposite Dongxing People's Court, there was the office of Dongxing Upright & Oblique Lawyers, where only two lawyers worked. Haonan sat on a sofa and told one of lawyers, Rong Benliang, what had happened. Rong Benliang was a thin man in his forties with eyebrows which were constantly moving, which annoyed Haonan. He did not take to him at first, but he believed that most lawyers were honest and he shouldn't judge Rong by his appearance. Besides, like a patient needing to see a doctor, he had no time to find someone else.

Seeing the contract Haonan provided, Rong drew out a copy of a "Letter of Witness", on which he stamped the seal of his lawyer office. He told Haonan, "With this document you'll win the lawsuit." Rong wanted to charge 20,000 yuan, but after Haonan had bargained as hard as he could, it was lowered to 10,000 yuan, and they reached agreement.

Haonan took Rong to Luofu goods yard to check the timber. Every time they met a stranger Rong wanted to know along the way, Rong would hand them his business cards. When they reached the pile of timbers, Guangwei was also there. He shouted, "You'd better get ready! I'll let the judge confirm that you'll have to pay me that 400,000 yuan!"

Haonan was surprised and did not know how to reply. Now it seemed doubtful if Guangwei sincerely meant to purchase the timber.

Rong walked up to Guangwei and politely presented his name card, which astonished Haonan. What kind of lawyer was he? Haonan had just paid this lawyer to lodge a lawsuit against Guangwei, but now the man was dealing with Haonan's enemy.

"That's good. I'll contact you," Guangwei said to Rong with a smile.

"I'll be pleased to provide a service," said Rong, shaking Guangwei's hand. They were like old friends who had not seen each other for a long time. Haonan, standing on the sidelines, felt as if he had served as an unintentional matchmaker.

Time passed, like a countdown towards Haonan's inevitable bankruptcy. Guangwei delayed asking for delivery, and it was obvious that he did not want the goods. Meanwhile Yefeng reminded Haonan ceaselessly that the cargo must be delivered as soon as possible because it was nearly the end of the month. But Haonan saw someone else in the Luofu goods yard checking the cargo.

Every day when he left the Shanghai Beach Hotel, he was very careful. He thought that what Jinxiong had said in the Donghai Hotel was probably an empty threat. However, he had to protect himself in this strange city, so he hid his stainless steel Nunchakus under his clothes.

In the Luofu goods yard, new loads of timber were arriving from Vietnam and some were being picked up to be transported away. Haonan's stack of *Dalbergia* remained, now covered with dirt after months of wind and rain. The customs clerks and workers who passed them there wondered why they had been stored for such a long time. Sometimes Haonan circled them purposelessly, and sometimes he phoned Guangwei and said, "When will you deliver?"

"I'll tell you at the appropriate time," Guangwei said coldly.

Although the delivery time and validity time hadn't been stipulated in the contract, the buyer had to deliver it within a reasonable time. He could not delay indefinitely unless the cargo was not available from the seller; Haonan understood this from the law. He visited the goods yard every day to wait for Guangwei's delivery, witnessed by the customs clerks and the workers there, to demonstrate that it wasn't that he didn't have goods to supply but that Guangwei was deliberately not making the delivery. He asked Rong Benliang to record this in a "Letter of Witness" for use in the forthcoming lawsuit.

On the fourteenth day after signing the contract, Haonan appeared in the goods yard in the early morning as usual. It was chilly and Haonan wandered beside the timbers. There were fewer workers now, and a crane in distance was moving cargo.

From the entrance of the goods yard, five young men appeared. They were tall and very dark-skinned, indicating that they were from Vietnam. They said nothing, but walked directly towards Haonan, staring at him. Suddenly Haonan sensed danger. Sure enough, as they approached, two of them pulled out wrenches and short sticks. At once Haonan stepped back, stretching out his hand to take out his Nunchakus from behind his waist. Then he faced them with his right flank. He thought of General Macarthur's words: "Only the one who doesn't fear death is qualified to be alive." He braced himself.

The five men had clearly never seen such a weapon, and were puzzled. However, they remained confident, being five against one. They whispered some words in Vietnamese and separated to attack him from different directions.

The first man dashed at Haonan, raising his wrench and aiming at Haonan's head. Haonan dodged it and raised his right hand a little. The B stick stayed in this hand, but the A stick flew out and struck the lower jaw of his opponent. The wrench clattered to the ground and he clutched his swollen jaw.

Using the inertia of the A stick, Haonan swung it behind his right shoulder. When the second man was about to hit him, Haonan, taking strength from his waist and leg, he held up the A stick from his back and chopped down the front in the shape of a semi-circle. The A stick hit his opponent's left shoulder and so hard that he grasped his shoulder and let out a loud cry. Haonan withdrew the A stick and his right hand seized the B stick for the next man.

One of the other three men dashed at Haonan from the left. Haonan threw the A stick over his right shoulder and followed with another move in which the stick was concealed. His opponents paused. Then Haonan twisted his waist and turned his hip, and the A stick struck the next man's leg. The Nunchakus attack, fast, powerful and with perfectly uniform speed, strength and angle, was beyond the Vietnamese man's understanding. He was unable to dodge, and it thumped the vein on his leg so hard that he hugged the leg and hopped around on one leg. Seeing this, the other two men fled.

Haonan did not try to follow them; he just smilingly thought to himself: *Once the Nunchakus is in my hand, then unless you have a gun...*

The workers watching was amazed that in one minute one man had defeated five.

The next day there were only two days left before the validity deadline, and Yao Jiqiang and Chen Yiquan, Yefeng's partners, returned to Dongxing from Vietnam. Yao Jiqiang, who came from Jiangsu Province, had a slight stutter. As soon as he saw Yefeng, he asked what had happened, then called Haonan's phone, "Why did it go wrong? Doesn't business require fairness and sincerity?"

"Of course I obey these principles," Haonan said. But how could he possibly talk about "fairness" and "sincerity" with men like Guangwei and Jinxiong?

"This cargo of ours has been stored for more than six months," said Yao Jiqiang. "We wanted to make delivery early. I've contacted Guangwei. He says that if you hand the deposit to Jinxiong and let him handle this business, he will deliver the goods tomorrow."

When he heard Jinxiong's name, Haonan was uncontrollably angry. It was clear that Jinxiong had already colluded with Guangwei. From the beginning Jinxiong had insisted that this deal must be handled by him and if he hadn't briefly gone to Indonesia, Haonan wouldn't have had the chance.

Seeing no reaction from Haonan for some while, Yao Jiqiang said, "I know you're unhappy. But this is the right of Guangwei, as buyer. Everything was controlled by Guangwei. And Jinxiong had guaranteed that the profit would be shared half and half with you after finishing. Actually you must think about the overall situation. You may imagine that if you don't hand in the deposit and two days later, our goods will be sold to other buyers, then you'll have to pay 400,000 yuan to Guangwei – is it deserved? You think it over first, and call me back later."

Four hundred thousand yuan! This was no small sum. If there was a lawsuit, he would try his best to refute it and he certainly would not pay compensation. But how much energy and time would it cost him? Apart from this, what would Rong Benliang do? He might have colluded with Guangwei too. Haonan had to think hard about it all.

That afternoon in the coffee shop of the Donghai Hotel, Haonan, Jinxiong, Guangwei, Yefeng, Yao Jiqiang, Chen Yiquan and Chen Xinsui gathered around a table. Jinxiong was still arrogant, and Haonan would have liked to punch him. But he had to control himself. After receiving the phone from Yao Jiqiang that morning and after consideration, he had made a concession.

He said, "I hope Jinxiong can write me a letter guaranteeing that he will share the profit with me fifty-fifty after finishing this deal."

"All right," Jinxiong said, smiling faintly. He wrote the letter and gave it to Haonan. "Now let me have the deposit." He was impatient.

"I must declare," Haonan said, "that from the deposit, 10,000 yuan has been paid for the 'Letter of Witness' and 4,000 for the warehouse rent. Hence, the balance is 36,000."

Jinxiong looked very unhappy, but thinking that little was better than nothing, he said, "All right."

"Now it's time for me to take back the deposit receipt of mine," Haonan said to Guangwei, who was still smiling. He slowly looked for the receipt in his file bag. Suddenly he cried, "Sorry, I forgot, it's not here."

Haonan felt anxious.

Everyone watched Guangwei.

Presently Guangwei smiled. "Here it is," he said. He fished it out and presented it to Haonan. After checking it, Haonan put it on the table. Meanwhile, he drew out 36,000 yuan from his pocket and put that down on the table. Jinxiong picked up the cash, and Haonan tore up the receipt into strips as they watched. The strips were thrown into the garbage. At that moment, Haonan felt as if a heavy mountain which had been pressing upon his chest for more than two weeks had finally moved away.

Early the next morning, the day of the deadline, Haonan called Jinxiong. "I'm at the Luofu goods yard waiting for your delivery," he said. Jinxiong replied, "All right." Haonan called Guangwei, but Guangwei only gave a hollow laugh.

There was no delivery that day, so when the deadline had passed, the timber was still piled there. Haonan had guessed that Guangwei wouldn't deliver it at all. Nor did Jinxiong ask Guangwei to deliver. Jinxiong just wanted to take back the deposit, with the aim of not letting Haonan obtain a penny of the profit.

One thing which made Haonan doubtful was that Guangwei had received the 200,000 yuan deposit from the next buyer – the old man. Since Guangwei hadn't delivered the goods to him either, why didn't the old man make a claim against Guangwei? If that had happened, why did Guangwei always appear so happy? Pondering on these puzzles, Haonan returned to Shenzhen on the midnight bus, as if fleeing from a plague.

Chapter 34
Special Rent

The year end was approaching and the spring flowers would soon blossom again. The spring festival of 2008 was coming.

"Never suffer, never learn." Haonan, returning to Shenzhen from Dongxing, bitterly recalled his past pain. He was working as an executive in a new foreign trade company based on zero salary and a half-share profit, relying on the Alibaba export platform, and business was going well again. After finishing two export orders and paying his personal income tax, he had made 150,000 yuan.

At 10 o'clock that morning, he called his mother as usual. A'shen did not have to use the public phone any longer; instead she had her own mobile phone to answer Haonan's call. Every time he dialled it, he cut it off at once, to remind his mother, and then he would call again five minutes later. Once again A'shen urged him do something about getting married, and to console her, he promised to bring a girlfriend home in the Spring Festival holidays.

Now Haonan had a problem. How could he produce a girl so soon? But he heard that someone had hired a "girlfriend" to take to his home town for the year end, and this was now so urgent that it occurred to him that he had to do the same. So he advertised on the internet, and soon received a response. A few days later he went to a coffee shop in Futian to meet the first person who had responded.

When Haonan arrived at the coffee shop and approached the table as arranged, he had a big surprise. Sitting there was Li Shuwen, the girl he had once shared an apartment with in Huaqiangbei. He had certainly never imagined meeting her again like this after losing touch for so many years. She looked as beautiful and fresh as Haonan remembered her.

As they started to talk, they both felt as if they had been separated for a generation. He was surprised that she had not married yet either, so she met the requirements of Haonan's advertisement. She told him that shortly after he had left her in Shangbayue village, she had been forced to return to Chengdu City, her home town, but she had returned to Shenzhen several years later. Now she worked as a shipping clerk in charge of bill of lading inspection and allocation in a large shipping company in Futian. She was not planning to go back to Chengdu for her yearend holiday because she had no boyfriend to take, so when she had seen an unknown man sending this invitation on the internet, she had responded immediately.

"That time in Huaqiangbei I leased half a home and half a bed to you. Now you're leasing me, but still not my body," she said.

"I understand. This time I need you for ten days. I'll pay you 300 yuan per day and cover all costs," Haonan said. "On the day when we set off, I'll pay you 30% deposit, and the rest will be settled when we come back to Shenzhen."

"Ok. Let's call it a deal."

Three days later, in a new saloon car, a black F6 from the BYD series, Haonan drove from Gang'xia to Xinzhou village to pick Shuwen up. They drove on to the Guangzhou-Shenzhen highway and through Humen Town and Zhongshan City towards West Canton. Six hours later the car left the highway from Guangzhou to Zhanjiang at the Huazhou exit. They were getting close to Nawu Town in the north of Huazhou.

His home town soon appeared in front of him. The high peaks of the Liuhuang Mountain were rich with the green of spring, and the blue water of the Ling River flowed slowly past. Along the road there was a chain of shops choc a bloc with festival firecrackers, making a lively scene to welcome the new spring.

Haonan drove the F6 straight to the house of his elder brother in Nawu. Three years before when his father had passed away, A'shen and his elder brother had moved from Chengbian village, Changling to Nawu. When they arrived, Haonan saw A'shen waiting at the door holding a crutch. The car stopped and Shuwen got out.

"Nice to meet you, grandmother!" she said.

"Why did you say 'grandmother'?" asked Haonan in surprise. "She is my mother, not my grandmother!"

"Mother? Oh no!" Shuwen was astonished. Her hand covered her face and she hurriedly apologised. However, she couldn't imagine how such an old woman could be Haonan's mother.

"My family has an unfortunate history, I'll tell you later," Haonan said.

A'shen had got used to this kind of embarrassment, so she didn't mind, and she continued to smile. Her eyes were glued to Shuwen. Clearly she had taken a liking to this prospective daughter-in-law. Shuwen was kept busy answering endless sharp questions from A'shen, and Haonan acted as an interpreter from the Huazhou native dialect into Mandarin.

Not long after, Haonan's nephew and all their neighbours arrived, circling Shuwen and ceaselessly asking questions. Shuwen was embarrassed and lowered her head. She was looking as fresh and beautiful as a fragrant lotus with petals moist with dew.

This house of Haonan's elder brother had four and a half floors. In the evening A'shen brought a pair of dark-red flowered pillows in the shape of mandarin ducks, which she had washed and dried, for Haonan's bed. Many days before she had already prepared this pillow, of a kind ordinarily used by a new couple when they first entered the bridal chamber.

Seeing it, Haonan was dumbfounded, and Shuwen, who sat on the chair, blushed again. Haonan thought for a while. He could not refuse. Then he put them down beside the bed.

On the fourth floor there was a suite of two rooms and one hall. In the evening, Haonan and Shuwen had a heart-to-heart conversation with A'shen. Under the bright light A'shen looked older than before. Haonan asked her questions, but A'shen ignored them, instead asking Shuwen how far it was from her home town to Shenzhen, how many brothers and sisters she had, how her parents were and so forth.

Soon A'shen said, "Tomorrow it will rain again."

"How did you know?" Shuwen was surprised.

Haonan explained. "She often went to cut and gather the firewood and do farm work when she was young, and her clothes were constantly getting wet, which caused rheumatism. So if she has an ache in her leg, we know it will rain the next day." He took a small wooden hammer and tapped A'shen's leg. "It's late now, let's talk tomorrow," he said to her.

A'shen nodded.

He held a basin of hot water and helped wash A'shen's feet, then massaged them. After that he put a charged-up hand warmer into her quilt and arranged for her to lie down. Shuwen, silently watching all this, felt warm in her heart.

The water-heater wasn't so good; sometimes the water temperature was too high, and it was hard to adjust because the water pressure was too low. Shuwen got used to showering. So before she took a bath, he didn't let her get in until he had adjusted the water temperature for her. While she was inside, he stood outside speaking to her from time to time, to make sure she had not suffered from carbon monoxide poisoning and passed out.

After she completed her toilet, they went into the bedroom. Seeing the bed, he said, "It isn't a high-quality mattress, you may not like it."

"When we were in Huaqiangbei our living conditions were poorer than this, but we could still live," she said, smiling.

"No, now you're going to sleep on my bed, alone."

"Then where will you sleep?"

As the proverb goes, "A night after a long absence is better than a wedding night", and

Haonan was desperate to hold her and sleep with her all night long. But they had an agreement. He pointed to a long sofa in the corner and said mysteriously, "Now we sleep according to the agreement between us. But at daybreak, we must put my blanket on your bed, as our quilt. I think you can understand."

Suddenly she pointed to Haonan's pillow. "Isn't this the pillow you used when we slept together in Huaqiangbei?" she asked. He smiled and nodded. "It's still so fresh, even though you've used it for many years. But what secret is hidden inside it? Chinese herbal medicine? But you don't suffer insomnia. Or maybe you have slept on it many lovers?"

Haonan smiled without replying.

The light fell down softly from above the mosquito net, and Shuwen, who had pulled the soft silk quilt up to her chest, slept silently. A curl of long hair crossed her face from the corner of forehead. She breathed sweetly. Meeting her again after so many years, seeing her sleeping and recalling the strange happenings in Huaqiangbei, everything seemed so sweet again, and he felt a sudden impulse to hug her. But thinking of the "gentlemen's agreement" between them, he turned off the light and went slowly to the sofa.

Shuwen was only pretending to be sleeping, and on seeing this she smiled secretly. Then, tired after their long day, they both fell sound asleep.

During the night A'shen got up to use the toilet. She went over to Haonan's door and pressed her ear to the door. She heard Haonan and Shuwen breathing; it sounded as if they were sleeping together. She smiled happily and went back to her room.

Just before dawn, Shuwen heard a firecracker go off outside, and could not sleep any longer. She woke up Haonan and they chatted. At last she asked him why his mother looked like a grandmother, and why he loved her so much. He opened his sleepy eyes, smiled mournfully and explained.

For families like Haonan's, it was a matter of history. Before the Chinese liberation, Zhou Weiluo, Haonan's father, who acted as the countryside primary school teacher, had been a cultured person, so he was selected as a village chief. During the days when he performed his duty, he never detained a man to join the army and there was never any corruption. But he had been in his post for only three days when the whole of China was liberated. Later on, seeing that the poor country people suffered from various illnesses, he became a doctor of traditional Chinese medicine. Every day he carried his medicine box marked with a red cross around the village houses and across ridges and mountains, saving many endangered patients, so he was praised in West Canton for being as highly-skilled as the famous

Bianque doctor in ancient China. But soon after that catastrophe broke out, and he could not deny his former status as "puppet village chief", so he was exiled to Hubei Province thousands of kilometres away and made to do hard labour, repairing Wuhan Yangtze River Bridge. A'shen had no idea if he would ever come back. After that A'shen painstakingly fed her mother-in-law, as well as Haonan's elder brother and sister. She also did heavy, dirty and demanding farm work, including rice-cropping, dung-carrying and so forth. She had to cope with hostile and contemptuous looks from others, being abused as a thief whenever she stood in the field.

During those years she received no news from her husband, but she could not leave her mother-in-law and two children at home and go to the far north to look for him. Nor did she have the money, and she could speak only a few words of the Huazhou native dialect that only the local people could understand. In any case she believed that Zhou Weiluo would disappear and felt she could only accept her calamity, and the responsibility of feeding her mother- in-law and children. She never thought of remarriage, and lived like a widow.

The days and years passed until she had cried her eyes blind. The children grew up steadily with nothing to eat but sweet potato, grass roots and even tree bark in the hungry days.

One day after three years, at the request of her mother-in-law, A'shen had to set up a dead spirit tablet for her husband. Then she held a memorial service, in tears and murmuring. Often when the cocks crowed at midnight she burned incense and held a memorial ceremony. She hoped that by doing this she could at least save the soul of her husband. Towards the year end and the Qingming Festival, she did it more frequently.

One morning eight years later the sun perched high in a topaz sky as A'shen went out to do her farming work, she was amazed to see the thin figure of her husband at the village entrance. His legs were scarcely thicker than the crutch he held, one sandal was broken and his right foot wore a slipper whose heel was thinner than the front. He wore torn clothes and had a vacant expression, like a ghost from a graveyard.

A'shen threw her hoe to the ground and ran towards him, and they hugged tightly at the village entrance, fixed in time like a sculpture. Neither had imagined they would ever see each other again.

On that day in front of the door of their tiled cottage, thundering firecrackers exploded. The family butchered the pig and chicken – though they were lent to them only – to celebrate. All the Changling villages, indeed the whole Nawu community, was full of excitement, because nobody had imagined that Zhou Weiluo could come back after disappearing for eight years. He said that only by relying on his strong willpower and his deep love for his family had he survived in Hubei Province. When he had come back to Guangzhou, he had walked back for over a thousand miles, sleeping beside the road like a beggar. After more than a month of walking, he had finally reached Nawu.

It was the next year when Haonan was born, an unplanned birth, but a specially happy event for the family. So there was a fifty-year age gap between Haonan and his father, and forty with his mother. When little Haonan played in front of his home, strangers came to see his doctor father, and they would ask Haonan, "Hello son, is your grandfather home?" Haonan then angrily stopped playing, looking at his father who just came out from inside the home and corrected them, saying "He is my father, not my grandfather." People would be alarmed, thinking it was unusual for such an old man to have such a small son. When they heard the story, they would know how bitter Haonan's parents' experience had been. So Haonan envied other children for their young parents.

After Haonan's father returned, he always lived healthily. However, because A'shen had been living as a widow for eight years, some people called Haonan "a child born after the death of his father". From his junior years on, Haonan was often bullied by the others. His father's eight years of suffering deeply hurt Haonan's heart, so he greatly treasured the days with his parents.

Finally, Haonan told Shuwen, his father had died three years ago at the age of 88.

Shuwen said nothing for a long time. Presently she turned her body and buried her face deeply into the pillow. She couldn't sleep any longer. And then it was dawn.

Chapter 35
Marriage

The next morning when Haonan got up, he boiled oatmeal for A'shen. She suffered high cholesterol, so he urged her to eat oatmeal every day, as it was not only breakfast but a food which helped to reduce blood fat. After that, he began to sweep the floor and wash Shuwen's clothes. Shuwen hurriedly got up to look after her own washing, embarrassed that he was washing her briefs. However he had finished and hung them up on the balcony. She couldn't help smiling. Their "renting agreement" wasn't perfect because laundry had not been covered. Haonan chuckled.

After breakfast, A'shen advised Haonan to go back with Shuwen to the Miaoshanbei Temple in Haonan's birthplace to burn incense and pray to God, a local tradition. A'shen thought that in this way the marriage of Haonan would be more secure.

It was raining a little as Haonan drove slowly back to his birthplace. The mountain road was rugged, and Haonan told Shuwen about the scenery as they went. It was this road from Nawu to Changling along which he had walked to and fro carrying rice, dried radish slices and his textbooks twice a week until he had graduated from Nawu High Middle School. It was also along this road that A'shen had so often carried firewood on her shoulders to Nawu market to earn a little income to support the family. Now it was a county-class cement road fifteen metres wide, carrying cars driving back from Guangzhou, Shenzhen, Dongguan and Zhuhai, and container trucks loaded with china clay, kaolin, for export to Europe and America.

Several minutes later the F6 reached the Miaoshanbei Temple. In front of it there had once been a big river where Haonan and Fuqiang had caught fish and shrimps, regarded by the local children as a good place for swimming. With bare bodies they would dive from the bridge several metres high in sequence into the river, then bob up more than ten metres away. But now the river had narrowed to a small stream, and no fish or shrimps could be seen.

At the year's end there were many country people and neighbours coming to pray. In such a gathering they would congratulate each other for completing a new building, for a family marriage or a new daughter or grandson. Haonan arranged the prepared chicken, pork and fruit on the prayer table, then burned incense and prayed. Shuwen stood nearby, A'shen lost no time in praying, saying, "God above, please bless Haonan and

Shuwen and let them get married at an early day and give birth to a baby as soon as possible".

Haonan was surprised, and Shuwen opened her eyes wide. He prayed sincerely, "I hope God blesses my mother with good health to enjoy her old age, and blesses Shuwen." Shuwen hurriedly prayed in a low voice, "God above, I want to explain that it isn't yet a marriage relationship between Haonan and me..."

After they had finished, many country people gathered, asking Shuwen many questions. If somebody asked when they would apply to get married, he replied that she had not yet got used to the local dialect; if someone asked her when the wedding banquet would be held, he replied that she had only just come back to Nawu, and so on. He suggested to Shuwen that she should just nod and not say anything.

But suddenly A'shen was angry. She felt that Haonan and Shuwen both lacked sincerity, so she pushed them in front of the prayer table. First she knelt down and asked the two of them to do same, saying, "Please follow me to speak!" A'shen then closed her eyes, crossed her palms and said loudly, "God above, this is Li Shuwen, please give your blessing for Haonan and me to get married soon, and give birth to a baby as soon as possible!" Hearing no sound from Shuwen, she then told Haonan to translate to Mandarin and asked Shuwen again to follow.

Haonan and Shuwen hesitated.

"Please!" A'shen urged.

"I..." Shuwen's face turned redder. She stared at Haonan. Haonan tried to signal to her that since A'shen was so old and bitter, to sweeten her heart, could she please speak accordingly? Meanwhile many country people and neighbours looked on. Shuwen then had to do so, and so did Haonan. They both kowtowed three times. Having seen that, A'shen added, "God here is very effective and accurate."

"Oh?" Shuwen was surprised. But A'shen was satisfied, and so were the others.

However, that night as A'shen was about to sleep she cried faintly. Haonan and Shuwen heard this in the next room. Afterwards Haonan's elder brother, sister-in-law and nephew all asked what had happened. In fact A'shen felt sick at heart. She had seen through the lie that Shuwen was her son's girlfriend. But she understood that she should bear full responsibility, so she blamed herself. She felt it was because of her poor birth background that Haonan had been born into such a humble rural family, and had not still met a love partner.

Hearing this, everybody looked at Haonan and Shuwen in alarm, but they all comforted A'shen as much as they could.

Haonan and Shuwen walked out of the room, lowering their heads. After a short discussion, they came back. Haonan denied what A'shen had said and explained that as a new girl, Shuwen had felt out of place here. If nobody believed them, they would hold the wedding ceremony there the day after tomorrow.

"Really?" hearing this, A'shen got up all of a sudden, her sorrow changing to happiness as if she had suddenly recovered from a sickness. The others all looked at them doubtfully. But Haonan still insisted that they could do so.

So the wedding ceremony for Haonan and Shuwen was held in a big room at the Julongxuan Restaurant in Nawu, where they both wore wedding clothes. Only three dining tables were set for the banquet, to which they did not invite too many relatives and friends. A'shen, sitting among them, saw that Haonan and Shuwen worshipped each other. She smiled with relief.

In the blink of an eye, the Spring Festival holiday was nearly over. Before leaving, A'shen had prepared a variety of local specialties for Shuwen, such as dried longans, olive and mango. Haonan and Shuwen said goodbye to his brother and sister-in-law and were ready to set off. A'shen followed the car shakily on her crutches. Haonan wound down the car window and stared at his mother with her white hair and wrinkles. It reminded him of the times when she had seen him off to school and waved to him without stopping every Sunday evening. He had always stared at her like this, as if hoping to imprint the image of her on his mind forever. As for A'shen, she showed all the sorrow of separation.

A'shen thought that she would now be waiting for the birth of her grandchild. "Don't drive too fast!" she urged Haonan. He nodded. "Stop if you get to a red light, be careful to dodge other vehicles, and beware of the bumper men!"

"Where did you learn such phrases?" he asked her.

"I stroll together down the road every morning with the other old grannies. All their grandchildren can drive. I learned from them," she said, smiling.

In fact when Haonan had taken his driving tests, he had passed all the parts at once. Except for the first year when he had had a minor collision, he had always held an excellent record, with no accidents and no insurance claims. However A'shen, who had never touched a steering wheel, still wanted to tell him how to drive, like a daughter-in-law trying to teach her mother-in-law how to give birth.

"You must use the indicators if you want to change lanes, and don't forget that Shuwen is in the car too."

The F6 moved forward slowly, A'shen still following. She said, "As soon as you arrive in Shenzhen, you should buy a house".

Why not? Haonan thought to himself. But then he felt crushed by the thought, like a crab under a stone. A house! He'd been working for one for so many years, but always failed. He could only say, "Yes, I will."

Shuwen listened silently to all of this.

"A'shen, when I come back home next time, I'll buy a visual mobile phone for you, so we can see each other when we talk," Haonan said.

"Is that possible?" A'shen was surprised but excited.

"Yes, they'll be available soon," said Haonan happily.

"It'll be wonderful if your mother can use QQ, so both sides can talk and see each other," said Shuwen.

"Yes. But how can she do that, unless a young man nearby can assist her," said Haonan.

"Yes, let your nephew help," Shuwen suggested.

Haonan thought this was a good solution.

Soon they heard the horns of a line of cars and motor-bicycles behind. The F6 was obstructing the traffic. Haonan accelerated a little, leaving A'shen behind. Even so, she still tried to follow slowly. Presently she stopped and stood by the roadside, her chest heaving. She still stared after the car, her left hand gesturing. She was probably trying to warn him not to crash into the oncoming cars.

With one hand on the steering wheel, Haonan rubbed his eyes with the other hand. Shuwen hurriedly took out two tissues, one to dry his eyes and one for hers.

Chapter 36
The Lawsuit

The next April, Haonan was surprised to receive a summons from the People's Court of Futian District. When he opened the envelope, his heart was thumping wildly. Had his mobile messages failed to beat Guangwei? But if Guangwei was taking action against him now, he would be ready.

But when he opened the summons, he was dumbfounded to see that the one who was taking him to court was Jinxiong. When Jinxiong had come back to Shenzhen from Dongxing, he still felt angrily that the 50,000 yuan deposit should be his own. Haonan had only given back 36,000. So he had issued a "Letter of Civil Lawsuit" claiming that he and Haonan had borrowed 1.6 million yuan from others when they were in business cooperation, and according to the principle in their agreement that both parties should jointly bear the debt, he was demanding compensation of 0.8 million yuan from Haonan. Jinxiong clearly knew that Haonan was unable to repay, so he would have to go to jail.

Haonan had never imagined that while he had not sued Jinxiong, instead Jinxiong would sue him.

But he wondered why he had not heard about a 1.6 million yuan loan before. He then concentrated his efforts on researching the law.

The day came when he entered the second floor of the court building where the second civil section was located, and the solemn national emblem stood high above the centre of court. The chief judge, judge, secretary and recorder all sat down in readiness. Haonan silently sat on the defendant's seat. He had not employed a lawyer and would defend himself. The plaintiff did not attend but had fully entrusted an agent lawyer, who – when Haonan turned to look – was unexpectedly the man who had been entrusted by Haonan in Dongxing, the cunning Rong Benliang. Haonan was alarmed. He also saw another man wearing a big neck chain, sitting there with a classical mobile phone as big as a brick. It was Guangwei. He inclined his head to smile malignantly at Haonan.

The gavel was banged and the chief judge announced, "Begin!" Then he said, "As defendant, did you, Zhou Haonan, have a foreign trade business cooperation with Leng Jinxiong from January 1, 2007 to December 31, 2008?"

"Yes," Haonan replied.

"Did you sign the agreement?"

"Yes."

"Is it valid for two years?"

"Yes."

"On September 13, 2007, Jinxiong, ie your partner, borrowed 1.6 million yuan from others to pay for a quantity of Vietnamese anthracite goods. Here is the original contract. According to 'The Liability of Partners', the 35th clause of 'The Law of Enterprise Partner of The People's Republic of China' states that the partner's debt, agreed as per their investments and/or agreement, is to be paid off by their respective properties, and you should bear half the debt. Did you know that?"

"I don't know about this loan. And please allow me to explain one thing," Haonan asked.

"All right," the chief judge agreed.

"During August of 2007 I handled a charcoal importing business in Shenzhen. Jinxiong supplied a batch of dark-red *Dalbergia cochinchinensis* in Haiphong, Vietnam, which was imported via the Dongxing checkpoint. We should have shared the profit, but he didn't share it with me, which broke our agreement," explained Haonan.

"Where is your evidence?" the chief judge asked.

"I have the agreement between us."

"But where is the evidence that supports the agreement?"

"I don't have any evidence," Haonan said. He regretted having no evidence, but he had never thought he would be sued like this.

"Since the defendant doesn't have evidence, we can't support this appeal," the chief judge said.

Haonan went on, "During November 2007 in Donghai Hotel, Dongxing, Guangxi, Jinxiong and I lived together in one room. That time because we had a business disagreement and I had taken a sleeping pill, Jinxiong attacked me by punching my head, which violated the criminal law of China."

"Did you call the police at that time?"

"No. It was too sudden for me to think of it." He wished now he had called them.

"Do you have it on video?"

"No. I didn't think of that either, and it was too late by then."

"Do you have any medico-legal evidence for your wound?"

"No. But I have witnesses." Haonan thought that was too late as well because the witness was not in Shenzhen.

"The defendant's evidence is lacking, so his appeal is not valid," the chief judge said.

Presently Rong Benliang stated, "On the Debt Note provided by the plaintiff, there are the signatures of Jinxiong and Haonan, along with the stamp of the Hong Kong An'niaoda Resource Group established by the plaintiff. Now on behalf of the plaintiff, I request that this Debt Note is recognised."

Haonan then took out his agreement and said: "According to the second clause of our agreement, Party A (Jinxiong) and Party B (Haonan) should mutually use the Hong Kong An'niaoda Resource Group, which must have the qualification of a legal taxpayer. However, this Vietnamese anthracite was not delivered. In the meantime, Hong Kong An'niaoda Resource Group operated by Jinxiong is only an offshore company. This 'empty-shell company' was registered in Hong Kong but paid no tax, in mainland China or in Hong Kong, so it doesn't have the qualification of a taxpayer. Jinxiong is a 'commander without any army'. Yearly he paid 1,500 yuan to a lady in Hong Kong, who was in charge of receiving and answering the telephone. If someone phoned for Jinxiong, she'd say 'He has just gone out on business to mainland China, please call his mobile phone' and the like. Actually Jinxiong never stayed at the location of his company and this company has no legal office. Hence, this 'Debt Note' has no legal status."

Haonan presented to the chief judge via the court officer the agreement and the evidence from Hong Kong Tax Bureau.

After inspection, the chief judge said, "We do not support a foreign trade business performed by an offshore company which does not pay tax legally. So the appeal of the defendant is valid."

"Look at our evidence here," said Rong Benliang, hurriedly presenting the original Debt Note, on which there was Jinxiong's illegible signature. It surprised Haonan to see that it was accompanied by Haonan's own signature. Haonan clearly remembered that Jinxiong had never mentioned such a loan and even if he had, Haonan had never made such a signature. So where did Haonan's signature come from?

"This 'Debt Note' is fictional," he said. "I hope the judges will check it carefully. I have evidence, which is the certificate I once won for First Prize in the Chinese National Hard-Pen Calligraphy Competition years ago, on which there is the stamp of the China Calligraphers Association and my personal signature. By this, we can see that the two signatures are different." He presented it to the court.

Seeing this, the chief judge smiled. When he had read the case papers he had felt that the name of Haonan was somewhat familiar to him. Now he had seen more of Haonan's work, in which *The Poem of Everlasting Hate* by Baijuyi, a Tang Dynasty poet, was written. As it happened a calligraphic version of this poem hung in the chief judge's own home. As an admirer of calligraphy, the chief judge could see the difference between the two signatures.

Now it seemed as if everyone in the court was seeing a calligraphy exhibition. However Haonan suddenly had an ominous feeling that the original "receipt" he had written for Guangwei was still in Guangwei's hand. Perhaps they had successfully faked it. Haonan thought for a moment, then said to Rong Benliang, "Now that the plaintiff has said that the loan was used in payment for the Vietnamese anthracite, can you show the Customs Clearance Sheet of Import Goods, together with the payment document for Import Tax and Value Added Tax?"

"No." Rong Benliang looked confused.

"Do you have evidence that the above taxes have been remitted to the national central bank?"

Silence. Guangwei, who sat in the public gallery, didn't look so arrogant now.

Finally the chief judge announced an adjournment, and said the judicial decision would be announced on another day.

Fifteen days later, the court pronounced the sentence. The request for compensation of 0.8 million yuan from the plaintiff was rejected on the grounds that the loan contract was not valid and there was no evidence to support the loan of 1.6 million yuan. Furthermore, the law had been broken because Haonan's signature had been faked on the Debt Note, giving the defendant the right to lodge another lawsuit. Jinxiong had lost his case.

Jinxiong, who knew that he was in the wrong and unable to win, gave up the right to lodge a further appeal in Shenzhen Intermediate People's Court. It turned out that Haonan's signature on the "Debt Note" had been faked by another person entrusted by Guangwei. However, in the end, Haonan decided not to sue Jinxiong.

Chapter 37
Love and Business

On a summer day Shuwen arranged to meet Haonan in the mangroves of Futian. She wore a white dress like a lily petal and her long hair fell down to her shoulder, and she looked relaxed and unhurried. The sun was shining and the tourists gathered in groups gossiping, playing cards, flying kites and so on. The sea lightly caressed the shore and many sea birds flew to and fro. Haonan and Shuwen strolled along the shore. Raising his head, he saw the West Bridge in Shenzhen Bay standing magnificently between Shekou and Hong Kong. In the west was Dongjiaotou, where he had once embraced Laizhen. It was fifteen years since Haonan had last been to Shekou in 1993.

While they walked, they talked softly. She said, "I'm a gracious girl who always listens to the words of my parents. However, I'm getting older year by year, and if I don't get married soon, it will be considered strange."

"Maybe," was his reply.

"If I delay any longer, I'll be an old spinster."

He agreed, laughing.

"This Spring Festival, you took me to your home town. Now I want to take you to my home town to meet my mother, OK? She too hopes I will take a partner to fulfil her wishes."

This surprised Haonan somewhat, and he hesitated before saying, "Yes, I could."

Shuwen already appreciated his honesty, kindness and sincerity. But the most important thing was that she saw his filial devotion to his mother.

"I'm glad I have met a man who holds a gem in his bosom and grasps jade in his hand," she said. She could not conceal her happiness.

"How long will you hire me for then?" he asked, smiling.

She seized his hand, dragged him to a stone stool and sat down. Then she said bravely, "I'll hire you for the rest of your life."

"And how will you pay the rent?" smiled Haonan.

"You should pay me!"

"It's you who's hiring me, so why would I pay you?"

"You should think seriously about that."

They clasped all four hands together and hugged tightly, his big strong hands on her small, gentle ones. She had the white and tender skin of Sichuan girls. The sea breeze blew lightly and her hair and clothes spread a faint fragrance like lavender. He sat beside her, wishing he could fully enfold her. But they were sitting in public and it was early in their relationship, so he had to control his desires.

Time had now weakened the image of Laizhen in his heart, which was like a pool full of dirty water which had been replaced with fresh.

A few days later, Kuang Dawei, Haonan's former colleague, made an appointment to meet Haonan in the coffee shop of the Shanghai Hotel. As soon as Dawei sat down, he said, "I'm going to buy a house in Futian soon. If you want, you can arrange some invitation letters for me. I'm only interested in getting letters from French companies. I'll pay you 2,000 yuan for each and I'll pay for as many as you can get."

Getting invitation letters is too easy, thought Haonan. In the ten years of his foreign trade career he couldn't count how many invitation letters he had sent and received. "It's easy for me, I'll just ask French clients to send them."

"Great! Just do it as soon as possible," said Dawei.

Haonan began working on the invitation letters the next day. The first French client he contacted by email was a woman called Mademoiselle Lagrande, to whom he said that he wanted to import her lubricating oil to China. Mlle Lagrande was delighted, for she had always wanted to exploit the huge Chinese market. Then

Haonan pretended to enquire about price, packing, technical data and so on. He said he wanted to explore in France, along with three assistants, at their own expense, so he asked her to send out an invitation letter. Without further ado, Mlle Lagrande prepared an English invitation letter, then scanned it and emailed it to Haonan for checking. Once Haonan had confirmed it, she dispatched it by courier. When he received it he presented it to Dawei, who immediately gave him 2,000 yuan.

Haonan asked what the letter was for, but Dawei would not say. Haonan did five more invitation letters in the same way, and was paid 10,000 yuan. Then Haonan told Dawei that he would not do any more until he had been told what they were for. Dawei told him he was arranging the emigration of some Chinese peasants to work in France, and their names were attached as Haonan's assistants on the invitation letter for applying for seven-day commercial visas. However, Haonan did not need to apply for it because it was unnecessary for him to go abroad, so his application was not use.

It turned out that these peasants would have a good income in France. According to French law, they could only stay seven days there, but they would not return to China when their time expired. Instead they would apply for shelter in France, and normally they would be successful. As a matter of fact, when they landed in France, there were people waiting to give them illegal work.

Dawei said he had many passports, and many more peasants wanted to go to France. Dawei said he only needed invitation letters rather than peasant passports. Haonan suddenly said that he was afraid of being involved in this work, and Dawei retorted that what they were doing had been agreed, so what was the problem?

It emerged that arranging for one peasant to emigrate from China to France could earn thirty to ninety thousand yuan, or even more. With such huge profits, how could he fail to get rich?

Dawei controlled the passport business and Haonan was unable to share in that, for he was reluctant to let Haonan share the profit. So Dawei only wanted Haonan to look after the invitation letters.

But the next day, the newspapers reported that there were a great many illegal Chinese emigrant workers rushing to France and some Snakeheads were arrested by the Shenzhen police authority. Haonan then realised the risk he was taking.

He had received no news from Dawei for a long time. When he enquired, it turned out that Dawei had been arrested by the police and all of his property confiscated.

Haonan felt as though he had been soaked by a basin of icy water. After immediately giving up the "invitation letter" business, he was recruited as a foreign trade executive by Shenzhen Anhan Steel Trading Co., Ltd. As this company was based in Xi'xiang in the Bao'an District, he moved from Gang'xia to the company's public dormitory in Xi'xiang. In the day he was busy with foreign trade business, while in the evening he sometimes wrote a diary.

March 10 2009, Ban'an, Shenzhen, overcast

Steel exporting is a big business, in which a great deal of operating capital, normally several million yuan, is required. The general manager of our company, Wang, is very young, but he drives a BMW 760. If this affluent second generation man from the East of Canton can inherit his father's business, he will do well. This company engages in the domestic steel trade with no import or export business. After two months' work I have got the I/E right, along with the foreign exchange account.

In the fourth month I got in touch with CRC Group, a customer in San Jose, the capital of Costa Rica in Central America, through the Alibaba export platform. They wanted to import 1 x 20' container of galvanized steel coils, which would be handled by Miss Ana in their Shenzhen office in Nanshan District. Ana speaks Spanish but is poor in English. I drove her to our company's warehouse to get and seal samples, and will soon sign the contract. Presently she instructed her headquarters to open a confirmed L/C for the amount of US$36,316.00. Provided we perform the contract and present the export documents to our negotiation bank, Citi Bank, Shenzhen Branch, this goods amount will be received on time.

As bulk goods, there is also "one price for one day" in the steel market. A steel trader like us doesn't have the right to fix the steel price, instead it's decided by the steel manufacturer. After we receive the L/C, the price of galvanized steel coils doubles, and accordingly the total amount of our contract has increased to US$7,895.00, so if we export them, we'll lose; but if we don't, it means we'll breach the contract. So, what can we do?

I discussed this with Wang and he smiled like a Western philosopher, saying, "The solution is always greater than the difficulty."

I can recite more like this from Newton, Hegel, Galileo, Aristotle and so on, excerpted in our "Reader" magazine. But what's the solution? Wang did not say. Seeing my doubt, he said, "Do you understand what I mean?"

"I do, I do," I replied in a routine manner, and left.

By chance I wrote in our contract beforehand that after signing the contract, if the world steel price fluctuated the contract price would be renegotiated accordingly. So I suggested to Ana that the additional rise of US$7,895.00 should be

413

considered as a down payment of the T/T amount, which was independent apart from the L/C. They agreed. Then I sent them the banking information of our company by email.

Contact between Ana and me is mainly by email. Normally, underneath her emails is the previous email I sent to her. I have a habit of checking past emails from time to time. That night I suddenly noticed the following underneath Ana's reply:

Bank: Hua Nan Commercial Bank Ltd., Taiwan

Account: 107970020298

Beneficiary: De Pony Enterprise Co. Ltd.

Best regards
Bruce Zhou (Haonan)

When and how did I send the above banking details? I was terrified. They weren't those of our company! It turned out that someone had used my name, asking Ana to remit the down payment to another account; the hacker has been keeping a close watch on me and used the "Trojan horse" technique to steal the password from my email box, so he was watching what I did all the time and at the moment of payment, he took action. Ana and her *company trusted me so much that they would immediately make the payment.*

All of a sudden I felt that my heart was burning. It was like many years ago when I had to phone Zhu, telling him that he must stop that payment of 120,000 yuan. I hurriedly dialled Ana, telling her what had happened. She replied that she would immediately tell her headquarters to stop the payment. However, as there are twelve hours of time difference between Costa Rica and China, her colleagues were all in bed and they would not be up until Chinese noon tomorrow. So we had to wait.

What a hateful hacker! What a foul cheat!

That night I was sleepless, fearing that the CRC GROUP had completed the payment. The next morning I kept dialling Ana every few minutes. No answer. Finally at 2 pm she answered, yawning. She claimed to be recovering from jet lag. I then urgently asked her the result, and she said slowly, "It's not paid yet."

I asked one more time, "Really?"

"Yes, not yet."

At last the heavy weight which was pressing on my heart was removed.

After that, only by resetting the computer, doing an anti-virus check and amending the password could I re-use the company's email box. I reported it to the police, but I couldn't find out who or where the hacker was. I must report this case to all my friends in foreign trade.

April 10, 2009, Ban'an, Shenzhen, overcast

After receiving the down payment from the CRC GROUP, it's time for us to fight cheats like Ana, for it was she who carried out another deception. She visited our company three times, but every time when I drove her back to her company, I asked if I could visit her office, but like Jinxiong before, she always refused with different excuses.

Ana's headquarter had opened a letter of credit to us with many errors inside but refused to amend it. I think she would pick our goods up in her destination port without paying the letter of credit with the excuse that there would be discrepancies in our shipping documents under the letter of credit. We, however, did not ship the goods on board in the end.

Ana soon claimed double compensation from us on the excuse that we had received her deposit and failed to deliver. However, we insisted that our goods were always available in our warehouse and welcomed her to collect, on the condition that she should amend the letter of credit.

Ana refused to do so, so we confiscated her deposit as profit and won in the end.

Chapter 38
A'shen's Deathbed

On an afternoon in early autumn 2010, Haonan was about to fly to Shanghai, for he had six twenty-foot containers of galvanized steel coils to be loaded at Yangshang port, Shanghai and shipped to Helsinki, Finland. As a foreign trade executive who had just joined Shenzhen Hua-Steel Group, within the previous two weeks he had discussed an order with Mr Bora, a Finnish buyer, their MSN messages extending to over 300 pages, and finally signed a contract. Then he had received a 20% deposit from Bora by T/T. Ten days after that, the goods and shipping schedule had been booked, and customs clearance would soon be made.

"Attention please! Flight No. 4365 from Shenzhen to Shanghai is now boarding," the loudspeaker announced. Haonan went over to join the queue. Suddenly his mobile phone rang. Dragging his luggage with his left hand, he grasped the phone with his right.

"Mr Zhou, the new house you bought will be available in five days' time," a salesgirl said.

"All right, thank you!" Haonan was overjoyed. At the end of the previous month he had made full payment for a suite of two rooms and one hall in Huaqiangbei Garden. Now, after nearly twenty years in Shenzhen, he at last owned his own house. Once he had moved in, he planned to pick up his mother and bring her to Shenzhen, so they could live together.

Just before he reached the boarding gate, his mobile rang again. He thought it must be the salesgirl wanted to add more information, but it was his elder sister. She said hurriedly, "A'shen fell down six steps on the stairs. She has suffered a stroke and fainted!"

Haonan's heart sank with a jolt. He asked, "How can that be? I spoke to her at ten o'clock this morning." He remembered that A'shen, who was now 84 years old, had spoken clearly at that time. How could this have occurred so suddenly?

"It's true," elder sister said. "The doctors in Nawu Town Hospital say it's impossible to save her. She has already been settled in the hall of our ancestral house in Chengbian village. You must come back right now!"

The words "impossible to save her" echoed in Haonan's ears. He knew that if someone had been settled in the hall of the ancestral house, it could only mean the end. What could he do? He had to go to Shanghai to load the goods, because he had put so much time and effort into this export business, yet if A'shen passed away, he would no longer have a mother. He at once made up his mind; he would have to go back home. Dragging his luggage, he ran out of the airport.

A new moon hung high in the sky as Haonan drove the black F6 at 120 kph west on the Guangzhou-Shenzhen highway. It began to drizzle, and the wind whistled. He began to sob. His beloved mother was on the verge of death. He asked the world: if my mother passes away, would I have wealth, even if my property were worth ten million yuan?

In the faint light of dawn the next morning, Haonan arrived at Chengbian. In the west of the hall on the first floor, there was rice straw and a cotton quilt laid on the cement floor, plus a mat, and inside a mosquito net temporarily set up, A'shen was lying unconscious. Seeing that Haonan had come back, everyone cleared a way for him. In accordance with tradition, Haonan took off his shoes as soon as he stepped into the house and walked barefoot to the hall. He went down on his knees in front of A'shen, tears streaming down his cheeks. He cried loudly, "A'shen!"

There was no reaction from his mother. Her eyes were closed tightly in her old and wrinkled face. The cotton quilt that covered her was fluttering up and down. He tried to lift her hand, but it fell back, as lifeless as a dead leaf.

"Since yesterday afternoon she has been in a deep sleep. She has not opened her eyes once," said his elder sister.

Haonan carefully pulled A'shen's right hand. He saw her mouth move a little in pain. It must be this hand that was hurt. "She can still feel!" Haonan shouted, but in his heart the pain continued. "A'shen, I've come back, do you know?" he said. "Your Haonan has come back from Shenzhen."

A'shen's mouth again moved slightly. He put his mouth to her ear and said, "A'shen, I've come back. If you can hear me, please open your eyes!"

A'shen's eyebrows moved slightly. Haonan rose to his feet, clenching his fist, and said excitedly, "She still has feelings. We can't let her leave us like this. Let's call the doctor right now!"

About ten minutes later an experienced doctor arrived. After assessing A'shen, he put up drips for the injection of fluids.

A'shen had always lived with Haonan's elder brother and sister-in-law. Yesterday his elder sister had happened to visit her. It seemed that A'shen had gone upstairs alone, perhaps to take Haonan's quilt to the top floor to clean it. Two hours later when she went up again to turn it over her blood pressure had suddenly shot up, making her dizzy, so she had lost her balance and fallen down the stairs.

At noon the hanging drips had almost dropped out. A'shen's eyes had half opened, but she still could not speak. The country people came to see her one by one and they all sighed, wrung their wrists and stamped their feet.

In the afternoon Haonan tried to feed A'shen. She could only half-open her mouth and only ate a tiny portion of rice soup.

Suddenly Haonan's mobile phone rang. He put down the bowl and soup spoon. The call was from Miss Sun at the Shanghai Wantong Shipping Company. She asked, "Mr Zhou, didn't you say that you'd come to Shanghai to load the goods? Why haven't I seen you yet?"

"I'm awfully sorry. I had to come to my home town for an urgent family matter and I forgot to tell you. Sorry!"

"Then what are we going to do?"

"Let me think, and I'll come back to you soon."

The customs clearance for this batch of goods would be made in the name of Shenzhen Hua-steel Group. Now that Haonan could not handle this, he had to entrust his colleague, Miss Wang, to do it. He at once contacted her and asked her to arrange for the other set of customs clearance documents to be sent out to Miss Sun, then all the formalities would be handled by Miss Sun, and he would control it by phone.

That evening, moths and mosquitoes circled the dim lamp. In the hall A'shen was still in a deep sleep. Haonan sat sadly beside her. Late in the evening he boiled some water and cleaned A'shen with a towel, then changed her soiled underclothes. She groaned at the pain, which made Haonan feel more pain himself.

He thought painfully: *When I was a baby, A'shen, I don't know how many times you had to do this for me, but now it's my turn. Why did this happen so fast?*

He put a sleeping-chair beside A'shen's bed, then lay down in it. Yet although he had driven through the night with no rest, he had no desire to sleep now. He kept wondering how A'shen had fallen. Had she forgotten to take the medicine for her blood pressure? He tossed and turned all night long.

The next day the doctor came again to renew the drips and said to Haonan and his elder brother, "Her vital signs are still positive, but you must be prepared for the fact that she can only last for a short time. Even if she does recover, she may be bedridden."

"No! I want her to be able to walk!" Haonan shouted.

"That's almost impossible," was the doctor's reply.

"Do we have to watch her die like this?"

"If she can't eat rice, that's what will happen," the doctor said, shrugging.

There was silence for a moment.

"You're very tired. Let's take this in turn," one man suggested to Haonan.

"No, I'll manage," said Haonan. He felt that only he could manage A'shen properly.

It would soon be lunar August 15, the Mid-Autumn Festival. According to the weather forecast, a tropical cyclone had formed and Typhoon *Fanyabi*, the most severe for thirty years, would wreak havoc in Canton Province. It was now extremely hot.

Haonan cleaned A'shen's body and changed her clothes every day, for he knew how A'shen loved to be clean. He could only feed her milk. On the fourth day, when A'shen was still sleeping, he found that she had a bedsore on her back. He hurriedly painted her skin with gentian violet, to stop the sore spreading. From then on, he knew the most important thing was to let her sleep on her side.

Haonan stared at A'shen, feeling confused. She was sleeping on her right side facing the wall. Sometimes her eyes opened a little, but they soon closed again. Her right toe moved ceaselessly. Her right leg was weighed down by her paralysed left leg, so she could not move it. Looking at A'shen lying there so powerless, Haonan was lost in thought.

423

Suddenly he realised that A'shen wanted to turn herself over by pushing against the wall, but she could not speak. He hastily knelt down by the bedside, and carefully and painfully helped her to turn onto her left side. Meanwhile he was told by the doctor that her left side was without sensation, so if she slept deeply like that, her heart would be put under pressure and her face would be buried deeply into the pillow, so she could be suffocated. After that he decided to change A'shen's sleeping posture every one or two hours, especially when she slept on the left side.

"With her looked after like this, I don't know how many days it will take," said Haonan's elder brother.

"I'll keep on for as many days as it requires," said Haonan, without raising his head.

At this point Haonan's mobile phone rang. It was a call from Lu, the general manager of Shenzhen Hua-Steel Group. "What's happening with the deal in Shanghai?" he asked.

"I've entrusted Miss Wang to carry out the matter. The buyer has already paid 20% deposit, so he can't pull out. Don't worry!" Haonan said.

"No problem. But the leave you asked for has expired," Lu said.

"Unfortunately my mother is seriously ill now. Can you put it off for a few days?"

"No, you can't do that. It won't work even if you are away for a single day," said Lu, who cared only about his business.

Haonan held the phone and looked at A'shen, who was no better. He calmly said to Lu, "Then I will resign."

"Really? You can't do that!" Lu was surprised.

"Yes. I'm resigning, right now."

Six days after A'shen had begun her sleep, Typhoon Fanyabi struck. It did not hit West Canton but instead landed on East Canton and the south of Fujian Province. Rain poured down uninterrupted, bringing a chill wind. Haonan hurriedly covered A'shen with a cotton quilt.

On the eighth day Haonan had a fresh thought. He summoned all the family together in the hall to talk. He said, "I've decided to accompany A'shen to Maoming People's Hospital because there she has a better chance of being saved. It's very regrettable that she could not be driven to the big hospital when this first happened."

"That's no use now, it's just a waste of money," said his elder sister.

"All the charges will be borne by me," said Haonan.

"It's a long way, at least 80 kilometres. God knows whether there will be a problem on the way. And all old people would rather die in the ancestral house than on the way to hospital."

"But would A'shen want to die like this? Of course we must be careful on the way, but we have to fight for her," Haonan said tearfully. "If her condition is really hopeless I'll have to accept it. But if we miss a slim chance of saving her, I'll regret it all my life."

"Even if she can be saved for a few months, in the end she can never avoid dying," said his brother.

"Don't you want to rescue her? Then everyone had better die as soon as they are born? Or better, not be born and just die in their mothers' bellies?" Haonan said, sobbing. "I'd like to take care of A'shen indefinitely. As long as she is alive, even if she lies on the bed or sits in a wheelchair, I will take care of her."

"More and more money will be required," said his sister-in-law.

"I will pay it. If I don't have enough, I'll sell my car and my house in Shenzhen. I must save A'shen!" Haonan shouted.

The others were silent. They had no words to answer him.

Just then A'shen suddenly murmured, "Ah!" and opened her mouth. Everyone was astonished and hurriedly turned to look. But she was silent again as before. Haonan felt that she had tried her best to say something, but failed.

"Now that you have said this, I won't stand in your way," his elder brother finally agreed. There is a saying that the eldest son is regarded as a father, and nothing in the home can be carried out unless it has his approval.

"Then I will now call the ambulance. And to make sure nothing unexpected happens on the way, we will invite that old doctor to go with us tomorrow. And early the next morning, no matter how strong the wind and how heavy the rain, we must set off." Haonan spoke like an army commander.

Once everyone had left, Haonan began to feed A'shen the rice soup again. Strangely, she decisively closed her mouth in refusal. It was the same with milk, no matter how Haonan begged. Why did she refuse like that?

Later that day the country doctor put up more drips, of concentrated glucose and sodium chloride. He said A'shen's veins were constricted and many organs were on the verge of collapse and could not easily absorb medicine, so the drips operated very slowly.

At nightfall, as Haonan changed A'shen's clothes, he said to her, "A'shen, you must hold on a little longer. Tomorrow I'll accompany you to Maoming People's Hospital. Please hold on, you'll soon stand up again." A'shen was unable to move, but it appeared that her breathing was more urgent. Haonan could only sigh, again and again.

Late that night the wind was still strong; sometimes it rained heavily and sometimes it stopped. In the dark under the eaves of the hall door, Haonan, distressed and helpless, suddenly knelt down on the ground, his forehead striking the stones. He bowed repeatedly, mud and rainwater covering his forehead, which was soon smeared with blood. He disregarded this as he begged, "Almighty God, please save my poor mother! I would shorten my life to give some of it to my beloved mother! Please, please, please!" He rose to his feet, then quickly knelt down again. "Great Jesus!" he prayed. "For three short months I was once a sincere Christian. I pray you forgive me for not praying after that. Now I beg you please to rescue my mother. Amen!"

When he had finished begging, it seemed he could hear A'shen behind him faintly shout "Ah!" He stood up and turned. Under the burnt and blackened light, which was nearly covered by moths, A'shen closed her mouth again, motionless. But her chest was palpitating fiercely. Then she opened her mouth wider to breathe harder, looking more and more strained. This behaviour made him feel strange, but he couldn't think clearly why. Hanging his head, he recalled again the heartbroken sight of A'shen as a younger woman carrying a pile of firewood all the way to Nawu.

Twice a day, Shuwen phoned him inquiring about A'shen's condition. Sometimes he put the cellphone to A'shen's ear so that A'shen could hear Shuwen's concern, although A'shen could not say anything. He heartily thanked Shuwen for her greetings.

Soon A'shen had been sleeping for eight days. Haonan wondered how a weakened 84-year-old woman who had not eaten a grain of rice could sleep without waking for so long.

The ninth day was lunar August 16. In the morning Typhoon *Fanyabi* had just gone and the storm had stopped. But people were saying that in many places in West Canton the turbulent mudslides caused by the typhoon had caused serious injury and the deaths of both humans and animals.

Half-circling in front of A'shen's bed, Haonan, together with all his relatives, were preparing to leave. At that moment he noticed that A'shen's face had become redder, and then she suddenly opened her eyes.

"Aaah..." A'shen had miraculously opened her mouth to speak. Haonan hurriedly went over and squatted by her bedside.

She began to speak. "Haonan... you — couldn't resign, couldn't— sell car either, nor sell — house," she muttered.

Haonan was astonished. "A'shen, how did you know these things?" he gasped.

"Don't save... me," she went on, speaking each word with great labour. "You must... keep car and

429

house for marriage to Shuwen. You cannot get married unless you have... a car, a house. I have nothing to leave you. I'm sorry."

That year after he had held the fake wedding ceremony with Shuwen, Haonan had gone back home to sacrifice to his ancestors before the *Qingming* Festival. When he was asked by his mother whether he had made Shuwen conceive a baby, he couldn't answer. He could not continue with the lie, so he had told his mother the truth. Puzzled, A'shen had sat down heavily. Haonan had at once knelt down in front of her and explained that he had a loving relationship with Shuwen, and they were getting closer little by little. A'shen had no choice but to believe her son. She had smiled, then resigned herself to waiting patiently for further good news.

Now A'shen lay silent for a while, still breathing painfully. Then she said, "Haonan, I heard your prayers — last night. My son, — it's enough to me that — I gave birth to you."

A'shen's logic was clear, and Haonan finally understood. Throughout the past nine days, her subconscious mind had been working clearly. She had heard everything that had been said in the hall, but had been unable to speak. It looked as if the miracle really had happened. Haonan knelt down on the mat and shed tears of happiness and joy. It seemed that the heavens and Jesus had been touched by his devoted begging and praying.

Again A'shen spoke. "I don't — want to go to the hospital. I won't — have a chance to go to — Shenzhen. It is such a big city. You must work well — there. Don't waste money — for me any longer. Let me — go. I don't want to — to hold you back."

For an instant they all looked at each other in surprise. Haonan heaved a long sigh. Now he understood; she did not want to become a burden on them. That was why she had refused to eat again when Haonan had tried to feed her yesterday; she had decided to die. And her recovery just now was only a last transient revival, like a meteor shooting across the sky before burning out and disappearing forever.

"You've — managed me — for so long," she gasped. "You must take — good care — of Shuwen." Haonan bent down, hugging her tightly. "I will — go now," she said, so faintly he could hardly hear her.

At this instant A'shen's mouth suddenly foamed with saliva, and she gasped for breath. Willing hands helped her to move to her left side, so that she could discharge the saliva. Haonan took handfuls of tissues to sweep the saliva away. But not long after that, A'shen's breathing stopped and her eyes rolled upwards.

At that instant the whistle of an ambulance was heard, and in a flurry of footsteps, the doctor and nurses arrived. The doctor quickly checked

431

A'shen's breath and pulse, then stood back and shook his head. "She is gone," he said.

"NO!" Haonan screamed from the bottom of his heart, the most desperate sound he had ever uttered. With that, all the people in the hall burst into tears. Haonan, his brother and all the other relatives got down on their knees in front of A'shen and buried their heads in their chests. And in Shenzhen, when Shuwen heard this heartbreaking news, she burst out crying in public in her office.

Chapter 39
Shaking Heaven

Those who had just been enjoying the Mid-Autumn Festival still retained the balanced deliciousness of last night's moon cake on their lips. The moon itself had been hidden behind heavy clouds because of the typhoon and the rain. Haonan's heart was filled with a collapsed and torn feeling.

All the birds in the mountains had flown away,
And all the men on the paths had escaped.

In the hall of the ancestral house A'shen lay silently in the smart blue clothes Haonan had dressed her in. Her eyes and mouth were tightly closed. Her face still carried the pink glow of life and her white hair had been combed. Her face appeared so calm and content that Haonan felt that she was just asleep.

After one group of men left, another came to honour her. In this normally quiet village of West Canton, Haonan saw that many country people had suddenly emerged, old and young, men and women, all of them wanting to take a last look at this old woman, and all bursting into tears.

Haonan walked out of the house alone. After eight restless days of taking care of A'shen, his steps were heavy, but his heart was heavier. He took out his mobile phone to call a manufacturer of anti-corrosives in Shenzhen.

"Confirming my earlier call, I'd like to purchase a glass box," he said. "It must be 1.7 metres in length, 0.75 metres wide and 0.75 metres in height. And I want a set of preservatives consisting of formalin and a chemical to keep insects away, with high long term effectiveness, along with the necessary assembly tools. Please send it by express delivery, extremely urgent – I will pay cash on delivery. The goods must reach us tomorrow and my address and telephone number will be sent to you by text at once."

"All right. Since you expressed your intention to purchase several days ago, the goods will reach you tomorrow morning," the other man replied.

Haonan's elder brother then took his son to a mountainside a kilometre away to the east, where A'shen had once cut firewood, to find a grave for A'shen. When they returned, there was a discussion about the funeral arrangements. The elder brother summoned the Taoists to arrange a funeral ceremony the following night.

"I don't want to put her in a tomb," Haonan said suddenly.

"What?" Everyone looked at Haonan, surprised.

Haonan explained that he did not want to leave his mother like this. He still wanted to see her when he returned home later. So he quietly announced his startling plan, a plan which had been hidden in his heart for a long time. He wanted to put A'shen's corpse in a glass box and preserve it forever in the hall of the ancestral house.

All those present were shocked. They looked at each other dumbfounded.

The 70-year-old village chief spoke up first. "Doing such a thing is something we have never heard of anyone doing before," he said. "As village chief, I can't take responsibility for this. If you go ahead with this plan, you will not be allowed to come back to our village and your name will be struck off the role of the clan of Zhou. The civil administrative office in Nawu Town won't permit you to do it either, and you'll be severely punished."

Haonan said, "I don't mind. I just want to see my mother when I come back here."

The village chief was so angry that he turned and left.

Someone else said, "Aren't you afraid that the body will decay?"

Haonan replied, "The science for this is very advanced now. I've researched it. Provided the preservative is properly prepared and sealed, the corpse will be preserved forever, just like a sleeping person."

"But a corpse lying in the hall is unlucky, and it will threaten others," said his elder brother.

"On the contrary, our mother will guard her son and daughter," Haonan replied.

"But no one has ever done this here before," said one man.

"Then I shall be the first one. I hope all of you can give me your understanding. Now I will tell you two stories." He went on to relate the following:

In the ancient Wei and Jin dynasties of our nation there was a man named Wang Pou from Shangdong Province, whose mother feared thunder. After she died and a thunderstorm was coming, Wang Pou hurried to her tomb in the nearby forest, consoling her by saying, "Your son is with you now, so don't be afraid".

The other story was called "Carving wood to worship a parent". A man named Ding Lan from Henan Province in the ancient Eastern Han Dynasty missed his dead father, so he carved the figure of his father on wood, and used this to pretend that he was still alive and with him. Every day he did not eat until he had worshipped his "father", and he also reported to the effigy every time he left home. It was said that later on he saw the effigy shed tears.

The people listened, wide-eyed and motionless. They all sighed when he had finished, but still none of them would agree to Haonan's bizarre plan.

In the evening Haonan hugged A'shen's corpse again, in tears. He was surprised to find that she still felt warm. He couldn't help wondering if she was still sleeping, or if somehow her indomitable vitality still remained in her body. He asked the doctor, who confirmed that A'shen really had passed away, but he admitted that he was puzzled that she was still warm. He told Haonan that the corpse could not be put into a coffin until it had completely cooled down, otherwise it would be regarded as rebellious and failing in duty to his parents.

Haonan slept by A'shen's body until late that night. The next day, his extraordinary wish was finally agreed by his elder brother, his other relatives and the villagers. Haonan was relieved.

Then an express delivery van drove up to Haonan's ancestral house, and the great glass box was delivered. Everyone worked together to move it into the hall. Haonan had already researched the process of preserving a corpse, and he now set to work. After working for nearly an hour, he was ready to lay A'shen in the glass box.

By A'shen's left ear he placed a black mobile phone, with a battery which could last for six months. He intended to dial it every morning at 10 o'clock to ask A'shen, "Did you have nice sleep last night? How is your blood pressure? Did you boil and eat the oatmeal?" On the day when the battery finally ran flat, he would hear the recorded message: "The number you dialled has been switched off, please call again later". Then he would know that A'shen had not used the phone and must still be asleep.

A'shen slept face upwards in a red shroud in her glass box. Her face was still calm as if she was only in a deep sleep. That evening, a group of Taoists wearing red and green and burning incense and candles conducted a funeral ceremony for A'shen. That night the bright moon hung above the heavens and the air was clear, as the sounds of a gong and a wooden hammer and of murmuring and singing drifted into the heavens above Chengbian. Haonan's relatives worshipped all night long with red and swollen eyes.

After the Taoists left, everyone solemnly stood in front of the glass box. Haonan fell on his knees and kowtowed, howling like a monkey, "A'shen!" and then his elder brother, sister-in-law, elder sister and nephews burned incense and memory paper and knelt down to worship A'shen. Haonan then confusedly murmured the *Elegy*:

The relatives probably remained in sorrow,
But the others had already sung the happy song.
What to say to the dead?

438

Only the corpse is left to be buried under the mountain long.

On a board behind the glass box a poem was engraved:

Inside and Outside

By Zhou Haonan.

In the far and remote village of the west of Canton Province,
When my mother conceived me,
I curled up inside her tummy,
My mother bulged outside.

After I was born, crying,
I often slept in a cradle bearing a mosquito net.
My mother sang baby songs ceaselessly,
squatting down outside.

When my mother carried me to transplant the rice seedlings,
clout the ripe paddies and lay the grain to dry on the ground,
I lay down inside the carrying-belt on her back,
While my mother was busy outside.

When I grew up, during in my childhood,

I sometimes wandered, playing with my little friends on the mountains,
While my mother constantly missed me at home.

When I went to study at Changling primary school,
I sat in the classroom to listen to the lessons.
My mother, who let me grow then,
often watched me from outside.

Afterwards I went alone far away to study separating from my mother.
Then I stepped into society.
I always struggled outside.
But my mother, who still ploughed in the fields,
Always kept waiting for me at the village.

I'd always been longing to purchase a house in Shenzhen,
In which we would live together.

There was, however, one day before my wish would be fulfilled,
It was this day when
the relationship between my mother and me changed forever.
It was this day when
my 84-year-old mother suddenly passed away.

So from then on, my mother would lie forever
inside the "tomb".

At that time under the heavens the crow was
crying,

the leaves were falling, and the incense and
paper were burning.

We, who were grovelling with red and swollen
eyes,

tremblingly knelt down by the "tomb",
outside...

"Alas! A'shen, why did you leave like this?"
Haonan exclaimed tearfully. "A'shen, what a
tragedy that I never took you to Shenzhen!" He
had struggled in Shenzhen for so many years, but
he had never taken her there.

At that moment Haonan had made up his
mind that just before his turn came to die, he
would arrange for a grave to be dug in the hillside
at the spot where his mother had once cut the
firewood. Inside the grave he would be buried with
his mother by the villagers in the same glass box.
In this way the two of them would stay together
forever.

Chapter 40
Encounters in the Canton Fair

When Haonan had bade his mother farewell and moved to the new house in Huaqiangbei garden, his heart was heavy. He had just resigned from the Shenzhen Hua-Steel Group. Now he had given up almost everything except the pillow he had brought from Anhui Province. This new suite contained two rooms, and one had originally been prepared for his mother. He had chosen this place near Shenzhen Central Park because he had wanted to stay in an area where his mother could have a nice place to stroll every day. However, "Man proposes, but God disposes". Now he would rather have his mother still alive and well than have a new house.

Shuwen ceaselessly called to console him as much as she could, and he thanked her. He needed to get himself going again. He had decided to give up the messy steel trade, and having found that the electronic and digital industry in Huaqiangbei was booming, he registered Shenzhen Lantian Technology I/E Co. Ltd, with only himself as director, mainly to export PC accessories. Because of an arrangement with the factory, his company could claim to be a manufacturer.

When the goods had to be checked and loaded, he drove to the factory. Normally he used his home as his office, but he also used his car as a mobile office, accessing email and QQ messages from his car on a notebook computer, and using a mobile broadband service to connect to the Internet. To start his own business, he urgently needed a platform from which to generate foreign trade. Since it was impossible for him to apply for a booth in the approaching Autumn Fair as it would be too expensive, he decided to do it his own way.

So when the 108th session of the China Import and Export Commodity Fair opened in Pazhou, Guangzhou on October 15, 2010, and the exhibitors and buyers swarmed in, Haonan was inside too, hanging an "Exhibitor" badge on his chest for which he had paid 300 yuan per day, and with a case for his product catalogues, name cards, calculator and notebook.

He knew that the second floor of Hall No. 5 was the Computer and Communication Exhibition Hall, so he first spent an hour and a half walking around and looking at all the company names and foreign trade executives in all the booths. He found ten enterprises exhibiting computer mice, so he chose one in a good position and stood beside it.

"Comrade, your badge!" an armed policeman suddenly called. Haonan was alarmed, because he knew no one was allowed to distribute publicity material inside the exhibition hall. Fortunately the policeman just said, "Your badge is upside down."

The booth belonged to an import-export company from Shenzhen which offered every kind of computer mouse. Haonan saw a little fat buyer step out from inside the booth and quietly followed him. Haonan rapidly stepped past him and asked him, "Hello, are you in the mouse business?"

"What?" The man was taken by surprise. Haonan hastily explained that he too dealt in computer mice, and he wanted to present his product catalogue.

"Are you a manufacturer?" the buyer asked. Haonan was only a trader, but he had to make the man think he had a factory, otherwise the catalogue would never be accepted. Haonan said he was, and the man happily took it and put in his case.

Presently there was a noise from a corner of the exhibition hall, and Haonan saw two guards pulling a young man away. It was clear that this man had distributed many catalogues to foreigners, so he and his catalogues were seized, his exhibitor badge was confiscated and he was expelled from the fair. Only then did Haonan see a notice on the wall, part of which read: "Distributing publicity documents in the aisles is strictly prohibited".

Haonan shivered. It seemed the rules here were stricter than at the last fair he had attended.

He subconsciously touched the catalogues inside his satchel, realising that he couldn't casually take them out. But he also had a solution. Provided he didn't stand motionless but wandered around freely, and as long as he did not give a catalogue to anyone unless he got confirmation that it was wanted, there should not be a problem.

Suddenly from another booth walked out a man who looked like a European. Haonan felt he could not miss this chance. He followed close behind, but the man kept walking fast, talking on his mobile phone. Haonan speeded up to keep pace with him until he reached the Arts & Ceramic Exhibition Hall. Suddenly the man stopped. It seemed he was looking for a colleague. Seeing this, Haonan approached him and asked, "May I present our computer mouse catalogue?"

The foreigner was astonished. Then he declared that he did not deal in computer mice.

Haonan felt cheated. He had clearly seen the man checking mouse samples in the booth, taking photos of them and bargaining with the vendor. But there was nothing he could do. He just had to say "Sorry" and return to the hall.

He strolled slowly back to the Hall 5. Beside the entrance were two chairs for people to take a rest. It occurred to Haonan that most of the foreigners who entered this hall were buyers of computer and communication items. Just then, a black man sat on one of the chair. Haonan hastily

445

sat on the other, then leaned across and said to him, "Hello, Mr Latoku, nice to meet you here!"

Mr Latoku assumed Haonan must be someone he had met before. As a matter of fact Haonan had simply looked for his name on his badge.

Haonan took out a catalogue from his case and asked, "Are you interested in computer mice?"

Mr Latoku took it. In fact he was an importer of computer accessories from Sudan, Africa, and he had come to the exhibition to look for a manufacturer. For an optical mouse, for instance, the CIF price given by Haonan was US$2.20, but Mr Latoku could sell it for five dollars in Sudan, a profit of over 120%.

Haonan spent the day cruising the aisles of the exhibition hall in this way. If he was tired, he would go back to the chair to take a rest. He only focused on those foreigners who had enquired, checked and negotiated in the mouse booths.

At 12 noon on October 17, the third day of the fair, he noticed that a foreign couple had been sitting on a stand for a long time. They were trying mouse samples on the table and taking pictures. There was clearly some dispute between the two, as they were ceaselessly comparing the samples and discussing prices. It was obvious that they were thinking of buying.

Haonan gazed at all of this with eagle eyes. He had to talk to these two potential customers. He decided to wait until they left the booth, then follow them and talk to them.

Suddenly his mobile phone rang; it was Shuwen. In her gentle voice she asked how things were going at the fair, which made him feel encouraged and empowered. Even so, his eyes never moved away from the target. When he saw that the couple were going to have lunch, he realised that he was now very hungry, and he longed for a drink of water. But he could not leave. The more reluctant the foreigners were to leave, the more likely they were to be serious customers.

Finally at 4 pm, they stood up to go. Haonan followed them as they left the hall and walked all the way to the Xinggang East metro station. He wanted to talk to them in a quiet spot with no one else nearby, so he bought a ticket and followed them on to a train. He stood by them on the train and heard them apparently talking about Guangzhou and the coming 16th Asia Games that would open there soon.

When they got off the train and headed for the exit to the station, Haonan still followed them, but he hung back a little. They crossed the road, dodged the bus and finally reached the Liuhua Hotel, where they sat on a long sofa in the lobby. Haonan caught a whiff of the woman's expensive scent. Pretending to read a newspaper, he waited.

Finally the couple went into a nearby Western restaurant and sat at a table. Five minutes later,

Haonan followed them, seized by a fierce hunger. He ordered a fast food dish of sautéed beef tenderloin with black pepper at a price of 50 yuan. He had to ask for a free extra bowl of rice before his hunger was satisfied.

It was nearly eight o'clock when the couple headed for the elevator, and Haonan ran up to get in with them. The man pressed the button for the 11th floor.

Haonan breathed deeply, then went closer. "I'm sorry to bother you two," he said.

They were startled by his approach. "What's the matter?" said the man.

Haonan said, "I saw that you are involved in computer mice, so I followed you from the Canton Fair."

The couple were very surprised, but they realised when they looked at Haonan that they had indeed seen him at the fair. They said they had met many Chinese foreign trade businessmen who distributed catalogues in the Canton Fair, but it was the first time anyone had followed them like this.

When the elevator stopped at the 11th floor, they all got out and stood in the corridor talking. Haonan asked, "Can I present you with a copy of my mouse catalogue?"

The man accepted it, and asked, "Your name, please?"

"Bruce Zhou," said Haonan, and they exchanged business cards.

"You must know of Bruce Lee," said the man.

"Of course!"

To Haonan's great surprise, it turned out that they were fans of Bruce Lee and his films, so they had plenty to talk about. They invited him into their room and introduced themselves as Mei Renaj and his partner Caroline.

It was 11 o'clock at night when Haonan returned home. His tiredness passed as soon as the phone rang and he heard Shuwen's sweet voice, filling him again with warmth and power.

On the last day it seemed that God was helping Haonan. He was very tired, but he could not afford to rest. In front of him he saw a black man of medium height and noticed that a mole as big as a mushroom was growing on the back of his neck. It suddenly took Haonan's memory back through time. He knew this man.

He tapped the man's shoulder and said, "Mr Pario?"

"Hello?" the foreigner replied, turning his head with a smile. Yes, this was Pario, the man from Portugal who had let him down by paying for two shipments, then received the third and disappeared without paying for it. Haonan did not know how many Chinese exporters had been swindled by this man since then.

When Pario realised who Haonan was, the smile vanished from his face. Suddenly he got up, pushed his way through the crowd and rushed out of the hall and along Xinggang Road East.

Haonan followed him, running at top speed. The crowds got out of the way, wondering why these two men were running like this. Pario ran straight across the highway, ignoring the cars, but Haonan was close on his heels. Some of the cars had to brake urgently, leaving long black skid marks on the road.

Pario was heading for the Xinggang Hotel, where he was staying, but in the chase he had lost his way. Still trying to escape from Haonan, he rushed into a nearby hospital which was full of people. He turned a corner, then disappeared among the patients, doctors and nurses. Haonan looked left and right, but he couldn't tell which way Pario had gone.

Thinking he had escaped, Pario stopped, his chest beating wildly. At this point a patient passed by, holding by her hand a plastic bottle full of yellow liquid. Thinking it was orange juice, Pario snatched it from her.

"You can't drink that!" the lady shouted, but Pario did not speak Chinese. "You cannot drink it!" the lady shouted again, but Pario had finished it. The woman did not know whether to laugh or cry. "Why did you drink the urine I need for my health check?" she said. Some people nearby laughed out loud.

Hearing the noise, Haonan knew which way to go. His right hand, as strong as iron pincers, grasped Pario's hand and dragged him to the public seating area. He sat down, panting with exhaustion. The people in the public waiting area looked on.

"I'm not the Pario you're looking for," Pario said.

"Then who are you?" Haonan was surprised.

"I'm his cousin."

"Then why did you run?"

"Because you chased me, of course."

"Then why didn't I chase anyone else?"

Looking at him, Haonan realised that there could be other people with moles like that on their necks. A thought came to him. "I want you to sign your name," he said. He remembered that Pario was left-handed and he recalled that in the past when Pario had written the "r" in his name, it was in smooth, beautiful handwriting, like a little snake raising its head in the grass and putting its tongue out. The only one Haonan knew who could write such an excellent "r" was Pario.

Sure enough, the man used his left hand to sign. As soon as Haonan saw the signature, he knew it really was Pario and not his "cousin".

"According to law, I can present this signature, along with the one on our previous contract, to the

451

evidence centre for authentication in Guangzhou," he told Pario. "If they agree, you will have to compensate me for my loss."

Never had Pario imagined that a signature alone could be used to identify handwriting, let alone that Haonan was such an expert on the subject. He had to admit his identity.

"Now we have to discuss that contract," said Haonan. "I do not think that this business should be dealt with by the police."

"Those goods of yours had discrepancies." Pario was cunning.

"But you had already accepted them. There was also a clause in our contract that stated 'If a quality problem is to be found after receipt of goods, this must be reported within seven working days,'" Haonan replied. "You did not do so. And why were your telephone and fax numbers cancelled?"

Pario had no answer. Under the eager eyes of all the people present, Pario, his face as pink as an azalea in June, was forced to take out 32 green US dollar bills from his pocket, each for a hundred dollars, and hand them to Haonan.

Haonan took one of the notes and wiped it on a piece of white paper. A faint green mark appeared. Then he grasped the two ends of the bill and rapidly pulled; there was distinct "crack!" He studied the note further. They were genuine. He wrote out a receipt for Pario and handed back one of the bills. "I don't have change for the balance of seventy-six dollars, so please take it."

Pario stretched out his hand silently for the note.

"You are welcome to place a new oil painting order," said Haonan. "I will ask our artists in Dafen village to paint a portrait of you." Haonan took Pario's hand and shook it. Pario said nothing but stood with bowed head. Then he sulkily walked out of the hospital.

That night Haonan told Shuwen what had happened that day. She felt happy for him and praised him for his actions.

Chapter 41
Pretending to Be a Manufacturer

The first enquiry Haonan received after he went back to Shenzhen from the Canton Fair was not about a mouse, but another item. The enquiry over the phone from Miss Chin, a customer in Bangkok, was: "Can you supply a biological microscope?"

"Yes, certainly," replied Haonan.

"But you must be a manufacturer. If you're only a trader, I don't wish to talk to you."

Haonan hesitated for only two seconds, thinking quickly. "Yes," he said. "I have the sole agent rights to Thailand from Guangzhou Yuri Optical Factory, which specially produces biological microscopes. I can send a copy of the certificate."

"All right, I require 800 sets, and please quote me CIF Bangkok."

Of course Haonan was not the sole agent for this factory, but the longer he had worked in Huaqiangbei, the more flexible he had learned to be. After putting down the phone he dialled Zhu, the managing director of Guangzhou Yuri Optical Factory, asking for a certificate for the sole agency rights for the Thai market. Zhu agreed because her products had not yet penetrated the Thai market, but she stated that the export order had to be signed within three months. The next day Haonan received the sole agent certificate from Guangzhou by express mail. He then sent a scan to Miss Chin by email, along with a quotation for biological microscope No. L2100. Within two days, they had discussed the order three times and signed the contract. Miss Chin said she would use L/C payment terms, which Haonan regarded as reasonable. Nevertheless Haonan still persuaded her to accept a clause providing for 50% to be remitted after signing the contract and the balance before the goods were loaded.

However, Haonan was at a loss about the quantity: should the 800 sets be shipped all at once or in lots? He felt it was best to ship them as one lot, and by sheer coincidence, there were 800 sets ready in the factory now. None the less, this was a new importer, and the greater the quantity the more risk there was and the more responsibility he bore. Finally he decided to ship them in two lots, 200 sets followed by 600 sets.

There was only one worrying clause; Miss Chin required that a QC tag must be hung inside the goods, which Zhu strongly objected to. Zhu announced that she would rather give up the order. But she invited Haonan, together with the importer, to visit her factory to negotiate. Haonan was reluctant, because at this point it was impossible for him to bring the importer to the factory. Presently he accepted Miss Chin's requirement.

Several days later, 200 sets of goods arrived at the warehouse he had rented in Huaqiangbei. Haonan went over and opened the 200 cartons of goods one by one. He then took out 200 QC tags which he had printed in a printing factory beforehand and hung them on the lens mounts of the microscopes one by one. Then he packed the goods up again carton by carton; it took him three days. After he had confirmed that the 50% balance payment had been received, the goods were loaded on board smoothly.

To his surprise, when the goods were exported, he received another enquiry for biological microscopes, from a man named Mayachefsk, with whom he had had lunch in the Canton Fair. Mayachefsk was from Russia and at that time they had only exchanged business cards. After returning to Russia, Mayachefsk was prepared to purchase 40 sets of large biological microscopes. He stressed that if Haonan was not a manufacturer he would not discuss it, and in any case, before placing the order, he would fly over ten thousand miles from Moscow to China to inspect the sample and check if the factory existed or not. Mayachefsk emphasized again and again that he absolutely refused to do business with a middleman.

The biological microscope was the key product of the Guangzhou Yuri Optical Factory. Haonan felt that it wasn't reasonable to invite Mayachefsk to visit the factory, and it would pave the way for others, because an I/E company named LQ was based there. If Mayachefsk visited, LQ would certainly gain him as a customer.

What should I do? Haonan thought. He knew that the Guilin Optical Factory in Guangxi and Guangzhou Optical Factory were both professional factories with 20 years of production behind them, but Guangzhou focused on biological microscopes and Guilin on stereo microscopes. These two types were almost the same, and only an expert could tell the difference.

Haonan then rang Mr Zhang, the managing director of the Guilin Factory, saying, "Can you accredit the Shenzhen Lantian Technology Company as your Shenzhen export office? And can you issue a certificate valid for three months?"

Zhang replied, "I'm pleased to hear that you've signed a big order for 800 microscopes with Guangzhou Yuri Optical Factory. I also want to establish an export agent office in Shenzhen. But regarding the certificate, you cannot simply have it whenever you like. You and I must have a business relationship first."

"How can we do that?" asked Haonan.

"You should purchase from us to create a sales record," Zhang said.

After putting down the phone, Haonan thought hard. Ten minutes later, he dialled Zhang again and said, "I will now place an order for 20 sets of stereo microscopes No. GL-99TI. My payment will reach you this afternoon and in a few days' time, I'll bring my client to visit your factory."

"So soon? All right. Once your payment reaches me, I'll issue the certificate to you." Zhang was startled by such speed. Of course it was impossible for Haonan to have found a buyer in ten minutes. But this buyer was actually the Lantian Company, ie himself. In fact he was only buying the 20 microscopes for stock in his house, for he knew that such products were always in demand from the factories and merchants which produced bare IC, LED and PCB boards in Huaqiangbei.

Several days later, Haonan brought two Russian customers to the Guilin Optical Factory. Mayachefsk was huge with brown hair. The other man was small and fat; this was his assistant and engineer, Cbzi, who spoke fluent English.

Haonan and Zhang accompanied the two buyers to the large and advanced workshops and the warehouse. Zhang had once worked in all these workshops. When the factory was reformed he had become the president there. Haonan took them into the wide sample room, where there was every kind of stereo microscope and accessories such as lenses, eyepieces, halogen bulbs and cold light resources in the cupboards.

On an exhibition stand in the centre was placed a big, heavy biological microscope. Cbzi inspected a blood specimen with it, adjusting all the settings. Finally the two men agreed that the sample machine was OK and they would buy this one and take it back for comparison with the mass-produced goods. So the first round had been won.

That afternoon Haonan accompanied the two Russians back to Shenzhen. After returning to Huaqiangbei, he persuaded them to buy various everyday electronic items, then invited them to a banquet in the Pavilion Restaurant.

Late that night when Haonan stepped out of the restaurant to answer his mobile, he suddenly saw that Cbzi was also on the phone in the doorway. To Haonan's surprise, Cbzi was now speaking pure standard Mandarin. He had always spoken English before, so Haonan had thought he spoke only Russian and English. It seemed that Cbzi had pretended not to know Chinese in order to spy on his rival's business secrets. Haonan decided to be more careful in future. It was fortunate that he had not given away any business secrets in the conversation today.

The next morning Haonan saw the Russians off at Bao'an airport and then returned to his office.

On board the plane, Mayachefsk was delighted with the biological microscope sample. He planned to exploit the electronics market in Russia, but he and Cbzi did not know that the microscope he had bought was really from the Guangzhou Yuri Optical Factory, not the Guilin Optical Factory. It was of course the sample Haonan had bought from the Guangzhou Yuri Optical Factory and taken to Guilin Factory himself, hugging it like his own baby. At first Haonan was worried about the deception, but he told himself that it did not matter which factory it came from; after all he could guarantee that the goods would exactly match the sample, so the contract would not be breached.

After returning to Russia, Mayachefsk signed the contract with Haonan by email and remitted 30% deposit payment by T/T. After that Haonan placed an order for 40 sets with the Guangzhou Optical Factory. One month later the microscopes had been completed, and after Haonan had received the balance of 70%, they were smoothly shipped on board. The order earned a total net profit of 400,000 yuan, 10,000 per set. However, the balance payment from Thailand for 600 sets of biological microscopes had not been received.

Haonan then received three enquiries, two of them from India and Pakistan. It seemed that only an enquiry from Holland was workable. At 11 o'clock that night, therefore, he dialled the Dutch buyer on Skype at home.

"I have the catalogue you presented to me in the Canton Fair," said Mohammed, the Dutch importer.

"Mohammed? I think I remember that name. Were you engaged in the hardware business in January 1992?"

"Yes. But how did you know that?"

"Did you ever sign a contract with Bruce Zhou, a foreign trade executive with the China Merchants I/E Trade Company at that time? In the Shanghai Restaurant in Shekou, and you wore a white gown?"

"Let me have a think. I have visited China three times... Bruce Zhou? Are you..."

"Yes, I'm Bruce Zhou, the man who met you right then."

"So it's you!" Mohammed was excited. "In that year after I signed an order with you, I was unable to get in touch with you. Then I gave up hardware. Now I deal in computer accessories."

Haonan replied, "I hope we can do further business."

Mohammed said, "Your previous company was only a trader. Now I must deal with the manufacturer."

Haonan was slow to reply. But he soon thought of a solution and said, "I have my own factory now. You need not sign the contract until you visit my factory."

"I have a Chinese representative in Huaqiangbei," said Mohammed.

In reality Haonan's company traded only in computer mice. If this business could be done, he would place the order with a mouse factory in Xi'xiang in the Bao'an District.

He then phoned Mr Wen, the factory's managing director, to ask about foreigners visiting the factory. But the factory name was completely different from Haonan's Lantian company. What could he do? Perhaps there was a way round this...

Several days later Haonan brought Mr Eli, Mohammed's agent in China, to see his company. Eli had blue eyes and a high nose and spoke fluent English, and Haonan assumed he was from Europe. It was clear that he did not speak Chinese. After a short visit to the company, Haonan drove him to the factory in Xi'xiang. The F6 raced along the Beihuan Boulevard, and forty minutes later they were in Xi'xiang.

Haonan led Eli to the factory building and walked to the office with him. At the entrance to the second floor hung a board which read "Shenzhen Lantian Technology I/E Co. Ltd." in Chinese and English. Eli stopped and stared at the board. "What's the style of calligraphy here?" he asked.

"What do you mean?" Haonan was flustered.

"I'm going to learn Chinese in Huaqiangbei next week, along with calligraphy. I like Chinese calligraphy very much."

Haonan then felt relieved, and told him the truth. "This is the Liu Gongquan style from our Tang Dynasty. With regard to the English, as you know, it's a handwriting variation of the most beautiful typeface, Times New Roman. And to be frank, the Chinese and English words were all written by me."

"By you?" Eli looked at Haonan in astonishment.

"Yes. Having my own calligraphy used in my factory will mean more to me."

Haonan guided Eli to the office of the managing director. He sat on Mr Wen's big chair and ordered Mr Wen to serve tea to Eli. Then he explained the production equipment, such as the SMT machine and mouse materials like IC chipsets, to Eli, along with the production process. Hearing this, Eli opened his eyes wide and nodded from time to time.

Mr Wen continued to assist Haonan by pretending that Haonan was his boss, and busied himself serving tea and water. As to the board hanging on the wall, before Eli arrived Mr Wen had taken off his own board and hung up Haonan's instead. Once Eli had left, Mr Wen put his own board back up. When it was time for Eli to come back to the factory to inspect the goods later,

Haonan and Mr Wen would perform the same tricks again.

Finally Haonan invited his guest to a McDonald's. As Eli ate his hamburger, he reported to Mohammed, his boss, by telephone, "Haonan really is a manufacturer."

And so the mouse order was finally signed.

Day by day Haonan had become smarter and more successful in the business. So when he met Shuwen by the sea at Xia'sha in Futian the next weekend, he finally asked her to marry him. To his joy, she accepted on the spot. They hugged each other warmly, knowing finally that they would live together and love each other for the rest of their lives. The sea wind blew and the waves lightly washed the seashore as they walked along arm in arm. Their excitement lasted all night long.

Chapter 42
The Secret of the Glue Bottle

That September, Haonan suddenly received an urgent call from Chen Yiquan, a middle-aged merchant whom he had once met in exchanging a deposit and receipt in Dongxing four years before. Chen Yiquan, who had just come back to China from Vietnam, first congratulated Haonan on the lawsuit against Leng Jinxiong, then said he had brought from Vietnam two small glue samples packed in plastic bottles which he had got from Ruan Mianmian, a Vietnamese merchant in Ho Chi Minh City. As a daily use item, this kind of glue had been sold out in Vietnam and nearby Cambodia, with huge demand. As no such factory was available in Vietnam, it had to be purchased from neighbouring China. Ruan, who had good relations with both the Vietnamese and Cambodian governments, had signed long-term sales contracts with buyers in these two countries. He had agreed to buy glue from China weekly, 100 cartons per batch with 1,200 units per carton, totalling 120,000 bottles of glue per week. He would import four batches per month, namely 400 cartons or 480,000 bottles, which would be delivered at the China-Vietnam border, then taken through customs clearance and exported to Vietnam. Chen Yiquan said he would send the samples to Haonan by courier, exhorting him to try to find such goods as quickly as possible.

Originally Haonan, having focused on electronic and digital items, had agreed with Li Shuwen's suggestion that he should not deal in too many complicated items. However it was not difficult for him to spare some time to look for a glue supplier. Two days later when he received the samples, he found that they were just like the national glue 502, which was mainly used to stick metal, plastic, rubber and leather etc. He first searched on the internet, asked in general stores and enquired from some friends. But no factory matched the requirements.

He then told Chen Yiquan what he had found. Chen Yiquan replied that Ruan had said that if a supplier or factory could not be found, he should call him without delay. He gave Ruan's mobile phone number to Haonan.

The international call from Shenzhen to Vietnam cost six yuan per minute. During the phone conversation, Ruan could only speak Vietnamese. Haonan smiled. He could use Vietnamese to deal with the business in future. Ruan told Haonan that he had a mobile phone number for Liu Rongming, a Chinese glue supplier.

He had stolen the number from the GI company, a big glue importer in Vietnam. However, Ruan had never met Liu Rongming and there had been no telephone contact either. Ruan also insisted that Haonan could not reveal who had given him the number, let alone give it to anyone else.

When Haonan dialled the number, it turned out to be registered in Haikou City, Hainan Province. When the other man opened his mouth, he laughed and said. "You have been lucky to find me, I'm a supplier that you never expect to meet."

"Great! Do you know Ruan Mianmian, a Vietnamese merchant?"

"Oh no. But there are countless Vietnamese who know me," Liu Rongming proudly responded. He explained that his factory in Haikou City imported fine natural rubber materials from Vietnam, so its quality was the best in China, and the 502 was matchless. Meanwhile, he said that his sole agent in Vietnam and Cambodia had already been bought by the GI company, the glue importer in Vietnam. This meant that except for the GI company, no one in Vietnam could buy this item from him. However he suggested that he could supply the goods to Haonan in Pingxiang, another checkpoint between Guangxi and Vietnam, if Haonan paid immediately without a contract. But the goods could be checked before payment. When Haonan became experienced in dealing in this business, Liu Rongming could authorise

Haonan as his general agent along the Pingxiang route to Vietnam and Cambodia.

Haonan hastily asked the price, and Liu Rongming told him it was 3.60 yuan per bottle. "That's higher," said Haonan. But Liu Rongming responded firmly, "I can't reduce it even by a penny. It's only because of your sincerity that I talked to you. You are lucky that I will supply these goods."

Haonan noticed that there was a red label on the sample stating "Suggested price RMB4.60/pc". Haonan calculated, basing on his selling price of RMB3.95/pc and the middle-man commission of RMB0.05/pc to Chen Yiquan, that he should offer Ruan RMB4.00. He was very surprised that Ruan at once accepted this price, declaring that he only cared about whether Haonan could supply the goods and not the price. Never in Haonan's foreign trade career had he experienced such a straightforward buyer. Haonan calculated that he would make 168,000 yuan, and his whole-year profits would be up to two million.

Haonan was stunned. He had travelled to Vietnam so many times without success, and now there was the prospect of a fruitful deal at last. In fact the profit was so much higher than the electronic digital items he was dealing in that he wondered if he should engage solely in exporting glue.

Haonan and Shuwen were now married, and Shuwen had resigned from the shipping company and was working with him. Just then, having just finished her work in the tax bureau, she pushed the door open. After listening to Haonan's story, she sat down and carefully calculated the whole budget. But her reaction was calm. She didn't believe it could be so profitable.

The next day Chen Yiquan called Haonan, saying that the deposit of 48,000 yuan for the first batch of goods from Ruan had been brought in by the Vietnamese women in Dongxing who were dealing in exchanging currency and waiting for Haonan to confirm receipt. Before this, however, Haonan must guarantee he would have the goods. Haonan was pleased, and he knew that the deal would be successful. He was always aware when dealing with the Vietnamese that a deposit was a must, no matter how the contract was worded. Of course this deal would be completely different from the timber deal in Dongxing four years ago.

At dusk Shuwen cooked a pot of sweet potato, a dish Haonan loved, to take with them. In the evening they set off from Shenzhen, driving the F6 along the Guangzhou-Shenzhen and Zhongshan-Jiangmen highways. At midnight when they arrived at the Liangjinshan service area, he slept for forty minutes across her warm thighs. Then they drove on, past Zhanjiang City, Xiuying Port and Qiongzhou Strait.

Early the next morning when they arrived in Haikou City, they planned to visit the factory of Liu Rongming. In fact they were invited to meet him at a KFC branch, and Liu Rongming, thin-faced, pointed to a van parked in front, stating that there were 400 cartons of glue goods waiting for Haonan to carry out a random check. Haonan did so and drew out 10 samples. However Liu Rongming refused to show his factory to Haonan and Shuwen, on the pretext that his production technology and intellectual patent must be kept secret. He declared assertively, "You have seen my goods, don't you believe I have a factory?" Haonan had to accept that.

During the meeting, internet messages from Ruan in Vietnam ceaselessly gushed into Haonan's mobile phone, urging him to get the goods ready as soon as he could. Liu Rongming swore that his goods would be supplied as long as Haonan arranged payment.

At noon, after coming back from Haikou City, Haonan put the sample upside down on the table, and stared at it. Suddenly he noticed something glinting on the bottom of the bottle. He immediately called to Shuwen, "Look at this!"

They hurriedly examined it with a microscope. It could be seen that on the bottom of the bottle a factory telephone number was carved in tiny writing: 071× 6633××9. In fact the number had been carved with the skilful use of fluorescent light, so it could only be seen if the sample was put upside down and seen at an angle of 45 degrees with a microscope. It was only by chance that he had noticed this number.

Their hearts sank. Shuwen said, "The more profitable the deal appears, the more careful we should be." Haonan nodded. He decided not to dial the number directly; instead he asked Shuwen to use a mobile phone registered in Guangzhou. They finally established that the glue had been made by the Yitong Paste-King Glue Factory in Hubei Province, and it had been sold for only 0.40 yuan. So if Haonan sold four batches of goods to Ruan in a month, he would make 1.7 million yuan at the huge profit rate of 900%, and a year's profit would be an unthinkable 20 million!

Twenty million! They were dumbstruck. This was the kind of fortune no one could dream of, unless one won the first prize in the current "Double Colours Balls" lottery in China.

When Shuwen contacted the glue factory in Hubei Province, she emphasized that she was in Guangzhou and asked them to send six samples to her cousin there. When her cousin received them after the National Day holiday, she sent them on to Shuwen. Then Haonan took six of the samples from Liu Rongming, together with those from the Hubei factory, totalling 12, and sent them to Ruan via Chen Yiquan in Dongxing. Several days later he received a reply from Ruan that all 12 samples had been confirmed. Haonan then asked Ruan to sign, sealing the samples and copying his passport, and send them all back together.

The lesson Haonan had learned with the ramie fabric business many years before had taught him to be careful. Ruan confirmed all the requirements lodged by Haonan, then stressed that the goods must fully conform with the sample without indicating any information such as name, telephone number and address of the producing factory – this was called "neutral packing" in international trade. Only then could Ruan, after receiving the goods, stick on his own registered logo printed in Vietnamese and Cambodian, otherwise he would be unable to sell them. In the end he urged Haonan again, "When will you have the goods ready?"

Haonan then asked Shuwen to check this point. But the Hubei factory then said that they had no stock. The goods were so hot that buyers were waiting in a queue for them. What was more, the full amount must be remitted before they would begin to produce, and no matter what the quantity was, delivery would be one month later.

When Haonan spoke to Ruan again, Ruan stated that once Haonan had got his deposit, the goods must be delivered on the same day. It seemed that Ruan had forgotten all about production time but was only making the excuse that the glue market was going up, and his buyers in Vietnam and Cambodia all just wanted to buy the stock or he would compensate by paying five times the deposits he had received from those buyers.

Haonan and Shuwen did not know what to do. In these circumstances he could only consider Liu Rongming, who had stock at any time and any place. Despite the fact that his price was on the high side, a profit at the rate of 10% was still obtainable. The most difficult part of every business was the beginning. He decided to buy his stock from Liu Rongming, then supply to Ruan, and from the second deal on, he would buy the goods from the Hubei factory instead.

Haonan and Shuwen were busy until midnight. He was about to rest, but when he came closer to her exquisite body, he was aroused again. He embraced her from behind, his hands tightly upon her breasts and his head on her shoulder, breathing in her aroma. She stood still, half-closing her eyes and letting him fondle her gently. It was only a few steps from the office tables in the hall to the bedroom. They both took off their clothes, and after a hurried bath they entered the bedroom. She was naturally beautiful, and her small red nipples formed a bright contrast with his bronze skin.

After two hours of rolling on the bed, they felt relaxed at last. They stretched out their arms and legs on the bed. She asked, "Don't you feel tired? You have made love for two hours, and you have a long way to drive tomorrow."

"I'd be crazy not to make love for two hours. How would I discharge all my powerful energy?" he said, smiling.

She pinched his ear. "But I'm tired, even if you are not."

He turned and pressed her under his body. "If you don't agree, I'll make love for three hours. You know I can control the time and tempo."

"You really are a love machine," she sighed.

The western end of the Shiwan mountain range stretches up to Pingxiang City in Guangxi, and its limestone landscape could be seen inside the car along the highway, together with the strange forms of the stalactites and funnels. All the mountains and forests made it feel like early winter, although it was still autumn. Haonan felt cold, but Shuwen in the passenger seat gave him warmth from time to time. She put a peeled sweet potato into his mouth, then unscrewed a bottle of mineral water and handed it to him. Then she gave him a piece of folded tissue to dry his mouth.

Thanks to these supplies, Haonan felt neither tired nor hungry. After a while she sat on the rear passenger seat, massaging his shoulders, and this gave his body more energy. If he had not been driving, he would have made love to her again there.

At last they saw the high martyrs' memorial at Youyiguan on the Chinese-Vietnam frontier, where armed police were on duty. Haonan's car drove into the open place in front of Youyiguan checkpoint. The sun was warm. Nearby they could see a dark, middle-aged Vietnamese man in sunglasses; Ruan.

"Nice to meet you!" said Haonan in Vietnamese, and the two men shook hands. Then from their leather suitcases, they pulled out the import and export contracts which they had signed by email beforehand.

"This deposit was returned to Vietnam from Dongxing and I exchanged it again, then brought it here," Ruan said. He took out 48,000 yuan from his leather suitcase, the first instalment. In fact, in order to obtain the Chinese notes, he had taken heavy bags of Vietnamese currency to Tongdeng, a frontier city in Vietnam. In accordance with their previous agreement, after Haonan received this payment, Ruan would check the goods, and provided they conformed with the contract, Ruan would pay the balance of 90% on the spot.

Shuwen, in her sports shoes and jeans, helped Haonan to take care of the deposit. In between

475

presenting him with the documents, she warily observed their surroundings.

After Haonan had checked the deposit, a car drove up at speed. The driver got out and opened the doors, revealing 100 cartons of the glue product. It was Liu Rongming, and there were another three men in the van. Liu Rongming had arranged to meet Haonan to exchange the money and goods simultaneously.

Haonan calmly opened the carton and took out six glue bottles. He put them upside down, laid horizontally, placed them at an angle of 45 degrees, then took out his microscope and examined one of them. He pointed to the bottom of the bottle and said to Liu Rongming, "There is a factory telephone number on it, which means it does not meet the neutral packing requirement between me and Ruan. I can't accept these goods, you must take them back."

Ruan was dumbfounded. He had never imagined that Haonan would find the secret telephone number. Then Liu Rongming suddenly shouted angrily, "So you conned me? The samples you took previously weren't from this batch of goods?"

"Yes. But who played who? When I drove a thousand miles to Haikou City, you didn't even let us enter your factory. In fact, do you even have a factory?"

Ruan and Liu Rongming looked at each other in silence. Seeing this, Shuwen hastily got the contract ready and gripped the leather suitcase, standing by Haonan's right side. Then Haonan stretched up his hands and clapped his palms three times. At this signal, a van which had been parked a short distance away drove up. The driver opened the back, where it could be seen that there were another 100 cartons of glue. These were the goods produced by another factory in Shenzhen, which Haonan had purchased at the price of RMB0.30 before going to Pingxiang.

Haonan pointed to the goods. "This is the sealed sample I got from Ruan, along with your passport information, on which there is also the official report issued by Shenzhen Import and Export Commodity Inspection and Quarantine Bureau, proving that the quality of these goods is in full conformity with your sample. Isn't it ordinary glue? Why did you make it so complicated? If it includes epoxy resin and the viscosity can meet the standard, it'll be OK. Of course if you don't accept, you can randomly take the sample, then we will mutually seal it and present it to the Foreign Trade Section of China International Trade Promotion Council in Beijing for arbitration."

Ruan and Liu Rongming, together with the other three men, were caught off guard, and did not know what to do. Haonan explained that although Ruan, Liu Rongming and Chen Yiquan had all declared in phone calls that they did not recognise each other, he had worked out what roles they had played. He had realised that "Suggested price RMB4.60/pc" had been stuck on to falsely increase the price, because Haonan had found, after a great deal of market investigation, that the same quality and volume of glue was sold at only one yuan to Vietnam and Cambodia, comparatively poor countries, so how could they accept such a high price as RMB4.60? If so, why wouldn't Chinese people all go to Vietnam and Cambodia and sell this item in the streets?

Haonan also understood that the invisible telephone number printed on the bottle bottom was originally an anti-fake device for the factory moulding. Chen Yiquan had deliberately introduced this business to Haonan. After comparing it with the strict trade terms of the Hubei factory, Haonan would be forced to buy the goods from Liu Rongming, and once he did so, Liu Rongming would get a profit as high as 384,000 yuan at a profit of 800%. But Haonan would have been unable to sell the goods.

At this point Ruan walked up to the goods which Haonan had bought from another factory in Shenzhen. He opened the carton, took one bottle out, and checked as Haonan had done. He found that unlike the product from the Hubei factory, there was no logo or other wording and no phone number appeared on the bottle bottom. Now he was more confused. He had planned this trick so that he could refuse Haonan's goods and claim back the deposit, with the excuse that Haonan was unable to supply the goods required, so that, as with the Dalbergia in Dongxing, he would force Haonan to lose double his deposit. Now Ruan had no excuse for refusing. In practice he did not have the money to pay the 90%; in fact he had never planned to pay it at all.

Haonan was prepared. He had concealed a pair of Nunchakus behind his back, for use if required. But he was not going to force Ruan to pay the balance, because he knew it would be useless. He regarded the deposit as all the money he was going to get from him. In the meantime he was paying the full amount for the goods to the factory in Shenzhen. He could still make about 6,000 yuan, and after deducting commission to Chen Yiquan and his fuel and travelling expenses, he could still earn a little.

Haonan then announced that if Ruan did not stop what he was doing, he would enforce the contract and lodge a legal claim for the balance through the Vietnamese government and commercial chamber. Ruan had to agree; he had no alternative.

Haonan then got into his car with Shuwen and drove away. But as they left he noticed that there was a saloon car nearby and inside was sitting Chen Yiquan, together with a big man who looked like Leng Jinxiong. The two of them were looking at Haonan too. Shuwen was wondering what was happening, but then the F6 accelerated onto the Nanning-Youyiguan expressway, heading for Shenzhen. Shuwen gently fingered her shoulder-length hair and smiled.

Haonan later found out that the Hubei factory did not exist.

Chapter 43
Coming Back to Shekou

There were so many times in dreams when I came back to Shekou,
I tightly hugged the huge Nan Mountain with my hands.

In the early autumn of 2011 when Haonan had returned to Shenzhen from Pingxiang, in order to fulfill an appointment with a Vietnamese merchant, he returned to Shekou after an absence of eighteen years. He drove into Shekou along the Nanhai Boulevard. Nearby was Sihai, the largest dormitory area for immigrating workers in Shekou, and crossing above the Nanhai Boulevard, the big blue board with "China Merchants (Shekou) Industrial Area" printed in white had been removed. The familiar No. 204 bus station had been moved to Mawan, and the New Times Plaza had been erected there. The high buildings such as the Sea View Building, the Minghua Centre and the Overseas Building were like stars surrounding the moon. The China Merchants Plaza nearby had undoubtedly become the brightest new landmark in Shekou. The slogan "Time is money, efficiency is life" still shone there. Everything in Shekou was still so vigorous and green.

It was the first time Haonan, who always tried to drive smoothly, had wished for red traffic lights, to give him time to look at the new scenery. Only when he stopped at a red light did he have the chance to look left and right, absorbing all the beautiful roadside views and comparing them with his memories of the old Shekou.

Presently he passed the Shanghai Restaurant, a place he had dreamed of every night before his marriage, and his heart shivered. The restaurant had a new owner and it had been converted into a leisure club. It was here eighteen years ago that he had met Laizhen, and apart from a glimpse of her in the Fierce Dragon Night Club in Futian, they had gone their separate ways. The past was still clearly visible before his eyes and it all seemed to have happened yesterday. He felt silently depressed, like Rochester looking at the ruins of his manor house in *Jane Eyre* by Charlotte Brontë.

After a while, his phone came to life with the ringtone tune *You Were My Everything*. It was the Vietnamese merchant, who asked, "Where have you been?"

Haonan was surprised to find that he could also speak a form of Mandarin. He replied, "I'm in Shekou. I'll be at your office soon".

Some time before, an urgent notice had been published in all the main media in Shenzhen stating that a Vietnamese merchant was on the verge of death because he was suffering from acute lymphoblastic disease, so a bone marrow donor was urgently wanted. But none could be found. Aware of this, Haonan went to the hospital to have his blood tested. He had been donating his blood without remuneration for fifteen years. They found he was the only one whose match with the patient exceeded six points, so he was the ideal donor. Marrow was extracted from him and transplanted into the Vietnamese man, and he was saved. He wanted to meet the donor through the hospital, and although the blood-donation regulations did not allow this, he insisted, so in the end the hospital made an exception and gave Haonan's contact information. When Haonan learned that the merchant was also named Zhou, he realised that five hundred years ago they must have been members of the same family.

Finally they met. The Vietnamese merchant was of middle height and looked old. His dark skin indicated that he had lived in a tropical area such as Saigon. At first glance, Haonan found that the man looked somewhat like his father. Haonan said to him in Vietnamese, "It seems you speak Cantonese."

"I come from Canton Province," replied the Vietnamese in Cantonese. After this the two of them continued to speak in Cantonese.

"Really?" said Haonan. "You're from Saigon, why did you come here to set up a factory? There are very few Vietnamese factories here."

"Though the tree may be a thousand feet high, its leaves have to fall down to its roots, as they say. Before the Chinese liberation I escaped conscription to the army by the Guomin Party and fled with my countrymen to Brunei, Indonesia, then Malaysia, and finally settled in Vietnam."

"Why did you want to set up a factory in Shekou?"

"I escaped along the Shekou water channel to the South Pacific, so I came back here for the sake of memories."

"Judging by your dialect, you must be from Huazhou in West Canton," said Haonan.

"Yes. When I have recovered and the factory is running smoothly, I'll go back to my home town. I have never seen it since I escaped to the South Pacific."

"Where is your home?" Haonan asked.

"Chengbian village in Nawu."

Haonan was staggered by this news. He said, "So your name is Zhou Weiding. Your elder brother is called Zhou Weiluo, right?"

"How did you know?"

Haonan suddenly stood up and hugged the Vietnamese. "You are my uncle! Zhou Weiluo is my father, and I am your nephew!"

Weiding was dumbfounded. "I can't believe it!" he said. "How are my brother and my sister-in-law?"

Haonan couldn't help but say sadly, "My father passed away in 2005. My mother died last autumn."

Zhou Weiding gave a long sigh. "I came back too late, too late," he said. He went over to the window, gazing at the sea. "When I arrived in Vietnam I always did business in rice, rubber and timber. Now I deal in electronic computer accessories, exporting Chinese electronic products to Vietnam," he said.

"What kind of timber did you handle?" Haonan asked.

"I dealt with rosewood and red sandalwood, but mainly I dealt in dark-red *Dalbergia cochinchinensis*. Sometimes I also dealt in rare yellow rosewood."

"You once dealt in dark-red *Dalbergia cochinchinensis?*"

"Yes. In 2007 I sold 20 containers a month of this wood to China, mainly bought from Laos."

Haonan was lost in thought.

"Are you interested in *Dalbergia?*"

"Yes. In 2007 I also dealt in it in Dongxing, Guangxi."

485

"You also dealt in it? In fact all my *Dalbergia* was exported to Dongxing at that time."

"Does it look like Swartizia from Tanzania?"

"Yes, most people can't tell the difference. I was so familiar with *Dalbergia* that I ventured to engage in Swartizia. In 2007 I imported six containers of Swartizia to Vietnam, then sold it to Dongxing."

"You also sold Swartizia to Dongxing?"

"Yes. The first three containers were sold to a merchant by the name of Leng in Shenzhen, the other to a man called Yefeng, who was from Guangxi."

"With Leng and Yefeng?"

"Yes, let me have a think – he was Leng Jinxiong, and Yefeng..."

"Did you really sell Swartizia to these two men?"

Haonan felt a mixture of emotions: *Why couldn't I have met my uncle several years before?*

"What is troubling you?" his uncle asked, seeing Haonan's pain.

Haonan then explained what had happened in Dongxing that year.

Zhou Weiding heaved a deep sigh and shook his head. "If we could have met that year, I could have supplied three hundred containers of that timber, not just three. And I could have supplied the *Dalbergia* as well. At that time the price was

486

30,000 yuan per ton, but Swartizia was only 2,000 yuan."

Haonan shook his head sadly.

They were silent for a moment, then his uncle suddenly remembered something. "I kept the I/E contracts with Leng Jinxiong and Yefeng," he said. "There is also the banking slip of payment from Leng Jinxiong to me, and the C/O and export customs clearance sheet and so on. You can take them and I can be your witness."

Zhou Weiding asked an assistant to seek out these papers and soon they were ready for Haonan on the table. Studying the documents, Haonan saw that one of them was an original I/E contract in Chinese and Vietnamese versions, signed ON August 13, 2007. There was Leng Jinxiong's illegible signature, which was familiar to Haonan. It confirmed that Jinxiong had first dealt in Swartizia, but it was described as dark-red *Dalbergia cochinchinensis* from Laos and was being sold to Mr Deng, a timber dealer in Xinhui, Canton Province. Mr Deng could not differentiate between the timbers, so he paid up.

Haonan said, "The court won't accept a civil lawsuit because it is more than two years ago. So I must forget it. I just have to regard it as an important lesson."

"There are many cheats in Vietnam," said his uncle.

"But one thing is still not clear to me. I told you just now that after I received the 200,000 yuan deposit from Chen Guangwei, if I was unable to supply the goods, I would have to pay compensation of 400,000 yuan. But I knew that this 200,000 deposit of Chen Guangwei had been received from his buyer. Now that I couldn't supply goods to Chen Guangwei, and likewise he couldn't supply to his buyer, Guangwei must also pay 400,000 to his buyer. Right?" Haonan was confused.

"That's right. In the import and export business between China and Vietnam, we also call it 'border trade'. Some cheats played the double deposit game. According to my judge, Chen Guangwei, his buyer and Yefeng recognised each other beforehand and they are a group of gangsters. The 200,000 yuan deposit is in fact their joint money. They had formed an alliance to trap you."

Haonan's eyes opened extremely wide, and the tea in his cup splashed over the ground under the table.

His uncle went on, "When you signed a contract with Chen Guangwei, they distracted you so that you made errors. If there was any disadvantageous clause in the contract, Guangwei wouldn't sign it, and even if it was signed, he would be reluctant to hand the deposit to you, so the contract would automatically be invalid. But you stayed in the Luofu goods yard, and formed an effective evidence chain. So if they lodged a lawsuit in the court, they probably would not win. You were lonely and helpless in Dongxing, and they threatened you and attacked you. But they had to sacrifice some deposit for you."

Haonan reflected that when he was signing the contract, Guangwei was wandering to and fro and opening his bag to show the cash to Haonan. He had also said that the deposit was about to be paid so the contract was only a piece of paper. The prospect of the deal being concluded and the profit being paid had made Haonan forget his awareness of contract law.

"I understood in the end that Leng Jinxiong had an alliance with Guangwei. At the time Leng Jinxiong invited me to be his business partner because he had been secretly entrusted by Guangwei," Haonan said.

"Maybe they are still in Dongxing playing the same trick," his uncle pointed out.

"We fought against them again in Pingxiang last month. Who knows how many people had been trapped by them again?" Haonan heaved a sigh.

A few days later Haonan accompanied his uncle back to Nawu. First he introduced him to his elder brother, sister-in-law and nephew, then the two of them went back to Changling, the town of their birth. Haonan silently kowtowed to the corpse of his mother, which was still kept perfectly preserved in the hall of his ancestral house. Her face was the same as he remembered it. His uncle was staggered by what Haonan had done with body of his sister-in-law. Then Haonan guided him to the mountain a kilometre away from his ancestral house, where his uncle burned incense in front of the tombs of his mother and elder brother.

His uncle knelt down, murmuring constantly, blaming himself for not having performed the filial duty. After a long time he rose to his feet and raised his old head to the mountains and the heavens, sighing at strange affairs of the world.

Upon their return, Haonan walked with his uncle around the fields and visited some of the country families.

When the expatriate Chinese in Vietnam had been expelled back to China, Zhou Weiding's wife, son and daughter had all been trampled and beaten to death in the riot, so he had no descendants. Accordingly he regarded Haonan as his sole offspring. Haonan's marrow had allowed his blood to regenerate. Zhou Weiding knew now that health was priceless, safety was happiness and wealth could not be brought in with a person's birth or taken away with death. He said that after a year or so he would build a small house in their home town, and an area of vegetable field would be hoed and pigs and chickens fed there during his remaining time. He hoped to be buried next to his mother and elder brother after his death, and so be with them forever.

When they returned to Shenzhen, Zhou Weiding handed over the management of his newly-established developing factory to Haonan so that he could retire. From then on Haonan managed the Lantian company, with a showroom in Huaqiangbei and a base in Shekou. At last he had become a manufacturer.

He then went to the Shenzhen Branch of the Singapore Union Bank to officially open a deposit account for the factory, through which all export settlement business would be handled. He met President Wu, who had retired but visited the bank again from time to time, and that evening, since Wu had to go back to Singapore, Haonan invited all his former colleagues to a lavish banquet.

Chapter 44
Atonement and Revelation

In the late autumn of 2011, Haonan returned to Gaoliang County in West Canton.

The Jianjiang River, which originates from Yunkai Mountain, the border between Canton Province and Gaungxi, runs through Gaoliang County. In the south-east of this county downtown the square teaching block of Gaoliang Middle School stands by the river bank. Now in front of it thousands of teachers and students formally gathered on the playground. A banner hung above it which read: "The Donation Ceremony for Zhou Haonan Who Has Honourably Returned to His Mother School!"

On the lectern Chen Wenchao, the headmaster, picked up a microphone and said, "In the college entrance examination in 1987, Mr Zhou Haonan entered Guangzhou Foreign Trade College with the highest score in our middle school. Afterwards he worked hard to make a career in Shenzhen. Today he wishes to donate three million yuan to set up the 'Haonan Scholarship'."

Following this, two members of staff held up a giant cheque for three million yuan, signed by Haonan. Everyone applauded, and the noise was a roar like a tsunami.

Haonan sat beside Chen Wenchao, wearing an autumn suit. He was smiling but he looked tense. Soon it was his turn to speak.

"There is a saying, 'The sheep has the filial duty to kneel down to be fed, and the crow in turn nurses its parents'. I hereby express great thanks to my mother school, the most famous key provincial middle school in West Canton, where intelligence and elegance is cultivated generation by generation. From here many students have gone on to Peking University and Tsinghua University. In particular, two students got the highest score in our province in the college entrance examination in successive years.

"When I stayed in Shenzhen, it was Shenzhen that made me succeed, but only after my studies in Guangzhou. Before this, when I graduated from Nawu Middle School in 1986, I was lucky to study here. However I actually could not do so because my score was one point short in the pre-exam for college entrance examination in 1986, and the applicants to study here must have got close to the college entrance examination score to be admitted by the college. So I feel very guilty. I must therefore now make atonement."

He rose to his feet, went forward, and knelt down before all the people. His head and hands hung down and his neck stretched out, looking as if he was inviting it to be cut through.

Everyone was stunned. Chen Wenchao hastily went over and dragged him up, saying, "Please stand up! Your gift is the biggest we have ever received. Why are you kneeling?"

Haonan refused to stand up. He still lowered his head, saying, "I wish to express my regret. For twenty-five years I've been carrying a heavy burden of guilt. Today I must explain thoroughly so that I can be forgiven by all of you, or my guilt will follow me throughout the rest of my life."

A deputy headmaster then went over, together with Chen Wenchao. They pulled up Haonan and said, "Please sit back in your seat before you say any more".

Haonan finally rose to his feet and returned to his place, still bowing his head. "Thank you," he said, a little calmer. He went on, "At that time, I was a peasant student without any social background. If I failed in the college entrance examination, I would have to labour in the field the rest of my life. So the college entrance examination was the weathercock of my fate and the decider of my future. However, I failed the pre-examination, by a single mark."

Haonan began to explain to the listening crowd. He told them that on that morning of 1986, the sun had shone. He had fled from Nawu Middle School carrying heavy books and other luggage, and walked back home like a wounded soldier retreating from the battlefield. At noon, when he was within a kilometre of his home, he had not dared to move any further, because it meant facing many of the other country folk.

He stood foolishly by the roadside. Suddenly he saw Fuqiang walking towards him. After Fuqiang heard what had happened to Haonan, he heaved a deep sigh. The pair walked into the nearby woods and sat with their backs against a big longan tree. While Haonan poured out his bitterness, Fuqiang consoled him. Haonan, who was weak in maths, explained that he had neglected to answer one test question and when he realised his mistake, there were only eight minutes left. In a hurry he had tried to answer it, but he had run out of time.

Haonan and Fuqiang talked on until nightfall, when they knew they would have to leave. Fuqiang told Haonan, "If you still feel too guilty to go home, you can stay with me." But Haonan knew he could not escape from the reality. He had no choice but to return home.

When his mother heard his bad news, she suddenly fell down unconscious on the ground until she was revived by his father.

That summer, Haonan started to work out how he could somehow join the remedial class for the college entrance examination the following year. He longed to attend the brilliant Gaoliang Middle School. What could he do?

Another villager who studied at Gaoliang Middle School told Haonan which items had to be presented if applying to join the remedial class:

1) <u>A personal permit to enter the room for the college entrance examination;</u>

2) <u>A score sheet for the examination, printed by computer;</u>

3) <u>The student's learning record at middle school;</u>

4) <u>A residence identity certificate for Gaoliang County.</u>

After discussing this with Fuqiang, Haonan laid his plans. In that year the lowest admitting score for liberal arts at college in Canton Province was 520. Fuqiang and Haonan selected Zhou Xiaotian, a classmate with the score of 516, who normally had a good relationship with Haonan. Unfortunately Zhou Xiaotian's home was in Yangmei Town, over a hundred kilometres away. However, at four o'clock early the next morning, wearing a straw cap, undershirt and sandals, he arose and rode his father's bicycle in the direction of Yangmei Town.

It was dusk before he finally arrived at Zhou Xiaotian's home. But Xiaotian's parents said their son had gone to a relative's home in Zhanjiang City, about a hundred kilometres away. Haonan was dumbstruck, but he asked for the address, then rode on to Zhanjiang City.

As he rode along a stretch of road enclosed by mountains, sudden "ghost fires" rose from the tombs, and seemed to follow him. He lost his balance and fell. The "ghost fires" circled above his head. He sat on the sands with trembling legs, his elbow joint painful and bloody. After a while the "ghost fires" disappeared and he hurriedly rose to his feet, held the bike up and rode furiously away.

He was hardly able to move when he arrived in Liangdong Town. He had to get accommodation in an inn, which cost him three yuan. Early the next morning, he rode on, and at dusk he finally reached his destination.

When Zhou Xiaotian saw Haonan, he was as dizzy as Haonan had been. Haonan explained that he wanted to borrow Xiaotian's personal permit for the college entrance examination, because Xiaotian had already said that if he did not pass the college entrance examination that year he would not take it again but go into business with family members instead. Fortunately the permit was in his luggage, and Xiaotian took it out and willingly handed it to Haonan.

Haonan, very relieved, had a delicious meal and a good rest there that night. The following morning he started from Zhanjiang City, spending a day and a night there before returning to Huazhou County. Without taking any rest, he went directly to the offices of Huazhou Education Bureau for "Pre-investigation". Here there were many teachers, students and parents who were learning their scores in the college entrance examination, some happily, some tearfully.

At midnight it was moonless, starless and windy. Haonan stealthily climbed over the wall of the Education Bureau and tiptoed quietly up to the wall to which all the students' scores had been attached. By the dim light of the sky, he found the name of Zhou Xiaotian and gently cut the score slip off with a small knife. However, he also cut off those of eleven other students nearby, so that nobody would know which score sheet was required. Then he hastily hid the score sheet, climbed over the wall and left as silently as snow falling on the ground. He collected his bicycle and immediately began the long ride back to Nawu. He wanted to be home as soon as possible to catch up on his sleep. When he arrived home the next morning, he slept for a day and a night.

There were still many things to be done. When he awoke he unfolded Zhou Xiaotian's permit and carefully removed the photo, then replaced it with his own. After that, within the stamp of "The Admission Office of Huazhou Education Bureau", he used a toothpick dipped in red stamp-pad oil to rewrite the characters for "Education Bureau" which were missing because of the torn photo. When he had finished, it looked exactly like the original. Then he cut off Zhou Xiaotian's score sheet and stuck it on the permit. Haonan's mother was puzzled and asked what he was doing. He smiled, but did not tell her.

The next day he went to the village committee, asking the secretary to issue a certificate stating that in order to meet the learning requirement, he had now transferred his residence identity papers from Changling to Gaoliang County where his mother's brother lived. He explained to the secretary that because of the failure of the pre-exam, to change his fate, he had changed his name to Zhou Xiaotian. So the certificate was issued to "Zhou Haonan, also known as Zhou Xiaotian..."

Afterwards, accompanied by Fuqiang, he took a blank student's learning record form to Nawu Middle School to see Mr Zhu, the educational chief. He hoped that Mr Zhu would write good comments on his form.

Mr Zhu's office was on the second floor of the teaching block. Since it was the summer vacation, there were few people inside the campus. Sometimes one or two people walked past. Outside the landscape was golden with ripening crops, soon to be harvested. A hot wind was blowing. From the pineapple woods and longan trees, they heard the loud song of the cicadas. Mr Zhu's door was open wide and inside he lay asleep behind a board screen. His snoring seemed to match the rhythm of the cicadas.

"I don't know when he will wake up," said Fuqiang.

Haonan said, "Better wait."

Fuqiang suddenly saw that the drawer in Mr Zhu's desk was open. He winked at Haonan, and said, "I wonder if the official stamp of the school is in there." He peered over and saw that there was indeed a round stamp in the drawer.

Suddenly Mr Zhu turned and tossed, muttering something. Then he began to snore again. Fuqiang said, "Let's not wait. We can't be sure he will do as we ask. Let's do it ourselves".

Haonan was surprised. "Do you mean we should stamp the form ourselves, and write the comments ourselves too?"

"Why not?"

After looking to make sure that no one else was around, Fuqiang seized Haonan's hand and they tiptoed into the office. Fuqiang opened the drawer and picked up the round stamp. He was right. It bore the words: "Nawu Middle School, Huazhou County". Haonan unfolded his form, and Fuqiang swiftly made stamps in several blank spaces, as directed by Haonan. Then they put the stamp back, half-closed the drawer again and tiptoed out as silently as feathers falling to the ground.

Mr Zhu turned and tossed again, grunting, "Who?" Then he fell asleep again, snoring even louder than the cicadas.

Back home, Haonan entered comments on the form to match those of Mr Zhu and his teachers in his old school reports. Finally the work was finished.

Now it was time for the final step. He set out on another 100-kilometre ride to his mother's brother, then went with him to the local police station to apply for a temporary residence identity certificate for Gaoliang County.

That night he returned to the home where his mother's brother lived alone. After having supper, he asked if a bed was available for the night, and his uncle said that his own bed would be provided. Haonan quickly fell asleep.

At four o'clock when he got up to go to the toilet, he stumbled over a man in the corridor and was surprised to find it was his uncle. He asked, "Didn't you say had a place to sleep?" Pointing to the ground under his back, his uncle said smilingly, "This is also a place, isn't it?" It turned out that he had left his own bed for Haonan. Haonan was so ashamed that early the next morning he told his uncle that he would return to Nawu.

Instead, he went to Gaoliang Middle School. This was the first day when the students could apply to join the Remedial Class in Gaoliang

Middle School. Haonan was the first to report to the admission office and present his materials. As the result would be announced the next day, he could not go back to Nawu.

That night he slept on a stone bench in Panzhou Park until midnight, when the staff cleared everyone out before closing the gates. Then he climbed up a giant longan tree and went to sleep hugging its huge branches. At midnight he awoke to see that a crooked branch appeared to be moving towards him. But how could a branch move? Abruptly he realised that it was a snake – the animal he feared the most! He hurriedly scrambled down the tree and fell to the ground.

The next day he staggered off to Gaoliang Middle School. He soon saw that Chen Wenchao had written down on a public notice board the name he wanted to see: Zhou Xiaotian. Haonan had succeeded. He could not help smiling. But at the same time, he was fearful that he might be found out.

He returned to Nawu with his news, which shocked all his relatives, classmates and friends. After that, with a new energy, Haonan finished his heavy farming jobs with his family, his skin now tanned to the colour of chocolate.

When the new term opened, he explained to the teacher who took charge of his class, "My name is strange, because 'Xiaotian' means I laugh to the sky. I didn't get the score to pass the college entrance examination this year, so I want to change my name to 'Zhou Haonan'. Will you agree?"

The teacher smiled kindly. "Everyone's name is decided by himself," he said. So that was how Zhou Xiaotian once again became Zhou Haonan.

In the following school year, 1987, Haonan was able to enter and pass the college entrance examination.

Haonan finished his story and looked up at the watching crowd. "Today I feel so guilty for what I did. I have come back here to atone for my crime, like in *The Kite Runner* by Khaled Hossein, when Amir went back to Afghanistan from the USA to atone. My donation of three million yuan can never make up for it. If you think it was criminal, then you may refuse it. I just want to take this opportunity to beg my mother school to forgive me, to relieve me of twenty-five years of worry. I am willing to kneel down for three days and nights at the door of the school to repent. I hope all the students here will study well, but I pray to you not to learn from my example."

There was dead silence. The leaders put their heads together and murmured in low voices. After a while, Chen Wenchao said, "There is a proverb from the ancient days of our country that says, 'Not everyone is a sage, and which man never makes a mistake? It is great if you can correct your wrongs'. What Mr Zhou Haonan said today would never have been known to us if he had not confessed this story, and nobody will be able to investigate it. He spoke bravely, showing that he still has a conscience. So even though he did not donate, we can forgive him."

Everyone applauded. Some of the female students sobbed. Haonan raised head and looked around, finally smiled tearfully.

Not long after Haonan returned to Shenzhen, relying upon the annual tax-paid profit of his company, he at last got the quota he needed to move his residence identity materials to Shenzhen. When the flowers blossomed the following spring, he drove back to West Canton carrying the Transfer Notice from the Shenzhen Government.

He collected the files which had remained filed away for so many years. But he felt extremely sad when he left. As he returned to his F6, the bag felt like as if it contained his funeral ashes. He laid it on the passenger seat, but the contents fell out and scattered. As he was putting them in order, he saw the student's learning record form once jointly made by him and Fuqiang. When he caught sight of the pre-exam papers for his college entrance examination in 1986, he couldn't help but sob. Chinese Language, Maths, History, English... he read randomly through the faded pages.

Then he had a sudden thought and counted the scores with the calculator on his mobile phone. He shrieked in alarm. In the final scores for Chinese Language, he had scored 116 marks, but it had been wrongly added up as only 115. His heart nearly jumped out of his chest. He calculated it again, five times. Yes, it was true. He had scored the pass mark of 116.

Just for the lack of one mark, he had spent so long drifting miserably here and there. It had even taken ten years from his mother's life. Now, although the injustice had been exposed, twenty-six years on, he only felt powerless and sad. He slumped limply down into his seat.

Chapter 45
Everything Kills Everything Else

After bringing his residence identity information and personal work files to Shenzhen and presenting them to the relevant governmental departments, Haonan continued to maintain the overseas electronic buyers exploited by his uncle, and more importantly, to treasure the customer resources he had obtained by devious means from the Canton Fair.

At nine o'clock that night, he drove a newly-bought automatic F6 belonging to a friend from an electronics factory in Gushu, Xi'xiang to Huaqiangbei. In the right lane of Beihuan Boulevard, when he was about to reach the section of Caitian, he found himself following a slow-moving big black car with a "B" emblem. Haonan knew it was a Bentley, the famous British marque, with which neither the Mercedes S Class nor the BMW 7 series could compare.

They say owners of famous cars are always arrogant. No wonder this Bentley was being driven so slowly. Haonan followed for several hundred metres, and the Bentley continued at the same slow pace. Haonan switched on his left indicator, pulled out and drove into the middle lane. But the Bentley did the same, still staying ahead of Haonan and preventing Haonan from returning to the right. Haonan hurriedly kept a safe distance from it in the middle lane. Suddenly he realised that he had encountered the Bumper Men again. But tonight, he decided to challenge the arrogant driver of this Bentley.

There were few cars on the road. Haonan breathed deeply, then drove from the middle lane to the left, the middle, the left... the Bentley driver was getting confused. Presently Haonan left the Bentley behind in the right lane. Then he braked hard, turned on the hazard lights and stopped. Now the Bentley too had to brake urgently, otherwise it would hit the tail of the F6, and the accident would be the Bentley driver's responsibility.

Haonan quietly got out of the F6. He wanted to see what kind of holy heroes were sitting in the Bentley. He saw the driver and three assistants get out. The driver was a thin man whose mouth protruded forward like a troglodyte.

"*Diaotou!*" the man shouted. It was Zhang Fuqiang!

The three other men saw that Haonan was an acquaintance, relaxed and stood by the roadside. They all spat out something white and wiped their mouths with tissues.

"One night many years ago in Huaqiangbei I had a battle against a Bluebird in my Jetta," Haonan said.

"Was that you?" Fuqiang was alarmed, then understood. "No wonder you seemed so familiar."

"Don't tell me you were the driver of the Bluebird?" Haonan was just as surprised.

"Correct, it was me."

"So you are still in this business?"

"No, I just occasionally play with it when I am bored. Tonight, when I started to patrol with my friends, the first car we met was yours."

"What a beautiful car!" Haonan said.

"The acceleration couldn't compare with the new Bentley, but it depends on who's driving."

"Yes. But it's very risky doing this bumper car trick, you should stop. Now let's go to the Xia'sha village and have some Huazhou's Sliced Boiled Chicken. We haven't tasted it together for a long time. We shall have a good drink there."

Haonan went over to the front passenger seat of the Bentley, opened the storage box inside and took out three tubes of toothpaste. "Do you take such good care of your teeth normally?" he asked. He threw the tubes into the garbage nearby.

"Since you know so much, you must know what this toothpaste is for," one of the other men said.

Haonan knew the toothpaste trick. After an accident, the bumper men used it to pretend that they were seriously injured by foaming at the mouth. Haonan was looking for a bottle of red liquid, and he soon found one. After shaking it, he threw that into the garbage as well, saying, "It's fake blood. Are your blood types O or AB?" The men all blushed.

Haonan searched again, and found a bag of olive stones. These were thrown against the car to make a pinging sound, after which the "Bumper Car" group would point to a dent on their car, saying it had been made by the other car. This way they could easily get several thousand yuan from the unsuspecting victim.

Again Haonan threw the olive stones into the garbage and said, "I worry about the lives you are living. God in heaven watches what all people do on the earth. Most people playing the bumper car game get their arms and legs broken, or die young."

Then he noticed a number of black and orange Traffic Penalty Notices in the names of the traffic police in Guangzhou, Shenzhen and Dongguan. "You even pretended to be traffic police?" he said.

"No, I wouldn't do that." Fuqiang shook his hand. He explained that when he needed a parking space, he took out the relevant Traffic Penalty Notice, wrote the licence number of the car on it and put it on the windscreen. If a real traffic officer saw the car he would see the penalty notice already there and take no action.

Hearing this, Haonan sighed. "You should all join our company if you find it so difficult to make a living. Now let's go to Xia'sha village."

"All right, I accept," Fuqiang replied swiftly.

The previous night, in an apartment in Bao'an District where Leng Jinxiong temporarily lived, his mobile phone rang. The caller said, "Do you remember me? I'm Huang Ziliang and we once met in Vietnam. Do you still deal in dark-red *Dalbergia cochinchinensis*?"

"Of course, I remember you. And how much Dalbergia do you require?"

"Initially I require ten large containers. Where can you provide it from?"

"I have goods everywhere."

"Do you have a sample? I'd like to make a special journey from Hong Kong to Shenzhen to meet you. Ten o'clock tomorrow evening in the Dynasty Restaurant in Hubei Road, Dongmen, all right? I hope no one else will be there."

"Ok, I'll go alone. See you!"

They met as arranged at ten o'clock the following evening. Jinxiong brought the sample and after half an hour of discussion, they reached agreement. Huang Ziliang said, "I'll show the sample to my British customer, who is in Hong Kong now. Once it's confirmed, I'll sign the contract with you by email."

At the door of Dynasty Restaurant they separated. Jinxiong looked at the figure of Huang Ziliang, thinking that this would be the first deal he had done for a long time and he would earn a good deal of money soon. He was still selling Swartizia from Africa as *Dalbergia* from Laos. He imagined counting the money he would make and smiled. Then he turned to walk towards the bus station.

At this point a van drove up and stopped in front of Jinxiong. Someone inside the van called his name, and he replied. Abruptly the car door opened and two strong young men got out. They picked up Jinxiong and threw him into the van. Then the van drove off to the east.

The van stopped when it reached the doorway of a hotel in Dongmen. With the two men gripping Jinxiong, they entered the hotel. Jinxiong knew they would have hidden weapons, so he did not dare to shout or disobey.

They took the lift up to the sixth floor, entered room 606 and locked the door. Then Mr Deng walked in and sat on the bedside.

"Leng Jinxiong, we meet again," he said. "I dialled your mobile phone so many times, but you always ignored it. I've been searching you for a long time. As the proverb goes, 'A wise man doesn't do treacherous things'. Today we finally caught you. I think you can still remember that in 2007 you sold three containers of dark-red *Dalbergia cochinchinensis* to me. Now, I ask you: was it really *Dalbergia cochinchinensis?*" Mr Deng was a young bodybuilder, and he looked very strong to Jinxiong.

"How could it... not be? You... you signed for it," Jinxiong said, trembling.

"You pretended Swartizia from Africa was *Dalbergia cochinchinensis* from Laos. You swindled me." Deng slapped Jinxiong's face hard, then kicked him. Jinxiong fell down and struck his head.

"We've signed the contract... and you signed the...commodity inspection certificate," Jinxiong said, gasping for breath. He covered his face with his hands, his body shivering.

"Dark-red *Dalbergia cochinchinensis* was written on the contract, but the wood was not *Dalbergia*. You hurt me very much. I paid you 2.6 million yuan. You will not be allowed to escape from here until you pay." Mr Deng kicked Jinxiong again.

At this moment two of his companions took out a rope and tied Jinxiong's hands, then gagged him with cloth. Mr Deng said, "'Evil is rewarded by evil. No reward is nil, and now the time has come." Jinxiong collapsed, on the verge of death.

Just before midnight that night, Haonan, Fuqiang and three other men were enjoying Huazhou's Sliced Boiled Chicken in a reserved room in Xia'sha village. After chatting with them, Haonan knew that Fuqiang's three assistants were all from

Nawu. Fuqiang was smoking the "big bamboo pipe", while his men were discussing which monkey or horse would be bought in their lottery affairs later, which was none of Haonan's business.

Haonan saw that two of the men were somewhat familiar. When he asked, it turned out that one was Yang Wu from Haonan's neighbouring village and the other was Chen Lingfang, who had once bullied Haonan at Nawu Middle School thirty years before. After so many years they had all changed a great deal, particularly Haonan, who having trained as a *Kungfu* fighter, was no longer the weakling who could easily be bullied. Chen Lingfang, who had not entered senior middle school after graduating from the juniors, had drifted in society until he had joined Fuqiang's group. Once known as the "Fighting King", he could not now stand up to Haonan for 30 seconds. However, it was Lingfang who first raised a glass of wine and rose to his feet, apologising for the wilfulness and tyranny of which he had been guilty thirty years before. Now Haonan could be magnanimous because he'd experienced so much suffering, so they shook hands to draw a line under the affair.

Soon everyone was relaxed again. Another assistant, A'min, changed the subject by saying, "Fuqiang is really a master of playing the edge-ball".

"What do you mean?" Haonan was interested.

"Once he gambled with me that he could get a Mercedes S320 without payment," A'min said.

"A second-hand one?" Haonan asked.

"No, brand new."

A'min told the story. At that period Fuqiang, who had reopened his restaurant, was doing little business. One day he was bored,so he went into a Mercedes dealership in Bao'an, saying he wanted to buy a Mercedes S320 costing over a million yuan. Seeing such a wealthy buyer, a slender salesgirl in a short skirt gave him a warm reception. He checked the details of the car and asked to take a test drive. Then he took out a copy of his driving licence for registering and sat in the S320 with the salesgirl.

He drove the car along the road around the car market. However, he complained that he couldn't test the car at such a slow speed, and needed to try it on the wider national route 107. Thinking he was a serious buyer, the salesgirl agreed. He drove faster and faster, and then, holding the steering wheel with his left hand, he stretched out his right hand towards the salesgirl's leg and touched it. The salesgirl was horrified and shouted, "What are you doing? Stop the car!"

Fuqiang stopped and the salesgirl hurriedly pushed open the car door and ran off. Fuqiang put his foot on the accelerator and vanished from her view. Only then did the salesgirl understand what had happened. He had driven the Mercedes S320 to show it to A'min, saying, "You lose." A'min was dumbfounded.

In the end Fuqiang drove the Mercedes back to the car city, left the key inside and called the salesgirl to invite her to get it back. He apologised to her, but she had already reported it to the police.

Fuqiang laughed, and then muttered, "Even though I drove it away, I couldn't use it because I couldn't register it in the Shenzhen Car Management Office." The others laughed too.

But Haonan frowned. He knew that because of this illegal behaviour, Fuqiang had been detained by Shenzhen Police and all his property, including his mobile phone, had been confiscated.

It was getting towards midnight. When Haonan was about to pay for the meal, Fuqiang waved to the waitresses, saying, "Let me pay!" But as the girl waited, he seemed to have trouble getting his hand into his pocket. It seemed as if his wallet was too big or the buttons were too tight. Seeing this, Haonan understood. Fuqiang did not always behave badly, but perhaps because he had become poorer, he could not do what he used to do. Haonan swiftly fished out his wallet and made the payment.

"I've told you that it ought to be me who pays it," Fuqiang muttered.

"Same," Haonan smiled. Then he went back to his car and took out a new intelligent mobile phone which had cost 6,000 yuan. He presented it to

Fuqiang. It seemed to Fuqiang that he had been given the most valuable treasure.

Then Haonan's mobile phone rang. The caller said, "This is Deng from Xinhui in Canton Province. We once met in Dongxing. That year I was cheated a timber deal with Leng Jinxiong. Today, with the help of my two brothers, I have captured Leng Jinxiong and we are now in a hotel in Dongmen. It was said that he once harmed you, so if you want to beat him with me, please come!"

Leng Jinxiong! When Haonan heard that name, anger surged from his heart. Nevertheless he first asked curiously, "How did you find him?"

"You also knew Huang Ziliang from Hong Kong. It was he who lured Leng Jinxiong out on the pretext of purchasing some dark red *Dalbergia cochinchinensis*. It was so difficult for me to seize this swindler. I also have some cement and a bucket ready."

"What did you get such things for?" Haonan was alarmed.

"If he cannot pay us today, we'll take him to the seaside at Shenzhen Bay. You know what I mean," Mr Deng said with a grin. "The trick of 'Luring a snake out of its cave' was introduced by Zhang Fuqiang, your brother."

"Really?" Haonan turned to take a look at Fuqiang.

It turned out that Mr Deng had visited Shenzhen many times. On one occasion he had met

Haonan and Fuqiang. Then Fuqiang had secretly shown Mr Deng the above trick, unknown to Haonan. And now, they rolled their sleeves and were about to give Jinxiong a good beating.

But suddenly, Haonan hesitated. He said to the other four men, "One moment," then went away to phone Shuwen. He had got into the habit of consulting her first over important matters. After talking to her for a few moments, Haonan came back and said, "We are not going there, not now." Afterwards he called Mr Deng back. "Thank you so much for your invitation, but what you propose is not legal. Why don't you sue him?"

"How can I do that? He has no company, no address. He is just like a shadow. He does not appear in public," said Mr Deng.

"But what you're doing now is illegal," Haonan stressed.

"I don't care."

"Mr Deng, can you check his lips? Are they dark and purple?"

"Why do you ask this? All right, let me take a look. Just wait a minute... yes, they are very dark and purple," said Mr Deng.

"I can tell you that he has suffered from diabetes for many years. Actually the diabetes isn't too serious, it's the complications that are the most horrible. He also suffers high blood pressure, and if his medicine is not taken in time he will die. If so, it's not worth it to you."

This made Mr Deng hesitate. He started to pace to and fro. Jinxiong, sitting on the ground, did not understand their dialect. He just looked at the carpet.

"So, what's your idea now?" Mr Deng called back Haonan and asking.

"I think it's better to set him free now."

"Impossible!" Mr Deng howled. "I've been looking for this swindler for years. How can I set him free just like that?"

"I understand. In fact I hate him more than you, and I'd like to punch him dead. But forget it. He is over sixty and he won't have more days in the world. Don't take what he did too seriously. Just regard it as a lesson. And lodge a lawsuit as quickly as possible, please!"

What Haonan had said made Mr Deng calm down a bit. Finally he said, "All right, we'll do it your way. We'll deal with this old thief by using the law."

So at midnight, the weak Jinxiong was left alone in the hotel room. He soon became seriously ill. When the police from Dongmen arrived, called by Haonan, they took Jinxiong in a police car to the intensive care unit at Luohu District People's Hospital. Finally Jinxiong was pushed out from the door of hell.

A few months later Haonan received a strange phone call from Fuqiang, in which he was told that a foreign merchant would be waiting for him alone in the Fierce Dragon Night Club at three o'clock in the afternoon. He asked Fuqiang where the merchant was from, but Fuqiang was unable to tell him. However, Haonan always respected customers and arrived punctually at the club. When he got there he thought of the old days, when this had been the stage where he had fought and spilled his sweat and blood.

He entered to see a group of people gathered there in the smoky room. Two of them were thugs in black, looking like fierce fighters. Near them were Rong Benliang and Chen Guangwei in a heavy golden necklace, together with Leng Jinxiong, who sat in an armchair. But strangely, Fuqiang didn't appear. Haonan suddenly understood that he had been lured to come here and he turned to leave, but the door was shut behind him by another crew-cut minder. At once Haonan understood that a net was falling upon him, and he had nowhere to escape.

Guangwei first went up to Haonan, raised a sheet of paper in his hand and chuckled. "The receipt you wrote in Dongxing is still in my hand, so the debt between us has not been settled. Aren't you the winner of the China National Hard-Pen Calligraphy Competition? Aren't you the man who knows how to forge handwriting? But this is still what you wrote. And why didn't your special invisible pen work?" he laughed. "You have enough money, but now I don't require your compensation."

Haonan realised that the "receipt" he had torn up in Dongxing was really only a photocopy, which had been reproduced on a special photocopier by Guangwei. He had kept the original receipt. A clever trick. But none the less, Haonan was calm. He said, "This can't be supported in the court because it has expired, and in civil law it is only valid for two years."

"This is not a court," said Rong Benliang, giggling like a monkey. "If it is, then I'm the judge."

"Didn't you make a video?" said Guangwei. "Play it and let me take a look. And where is your witness? Haha!" Guangwei was as happy as a child on holiday. Even though Haonan had made a video, it had corrupted, and in any case it was many kilometres away.

"Didn't you say you would present my mobile phone messages to the court as evidence?" Guangwei went on. "All right, come on, summon the witness and show me the evidence!" Guangwei laughed and spat a pool of phlegm onto the ground. Rong Benliang did the same.

"Then what do you want?" Haonan asked.

Guangwei went up to Haonan and prodded his nose with a finger and said, "I want to destroy you and cripple you!"

It was like the quiet moment before an atomic bomb explodes. Haonan had no way of getting out of there, nor of dialling 110.

At this point one of the older bruisers rose to his feet. He said in a low and heavy voice, "Friend Zhou, sorry for offending you. Don't blame me, because I have been entrusted by boss Chen Guangwei, who has paid for one of your legs. At Luofu goods yard in Dongxing in 2007, we unfortunately underestimated you again. So now you have to accept your bitter fate."

It felt as if a sharp knife had been driven through Haonan's bones. In the faint light he suddenly recognised this man. It was Lei Dong, the big fellow Haonan had met when he had shared with Shuwen in Huaqiangbei. The other bruiser stood nearby. They simultaneously recognised Haonan.

Lei Dong laughed. "At that time I really didn't understand how that beautiful girl could have escaped," he said. "Then we realised it was you who helped her that night. You may have got away with it then, but all debts will be settled here today!"

Lei Dong stood by Haonan's left shoulder. He was a third taller than Haonan. He took out a roll of newspaper from the sofa, and drew from it a knife fully 75 centimetres long, thick at the hilt and deadly sharp at the point. He banged it down on a round table in the centre of the room. Then he paced back up to Haonan and said, "With this knife I set up my career in China, Vietnam and even in USA. It has followed me for many years. It cuts iron like mud. You are neither the first one nor the last. A litter later I'll use the fresh blood of your leg to make you pay your respects to this precious knife of mine!" He took a few steps away from Haonan.

Haonan still stood motionless, but he could hear his own beating heart. He was hopelessly outnumbered and knew he would be as helpless as a turtle in a jar. But still, he said to himself: *I must try as hard as I can to fight against them, I can't give in!*

Lei Dong and Haonan both stared at the long knife on the table halfway between them. Lei Dong had been dominating the situation, but now suddenly it seemed that they were equals.

Simultaneously, the two men lunged forward. But as Lei Dong's hand stretched towards the knife, Haonan's hand did not go in the same direction. He knew that if he competed directly with Lei Dong, there was only half a chance of seizing the knife first. Instead, with his right fist he thumped Lei Dong's right hand, preventing him from reaching the knife. Then, as quick as a lightning, he struck his adversary with a high half-round kick, striking him full in the face and knocking him to the ground.

The two men on the sofa jumped up to snatch the knife, but as fast as a swallow skimming over water, Haonan had already seized it and grasped its handle firmly with his right hand. Then he stood back a little, raising his left hand to defend his heart and holding the long knife in front of his chest with his right side facing them. The brightness of his eyes seemed to be reflected in the brightness of the knife. None dared to approach him.

Lei Dong, whose nose had been broken by the kick, was struggling to stand up. Without stopping to wipe the blood away, he staggered to the doorway and fled. His two accomplices followed. Then Rong Benliang ran off to join them, and they all disappeared.

With the knife in his hand, Haonan walked slowly up to Guangwei.

"My – boss, my, my – patron! Take it easy!" Like a eunuch meeting his emperor, Guangwei suddenly fell on his knees before Haonan. He begged in a choking voice, "If you – set me free, I swear that I will never hurt you again. I would sweep the dust from your shoes with my eyelashes. And here is the receipt for you."

What should Haonan do now? How was he going to settle the debts between them over so many years? So many scenes surged in his mind, but abruptly, like a reservoir releasing a flood,

Haonan raised his hand and snapped at Guangwei, "Stop playing the martyr! Get out of my sight!"

Guangwei scrambled to his feet and hurriedly fled. Haonan went over to pick up the receipt and walked slowly over to Leng Jinxiong, half-sitting in an armchair in the corner. Now he was the only one left. Seeing that everyone had been released except himself, Jinxiong believed it was only upon him that Haonan wished revenge. Terrified, he closed his eyes.

Holding the knife in his hand, Haonan walked closer and closer to Jinxiong. One step, two steps, three... the arm-chair shook. Haonan reached the armchair – and stretched out his hand. He did not thump Jinxiong but grasped the chair and pushed it out of the room.

Jinxiong opened his eyes and gazed in wonder. Haonan murmured, "All right! Where mercy is possible, mercy should be shown". Then he fished out his mobile phone and dialled 110.

By now some members of staff had arrived for the evening shift at the night club, and they had gathered together and watched the scene in terror. And now the police arrived. Haonan handed the long knife to one of the officers and told them to interrogate Jingxiong.

After leaving the police station, Haonan stood by the roadside on Shennan Boulevard. He took out the hateful "receipt". He studied his signature, then tore it into pieces and threw them away. He watched them blow up into the sky before falling into some garbage nearby.

Only now could he feel a sense of relief. The nightmare of the receipt was finally over.

Chapter 46
When the Sands Are Finally Blown Away

One day in the late autumn of 2012 Haonan came back to Shekou after driving a foreign merchant to Bao'an Airport for his flight. In this competitive era when everyone in China was dealing in foreign trade, he uploaded all his pictures of computers, accessories and communication items produced in Shekou to the export platform of Alibaba. Meanwhile, he had an official stand in the Canton Fair twice a year, so he was now part of "Official Army" rather than a "Guerrilla". Many foreign merchants sent enquiries, and some of them even visited Haonan's company and factory, where they checked the samples and signed orders. Haonan was so busy that he recruited two foreign trade executives who had graduated from international trade in Guangzhou.

When he filled up with fuel at Gushu filling station, he saw on the live news playing on the LED TV screen there that Shenzhen police had just detained a criminal gang, which, as internet hackers, often broke into business email boxes to cheat. Haonan recalled that he had encountered this trick on business in Costa Rica. When he watched further, a familiar face showed on the TV screen. It turned out that the backstage manipulator was Chen Guangwei. He was now going to be punished with several other criminals. Haonan was scared. Would he be dragged into this?

Afterwards the TV reported that a group of bosses had been detained after they fled, and Haonan saw the names and faces of Hu Hangong and Wang Gexin. He couldn't help but sigh; they had deserved it.

Haonan often stayed in Huaqiangbei and went to Shekou every other day. Every time he reached his office, he first opened his email box and MSN in the desktop computer.

Today at the factory he had received an email from Mohammed, advising him that he was satisfied with the Bluetooth goods he had received, and he was now placing a second order. The second email was from Mayachefsk, telling Haonan that he would place orders for 40 sets monthly from this month on, at the same price, unless the US dollar fluctuation exceeded 5%. Haonan was so excited that he clapped his hands and shouted "Yeah!" in the air, because from now on he would make a profit of 400,000 yuan per month.

Mayachefsk furthermore asked whether Haonan could attend the First Russian Electronic Exhibition to be held in Moscow soon. Haonan confirmed this, but one thing he was going to keep secret was that he was planning to bring a female Russian translator who would pretend not to know Russian.

His human resources chief came in, saying, "General Manager Zhou, a secretary clerk is waiting for a job interview, are you available now?" Haonan agreed and rose to his feet.

Through the glass window of the conference room, he saw a woman sitting inside with a boy. He opened the applicant's resume and photo, and all of a sudden, he gasped, "Lin Laizhen!"

"Zhou Haonan?" she rose to her feet and cried out too, astonished. She wore a long white skirt printed with flowers and her figure was now quite plump. She still had long hair down to her shoulders. Although the crow's feet of age had appeared on her face, her beauty had hardly faded.

He remembered how he had howled this woman's name among the trees, heartbroken among the sounds of the waves, and how on so many nights he had hugged his pillow and woken, thinking he was hugging dear Lin Laizhen once again. And now, after so many years, here she was in his office.

He put down the resume on the conference desk. Then he went over to the window, looking out at Shenzhen Bay. "It's hot now, too hot," he said. He went to the basin and splashed water on his face, or more precisely, on his weeping eyes. After that he took several tissues and dabbed them on his face. Then he went again to the window, looking at the bay and saying nothing.

She bowed her head. The boy beside her watched them curiously, but he too said nothing.

"Long time no see," he said at last, trembling.

"Yes, long time no see."

"You're applying to be a secretary clerk?"

"Yes." She bowed her head.

In that year after meeting Guangwei, Laizhen had immediately abandoned Haonan. Her only regret was that never again had she had the wonderful experience of making love for two hours, and certainly she had never had nine orgasms – not even one. Guangwei only had sex to enjoy himself, and he always accomplished it within a few seconds. Later on he did not go through with the formalities of marriage, so Laizhen had never fulfilled her dream of getting a Shenzhen Permanent Residence Permit and a house by marrying a local resident. Guangwei, seeking different beautiful girls day and night, had got tired of Laizhen and finally abandoned her, by which time she was pregnant with his child. She had had to give birth to her son alone in the hospital, and after that she rented in Shekou and did temporary work. As time had gone by, she had become a woman. It was difficult for her as a single mother to find a suitable man to marry.

But it had all gone wrong for Guangwei. It was said that after he was released from the police station he had lost a huge gamble in Macao, which had driven him bankrupt.

The boy beside her was about ten years old and not well grown. He looked like a small child and had poor eyesight. His behaviour was also very poor. He could not manage the toilet and would not wash his bowl or chopsticks after meals. All he did by day was to watch TV cartoons and play computer games. In order to feed this boy, she had to look for a job. And she had to take him everywhere with her, even to this job interview, otherwise she would not know which internet café he had disappeared into.

Seeing this boy, Haonan thought that if she had married him at that time, their children would be the same age. But everything was long gone, and he could only sigh from the bottom of his heart.

"How is your typing?" he asked. He was recalling the time when he had taught her how to type.

"Not bad, about 50 Chinese words per minute."

"That's a good speed, you can be employed here. But the secretary clerk isn't a technical job. The salary is 3,000 yuan, and you can ask for your specific requirements when you work later."

"Can you offer weekly pay?

"Not in principle. None of my 200 workers has ever asked for weekly pay. However, I can make an exception for you."

"Thank you so much. And when can I start work?" She was nervous.

"Any time you like."

"So, how about tomorrow?" "If you wish."

She nodded and got up to leave, dragging the boy behind her. In her sorrow, her expression appeared like the pear blossoming in the rain.

He saw them off as far as the factory door. Seeing her beauty and assuming she was the respected guest of General Manager Zhou, the doorkeeper smiled and saluted to them. The doorkeeper was Chen Lingfang. Haonan was paying him twice as much as he could get elsewhere.

For a time Haonan did not return to his office, but stayed in the conference room in the seat where Laizhen had sat, lost in thought. It seemed that he was trying to recapture her scent.

Finally the sound of his mobile interrupted his thoughts. It was from Mei Renaj, his German customer, saying he was sending an import contract for Haonan to check and countersign. He was ordering 5,000 computer mice, and if both sides were happy, he would increase this to 20,000 every month. Haonan couldn't help being pleased.

After checking that, he recalled that there was still one thing to be sorted out. He dialled Zhu, the managing director of Guangzhou Yuri Optical Factory, and told him how he had put the QC tags on the 200 sets of instruments. Zhu was surprised, but she smilingly responded that there was no problem and if Haonan didn't mention it, nobody would be aware of it.

Haonan then called Chin, explaining the QC affair to her. Chin replied that if the QC wasn't with the goods, she would not sell them. She expressed her thanks for Haonan's honesty and sent him 6,000 US dollars as the fine for her breaching the contract for the 600 sets of goods she was not purchasing.

Shuwen had now become the financial supervisor of Haonan's company. She had just given birth to their son, who weighed a healthy 4 kg.

Haonan often stared at the old building in Huaqiangbei where he had once lived with her. When this building had gone on sale by public tender, Shuwen had bid for it on behalf of Haonan, and against heavy competition she had won it for the price of 78 million yuan. All the financing was arranged through the Singapore Union Bank, Shenzhen Branch, where he had once worked, which he saw as his business reward to the bank. His fortunes had now entered a new era.

When he signed the relevant contracts in this bank, he happened to meet Xu Yanwei, his former colleague. Xu Yanwei had established his own company and set up a textile factory in Anhui Province, relying upon the letter of credit for mixed cotton and yarn from Pakistan which had been exploited by Haonan that year. The company was listed on NASDAQ in the USA.

At the end of 2016, a new 63-storey "CIF Building" rose up in Shenzhen. The excellent calligraphy of it, in the Liu Gongquan style, was clearly Haonan's work. It was his own building. From the first floor to the fourth were a range of electronic booths to be rented, and from the fifth floor, there were twin commercial and residential units, where Eli, in a suit, was the new Chinese Representative in the Mohammed's office. Fuqiang had finally been forgiven by Haonan because of their close childhood friendship even though Guangwei had once paid him 50,000 yuan to lure Haonan to that Fierce Dragon Night Club right then. Now, as a new driver, Fuqiang, and Luo Zhenfeng, as the canteen manager, had also been individually allocated apartments as shareholders, where their family members would live together. And certainly an apartment was available for Haonan's newly-found uncle, Zhou Weiding.

On the day when this building was officially opened, Haonan and his uncle jointly invited many guests, including Chen Wenchao, Zhang Fuqiang, Luo Zhenfeng, Zhou Xiaotian, Wang Zhengmao, Vice General Manager Wen, Chen Xiaomei, Xu Yanwei, Yu Minru, Fu Yanjie, Li Rentai, Kuang Ming, Li Feng, Huang Lijuan, Yang Xiaolong, Kuang Dawei, Managing Director Zhu (Anhui

Province), Managing Director Zhu (Guangzhou), Managing Director Zhang, Mr Wen, Eli, Mr Deng (Xinhui) and Lin Laizhen. During that day, the song Stepping into the New Era was played repeatedly.

Right then, to do more electronic importing business, he had registered a new company, Shenzhen Care E Health Technology Co. Ltd. He would build an advanced and healthy platform operated by an intelligent robot, an invention which would benefit every family and community in China, especially children and aged people.

When he had attended the American Consumptive Electronics Fair that year, he had been fortunate to meet Mr Frank Hester, an entrepreneur who owned and ran TPP, one of the UK's largest clinical software companies, and had been presented with an OBE, one of the country's highest honours, by the Queen. After acknowledging more global business opportunities brought by "The Belt and Road" Initiative of China, Mr Hester had flown to China to sign a business agreement with Haonan. Thus Haonan had introduced the cutting-edge technology of TPP to Chinese market.

As Fuqiang watched everyone clinking their wine glasses in celebration, he sighed and turned to Haonan. "Great! *Diaotou*! Now you don't need to advance secretly by an unknown path!"

Haonan, who had been donating blood free of charge for more than ten years, also used a room on the fourth floor to set up the "Shenzhen Friendship Club of Blood Donors", to allow anyone who had donated 400 ml of blood anywhere in China to read, surf the internet and practise keep fit without payment.

One weekend Haonan was thumping the punch-bag in the club and dripping with sweat. He was pelting the bag with straight, cross and round punches, push kicks and side kicks. Shuwen was playing with their small son. Suddenly three representatives of Futian District Blood Station arrived to see Haonan, along with a woman who looked somewhat familiar to Haonan. She was accompanied by a tall, slim and graceful young girl. They said they wanted to present a silk banner to Haonan, together with a bank cheque amounting to 50,000 yuan. Haonan had made an impression on these three people when he had donated blood there before.

The other woman was Fu Xiaohong, who had once cheated him out of his 40,000 yuan boxing bonus by pretending to be looking for romance with him. Her conscience had been troubling her ever since. She had tried to contact him but failed. Recently she had brought her daughter to Shenzhen and the girl had suffered an accident on the roller coaster in Happy Valley. She was saved by a blood donation, and like Haonan's uncle, she found that the donor was Haonan, so she wanted to thank him. She regarded the 50,000 as the debt she must repay to him.

The sudden appearance of Fu Xiaohong made Shuwen think, for she had heard Haonan talk about what had happened. Yet she felt no bitterness, no "vinegar bottle" in her heart. Although Haonan was reluctant to receive this sum, he could not refuse.

Soon Haonan and his family were living on the top floor of the CIF Building. It was a magical transformation from the humble life when he and Shuwen had been co-renting. In their spare time they often sat on the glazed-tile balcony with their son, looking down at the distant Shenzhen Textile Building, the Modern Window, the Seg Plaza, the high Pingan Financial Centre Building and the green Lotus Mountain. He told Shuwen that the new highest building in Shenzhen would be built in Luohu District soon. She was surprised again.

One day, Haonan decided that it was time to reveal the mystery of the pillow which he had always carried with him for more than twenty years. Everyone wanted to know its secret.

It was a normal single pillow made of bamboo strips and straw, with a floral edge. The foam rubber core kept the user's head warm in winter and cool in summer. As it was periodically washed by Haonan, it was almost like new and smelt fresh.

Even after he had got married and they bought everything new, the pillow was unchanged.

Haonan carefully opened the seal. Then from inside he took out a cloth bag the length and width of a mouse pad. Inside it was a further sealed bag. Haonan opened that one too. Everyone was astonished to see that it contained a handful of soil and a knot of grey and white hairs.

Haonan explained it all to them. This was the soil that he had dug under the *Bougainvillea glabra* when he had knelt down before leaving Shenzhen that year. At that moment he had never thought he would see Shenzhen again. This was the reason why he had brought the soil away, so that he could touch it at any time and feel better. When he had stayed in Anhui Province for two days, he had bought this pillow and stitched the soil inside it in a cloth bag. From then on, wherever he was, whether in Anhui, Shenzhen, Guangxi or Vietnam, this pillow and its secret had accompanied him at all times. When he slept on it he could feel that he was hugging Shenzhen, or, that Shenzhen was hugging him; he also felt that he was listening to the story of Shenzhen and touching the pulse of the city which had meant so much to him, and this made him indescribably happy. And this knot of grey and white hairs was his mother's, cut after her death. By sleeping on this pillow, he sometimes saw his mother in his dreams.

"How could you put a bag of soil into your pillow? *Diaotou!*" Fuqiang shouted and smirked.

"A poor girl like me cannot compete with a handful of soil!" Shuwen muttered.

"No, you're just as important," Haonan replied, smiling.

"So many years have gone by," Fuqiang sighed. "That saying of mine should be changed. I should say, 'Earning a little money is hard for me, but earning big money is easy for Haonan'!"

"Thank you! But that's not fair," said Haonan. Now let's look at this." He placed his right palm over his left fist to show satisfaction, as when Forrest Gump got a good harvest by feeding his shrimps.

Then Haonan pointed to the wall. Everyone lifted their heads. On it could be seen two deep lines, which had been newly inscribed by Haonan in the regular script of Liu Gongquan:

The gold cannot be seen until the sands are thoroughly blown away,
After over two decades my dream has finally come true today.

The end

Printed in Great Britain
by Amazon

56938230R00293